KILL
ALL
YOUR
DARLINGS

KILL ALL YOUR DARLINGS

DAVID BELL

BERKLEY

NEW YORK

BERKLEY
An imprint of Penguin Random House LLC
penguinrandomhouse.com

Copyright © 2021 by David J. Bell
Penguin Random House supports copyright. Copyright fuels creativity, encourages diverse voices,
promotes free speech, and creates a vibrant culture. Thank you for buying an authorized edition of
this book and for complying with copyright laws by not reproducing, scanning, or distributing
any part of it in any form without permission. You are supporting writers and allowing
Penguin Random House to continue to publish books for every reader.

BERKLEY and the BERKLEY & B colophon are registered trademarks of
Penguin Random House LLC.

Library of Congress Cataloging-in-Publication Data

Names: Bell, David, 1969 November 17- author.
Title: Kill all your darlings / David Bell.
Description: New York : Berkley, [2021]
Identifiers: LCCN 2020057068 (print) | LCCN 2020057069 (ebook) |
ISBN 9780593198667 (hardcover) | ISBN 9780593198674 (trade paperback) |
ISBN 9780593198681 (ebook)
Subjects: GSAFD: Suspense fiction.
Classification: LCC PS3602.E64544 K55 2021 (print) | LCC PS3602.E64544 (ebook) |
DDC 813/.6--dc23
LC record available at https://lccn.loc.gov/2020057068
LC ebook record available at https://lccn.loc.gov/2020057069

Printed in the United States of America
1st Printing

For Molly

In writing, you must kill all your darlings.

—William Faulkner

KILL
ALL
YOUR
DARLINGS

PART I

CHAPTER ONE

CONNOR
PRESENT

Grendel doesn't bark when my key hits the lock.

That's when I know something is wrong.

Grendel, an eleven-year-old beagle mix, still barks at the mailman, the neighbors, squirrels, cats—any strangers at all, despite his age and flagging energy. And I can count on him barking with joy when I come in the back door every evening. If not for him, I'd always be greeted by stone-cold silence.

And that's what I hear tonight.

I toss my keys onto the kitchen counter and slip my coat off.

"Grendel?"

Everything looks normal. Grendel's food bowl is nearly empty, which means he's eaten while I was out at the library. I usually manage to keep the kitchen clean, mainly because I don't cook. The appliances are here, and everything appears to be in order.

But something *feels* wrong.

Without Grendel's barking, the house seems unsettled.

Off.

A chill flash-freezes up my spine. I feel like an intruder in my own home, like I've walked in on something.

I move toward the front of the house, stepping carefully. The ancient floorboards squeak, each one sounding like a gunshot.

Grendel typically spends his time on the couch when I'm gone. When he hears something outside, he likes to lift his head and look out the picture window. He lets out a series of barks that make him sound much more vicious than he really is, and once that's out of his system, he flops back down as though he's just run twenty miles.

By now I should hear his collar jingling, his nails on the hardwood. *He's an old dog,* I tell myself. *Old dogs don't live forever.*

"Grendel?"

When I reach the entrance to the living room, I freeze in place.

Everything is where it's supposed to be. The lamp I always leave on is on. The furniture is arranged the way it's been arranged for years. Nothing is disturbed. Nothing is broken.

And Grendel sits on the floor, his tail flopping back and forth when he sees me.

Everything is where it's supposed to be except that someone is sitting in the recliner, legs crossed, hand gently scratching Grendel between the ears.

"Hello," she says.

My mind is slower than my body. My body reacts instantly. My muscles tense. My hands clench. My knees bend into a defensive crouch, and adrenaline shoots through me like rocket fuel.

But my mind is still trying to make sense of this scene before me. A young woman with long hair dyed an unnatural shade of red sits in my recliner petting my dog. And she greets me like she's supposed to be there, like I've asked her to wait for me to come home this evening. She wears a red coat, black jeans, and heavy boots, and her face is mostly obscured by large owllike glasses.

"Who the hell are you? You need to get out of here—"

The woman lifts her hand from Grendel's head and holds it up, cutting off my words. Grendel bounds over, sniffs my shoes. He would have barked when she first came in, because he always barks the first time he meets someone. Then he gets used to them. He looks happy to see me.

"You know who I am, Connor," she says, "and once you remember who I am, I think you're going to know why I'm here."

"I don't know who you are," I say. "But I am going to call the police if you don't get out. If you didn't take anything and didn't hurt my dog, you can just leave, and I won't press charges."

She ignores my threat. With a slow theatricality, she lifts the glasses off her face and folds them, placing them carefully in her lap. She blinks a couple of times but remains quiet.

"If you want food, you can take it. Or money. I'll give it to you. But you have to go."

"Connor."

And then I finally see it. Her face is suddenly familiar. The eyes are bright blue. The shape of her face. Thinner. Much thinner. But recognizable.

She must realize that I'm starting to really see her because she smiles knowingly, like a chess master who has just outfoxed a lesser opponent.

"No," I say. "No. You're not supposed to . . . I mean, you're supposed to be . . ."

She lifts her eyebrows. "You mean, I'm supposed to be dead? Is that it? I'm supposed to be dead."

"Not dead," I say, my voice lower. "Not exactly dead."

But she's nodding. "Oh, yes. I'm supposed to be dead. I'm supposed to be written off. Forgotten. Erased. Tossed in a ditch or a river or a forest, my bones scattered to the winds and slowly returning to the earth. Dust to dust and all that. Isn't that where I'm supposed to be?"

"Yes," I say. "That's what we all thought. I'm glad that's not true, but I'm . . . This is all very disconcerting. You're here. . . ."

She leans forward and reaches behind her. She brings out a familiar-looking object and holds it up between us. She looks like she's on television, presenting something to the viewing audience.

"Isn't this what we need to talk about, Connor?"

It's my book. The book that was published today by a major New York publisher. The one I was at the library reading from and signing. The one that represents a dream come true for me.

I don't answer her question.

I come all the way into the room and sit on the couch across from Madeline O'Brien. I sit across from my former student, the young woman who disappeared almost two years ago, just months before she was supposed to graduate.

CHAPTER TWO

"Madeline, are you okay?" I ask. "Are you hurt? Do you need me to call someone? My God, does your mother know you're okay? Do the police?"

She turns the book around and studies the front. She runs her hand over the cover in a small circle, her skin against the paper making a rustling noise. "We can discuss all that in a minute. I want to talk about this book first."

"How can we talk about anything except why and how you're here? People have been looking for you. They're worried about you. This is all a shock."

"All in good time."

Grendel has come back into the room, and he yawns and stretches out by my feet. He's already bored by the rare appearance of a visitor in the house.

"*My Best Friend's Murder*," she says. "That's a great title. Did you think of it yourself, or did the publisher come up with it?"

"It's my title."

"I remember you saying in class once that most writers don't get to use the titles they want. The publisher always rejects them or changes them, so good on you getting this one in."

"Do the police know you're . . . here? Alive."

"I've been following this," she says, tapping the book. "Just because I was gone doesn't mean I didn't know what everyone in Gatewood was doing. If you can get to a computer, you can visit social media. I could keep track of my friends and family. What's left of them. You. Other professors. You sure posted about this a lot on social media. Almost every day for the last six months. You must *really* want this book to sell. You used to tell us not to spend our time online, that social media is ruining us. I guess that all changes when you have a book coming out and you want to pimp it."

"That's part of a writer's job," I say. Like any teacher, I hate having my own words used against me.

"I guess so. Social media can be used for a lot of things. Promoting books. Searching for missing people."

When she speaks and gestures, I see the Madeline I once knew. One of my best undergraduate students. Bright. Talented. Elusive. She talked a lot in class and wrote raw, vivid stories about troubled families with absent fathers, and the mothers were always calling the police on their lousy new boyfriends. It was hard for me not to assume they were auto-biographical. In our conversations outside of class, she hinted at a difficult home life but never provided any details.

She looks like she's lost about twenty pounds, and I wonder what she's been doing for the past two years. Has she been in danger? Sleeping on the streets?

She also does one of the things I remember most about her, a nervous tic she occasionally resorted to in class. She did it only on rare occasions, usually when one of her stories was being discussed. Madeline reaches up and rubs her index finger across her right eyebrow and then pinches her thumb and index finger together, plucking a single tiny hair out of her skin.

"I bought a copy of the book this morning," she says, lowering her hand from her forehead as though she's just done the most normal thing in the world. "At Target. That's pretty sweet to get your book there. I started reading it in the parking lot, and I've been reading it all day. Except when I went to the library to hear you speak."

I thought so. She was standing in the back of the room, obscured by the people I knew and many who I didn't. I remember seeing the slim young woman with the bright red hair.

It turns out I *did* know the woman. She was Madeline.

"You left before the book signing," I say.

"I don't like crowds. And there were a lot of familiar faces there. I needed to be careful."

"How did you get in here?"

"The basement. You should get a dead bolt down there."

"It's Gatewood. Most people don't even lock their doors."

"That's a mistake," she says. "You never know who will come in."

It's strange. When Madeline disappeared at the age of twenty-two, I was anguished. Scared. Confused. Devastated that someone so young could fall victim to a seemingly random and horrible crime. Her disappearance—and apparent death—during her senior year of college brought back a lot of feelings I'd been working to move past, feelings that lingered from the losses I'd unexpectedly suffered when my wife and son died. For weeks after Madeline disappeared, I wandered around in a haze. And so did my colleagues on campus and my students. We were all shocked.

But I don't feel relief with Madeline sitting in my living room. Her reemergence is so abrupt, so disconcerting, that I scramble to think of ways to get her out of the house. If she doesn't want my help, if she won't let me call the police, then I'm not sure I want her here at all.

I don't want her here because I know what she really wants.

"I told you I started reading this book earlier today," she says. "And I haven't stopped. I haven't stopped even though I know every single thing that's going to happen."

CHAPTER THREE

MADELINE
SPRING, TWO YEARS EARLIER

Dubliners billed itself as an authentic Irish pub.

Madeline had never been to Ireland, had never been anywhere, really, but she felt certain the bar wasn't close to authentic. Posters on the wall showed foamy crashing waves and lush green fields. Or else ads for Guinness. The bartender sometimes spoke with an accent, although he once told her he grew up two hours away in Lexington, Kentucky. And that was about it for authenticity.

But the students didn't care about authenticity. The beer was cheap, and the pub was close enough to campus to walk.

Sometimes, when business was slow, the bartender didn't bother to card. It didn't matter to Madeline, who was twenty-two, or to her classmates in advanced fiction writing since everyone was a senior and old enough to drink legally. But it sure made Dubliners appealing to a lot of students, even though the place smelled like stale beer and fried food. And your shoes stuck to the floor pretty much everywhere you walked. *Step-stick. Step-stick.*

Dr. Nye—or "Connor" as he let them call him on those occasions when they all went out drinking—said anyone who was over twenty-one and wanted to go out for a beer should gather at Dubliners after their senior fiction-writing seminar. His treat. No student was going to pass up that chance. When professors offered to drink with students—*and to pay*—students showed up. Madeline had learned—from hard experience—there were professors she didn't mind being around when they were drinking and professors she knew she needed to avoid when they were drinking.

Madeline ordered a pint of Harp and stood at the end of the bar, tapping her foot to the Lynyrd Skynyrd song a guy in a red flannel shirt had played on the jukebox. She had been hoping to speak with Dr. Nye after class anyway. No, not just *hoped* to speak with him. She *needed* to speak with him. She *needed* his advice. That was why she had come to Dubliners more than anything else. Not for the free beer—although she certainly didn't mind that. But for his wisdom and knowledge.

Connor met her eye once but was surrounded by the three or four neediest students in the class. They were the ones who laughed loudest at his jokes, spent the most time in his office hours, wrote stories not because they wanted to write them but because they thought Connor would like them. Madeline felt certain he was smart enough to see through it. She gave him credit for being able to cut through the bullshit.

But she hung back, waiting. She wanted to talk to Dr. Nye, wanted to talk to him about her thesis.

She wanted to talk to him about so much more. But the thesis she'd turned in the day before was at the front of her mind. Almost the second she'd handed it over to him and walked out of his office, she regretted it.

She wished she hadn't written about things that were so real and raw, even though that was exactly what Nye always told them to do.

But Madeline feared she'd been just a little too real and raw. . . .

And it was going to bite her in the ass. Hard. And she was doing what she always did, what she'd been taught to do since she was a child—look for the exit. Find the fastest way out. Don't wait for trouble to pin you down.

No, she told herself. *Try to stay for a change. Try not to run. . . .*

Someone slipped up next to her, a guy she'd taken a few classes with over the years, Isaac Frank. Isaac wrote science fiction stories riddled with grammatical errors. Madeline wanted to pull her hair out when she read them. But he was a nice enough guy, someone she liked to talk to before class. Isaac was trying to convince his parents to pay for him to travel abroad over the summer before he went to graduate school. Not study abroad. *Travel* abroad. Travel. As in . . . just for fun. But Isaac had told her just the other day his parents were willing to pay for only three weeks of travel instead of the four he wanted. Madeline listened, pretending she could in any way relate to Isaac's first-world problems.

She hoped summer plans weren't on Isaac's mind in Dubliners. He leaned in close to Madeline at the bar, sipping from a Guinness, and she decided if he started complaining about not going to Prague she was going to dump a beer on his head. She just couldn't listen.

"Hey, Madeline," he said.

"What's up, Isaac?" she asked.

Madeline didn't listen to Isaac's response. She stared down the length of the bar where Connor stood with the sycophants. One of them, a sorority girl named Hannah, was going on and on about something, and Madeline watched Connor listening and occasionally smiling. But the smile looked forced. His mouth moved. His teeth showed. But his eyes remained flat.

"Should we go rescue Dr. Nye?" Madeline asked. "Hannah won't shut up. She literally hasn't taken a breath in five minutes."

"He's on, like, his fourth drink."

"He's a writer. What do you expect?"

"We've only been here an hour or so," Isaac said.

She started tapping her index fingernail against her glass. *Ping. Ping. Ping.*

"Nervous much?" Isaac asked.

"What?"

"You seem kind of stressed. Or something."

"I'm fine, Isaac." She realized she'd snapped at him. And he looked like a hurt puppy. Isaac was clearly one of those guys who couldn't handle a woman speaking harshly to him. "I'm sorry. No. I mean, I just turned my thesis in yesterday. It's a novel."

"Oh. Sweet. One step closer to graduation."

"Yeah. Maybe. It's pretty . . . Well, I put some stuff in there I don't know about. I want to ask Nye about it."

"Is it sex stuff? Nye doesn't care about that."

"Not sex," Madeline said. "Just . . . Well, I think I want it back before he reads it. I might change it. Maybe write something different. Something less . . . real, I guess. I'm afraid Nye will think the wrong things about me. And other professors might get the wrong impression of me."

"Really? He's pretty chill."

"Professors tend to stick together," she said. "They're like cops. You know? The blue wall?"

"They do that in the Mafia too. They call it omorta."

"You mean *omertà*. That's the code of silence. I read a book about it once."

Isaac glanced at Nye. "Well, he looks pretty sad," Isaac said.

"Wouldn't you if Hannah was babbling in your face?"

The music seemed to get louder. The TV showed the university's basketball team running up and down the court, shooting and passing. It looked kind of pointless to Madeline, all the back and forth, back and forth. But it was Kentucky, and everyone in the damn state talked about basketball all year round. Even Isaac watched it, his face deadly serious, like he was viewing a documentary about World War II or some other major historical event. Had she heard someone say it was an important tournament? Something called the NIT? Was that a big deal?

"It's not that," Isaac said, eyes on the TV. "He's sad because his wife and kid died. Tragically."

Madeline wanted to sigh, but she held it in. She'd been corrected by professors before because she sighed when her classmates said something particularly stupid. The rumor had been going around as long as she'd been an English major that Dr. Nye's wife and teenage son had died a few years earlier. Sometimes the story said they'd died in a car accident. Sometimes people said they'd been murdered. Once Madeline heard they'd both died when a neighbor's dog went mad and attacked them in the backyard. When Nye had come home from work that day, so the story went, he found the dog standing over their mauled bodies, licking his bloody chops.

"That's all bullshit, Isaac," she said. "He looks sad because he wants to spend more time writing novels, and he can't because he has to teach. He's into the tortured-artist thing. It's kind of appealing to be all sad and broody."

Isaac's lips spread across his face as he turned away from the TV. He looked like a condescending schoolteacher. "It's not a rumor." He sipped his beer and leaned his elbows on the bar. Isaac was a tall guy. Not overweight but kind of . . . doughy. He looked like he hadn't been outside in two months. More like Dr. Hoffman, although obviously Hoffman was a lot older. And just thinking of Hoffman made her shiver and remember what she had to talk to Connor about.

And Isaac wasn't like Dr. Nye. Or Dr. White. Guys who managed to stay fit even in middle age. Stay fit and look good.

"I Googled it one night and found an article," Isaac said. "I guess Nye's wife is—was—some kind of researcher. Like management consulting or something. She had to go to some conference up in Maine, and she took their son, who was, like, fifteen years old, with her. And while they were there . . . Well, it's really kind of a freaky story."

CHAPTER FOUR

Around ten o'clock, the students started to leave, dispersing into the cool early-spring night. Madeline was on her third beer, and when Isaac left, he offered her a ride because it was so dark. "Spring forward" had made the days longer—and cost her an hour of sleep—but not long enough.

"I'm good," Madeline said. "Thanks."

Isaac lingered, looking like he had something else to say.

"What?"

"Well, it's just . . . I wouldn't want Dr. Nye to know I told you that stuff about his family. He might think I'm talking shit about him, but I'm just repeating what I read online."

"It's cool, Isaac." Madeline turned an imaginary key over her mouth. "I'm good at keeping secrets. Trust me."

Isaac looked relieved and left Dubliners, no doubt to work on another grammatically incorrect story about an astronaut in the year 2347 having sex with a lusty robot.

Madeline checked her phone. Nothing. She felt relieved. She couldn't deal with anyone trying to get in touch with her. She wanted to be left alone. She hoped that might finally be happening. Maybe things would blow over and calm down.

She told herself that—but life had taught her something different. *If wishes were horses, Maddy girl,* her mother used to say.

She wasn't sure what she was going to do when she left Dubliners.

She knew what she *should* do—homework. But after she'd had nearly three beers and no food, her mind wouldn't be able to focus. If she tried to read or write, the words on the page might dance around like tiny hieroglyphs, mocking her with their refusal to form into anything sensible. And she'd been getting so little work done over the last week with everything on her mind.

Her eyes drifted up to the TV screen. For a moment, she felt curiosity about the result of the game, mild disappointment spreading over her when she saw that her school—Commonwealth University—was losing by five points with three minutes to play. She knew it was time to go when basketball started to get her emotionally engaged.

A stool scraped next to her.

She knew who it was before she turned. Connor Nye.

"You like basketball?" he asked.

"Not really. I don't know what's going on. Just a lot of running."

"My son loved it," he said. "Actually, my wife loved to watch it too. When we met in college, our first date was at a basketball game. Michigan against Purdue."

Something tugged in Madeline's chest. *Loved.* Past tense. A flush spread over her face, and it wasn't from alcohol.

"But my son had just grown taller than me," Nye said, "and I was having trouble beating him one-on-one." He held a full pint of beer, and just as she looked over, the bartender placed a shot of whiskey in front of him. Connor nodded toward his glass. "Want one?"

"Sure. Why not?"

Connor pointed, and the bartender filled a shot glass for Madeline. She picked it up and said, "What are we drinking to?"

"How about to you turning in a draft of your thesis yesterday?"

"Here's to it," she said, and threw the shot back. A pleasant burn in her throat. Her eyes watered. She swallowed beer to chase the shot. She'd just crossed the Rubicon and tipped over from slightly buzzed to starting to get drunk. "Although, I wanted to talk to you about that. I'm a little nervous about it."

"That's not unusual."

"It's not?" she asked. "There are some things in there . . . things that are personal. And pretty real."

"Sounds intriguing. I've read enough sexy robot stories for one lifetime."

"I think I should take the thesis back. I think . . . it's just too personal. In fact, I'm going to have to insist on getting it back."

"Sounds like you have cold feet."

"I have cold everything. I don't want . . . It's one thing for *you* to read it. But eventually there will be a whole committee. And these undergraduate-thesis defenses are open to the public. Sometimes a lot of people show up. Students and . . . other professors. So people, *certain* people, might think the worst of me when they hear about it. Am I making any sense?"

Madeline hated the pleading, defensive tone in her voice. After all—what did she have to apologize for? Once, in class, Dr. Nye had quoted Anne Lamott and told them the people in our lives shouldn't be offended by what you write. "If people wanted you to write warmly about them, they should have behaved better."

Madeline agreed with Nye on that. But the stuff in her thesis. The stuff she wrote down *in detail.* When she wrote it, she felt certain about it, certain she was writing down the truth. She still did. She just felt less certain about sharing it with the world.

With the community in the English Department. With others who might hear about it.

She felt her hand going up to her eyebrow and caught herself. She scratched her nose instead, hoping Dr. Nye hadn't noticed. Had he seen her annoying tic in class?

"Is there something sordid in the book?" he asked.

"No. It's kind of violent. A woman gets killed."

"Lots of books are violent. I can handle it."

"I know. . . ."

"I'm pretty surprised you turned in a mostly handwritten draft," Connor said. "What happened? Did your feather quill run out of ink?"

"Yeah, I meant to tell you about that." Connor had a way of jabbing at his students. He could playfully kid them but also let them know he disapproved. "I struggled to get this thesis going. I had about five thousand words done, and then my computer died. I mean, it just croaked. Nothing could be saved. It cost me a hundred dollars to go to the shop and have them tell me they couldn't save it."

"I'm sorry."

"Yeah. So I started writing by hand for a while. And . . . I don't know. It felt more organic or something. It connected me more to the words and the rhythm. Does that make sense?"

"It does. Sure. But I don't have to accept the thesis that way."

Madeline felt sick when he said that. Her stomach dropped to the floor.

He went on. "A lot of professors wouldn't take handwritten work at all. Maybe you should find a way to get it typed—"

"I can't afford a new computer. I mean, I *really* can't, not with all the loans and things I have. I need to bite the bullet and buy one, but the debt scares me. And my mom can't help at all." She looked away and swallowed hard. Why couldn't she have a parent with enough money to pay for basic shit? "I have to write at night because I'm working forty hours a week at the grocery store to pay for school. Sometimes more than forty. I write during downtime at the job. By the time I'm off work, it's dark. Sometimes you can be the only student in a lab at night, and that's kind of weird."

"You really don't have another way to do it? Even a friend's computer?"

"That can be tough. Everyone has their own work to do. Look, I don't feel safe walking around campus at night. A friend of mine . . .

Well, I don't want to say too much. I kind of based the thesis on something that happened to my friend. That's the violent part. And I'm worried it's telling her story in a way I shouldn't."

"If it affected you, it's your story too."

He sounded so wise. So understanding. Would she ever be grown up enough to sound like she knew what she was talking about? To sound calm and certain?

"I guess so," she said.

Nye looked like he'd decided something. "Okay," he said, "I'll accept *this* draft in handwritten form. You're lucky it's legible. But you'll have to make it a Word file for the Honors College. You've got a couple of months for that since the defense will be in early May. Then you can graduate."

"I know. That's how I'll revise it. On a computer. I promise."

"I flipped through it a little earlier. What's up with those pages near the end that are actually typed? For a while, I thought it was some postmodern intertextual commentary. Why did that happen? Did your computer rise from the dead for a few days?"

"No. I borrowed a computer . . . but it didn't really work out for the long run."

He drank his beer. His shoulders were slumped, and up close, he looked older than he did in class. Madeline saw lines around his eyes she'd never noticed before, the amount of gray in his dark hair. He'd told them he was forty-three, and that just sounded old. Madeline knew people in their forties could still have a good time, but Connor looked like a great weight was pressing down on him. And she couldn't stop thinking about what Isaac had told her.

"Is everything okay?" she asked.

He looked over, the light catching his brown eyes. "I'm drunk."

"Anything besides that?"

He lifted the glass to his mouth but stopped without drinking. "You mean, the haunting memory of my wife and son being devoured by a dog?"

Another classic rock song was playing, one Madeline didn't know. Something about a guy who kept moving on from one woman to another. Then again, maybe that was every classic rock song.

"I'm sorry," Madeline said. "I shouldn't have said anything."

"I'm kidding," he said. "They didn't get devoured by a dog."

"I know," she said.

He perked up some. "You do? What do you know? I'm always curious to hear what's being said about me. Each new class brings in a new rumor. So what is it now?"

Madeline knew she was getting in deep, that maybe it was time to make her exit. But she told herself to stay, to talk to Nye like he was just another human being instead of her professor.

"Drowning," she said. "They went to a conference your wife had to go to in Maine, and they went kayaking in the ocean. Some kind of crazy tide swept them away. A freak thing."

Connor turned back to his beer and took a long drink.

"It sounds so specific that it must be true," Madeline said. "That's how I know it's not a rumor. It's like in class when you say that the more unique a detail, the greater sense of truth it creates. Whether it's physical or emotional, the right nugget of information makes it seem like the writer has really been there and done that."

Connor finished the beer in one big gulp. He waved to the bartender and asked for the bill.

"That's what's going on with my thesis," she said. "It might be too real . . . some of those details I included."

"How can fiction be too real?"

"If it's based on something real, and that very realness hurts somebody. Or puts them in danger. Or makes the wrong person angry. Do you know what I mean?"

Nye leaned forward, like he was hard of hearing. "Danger? If someone is in danger . . . I mean, I don't see how a book could do that. A book no one has read."

"People have read some of it, or they will. I think maybe I just need to back away from the project, maybe write something else."

"You *can't* do that," he said. "You have to write what you want to write. I mean . . . after Emily and Jake died, and I tried to write, every story began the same way. With a mother and her fifteen-year-old child dying in the ocean on the first page. Over and over. Fifty different times." He stared into the empty glass in front of him, and his voice sounded weary. "God, I got sick of myself."

"My dad died when I was little. Very little. I used to try to write about that, but I never really could."

"It's too real. Or raw."

"Maybe not real enough," she said. "I didn't know him well because I was only three. I've never even been to his grave. Is that weird?"

Nye shook his head. "No. I go to my family's graves pretty regularly. It's peaceful. In times of stress it's calming . . . to be near them in a way. Sometimes I even go over there at night and sneak in when the gate's locked. There's a way to do it. A big tree about fifty feet down from the gate has pushed through the fence, and you can slip in."

"I'm sorry," Madeline said. She felt like an ass for pushing about things she had no business getting into. She always did that and never knew when to back off. She wanted to say more about her thesis, but her concerns seemed small next to a guy who'd lost his family.

"I'm drunk. My wisdom is sloshing around in my head. Pickled." Connor handed a credit card to the bartender. "It's okay. I have to get going. And if I want to talk, I'll talk to Grendel."

"Your dog?"

"He listens to me all the time."

"You're not driving, are you?"

"No chance. But that was the rumor one semester: that my family had been killed by a drunk driver. And the drunk driver was me."

Connor signed the credit card slip with a flourish. Madeline wanted to be able to sign her name in a book like that someday. Confidently.

Stylishly. Like she owned the world. Connor had published a book of short stories with a small press while he was in graduate school. Madeline had found a copy in a thrift store in town and bought it for a dollar. She'd never told Connor she'd read it, never asked him to sign it. That was the kind of thing the sycophants would do. But she loved the stories and wished she could get out of her own way enough to ask him about them. Where did the ideas come from? How long did it take to write them?

What was it like to see his own words in print?

"But the drunk-driving thing isn't true," he said. "The kayaking thing is right. A rip current. And it is so weird it sounds made-up, doesn't it? It's a heck of a lot weirder to try to live through."

Madeline watched him go. His shoulders were still a little bent, and he stumbled once before he reached the door. She knew he lived about a ten-minute walk from Dubliners. But it was already dark, and he'd had way too much to drink.

Once again Madeline asked herself—*Isn't this the kind of thing I should just stay out of? Back off and let things play out the way they play out?*

But if they reached his house, maybe she could ask for the thesis back. Maybe she could explain it all, and Dr. Nye would reassure her and tell her she was overreacting to everything. That what she thought she knew wasn't really true, just one gigantic misunderstanding.

She threw back the rest of her beer and grabbed her purse. She rushed to the door, following him.

CHAPTER FIVE

CONNOR
PRESENT

"Madeline," I say, "why don't you just let me explain what happened?"

She leans back, the book and the oversized glasses in her lap, and gives me a long look. "I think I know what happened. It seems pretty obvious."

"Yes and no," I say. I feel like a fool, trying to justify something that has no justification. I'm not even sure what my own defense will be, but I have to say something. "I really wasn't myself after Emily and Jacob died. To lose them in such a bizarre way, drowning in the ocean. I almost think if they'd died in a car accident close to home, I would have handled it better. I lost thirty pounds because I wasn't able to eat. I mean, I was really in a fog. Jake had just turned fifteen, and I know that isn't college age, but it was tough to go in and see all those young faces in class, faces that reminded me of him. I barely kept my job. Only through the good graces of my colleagues, who gave me a lot of rope. It's not a time in my life I like to think about. Even though those years define everything. I'd sit in faculty meetings and start to sob. I'd go days without bathing or shaving. I'd sit at home and go through a bottle of Jim Beam in one evening. None of it was pretty."

"I'm not trying to diminish your grief," Madeline says. "I saw what it was doing to you back then. Everybody did."

"When I read your thesis, Madeline . . ." I stand up and walk across the room. Grendel watches me, his mouth open. I rarely have company, so he must be wondering why a stranger is in the house. A nice stranger but a stranger. Emily had loved to entertain. Dinner parties, cocktails. She'd invite people over for the Super Bowl, the Derby, Halloween. Since she's been gone, I haven't done any of that. If people come over, it's random. Scattered. "Your thesis was so good . . . for an undergraduate to write so well. That's all I can say. The writing was so compelling."

I remember the story so vividly. And not because I was just talking about it at the library.

And not because I read and reread it as I revised the book.

I remember the story because it was so well done.

On the surface it appears to be a conventional thriller. Two women are friends in a small college town. One is a student, the other in her late twenties. When the older woman's husband starts to show an unhealthy interest in the younger woman, it threatens to tear their friendship apart.

But then the older woman ends up dead. Murdered in her car outside her place of employment. And the husband is the prime suspect. And since the younger woman is the only one who knows the troubles in their marriage, the husband may be coming after her next, hoping to silence her forever.

I turn back around. Her cheeks are flushed. Maybe in response to the praise? I remember what it was like to have a compliment from a professor.

"It's about so much more than the murder," I say. "You do so much with the friendship between the two women. Their class differences. One woman went to a really expensive private school and grew up privileged. The other is working her way through a state university with a crappy job. The way they confide in each other so intimately. Did I teach you how to do that?"

"Some of it, I guess. Some of it I just . . . knew how to do."

"I'd been trying to write for years," I say. "Even before Emily and Jake died, I'd been floundering. I'd started about thirty different novels. None of them went anywhere. When they died, there wasn't a chance I was going to write anything."

"You would have at some point," she says. "It takes time when you lose someone."

"That's what they say. I think that's one of those pieces of conventional wisdom that are bullshit. I don't know if we're ever the same."

"You might be right," she says.

I think I'm getting through to her. I take a couple of steps toward her and keep going. "You remember that night in Dubliners? That last night we saw each other."

"I remember that night very well," Madeline says.

Her words make me cringe. "Ugh. I really don't remember it all. I had a lot to drink—"

"I'm more interested in what you're saying about the book."

"Okay. I came home that night, and I fell asleep in that very chair you're in. I didn't have to teach the next day. I woke up, hungover, just after the sun came up. I walked Grendel, drank a bunch of coffee, and started reading. It started innocently enough. I made some notes on my computer, things I wanted to tell you. Just little suggestions. And I could see how some of the scenes could be slightly different. Tighter. Or more expansive. The story was already so good, so vivid. And I was so consumed with it. No thesis had grabbed me that way or made me care that much in a long time. Not many published books had. I sat at the kitchen table and read the whole thing in a day. It was amazing. It *is* amazing."

"Thank you," she says. "It was pretty rough when I turned it in."

"Sometimes raw and rough are better," I say. "Sometimes we just need to get out of our own way as writers. We have to try not to overthink it."

"That's what you used to say in class," Madeline says.

I always feel like a fraud when I say those things to my students. They listen to me eagerly, hanging on my every word. But who am I to hand out advice when I'm not writing anything either?

"I'd typed up all these notes and ideas about your manuscript," I say. "And I was going to see you in class the next day, and we'd be able to talk about it. And I thought to myself . . . I tried to convince myself that I'd really be happy if you had success with the book. That I could bask in your reflected glory because maybe I'd played some small role in getting you there. That's enough for some people who teach. But the truth is, I hadn't even helped you that much. I know I was disconnected. I know I wasn't mentoring you the way you deserved."

"Nothing ever goes as planned, does it?" Madeline says.

"No. Before I could reach out to you and tell you how much I liked the book, you were gone. Disappeared."

CHAPTER SIX

Now that it's out, I feel agitated, restless. My thoughts are a jumble.

"Do you want a drink or something?" I ask. "I think I need bourbon."

"Sure," she says. "I always drank when you paid."

I go back out to the kitchen, Grendel at my heels. It's cold out, and I'd turned the heat down when I left the house. But I feel flushed, sweaty. Almost like I have a fever. I open the corner cabinet and take down a bottle of Rowan's Creek and two glasses. When Jake was born, twenty years ago, Emily's brother gave me a bottle of Rowan's Creek, so whenever I drink it, I think of my son. My hand shakes as I pour.

Grendel starts eating. I hear his chomping in the corner.

"You were drinking a lot when I last saw you."

I turn toward Madeline. She's standing in the doorway from the living room, leaning against the jamb.

"I was," I say. "I've cut back. A lot. I had to." I hand her the glass, trying to control the trembling. "But I think I could use one or maybe two tonight."

"I guess it isn't every day that a ghost shows up in your house."

I swallow and lean back against the counter. "They looked for you, Madeline. Searches all over campus and town. It was on the news. Some people thought you just up and ran off on a whim. Some students do that. Impulse trips."

"Some kids can *afford* to do that."

"Right. But they looked in your apartment. You left all your books and clothes behind. You were an excellent student, an honors student, a few months away from getting a degree. And you stopped coming to class. The police questioned everybody who'd had any contact with you, including me. Especially me because we were all at the bar that night."

"And I left Dubliners right after you did."

"Right. Some of this is fuzzy. How I got home . . . how I even managed to get my key in the lock and get inside . . . I kind of think you came with me . . . but I don't know how far . . ."

"Out in the living room you were talking about the book," she says, arms crossed, glass in front of her. "After you read it and wanted to talk to me and I was gone."

I finish my first glass and pour another. *This is it,* I tell myself. *Just two drinks.*

"You know I have to publish to get tenure," I say. "That's the way to survive in academia."

"I've heard about that."

"Publish or perish, they call it."

"It sounds awfully bleak."

"It can be," I say. "And I hadn't published anything in the seven years I'd been here. That book of stories *Autumn Sunset* came out when I was still in graduate school, so it didn't count. If you don't get tenure, you get fired. And if I didn't get tenure here, I probably wouldn't get hired anywhere else. They'd see I failed to produce, and no one would touch me. Why would they want a middle-aged guy with a huge blank spot in his publication record?"

"You could tell them about your family," Madeline says.

"Sure. And the university here gave me an extra year for bereavement. I still couldn't produce a book or even a few stories." Grendel appears to be finished eating. He slurps some water, shakes his head, and goes back out to his perch on the couch. "Dr. White, the department chair, is a pretty good friend. And he really looked out for me. But he could only do so much. And he was really on me, reminding me what was at stake. He kept telling me, 'Just produce something, Connor.'"

"No pressure, right? Hurry up and write an entire book while you're grieving."

"Life goes on at some point." I drink some more. "The world doesn't stop forever. Six months had passed after you disappeared. Six months. No one really said it out loud, but everybody was thinking the same thing. After a few days—a week, really—people were thinking the worst had happened. That you weren't coming back. That you were dead. Murdered. Even your mom said it in an interview she did with the local paper. Does she know you're—"

"I'll call her soon," Madeline says, her voice sharp. "You just finish telling me about the book and how all of this happened."

We've reversed roles. She's asking the questions. She's playing the part of authority figure. And I feel compelled to answer her and give a full accounting of myself.

"I had your book," I say. "Almost all handwritten. And you were gone. And I had an agent interested in my writing from years ago, although I wasn't even sure she still knew I existed. I took your handwritten book and retyped it on my computer."

"You gave me a hard time about turning in a handwritten draft. I told you my computer died. . . ."

"It turned out to be to my advantage. I made some of the revisions as I went along. I kept telling myself I wasn't going to send it anywhere, that I was just going to type the book out as an exercise, a way to get my own creative juices flowing again. But the deadline was coming up for my tenure review. And I really wasn't sure how I would handle it if I lost this job. On top of everything else, to be unemployed with nowhere to go."

Madeline shows concern as she listens. She's nodding, encouraging me to keep talking. And it feels good, really good, to finally unburden myself of the secret I've been carrying around for the past eighteen months. Even if I am unburdening myself to the person most directly harmed by my actions.

"It's so hard to get a book published," I say. "What are the chances for anyone? It was a whim. A Hail Mary play. But my agent loved the story. And within a few weeks, an editor loved it. And bought it. I kept telling myself to speak up, to tell them it wasn't mine. But the train just kept gathering momentum and . . . I have to be honest . . . after everything that had gone wrong for me, after all my struggles with writing, to hear people saying such nice things felt really, really good."

I look at her, and she swallows some of her bourbon. The look on her face has shifted, from concern and understanding to something I can't really read. Her eyes look flat and cold, pale marbles staring back at me.

"I'm sorry, Madeline," I say. "I really am."

She takes her time responding, and then says, "Don't worry. I didn't show up here without a plan for how you'll make this all right."

CHAPTER SEVEN

CONNOR
SPRING, TWO YEARS EARLIER

I guzzled coffee in my kitchen. I was tired and had to get to class. And for a change, I wasn't tired from drinking. Or because I'd been up all night, tossing and turning, missing Emily and Jake.

It was because I was tired from reading Madeline's thesis.

She'd turned it in two days earlier, and I'd started reading it the day before after waking up in the grip of the mother of all hangovers. When I'd first started reading the book, my head thumping, my gorge rising and falling like waves on the sea, I worried I liked it so much because it was taking my mind off being sick from alcohol.

But as the day went on, and as the story gripped me more and more, compelling me to turn the pages faster and faster, I knew—I *knew*— my reaction was a true one. Madeline had managed to write an outstanding novel—one about a young woman being murdered in a college town—the kind of thing most people never wrote in an entire lifetime of trying. Somehow she'd managed to do it at age twenty-two, during her senior year of college.

I didn't know whether to be jealous or proud.

I went back and forth between both emotions. With a little shock thrown in. I'd never had an undergraduate student—or any student— write something so good. Had never imagined that an undergraduate at Commonwealth University in Kentucky would reach such heights at such a young age.

I'd needed the coffee when I finished with showering and shaving. My hangover from the day before had faded. The familiar thumping in my head, the roiling in my guts, was over. I poured food into Grendel's bowl and checked my phone. A missed call from one of my English Department colleagues, Lance Hoffman, which struck me as odd. Lance rarely called. He didn't even like to text.

"Why's he calling?" I asked the empty kitchen.

The dog gave me the side-eye, then bent to eat. Grendel moved in after Emily and Jake had been dead a year. My department chair, Preston White, rescued Grendel from the local shelter and then found out his youngest daughter was mildly allergic.

"I think he'd be happy living with you," Preston said when he showed up on my doorstep with a forty-pound bag of dog food, a leash, and a dish. "He needs a home. You need company."

I thought the allergy story was a dodge, a way to make the handing over of Grendel seem less like an act of charity and more like a necessity. But I didn't argue. I needed to get outside myself. I needed to have something to care for. Someone to notice if I came home at night or not. But sometimes I saw the way Grendel looked at me. Was it possible for the dog to show pity? To judge me?

At those times I would say, "Boy, you should have seen me in my prime. You should have seen me before the moon and the stars crash-landed on my head."

I finished the coffee, felt the tingling buzz as the caffeine perked me up. I unplugged the toaster and the coffeemaker, made sure Grendel had plenty of water. I'd see Lance on campus and could talk to him then. If I waited to leave, I'd miss out on prime parking. Whatever Lance wanted could wait.

"You keep an eye on the place," I said. "I'm going to be better from now on. The other night was a low point."

Grendel kept on eating. But he flapped his tail.

I took it as affirmation of the decision to turn my life around.

The front bell rang. Grendel barked three times in a row, food falling out of his mouth and onto the linoleum. I almost ignored the ringing and went out the back. I'd be late for class, and showing up late was no way to turn the page to the next chapter in my life. And for a change, I was eager to get to campus. I wanted to talk to Madeline, wanted to talk to her about the thesis. Hell, I wanted to pick her brain, writer to writer, and find out how the hell she had tapped into whatever current of inspiration she'd found and churned out that book.

Where had it come from?

But the ringing came again. Insistent. And nobody ever rang the bell.

"Shit," I said.

Grendel barked again but stayed at the food bowl, eating away.

I dashed to the front of the house. "All right, all right."

I expected someone selling something. Or the meter reader.

When I opened the door and saw a woman in a suit with a uniformed cop by her side, my mind flashed back to a place it didn't want to go.

Three years earlier, on that very stoop. Two cops and a social worker, knocking on the door. I knew. As soon as I saw them, I knew something was horribly wrong. And everything flashed before my eyes—our wedding day, Jake's birth, moving into the house in Gatewood just a ten-minute walk from campus.

And that spring morning, when a cop was there again, I knew. I tried to convince myself it was something simple. A misunderstanding. A parking ticket.

But it wasn't right.

None of it was right.

"Connor Nye?" the woman in the suit said.

"What's the matter?" I asked.

There was an advantage to not being that close to anybody. Except Grendel. The cop couldn't come to the door and tell me anyone else near and dear to me had died. There were no more bombshells to drop. No more family members to pick off. I tried to find comfort in that, but the thought only depressed me, dampened the good feelings I'd woken up with.

The woman asked me if I knew a student by the name of Madeline O'Brien. And when I said yes, of course, I could tell she already knew the answer. And then she insisted on the two of them coming inside the house and talking to me about her.

CHAPTER EIGHT

Grendel came out and sniffed both of the cops' shoes. The detective patted him on the head before she sat down and started asking questions.

"When did you last see Madeline?" The woman in the suit told me her name was Alicia Bowman, a detective with the Gatewood police. She wore her strawberry blond hair pulled back off her face, and her eyes were a pale blue, a far cry from the grizzled, world-weary detectives I saw on TV.

Why would she ask unless something was really wrong?

Why would she need to ask a student's professor when he had last seen her?

"What is it?" I asked. The caffeine and the fear shot the words out of my mouth faster than I could think them. "Is she hurt? She's in my advanced fiction-writing class. Can you tell me what's going on?"

Bowman waited a beat. "You haven't heard?"

"Heard what?"

I looked around, seeking help. I looked at the uniformed cop, who sat impassively in the chair. I glanced at Grendel, who just beat his tail up and down.

Bowman said, her voice as flat as the coffee table, "Madeline O'Brien is currently missing. She didn't go to any of her classes yesterday. She didn't go to her shift at the grocery store last night, which I understand is how she's paying for school. Her mother can't get ahold of her. No word to her friends. We're trying to determine if anyone knows her whereabouts."

The room spun. The caffeine, the adrenaline. The news. Was that why Lance was calling?

"Is it possible she just went away?" I asked. "Young people, college students, they can take off on a whim. I had a student once who stopped coming to class, and a year later he came back, and when I asked him where he'd been, he said surfing in California. Living in a tent."

"That does happen," Bowman said. "It's possible Madeline left on a whim. She had a rather nomadic life growing up. But given her dedication to her studies and the abruptness of her departure, we're treating it as a disappearance."

"Damn," I said. "I just saw her. . . ."

"When?" Bowman asked.

"Wednesday night. At Dubliners. The whole class went."

"Undergraduates?" Bowman asked.

"It's a class of seniors. They all had ID. Plenty of professors take their students out during the semester. I'm not the only one."

"What time did you leave Dubliners?"

"Nine thirty. Maybe ten."

"And was Madeline still there?"

"Well . . ."

"Well, what, sir?"

I saw where it was going.

"I left. And then she left right after me. She was worried because I'd had too much to drink. She didn't want me to drive."

"Did you?"

"I walked. I'd walked to campus that morning because I knew I'd be drinking later." I pointed to her right, in the direction of downtown and campus. "It's not far," I said, as though the cops wouldn't know.

"So did Madeline O'Brien walk you back here to your house?" Bowman asked.

I froze. The words that once tumbled so freely out of my mouth backed up like cars jammed on a highway.

I could only rip the Band-Aid of my drunkenness off and let the cops see the scab underneath.

I knew Madeline had walked with me. I remembered that clearly. We crossed the square together. I could remember the fountain, still shut down and full of dead rustling leaves although spring had just arrived. We went two blocks up College Street, the night cool, my jacket pulled tight around me. My hands stuffed deep into my pockets because I had forgotten to bring gloves.

We turned west on Eighth Street.

I didn't know if we talked. We must have. I couldn't imagine we walked side by side, even on a cool night, without talking at all. I liked talking to Madeline. She acted more mature, more worldly, than any other student I knew.

"So you don't know what you might have talked about?" Bowman asked.

"I have no idea. Maybe her thesis, since she just turned it in. Maybe how cold it was."

"This was just two nights ago, and you don't remember what you talked about?" Bowman asked.

"I was drunk," I said.

Two more blocks, and I saw my house. I'd left the porch lights on. I knew that. And through the alcoholic haze, I saw them burning. A beacon in the night.

When Emily and Jacob were alive and I'd turn the corner either in my car or on foot, my heart lifted at the sight of those lights. They meant warmth. Safety.

Home.

The basketball hoop in the yard, Jake doing his homework at the kitchen table. Emily on the computer in the other room, working on a management consulting project for a local company.

When I saw the lights with Madeline, I felt pretty certain I turned to her and told her that was my house. And that she didn't have to keep walking with me, I could find my way from there.

And we said good night.

I think.

"You think?" Bowman asked. "You need to be sure, Dr. Nye. A young woman is missing. Did you say good-bye on the street or not?"

I couldn't lie. Not to the cops.

And if Madeline was really missing—and in danger—then they needed to know everything they could possibly learn about what she'd been doing.

I had seen those porch lights. I pointed them out to her. I told her she could go on, that I'd be just fine the rest of the way.

I don't know what Madeline said. I don't remember anything else I said.

Had she come all the way *to* the door? *Inside* the door?

Had she been in the house with me?

"I don't know, Detective," I said. "I just don't remember. I can't even be sure about the part I just told you that seems kind of clear."

Bowman tapped her fingers, which were long and elegant, against her thigh.

"That's all there is, Dr. Nye?" she asked.

"That's all. I hope it helps."

"Oh, it helps," Bowman said. "As far as we can tell, that makes you the last person to see Madeline O'Brien alive before she disappeared."

CHAPTER NINE

CONNOR
PRESENT

Madeline finishes her bourbon.

She crosses the kitchen, brushing right against me, and I move out of the way so she can reach the bottle of Rowan's and pour a refill. She takes her time, her movements slow and deliberate. The bottle clinks against the rim of the glass. The liquid chugs. She's drawing out the moment, making me wait as long as possible before she speaks.

She finally turns around and leans back against the counter with the half-filled glass in her hand. I've scooted over to the kitchen table and stand next to it. Waiting.

"I get it," she says. "I do. Grief can drive people crazy. Especially when it's sudden and unexplained. My dad died when I was three. I barely remember him, but I do remember when he died. I just walked around the house, crying and crying. Saying his name. 'Daddy, Daddy.' I'm twenty-four now, and isn't it weird I can remember the feeling of loss more than I remember the man?"

"It's sad," I say. "I'm sorry. Maybe that's why the emotions are so real in the book. *Your* book. When your character Lilly remembers her family and childhood, the way *her* father died, I think the reader feels so much empathy for her. It came from a real place."

"And from *you*," she says. "That's why everyone is going to love the book. They'll hear your sad story about your wife and fifteen-year-old son dying and associate it with the characters. That's why it's smart you've talked about your tragedy on social media and in interviews online. People love to know the story behind the story. You should tell everyone what you told me—about sneaking into the cemetery at night. That's a great detail."

"I still do that sometimes, but I didn't want to talk about those things. I didn't want to use my loss to make money."

"But you did it anyway."

"I know it's crass, but I want the book to sell."

"Well, let's hope it does." Madeline's glass clinks against the counter when she puts it down. "I can't really resurface right now. It would be very, very complicated if I did. Dangerous, I would say. I think it's a risk for me to be in this town."

"Madeline, if you think someone wants to hurt you, then you should go to the police. Tell them the truth. Give them names. They can protect you."

She shakes her head, arms crossed. "You're so silly, aren't you? The successful middle-aged white man who naturally thinks if you go to the police, they'll help you with all your problems. Of course they'll believe you. Of course they'll take your side. Why wouldn't the good old police help the good old man? Right? Isn't that what always happens? A man can get away with whatever he wants. I've seen the police up close before. When I was a kid. They don't help."

"Okay," I say. "Then tell me what I can do."

"It's easy, really. A simple transaction. You give me all the money from the book, and I won't tell everyone you plagiarized it. Cash, of course. No checks. I know you had to give fifteen percent to your agent. And there are taxes and shit. Just give me the rest, since *I* actually wrote the book, and we're even. When the time comes, I'll write another book. And so can you. No one will know the real truth about this one."

I ignore the part about me writing another book. Whether she meant it as a dig or as a statement of fact, I can't bear to dwell on it. I just don't know if I can ever write anything else. If the past five years have taught me anything, it's that I may lack what it takes to finish a project I start.

As for the money . . .

"I can't do that, Madeline," I say. "This novel is my New York debut, and I didn't get paid that much for it. People always think authors make a ton of money, but I really didn't get a big advance."

"I grew up without money," she says. "I mean . . . *nothing*. So any amount will sound like a lot to me. Three or four digits is a windfall."

"I didn't grow up with money either."

"You grew up with more than I did," she says. "If your parents kept the lights on, you had more than me."

"The money is spent," I say. "Yes, I got an okay amount, more than I ever thought I'd get for a book, but I also owed a lot of people. I had a student loan from graduate school. When I got my PhD, I was married, and Jake was a kid. We had to borrow so we could eat. And since Emily died, I'd let things go on the house. She always kept an eye on those things. I neglected everything. The roof had a leak. The car was dying. Like an idiot, we didn't have life insurance, which really would have helped. Look." I point to the other room. "Just last year, Grendel had a tumor on his kidney. He needed surgery. Three thousand bucks. I had to do it. I couldn't let him go. I couldn't be alone. The money . . . it's pretty much spent."

"Don't bullshit me, Connor. I won't be lied to. Not again."

"I haven't lied to you. And I'm not lying now. If I had the money, I'd give it to you. It's rightly yours. I didn't publish the book to get money. I told you why I did it."

Madeline's jaw sets hard. Muscles twitch in her neck, and short, sharp breaths come out of her nostrils. She remains silent. She may not have anticipated this obstacle.

"Madeline," I say, "there might be royalties. Later. And it's a two-book deal, so there's more money when . . . *if* I write another book. And you can have all of that. They're hoping there might be movie or TV interest. Or the book could get translated into another language. If any of those things happen, you can have it all. I promise."

She turns to the bourbon. It looks like she's going to pour more for herself, but she doesn't. She makes a fist and knocks against the countertop once and then twice. A gentle knock while she thinks, and then turns back to face me.

"Or," she says, "I could go up to campus tomorrow. I could meet with the dean or the provost or whoever cares about things like this. And if I tell them you plagiarized this book and used it to get tenure, what will they think? What would your publisher do?"

"I'd lose my job," I say. "I'd have to give back the money. It would all be over."

CHAPTER TEN

"Look, Madeline," I say. "It's hard to put my hands on that much money. How much are you asking for exactly?"

"Whatever I'm owed."

Her response makes me sigh. "Okay. I can try, but you're acting like I have a pile of cash sitting around. Like the publisher just sent me a bag of gold coins. I can try to get my hands on some money for you, but it's going to take a little time."

"How much time? Tomorrow?"

I sigh again. "I'm going to have to go to the bank. Maybe I can get a loan against the house. There's a little equity there. Or maybe I can get some kind of home improvement loan. I can tell them I want to renovate the bathroom."

"I like the way you're thinking now, Connor. How soon?"

"I have to teach tomorrow. Then I have to get to the bank—"

"You could get a cash advance on your credit card. My mom used to do that when she was strapped. They kill you with the interest rates, of course. But it's fast."

"I'm not going to do that. I'll ruin myself."

"Ruin is definitely on the table, one way or the other," she says. "If you don't get the money, things could get very, very bad for you. In a number of ways."

"What does that mean?" I ask.

"Whatever you want it to mean."

I hold my hands out, asking for calm. "I said I'll try. How do I get in touch with you?"

Madeline laughs, like I'm the biggest fool she's ever met. "Sure, Connor, I'll tell you exactly where I'm staying so you can call the police. I'll find you. I know where you live and work. I know the places you like to go. I can watch for you. Maybe follow you. Maybe I'll even find you in the gutter outside of Dubliners. Or maybe at the cemetery. Okay? I'll track you down."

"You can't follow me."

"Oh, I can. And I will if I want to. I'm a ghost, remember?"

"Are you safe where you're staying?" I ask.

"As safe as anyone."

"What do you need the money for?" I ask. "Are you mixed up in something? I mean . . . is someone forcing you to do this?"

"I need it because it's mine. Because I earned it." She looks and sounds younger than she has since I found her in the house. "I think you have more to lose if I expose you."

"Maybe," I say. "I'd lose a lot if you went and told on me."

I let my words hang in the air between us for a moment. The sweetly smoky taste of the bourbon lingers in my mouth. Her face changes. The set of her jaw relaxes. She almost smiles.

"Madeline, how would you prove you wrote the book?" The thought pops into my head as the words come out of my mouth. I hadn't thought of it before this moment, and I feel gross saying it. But I'm trying to survive and buy time. "You turned in a handwritten manuscript to me. Remember? And I have the only copy now."

Her mouth opens, but she doesn't speak.

"Actually, I don't have that copy. I'm not an idiot. After I typed it, I burned it."

"That's fucking bullshit—"

She takes a lunging step toward me, but Grendel starts to bark in the living room.

Is he barking to protect me? Or for another reason?

I don't care. Madeline stops when she hears him.

I move over to the entrance to the living room. Grendel is standing on the couch, looking out. Headlights glow against the front of the house.

"Someone's here," I say.

I go to the window and look out, Grendel at my side. I see a couple of my colleagues coming up to the porch. Preston White and Lance Hoffman. At the library, they said I needed to break open a bottle of champagne, and when I said I didn't have any, they threatened to buy one and come over. I figured they were joking, but here they are. I unlock the door.

The two of them are better friends with each other than they are with me. But when Emily and Jake died, they kind of adopted me, making me a special project as I lifted myself out of the depths of grief.

I go back to the kitchen, and Madeline already has the back door open.

"Don't you want to stay?" I ask. "Weren't they both professors of yours? Maybe you can say hello. Tell them how you faked your disappearance—"

"I'm not letting this go," Madeline says. "Don't try to give me the shaft on this. I mean it."

She slips out the door and into the night.

Behind me, Preston and Lance come inside, talking loudly like a couple of students themselves. And that's how they frequently act when they're together and when they've been drinking.

I put Madeline's glass in the sink.

Preston comes into the kitchen, claps me on the back. He thrusts the bottle of champagne into the space between us. "Told you we'd be here."

"You're a man of your word."

"Where are the glasses? Whoa. What's this?" He points to the bottle of Rowan's Creek, the glass on the counter. Then he looks in the sink. "Two glasses?"

"I was thirsty," I say.

"You're not going to say who?" he asks. "Lance, the boy had company before us."

"Who?" Lance asks. He whips his head toward me. He actually looks serious. "A lady?"

I can't tell them.

"Just an old friend," I say.

"A female friend?" Lance asks. "A girl?"

"Just a friend."

"Well, well," Preston says. "The plot thickens."

CHAPTER ELEVEN

I've never liked getting out of bed. I've always hit snooze and buried my head under a pillow. I try to hide from the days as long as possible.

Emily was the exact opposite. She loved mornings and bounced out of bed with the energy of a kitten.

Some mornings she would turn off my alarm before it rang and then lean down and nuzzle my cheek with her nose or kiss me on the forehead. That was how I liked waking up. And I wish I still could.

But that time is gone. . . .

And I'm dragging when I walk Grendel at six forty-five the next morning. And I'm nervous, shaky. Madeline's words play over and over in my mind, her promise—*threat?*—to be watching me, following me, making sure I do what she's demanded of me. Is she out here right now, lurking in the bushes or behind a car?

My head thumps. A dull pain above my right eye. Champagne. It's been years since I drank it, and I downed several glasses with Lance and Preston last night. They thought I was celebrating. I needed the drinks to calm down after seeing Madeline.

It's cold, but Grendel takes his sweet time deciding where to shit. He seems to have become pickier in his old age. He prefers taller grass, but it's January in Kentucky. Good luck finding anything growing.

While he sniffs and contemplates, I look around, studying my neighborhood of small, well-kept bungalows housing professors and young professionals. I expect to see Madeline lunging toward me with the book in her hand, demanding money.

I try to convince myself it was all a dream, a guilt-induced hallucination that conjured her in my living room last night. But I know it's real. Her copy of the book still sat in the chair where she left it. Her glass remained in the sink.

For all I know, she's already gone to someone in a position of authority at the university.

Grendel drops his load, and I pick it up with a plastic bag. We start back. Snow flurries start to fall, swirling around us. Grendel lifts his snout and sniffs as though he's enjoying the scenery. His brown eyes are duller, the fur around his snout grayer. I tell him I'm running late. We have to hurry. And I give the leash a gentle tug, which moves him along.

I, of course, didn't mention Madeline to Lance or Preston. For the past few years, Preston has been encouraging me to date, to "get back in the game," as he puts it. A year and a half earlier, he and his wife, Kelly, set me up on a date with a professor in the Modern Languages Department, a woman my age who had recently divorced. I went along, more than anything else because I'd run out of plausible excuses to avoid it. The woman was pleasant enough, and our conversation about campus gossip and national politics demonstrated we had plenty in common. But that was as far as I wanted it to go. The idea of going any further, of letting my guard down and opening myself up to another person in a real way, still felt like a bridge too far. I never asked for a second date, and I'd heard the woman recently married a software engineer who works for a corporation in Lexington. "She's over the moon," Kelly said.

I reach the welcome warmth of my house. I feed Grendel and leave him to his messy chomping while I shower and get ready for a day of teaching, starting with a creative-writing class at nine. The hot water helps clear the cobwebs. The shaving makes me feel like a human being.

Preston didn't let the subject of my "friend" go last night. He kept asking who she was and what my intentions were toward her. I finally lied and said she was my neighbor up the street. I told him we were just getting to know each other, but nothing physical had occurred yet.

Preston slapped me on the knee and looked at Lance. "Can you believe the way the boy's life has picked up? New book. New ladylove. Tenure. What more could he want?"

"He smells like a rose, doesn't he?" Lance said in his arch way. "He wrote a book and got rich. It's better than having him moping around the cemetery late at night like a grave robber."

And we drank more, toasting my good fortune.

I felt like a fraud, accepting their praise. And I felt afraid, knowing Madeline was out there.

I dress quickly because I'm running late. My phone chimes. A text from Preston.

Got time to swing by before class? Need to tell you something.

What could he want?

Sure.

I have classes all day, and now a meeting with Preston in the morning. I tell myself to try to squeeze in a trip to the bank. Or at least a call to see if I can get my hands on any money. If Madeline wants proof that I'm not rich, all she needs to see is me rushing off to work the day after the book came out. That's life for most writers: squeezing a book release in between the day job.

I grab my coat and bag. I'll get a coffee on the way. No time to brew any. Grendel is still eating in the kitchen, and I tell him to keep an eye on the house. I remind myself to get a dead bolt installed on the basement door to keep out any other unwanted visitors.

Grendel yawns and trots off to his day bed in the front of the house. I take my key off the counter. I'm ready, just in time.

Grendel starts to bark. I assume it's someone going by, a jogger or a biker.

But the doorbell rings.

"Crap," I say. "Now what?"

What if it's Madeline? Back and more insistent—

I think about ignoring it, slipping out the back while whoever stands on the porch—a religious nut, a political campaign worker, my former student back from the dead—shivers in the cold. But there's always that doubt. . . . What if it's something important? I still hear from Emily's family. Her mother has been in shaky health—what if there's a crisis? I'd never forgive myself if I missed that kind of news.

Grendel continues to bark. The bell rings again. I look like a man ready to leave, so that will help me get rid of them. I rush to the front, wearing my coat and carrying my bag. Keys jangling in my hand.

I look out Grendel's window. It's a woman but not Madeline. Thankfully. This woman is about my age. Tall. Bundled in a long overcoat. Vaguely familiar. Do I know her from work?

Then I see the object in her hand. A copy of *My Best Friend's Murder.*

Really? Is this what it's like for writers? Fans show up on your stoop unannounced carrying the book? Sure, I can see it happening to Stephen King or Anne Rice. But me?

I undo the lock, pull the door open. The cold air blows past like the freezing breath of an angry winter god. It stings the tips of my ears.

"Dr. Nye?" she says.

I know why she looks familiar. I know where I've seen her before. It's been two years, but I can't forget her face.

"Do you remember me?" she asks. "Alicia Bowman with the Gatewood Police Department." She holds the book up between us. "I was wondering if we could talk about this."

CHAPTER TWELVE

Bowman comes in. She's my height, a little taller even. She looks long and lean under her overcoat. She might have a few more streaks of gray in her hair than two years earlier, but if anything, she looks like she's barely aged.

"I can see you're on your way to campus," she says. "This won't take long."

She bends down, scratches Grendel between the ears, which makes them friends for life.

"Yeah," I say, "I have a meeting and then class at nine. . . ."

"Who's a good boy, huh? Who's a good boy?" She straightens up. "Shall we sit?"

Bowman manages to make her friendly suggestion—*Shall we sit?*— sound like a command. And before I can answer, she's heading to the couch, taking off her coat, which she tosses over the recliner, and sitting down, the book in her lap. It's my house, but I follow her lead and sit as well, my coat still on, my bag at my feet.

"I'm sorry I didn't make it to your event last night. I had to work. But I bought the book right away. Ordered it early in fact so it would arrive yesterday. I read online that's best for the author."

"That's what they say."

"And I started reading it yesterday. On my lunch and dinner break. And before I fell asleep. It's quite compelling."

"Thank you."

"It's really impressive the way you were able to write about two female characters. Not every man could do that."

"Well, I was married. And when I was growing up, I was close to my sister."

Bowman studies the back cover of the book. She doesn't seem to be in a hurry.

"Do you want me to sign that for you?"

"Would you?" She holds the book out to me.

"Sure." I reach inside my coat and find a pen. Even after last night and the book signing, it feels strange to have someone want my signature. I'm still not sure what I'm supposed to write, with how much of a flourish I should sign my name. "To Alicia?"

"Alicia and Jenn. My wife."

"Sure."

As I write, she goes on.

"Jenn makes fun of me for reading these crime thrillers. She always asks me if I want a break from the kinds of things I deal with at work. But you know how it is in Gatewood. We don't get a lot of cases that would belong in a book. Mostly it's smaller stuff. Robberies. Drugs. College kids getting drunk and fighting. It's rare we get anything too exciting. Well, you know that. Your student a couple of years ago. Madeline O'Brien. That's the kind of thing that could make a good book."

I'm writing the date when she says Madeline's name. My hand clenches, and the pen slips, almost sliding off the page, giving the "y" in my last name a gigantic tail. I don't want to look up, don't want to see if Bowman notices. But I'm sure she does. She's a detective who probably notices every little thing.

I cap the pen and hand the book back. "There you go."

"Thanks."

"I appreciate you buying it. But I really have to get going—"

"Can I ask you where you got the idea for this?" Bowman asks. Her tone has shifted ever so slightly. We're no longer casually conversing.

She's friendly but moving toward some specific point. "I'm sure writers get asked that all the time, and you probably got into it last night at the library. But it's such a fascinating book, I wanted to ask."

I have an answer. Even though I didn't write the book, I prepared one because I'd heard from writer friends what I would be asked. They said that at every book signing and in every interview, someone would inevitably ask where the idea came from.

"I've always been fascinated by murder cases," I say. "And I've read about a lot of them. But also . . ." I clear my throat. Madeline was right—I do talk about Emily's and Jake's deaths a lot as a way to sell books. But it never feels natural to me. "Because of my own experiences with loss, I'm interested in the way people respond when terrible things happen in their lives. When something unexpected happens, and everything gets turned upside down, how do people find a way to keep going and move on?"

"Right, right. I can see that. Your character in here, Lilly, the younger woman in the story, she had the loss of her father when she was young. And then her friend Sarah gets murdered. A lot of loss." She taps her fingers against the book cover. Long, slender fingers I remembered from when Madeline disappeared. Fingers that would play the piano. *Tap tap tap.* "Do you ever use details from real murder cases in your writing?"

"Not directly. No."

Tap tap tap.

"I'm asking because . . . Well, do you remember Sophia Greenfield?"

"Sophia Greenfield? Is she a writer?"

Bowman smiles, but it doesn't reach her eyes. She shifts her weight on the couch, scooting forward. She holds the book in her right hand and points at it with her left. "Sophia Greenfield lived here in Gatewood, over off of Oak Tree Parkway. A woman in her late twenties. She was murdered in the parking lot of her office about two and a half years ago. She worked for a local nonprofit that promotes literacy, and she'd been at the office late, planning a fund-raiser. She told her husband she had a meeting, but nothing was listed on her calendar or her computer. No one seems to know who the meeting was with. Her husband told us she'd been pretty agitated and distracted in the days leading up to her death, like something was on her mind. But she never said what. This doesn't sound familiar?"

"No," I say. And I mean it. "You have to understand something, Detective. When my wife and son died, I was in a pretty heavy fog. For a long time. I didn't follow the news. I didn't socialize. There was an election for president, and I didn't vote. I didn't even pay attention to who won. I mean . . . I was deep in the depths of despair. A lot went on I didn't notice. I'm sorry."

"No reason to apologize. And I'm sorry for bringing up bad memories." But she really doesn't sound that sorry. "But Sophia Greenfield . . . You see, the details in your book and the real details of Sophia's murder are a lot alike. Strikingly so. In fact . . . it's almost like you were there when she was killed."

CHAPTER THIRTEEN

I'm still wearing my coat. Bowman wears a white shirt, a gray suit, and crisply cleaned brown shoes. A gold watch and a wedding band. She looks like she plans to stay a while.

My coat feels tight and heavy. The heat blows out of the register across the room, making a low rattling noise. It shakes the fake plant that's been sitting on the floor for years, gathering dust on its plastic leaves. I unbutton my coat and slip it off, feeling a little relief.

"You're asking me if I based the book on this woman's murder," I say. "This . . . Sophia . . . ?"

"Greenfield. I guess I'm not asking you that anymore, since you just said you've never heard of the case. Although it seems hard to believe. We don't have many murders in Gatewood, so the case got a fair amount of attention. Were you really in that much of a fog?"

"I almost lost my job, I was so out of it. I was lucky I held on. To anything." I hate thinking of that time.

"You were lucky not to have noticed who won that election. I'll say that. I still keep trying to pretend I don't know the results." She smiles at her own joke, but it looks forced. She clears her throat and taps the book with a long index finger. "In the book, you have a character named Sarah Redmond. And she gets murdered in her car in a parking lot. It's outside her health club in the book, but still . . . Sophia Greenfield. Sarah Redmond. 'Red' instead of 'Green.' See? And they're the same age. Twenty-seven. Right?"

"That's just a random number. A lot of people die when they're twenty-seven. Detective, I'm really not sure where this conversation is going, but I—"

She goes on like I haven't spoken. "Sure," Bowman says. "Like the Twenty-seven Club in rock and roll. Janis Joplin. Jimi Hendrix. Kurt Cobain. Maybe the age is just a coincidence. Maybe it all is. But Sophia's body was discovered in her car by her husband when he went looking for her. In the book, Sarah's body is found by her husband when he decides to go looking for her. Admittedly, the real Sophia had blond hair, and the fictional one has red hair. But they both have green eyes. Both tall. Athletic. Kentucky girls who like bourbon and yoga. Sophia's husband became the prime suspect. Sarah's husband did too."

"The boyfriend or the husband is always the prime suspect," I say. "That's true in real life and in every thriller. I don't know why you're here—"

"Of course," Bowman says. "You men haven't done very well by your partners over the years. Suspicion always lands on them, and for good reason. Sophia was found murdered in her car. She worked late and didn't come home when she was supposed to. Of course, her husband's fingerprints and DNA were all over the vehicle. He drove it a lot. And there were unidentified prints and other DNA in there—hairs, fibers— but they didn't match anyone in the system. So our killer, if it isn't the husband, is out there somewhere, and if we find him, we can match it. There's some evidence she may have been taken by surprise. Possibly there were two assailants. There are a variety of theories we've explored about the crime, but we've pretty much reached a dead end."

"Detective, it's possible I read about the case and didn't consciously remember it. Or maybe I heard someone talking about it. In the store or the barbershop. I once published a short story, in my first book, and I gave a German shepherd the name Hogan. A few months later I got an e-mail from someone I went to grade school with, and she asked me if I remembered that her dog when we were kids was called Hogan. I didn't remember until she said it. That detail was lodged in my brain somewhere, and I pulled it out subconsciously, completely unaware. It happens."

"I'm sure it does," Bowman says, tapping the book again. "I would imagine when a writer writes a book like this, there are so many details they have to choose. What characters look like. Where they work. What color their eyes are. Inevitably you have to draw on some things that are familiar to you."

"Maybe you should write a book, Detective," I say. "You must see a lot of interesting things in your work."

"I could never write a book. That takes a lot of discipline. And time. As I know you know."

I don't say anything. She's right—I *do* know what it takes to write a book. I know because I've tried and failed, many times, and nothing teaches you how hard it is to do something like failing at it.

But I can't tell her that.

Bowman scratches her chin. "We, of course, checked all the calls she made and e-mails she sent. Sophia made a few calls to the English Department. To the main line. Do you know why she might have called there?"

"I have no idea."

"She didn't talk to you?" Bowman asks.

"I don't know who she is. I have my own direct line to my office. Every faculty member does."

"True enough. Sophia called the main office, but then if it got transferred somewhere else, we can't see that on the records. So you don't know why she was calling the English Department?"

"I have no idea. What was this nonprofit she worked for?"

"It promotes literacy among at-risk youth. Reading programs, workshops, the like."

"Maybe she wanted help from the English Department. It seems like a natural match if she cared about literacy."

"That's what her husband said. I guess maybe a few English majors have worked there as interns over the years."

"That's possible. I don't know where every student works as an intern."

"And who handles the internship program?" Bowman asks. "Do you know?"

"My colleague Carrie Richter does."

"Yeah, we talked to her at the time of the murder. She and Sophia exchanged e-mails about the program."

"Okay, then."

"But you didn't talk to Sophia?"

"I didn't, Detective. She didn't call me."

"I thought I'd ask because you work in the English Department. But what stood out to me about your book, Dr. Nye, and this will be the last thing I ask you about because I know you have to get to campus. But what stood out to me was the *way* Sarah was killed in the book. When we investigate a serious crime like this, sometimes we choose to withhold certain details from the public. You'd be surprised at the number of people who want to call in to a police station and either confess or else turn in someone they know. We get unhappy wives who call in and say their perverted, cheating husbands must have murdered the young woman. Or we get unhappy husbands calling in and saying their pain-in-the-ass wives must have murdered the young woman out of jealousy. We'd spend all our time talking to these crazy people, time we should be spending on finding the real killer. So we hold something back, something only a few people know. And in the case of Sophia Green field, we never told the public how she was murdered. We said she died by strangulation, which she did, but we didn't say whether it was manual. Or with a ligature. You see where I'm going with this?"

"Is this a joke of some kind?"

"I wish it was."

"So a character in my book, Sarah Redmond, was killed with a scarf," I say. "A ligature, as you said. So what?"

"It's funny," Bowman says, but she doesn't look like she's amused. She looks like she just stepped on a tack. "Sophia Greenfield died in exactly the same way. Strangled by a scarf her grandmother gave her. And that's the detail that's never been made public before."

CHAPTER FOURTEEN

I could end the whole thing right now. Five words would do it:

Madeline O'Brien wrote the book.

I could tell Bowman that Madeline was alive, that she'd been here. She'd threatened me and promised to come back. Bowman could then focus her attention on *Madeline*, hunt her down, and find out what she knows about Sophia Greenfield's murder. I could forget about a home equity loan or a credit card advance or any other form of blackmail payment.

Five words that flash in my head like a neon sign: *Madeline O'Brien wrote the book.*

But I don't say them.

To say them would give everything away. The book, tenure, my job. Any stability I'd clawed to get back over the last five years. No, I couldn't lose all that.

"It's not such a big leap to imagine someone being strangled with a scarf, Detective," I say. "When I was a kid, I saw that Alfred Hitchcock movie. Which one was it? *Torn Curtain?* No. The one where the guy murders women with his neckties."

"*Frenzy.*"

"Yes, see, that's it. *Frenzy.* You see, maybe that movie was lodged in my subconscious, and I needed a way for this character to die, and there it was. A scarf instead of a tie."

"Yes, but her grandmother's vintage scarf? You just happened to think of that? And the book describes the color and pattern of the scarf pretty accurately."

"There are only so many ways to kill people in a book. Or in real life."

Bowman points at me. "I think you're reaching. But maybe you learned this detail another way. Maybe you wanted to do some research—I love it when writers do a lot of research—and you talked to someone who worked on the case. If that's so, then I want to know who that person is who was blabbing sensitive information around town that could jeopardize our ability to prosecute someday. That way I can terminate their employment with the police department. Is that what happened?"

"I didn't talk to any police officers," I say.

"Then there's another option." Bowman scoots forward more, until it looks like her butt is going to slide right off the front of the couch and onto my living room floor. I see crumbs on the floor by her feet. A stain on the upholstery. I need to clean more. "Maybe you know someone who told you this detail. Maybe *that* person knew something they shouldn't know."

Madeline O'Brien wrote the book.

Bowman holds my gaze, like a snake charmer. The moment hangs in the balance like her body on the edge of the couch. Will everything stay up or crash down?

"I made it up, Detective," I say. "I really did. I'm not sure what else to say, except I'm sorry anyone got hurt."

"I appreciate you saying that," she says. "But it wasn't just the scarf we kept from the public. In the book—*your* book—you provide a pretty detailed description of the position Sarah's body is in after she is murdered. Do you remember that?"

"Of course."

"You wrote that she was slumped over, her head resting against the right side of the steering wheel."

"Well, but that—"

"And her right hand was resting on the seat. Palm up. And her left hand was hanging limply at her side. The middle nail on her left hand broken from a defensive wound."

"Naturally she'd have defensive wounds—"

"All of those details were, pardon the pun, deadly accurate. Almost like you'd seen the crime scene."

My mouth is desert dry. My tongue is mummified.

"I . . . I don't . . ."

"Of course she'd have defensive wounds," Bowman says. "Anyone could guess that. But you gave her a very *specific* defensive wound. On the middle finger of her left hand. Just like the real Sophia. Who you say you don't know."

"I don't."

Bowman rubs her nearly flawless chin. She maintains her delicate perch for another few moments and then deftly rises off the couch and reaches for her coat.

"I'm sorry I bothered you so early in the morning," she says while she pulls one sleeve and then the other on. "I hope I haven't made you late for class."

I stand up too. So does Grendel, although he doesn't have anyplace to go.

"It's okay," I say, pulling on my coat. "I'll be fine."

Bowman holds up the book. "At least I got this signed. Thanks for that."

"Thank you for reading it," I say.

"Are you going to be in town?" Bowman asks when we reach the door. "Are you going off on a book tour or something?"

"No," I say. "My publisher isn't sending me out like that. I used to think I'd get to go on a big book tour, but it's my understanding they usually only do that for bigger-name authors. I'm doing some smaller events around the state, but nothing too elaborate."

"So you'll be in town?"

"I will. I have a day job. I have a lot of bills."

"Do me a favor. If you do head out anywhere, can you let me know? I want to be able to follow up with you about this if I learn anything else."

I can't stop my cheeks from flushing. And I'm sure Bowman sees what I can feel. "Sure. I guess so."

"Great." She puts her hand on the knob but doesn't turn it. "Say, Dr. Nye?" She lets go of the knob and straightens up. "It's interesting. When Madeline O'Brien disappeared, we did look into whether or not she and Sophia Greenfield knew each other. Sophia's murder and Madeline's disappearance happened about six months apart. It turns out they went to the same yoga studio. They were friends who talked from time to time."

"Curious."

"Did you ever go to Yoga for Life! here in town? Are you a yoga guy?"

"I can't even touch my toes anymore."

"I love yoga," she says. "But I go to the studio called Imagine on High Street. Jenn knows the owner there. It's good for you."

"I'm sure it is."

"You haven't had any other thoughts about Madeline's disappearance, have you? I know it's been two years, but you were pretty foggy about that last night you saw her. The last night *anyone* saw her, as far as we know. Anything on that?"

Bowman must now see my flushed cheeks. It feels to me like she must be able to hear my heart beating, as much as it's thumping inside my chest. Like a fist punching the inside of my rib cage, trying to break out.

"Nothing," I say through a mouth still dried by last night's alcohol and this morning's fear.

"Maybe that's another book," Bowman says. "I hear true crime is big right now."

Before I can say anything, she pulls the door open and leaves, letting in another blast of cold air against my burning cheeks.

CHAPTER FIFTEEN

Sartre said hell is other people.

But he never tried to park on the campus of Commonwealth University.

On a weekday morning after eight o'clock.

On days I ran late—and there were a lot of them—Emily used to drop me off before she went back to work. Those ten or fifteen minutes we spent together in the car, alone, were some of the best of our marriage. We developed the habit of finding a song on the radio to sing along to, and then we'd belt it out as loud as we could. Neither one of us could sing, but we let it rip anyway. Sometimes we'd pull up next to my students at a stoplight, and they'd stare with puzzled looks on their faces as we screamed "Livin' on a Prayer" or "Wake Me Up Before You Go-Go." Most of the time we laughed more than we sang.

Now I know *exactly* when I have to leave my house in order to make it to campus in time to get a parking spot close to Goodlaw Hall, which houses the English Department. Bowman's visit—and pointed questions—threw everything off. And I end up in the overflow lot at the bottom of the hill, which means I have to schlep about a half a mile in the biting wind, carrying my ancient university-issued laptop and a stack of student papers. The cupola bell tower on top of Goodlaw looks like it's in another county when I start walking, and by the time I reach the building, I'm winded like a man who just ran ten miles. I'm sweating under my clothes, and I can't wait to peel off my winter coat and drop my bag in my office.

And I'm almost convinced Madeline has already been here, telling Preston or the dean or anybody who would listen that I stole her book, that I need to be fired, that I'm the lowest form of life to ever live—

And I *am* intercepted right inside the door.

But it's one of my colleagues, Carrie Richter. She's a few years older than I am and teaches American literature. We've never really socialized, and I know she's divorced with a teenage son. Carrie and I have served on a few committees together, and I've always found her to take a reasonable approach to solving problems. She's standing inside the door as though she's waiting for me, although I'm not sure why. But when she sees me, she lifts her index finger as though testing the direction of the wind.

Does she know Madeline? Has Madeline talked to her?

Then I remember Bowman asking about the internship program. And whether I talked to Sophia about it. Bowman knows that Carrie did.

"I'm so glad to see you because I wanted to tell you something," she says.

"What's that?" I ask.

More questions about Sophia?

I'm trying my best not to sound out of breath from my walk up the hill. I always think my overall health is in the toilet if I can't walk up the hill without getting winded. I don't change my lifestyle any, but I do worry about it.

"I'm sorry I didn't make it out to your event last night," Carrie says. "I had some exams to grade. Besides, your book isn't really my kind of thing."

"Your kind of thing?"

"I know a lot of people like mysteries and thrillers and whatever. You know . . . books about women getting killed in awful ways. There's enough of that in the world."

I feel like I have to say something. And Bowman's visit had been running over and over in my mind as I drove to campus. "You knew Sophia Greenfield, right?"

Carrie's eyes widen. "I did. Well, to be honest, I only met her for coffee once. Mostly we e-mailed because she was trying to get us to send her interns." She visibly shudders. "It was ghastly what happened to her. Murdered that way. Disgusting."

"I'm sorry."

"Did you know her?" Carrie asks.

"No, no. I didn't."

"She was really kind. That's the impression I had of her. We talked about Anthony a little."

"Your son."

"Right. She offered to mentor him or something. He was having some tough times."

"Did she do that?"

Carrie's brow creases. "Why did you bring her up today?"

"Well . . . you mentioned a woman being murdered. And I knew about the internships. . . ."

My fumbling explanation seems to satisfy Carrie. "It's so sad. That's why I don't read books about serial killers."

"It's not about a serial killer—"

"I mean, I get it, especially if you're going to the beach. But . . . not for actual reading."

"I understand," I say, although I don't. "Thanks for telling me your thoughts."

I wait, wondering if she'll say more. Maybe . . . congratulations or something like that. But she doesn't.

"Well," I say, "it was a good event."

"I have to run. I'm off to talk about Edgar Allan Poe."

I start down the hall in the opposite direction, but then Preston sticks his head out the double doors that lead into the English Department.

"There he is," he says. "Our distinguished author. You've got time before class, right, champ?"

"I was just coming to see you," I say. Again my mind goes back to Madeline. Has she already spoken to Preston?

"Come on." He waves me in, so I follow. Preston wears skinny black jeans, and the sleeves on his checked shirt are rolled to the elbows with pinpoint perfection. He's a few years younger than I am, a guy who went straight from getting his undergraduate degree to earning his PhD and was on his way to tenure before he turned thirty. He runs the English Department through a combination of cool efficiency and ironic detachment. Everyone assumes he'll be dean or provost someday. If not at Commonwealth, then somewhere. Behind his back as well as to his face, his colleagues call him "Preston the Politician."

He closes the door to his book-lined office once I'm in and settled into a chair. Preston breezes around to his side of the desk and sits. He checks his e-mail first, clicks a few things, then turns to me.

"You kind of look like shit," he says. "You had too much champagne."

"And that hill is too steep."

"You need to get to the gym with me. Do some weights. Run a little. Now that so much is going right in your life, you need to rebuild the temple of your body."

"The temple has a lot of cobwebs and loose bricks, especially after a night like the last one."

Preston rests his folded hands on top of the desk, which is remarkably free from clutter. To his left sit three framed photos—one of him with his wife, Kelly, and then one photo of each of his daughters. They look perfect enough to have come with the frames. To his right, row after row of books. He teaches postcolonial literature and is known for his high standards, strict adherence to the rules of grammar, and dynamic lectures. Students love him or fear him. Or both.

"That's what I wanted to talk to you about," he says. "In a round-about way."

"Last night?"

"Your visitor," he says, his face becoming more serious. "The one you said was the neighbor up the street?"

I swallow hard. Why the hell is he bringing this up? And what does he know?

He unfolds his hands and rubs at a little speck of dirt only he can see.

"I just want to make sure you aren't getting into some kind of trouble you're not going to be able to get out of," he says.

And then I have to wonder—did he see Madeline leaving my house last night?

CHAPTER SIXTEEN

For the second time that morning, I find myself on the wrong end of an interrogation.

This time it's a friend, but that doesn't make it feel much better.

"I don't understand, Preston. And I do need to get some things done before class."

"Look," he says, "you and I are good friends. I probably know you better than anyone else in this department. And I mean it when I say I'm glad to see things turning in the right direction. You've been through hell. Really. I mean, there but for the grace of God, you know?" He cuts a glance at the photos of his family, then goes on. "But I do feel the need to speak up, to look out for you. And I couldn't say it last night with Lance there. I didn't want to embarrass you. And Lance . . . he's a little loose-tongued. I've learned I have to be careful what I say around him, especially when there's alcohol involved. He gets depressed as well. I don't think he's written a poem since he got tenure fifteen years ago." Preston rubs his forehead. "Between you and me, I wouldn't mind seeing him retire. But that's about five years away. And you just can't easily get a tenured professor to go. So we're kind of stuck with him. He runs his mouth to feel important, especially with students, so unless I want the whole world to know . . . Plus, I didn't want to ruin the good time you were having. It was a really big night for you. A book published. Most of us are lucky just to have enough articles published to get tenure."

On a few occasions, Preston has talked about writing a novel. He's even gone so far as to show me a few chapters from a work in progress. It seemed more theoretical than dramatic and completely plotless. I couldn't imagine anyone wanting to read it, but I gave him a few pointers, trying to help.

"You clearly had a woman there when we showed up," he says. "I could tell by how you acted when we came in. A man acts different when a woman's been in his house. It's just something we can sense instinctively. You said it was your neighbor up the street, but why would a neighbor slip out the back door like a thief in the night? Why wouldn't she want to stay and celebrate your big evening with you? With your friends?"

"She didn't—"

"Hey," he says. "I get it. I was single once too." He jerks his thumb toward the photos. "It's been a while, but I remember. I'm not trying to pry into your business, even though we are friends. A new relationship or whatever, you may want to keep it quiet. That's cool. And Emily was smart and beautiful, but it's been five years. That's a long time." He leans forward. "But I was thinking about it last night and this morning. And I talked it over with Kelly."

"You talked with Kelly?"

"Why would a woman run out like that? Why would you—or she—want to hide that way? I thought maybe the woman's married."

"No. God, no."

"And then I thought maybe it was a student."

"Preston—"

"You don't have to say anything. We're not talking in any kind of official capacity. We're talking as friends, even though we're in Goodlaw. And I hope they change the name because Hiram Goodlaw owned slaves. But that's neither here nor there. No, what does matter is that the campus environment has really changed in the last year or so. They were slow off the mark. A lot of old, entrenched attitudes that needed to change out here in the hinterlands. Now the university is really taking it seriously when it comes to relationships between professors and students. And they should. *All* universities should. It's about time we listened to women. This is a new era. It's here to stay. And I know you agree with me."

"Of course. But there was nothing like that—"

"After what you've been through, I wouldn't judge you for anything you did. But . . . even though you got the tenure vote, it can eventually be taken away if anything improper is going on. Tenure won't protect you, even with the book being published. I don't want to see that happen to you. And I don't want to see it happen to this department. It gives everybody a black eye. It really does. I don't want people to think we condone that behavior. I want this department to be out front, doing the right kinds of things. I want this department to be a model."

"I know you care about that."

"We all should. Speaking of that, Kelly has a new friend, a woman who just moved to town to work in IT at General Motors. She could set you up."

"Preston, you have to believe me. There's nothing like that going on. It really was just a friend who came by the house last night. I've never . . . I mean, I would never with a student. I don't believe in that any more than you do."

"Okay, good." He looks relieved, like a man who was just told he doesn't have any cavities. "I'm sorry. Maybe I was out of line bringing that all up. I want to make sure you get all the good things you deserve. And coming out of this funk you've been in . . . there might be temptations. Let's face it: These students worship you."

"They're kids. They don't know anything about the world."

"You're a published author and a professor. They look up to that."

"I guess so." I check the clock behind Preston. It looks like something he bought from Pottery Barn instead of the run-of-the-mill schoolroom clocks most of us rely on. "I really have to run. But I promise you there's nothing going on with any students. I wouldn't do that."

"Maybe I shouldn't have said anything," he says. "Maybe I'm an over-protective mother hen here in the English Department. But I worry about my people. Especially you."

"It's good to have friends." I gather my things and stand up.

"Madeline," Preston says.

When I hear the name, I spin around like he's fired a gun.

Madeline? Why?

"What did you say?"

"Madeline. Madeline O'Brien. *She* really worshipped you."

"She was very talented," I say.

"Right," Preston says. "She's an example of a smart, talented kid who really looked up to you. I'm just trying to let you know you've got a lot going for you. Everyone sees that. Even if you don't."

CHAPTER SEVENTEEN

REBECCA KNOX
PRESENT

It's freezing cold. Butt-ass cold for January in Kentucky. It's her senior year, her final one in college, and she doesn't remember it ever being this cold in Gatewood.

Despite this, Rebecca circles Goodlaw Hall once and then again and starts around a third time.

She knows Nye is in there, in his office getting ready for his next class. She knows when he's around because she was in his class early this morning, and she's talked to him plenty of times. About writing. About applying to graduate school someday. About life.

Why is it so hard for her to go in *this* time?

Why couldn't she just talk to him after class?

She wanted to but couldn't bring herself to do it.

Rebecca makes her third trip around, the snow flurries pelting her face. Her heart flutters like a flag in a strong wind. Flapping here and there and back and forth. She has friends who smoke. They claim it calms them down, helps them deal with stress. Rebecca has never smoked a cigarette in her life, never wanted to, can't imagine what her mom would say if she did, but if it brings peace and calm . . . She kind of wishes she did.

Just go in, she tells herself.

Do you know what you must look like out here? No doubt some student is bored in class and staring out the window while their professor drones on and on about Milton or Dante or dangling modifiers. And that kid is looking out the window and wondering why this girl is circling the building like a crazy person in the freezing cold. Anyone watching would think Rebecca was drunk or high or crazy.

"Screw it," she says out loud, and heads to the nearest door.

It's during class, so the halls are mostly empty. She hears a few voices lecturing, and her boots clack against the tile floors, echoing off the walls. She's in here almost every day, but the smell always gets her. Floor polish and old books. She thinks of this building as her home away from home. The oddball professors, the eager random students who talk about writing and movies. The English Department draws them all. Hippies and frat boys, Goths and farm kids. She could completely change her look and wardrobe every day and always find someone to fit in with.

Dr. Nye's office is at the end of the hall. She sees his door is open, the glow from a lamp spilling out. It's a gloomy day. There's not enough artificial light on campus to make up for that.

She steps into the doorway and knocks gently. "Dr. Nye?"

He's staring at his laptop, and her knock seems to startle him. He lifts his head like he thought he was alone in the building.

"What?" he asks.

"I'm sorry. I can come back."

"Oh. No, you don't have to do that. Sorry."

But he shuts the lid of his laptop like he's hiding something.

"Are you sure?" Rebecca asks.

"Please. Come on in."

Rebecca does, taking the seat across the desk from Nye, the one she's sat in many times while he's dispensed wisdom. But the way she seemed to interrupt him makes her even more nervous, and she wishes she'd just forgotten the whole thing. Instead of coming inside, she wishes she'd just kept walking around and around the building and then gone to her apartment and her idiot roommate.

But here she is. And Nye looks at her expectantly. Impatiently.

He seems tired, his eyes red. She's heard some of her classmates discuss how attractive they think he is, but Rebecca never really sees it. She thinks of him more like the cool-dad type. Or maybe the cool uncle, since she has a dad who is kind of cool. She knows Nye's wife and son died in some kind of weird accident five years ago. *A bike? A sled?* She thinks of them every time she comes in because he keeps a picture of them on the shelf behind him. A pretty woman, natural-looking with her hair in a ponytail, laughing on a beach. The kid next to her smiling. A cute boy with dripping-wet hair. Probably taken a few years before they died. She stares at the photo a little too long.

"I haven't finished reading your thesis yet," Nye says. "I meant to tell you after class this morning that I hoped to be through it by now, but you left before I could speak to you. Things have grown a little hectic with the book and everything. But I'll get it done by next week."

"Oh. Sure. That's not what I'm here about. I mean, thanks for telling me. There's no rush. I don't have to defend it until . . . When am I supposed to defend it?"

"End of April or the beginning of May should work. In time for your graduation."

"Cool. Yeah, that's fine."

Rebecca recognizes her missed opportunity and curses herself again for being stupid. She could have pretended she's here to discuss the thesis instead of what she's really here for. She could have said thanks and left, but she missed her chance. And now she sits across from Nye with him expecting her to have something else halfway intelligent to talk about.

Nye studies her. One of his eyebrows goes up, which is the look he gets when he doesn't understand something a student says in class and wants to express disapproval without being totally shitty or hurting someone's feelings.

"How are things going otherwise?" he asks. "Classes good? Life good?"

"Things are good, yeah. It's cold. Really cold."

"It's January. We'll start to get a break soon. I grew up in Michigan. If we were up there, we'd have a whole lot of winter ahead of us."

"Totally. Yeah."

"Did you just want to talk about the weather?" he asks. He has this way of low-key ragging on students when he asks questions. He's not being rude, but he's kind of saying, *Hey, do you really have anything important on your mind?*

Rebecca swallows. Her throat is dry. Chalky. Like she'd been drinking the night before even though she hadn't. And rarely did.

"It's about your talk last night," she says, impressed with herself for how steady the words sound.

Nye's eyebrow goes a millimeter higher. "What about it?"

"I really enjoyed it. I did. I liked the way you talked about the book and how you wrote it. And answered all those questions. It was interesting. I haven't started reading it yet."

"I'm sure you have plenty of other reading to do with graduation coming up."

"No doubt." She tries to generate saliva in her mouth and manages to summon a drop. "Anyway, last night. It's about the crowd, the people who were there. Well, one person who was there."

Nye straightens in his chair, tilts his head to the side. "What do you mean?"

"Okay," she says, plunging forward. "You're going to think I'm nuts, but I'm pretty sure I saw Madeline O'Brien in the back of the room last night."

CHAPTER EIGHTEEN

It feels good to say it.

Even though Nye stares back at Rebecca, his face showing nothing beyond the raised eyebrow, and even though he probably thinks she's the craziest, most irrational person he's ever met in his life, she's glad she said it.

Ever since last night when she went to the event, Rebecca has been turning over in her mind what she saw. The woman in the back of the room with the red hair and the glasses. At first, Rebecca assumed she was another student, someone she'd taken a class with but didn't really remember. One of those faces she sees around campus or at parties that looks vaguely familiar but she can't remember where she knows them from because maybe she was off in her own head in that class, or maybe the person never participated, or maybe Rebecca was a little drunk when they met at a party.

But then the woman did something familiar. She tugged at her eyebrow. It doesn't seem like much, and for anybody else, it wouldn't be. Except Madeline used to tug at her eyebrows when she grew nervous. Rebecca observed her doing it in class one day and locked eyes with Madeline, and then when they were walking out of the room, Madeline said, "I know that eyebrow thing makes me look like a freak. I only do it when I'm really nervous."

And Rebecca told her it was no big deal, that everybody has their little quirks. And she asked Madeline if she had a test or a paper or something coming up, and Madeline said, "Oh, no, it's something personal," and walked away.

And that was about a month before she disappeared.

So when that woman at the reading started tugging on her eyebrows, Rebecca really believed it was Madeline. And Rebecca shuddered and everything turned cold like she'd seen a body rise from a grave.

But she calmed down—a little—and after the event tried to catch up to the woman, to talk to her and find out if it really was Madeline, but the eyebrow puller was long gone by the time Rebecca made it across the crowded room and started looking.

And didn't that make her seem even more suspicious?

Nye continues to stare for an uncomfortably long period of time. Finally, he says, "Now, why would you say something like that?"

"Did you see the woman in the back of the room? With the really red hair? You must have seen her because she was right in the back. She would have been directly in your line of sight. Did you see her?"

"I might have," Nye says, sounding irritated. "You think that was Madeline?"

Nye's attitude knocks Rebecca off her stride. She could tell him about the eyebrow thing but wouldn't that sound as ridiculous—or more so—than everything else she's already said? Aren't there a lot of anxious young people who stand around at the back of crowded rooms pulling on their eyebrows? And the woman looked so much thinner than Madeline. And Madeline is supposed to be . . .

Besides, Rebecca knows people in power don't really like it when you bring up unpleasant or unusual things. They like to see the world a certain way, and they don't like to listen when someone has a different opinion. Nye isn't totally like that, she knows. He's pretty good about listening to students and trying to understand them. But still, he's a professor. And a dude. And they just don't always listen the way they should.

She wishes she'd kept circling the building. But she's in it now.

"Did this person talk to you? Or say something to you?" Nye asks.

"No, she left before I could."

Nye takes his time speaking. He scratches his head and seems to be carefully formulating a response. He looks like he wants to let Rebecca down easily, not just come out and say how ridiculous and immature she's being. And Rebecca would hate it if any of her professors thought she was immature. She's not that kind of student. She meets every deadline, comes to every class. Visits office hours for every professor, even those she really has nothing to ask.

When Nye does talk, the irritation is mostly gone. He sounds . . . Rebecca isn't sure. Does he sound relieved?

"So maybe you just *wanted* this person to be Madeline," he says. "Maybe you found yourself thinking of her because the book is about a murder in a town like Gatewood, and your mind played a trick on you, so you could only see what you wanted to see. Were you and Madeline good friends?"

"Not really," Rebecca says. "I liked her. But we didn't hang out much. Just one class. Sometimes I'd see her at a party. One party in particular . . ."

Rebecca doesn't want to say more. She won't get into that night. She won't tell Nye about Zach and the thing in the alley. She thinks Nye would understand better than most. She thinks Nye would be the kind of person to give her the benefit of the doubt and really listen.

But how could she be sure?

She remembers that woman in her dorm back during her freshman year. The one who transferred away . . .

Nye goes on, his words more forceful. "I *did* see that woman in the back of the room, the one with the red hair. I couldn't miss her, like you said. But I didn't think she looked anything like Madeline. Not at all. If you wanted to hide, you wouldn't show up with hair dyed that bright of a color. And I think we've all had to face the harsh truth that Madeline is probably not coming back. Not after two years. It's really unfortunate."

"Yes, I know the statistics."

Now Nye leans forward, his brow furrows. "Do you know something about Madeline's disappearance? Is there a reason why you think she would be here?"

Rebecca's heart resumes its flapping. It feels like it's going in four directions at once inside her chest. "No, I don't."

She thought Madeline was dead. Everybody did, and that was freaky enough.

But then what if Madeline was alive? And back?

Isn't that even freakier?

"I'm sorry you seem upset about this," he says. "It's hard when there aren't answers about someone. Maybe it's best to just chalk this up to a misunderstanding. And for you to concentrate on your own work."

Rebecca gets the message he's trying to send. And it's what she feared someone in a position of authority would think or say. *Just forget about it. It isn't your concern. These aren't the 'droids you're looking for.*

That's what they always say. . . .

"You're probably right," she says. "And I have to be getting to my class."

"Is there something else I can do to help with this?"

"No. That's okay."

"Good." Nye leans back. He looks more like his usual self. Chill. Easygoing. The cool uncle again. "And I'll get to the thesis soon. I promise."

"Thank you."

Rebecca exits his office and pushes through the double doors, back out into the cold. The wind blows stronger, and the flurries swirl faster.

She tries to take in what Nye said, tries to see it his way. After all, chances are Madeline is dead. And if she's alive, she doesn't want to come back.

But damn, Rebecca thinks.

The way she pulled on her eyebrows . . .

CHAPTER NINETEEN

CONNOR
PRESENT

I always enjoy talking to Rebecca. She's a good kid—a diligent student. A little shy but a hard worker. If every class had twenty Rebecca Knoxes in it, my job would be a walk in the park. But I can't wait for her to leave because I want to open my laptop and get back to what I was reading. I'd just found the article when she knocked on the door. And now it's cutting it too close. I have to get to class, or I'll be late.

And truth be told, I need the distraction. Rebecca's visit and her recognizing Madeline shake me more than anything else from this morning. But if Madeline's in town, even disguised, the possibility of her running into friends, students, professors, increases exponentially. It's a small community, with a limited number of places to go. The walls of my office look closer, like they've moved several feet forward during the course of the morning.

The classroom is a refuge even though I'm distracted. I head off to my next class, Introduction to Creative Writing, and half of that class is fiction and half is poetry. I know nothing about poetry. I've never written it. I've never even read it. But I have to pretend to be an expert for fifty minutes a day. While the students read their assignments out loud— and their readings sound like recitations of the tax code—my mind continues to drift back to what I was reading when Rebecca came in.

An article from the local paper about Sophia Greenfield's murder.

I'd only scanned the beginning when Rebecca knocked, but the details cycle through my mind like a GIF. *Twenty-seven-year-old Sophia Greenfield was found dead outside her job last night. Police have no suspects. Her husband, Zachary Greenfield, was working late. When she didn't come home, he grew worried and found her body in the parking lot. Her parents have been notified.*

A picture accompanied the article. A smiling blond young woman. Pretty. Bright. A life full of promise. All of it cast away in a few moments of struggle inside her car.

There's something more about her face, something I recognize. It feels like I've seen her before—*have I?*—but I can't say where. I don't think she was a student. I don't think I knew her from anything else.

Does she just look like all the other beautiful, smiling, healthy young faces populating this college town? The ones that always make me think about Jake?

But . . . Bowman is right. Her story sounds just like my story. Just like Madeline's story. A woman murdered in a parking lot. Her husband the prime suspect.

The scarf. The position of the body. The wounds.

What would I think if I were Bowman?

The room has gone silent. I've blanked out, gone off into my head. I look around. Nineteen faces watch me expectantly. I'm supposed to be saying something, leading the way. After all this time, it's still hard to believe I'm the authority figure. That I'm the one people look to for guidance.

"That was a great discussion," I say. And I have no idea if it was or not. I glance at the clock. Only seven minutes left in class. Close enough. I tell them what to read for next time and send them packing. I dash out of the room faster than they do, eager to get back and finish reading about Sophia.

As I navigate the halls, I look at every student's face more closely than ever. Normally I glide past them, nodding or saying hello to those I recognize, trying hard to remember names of students from past semesters.

But today I look. Closely. Is Madeline walking among them? Could her hair be another color now? Could she have changed her mind and decided to resurface on campus, blowing everything in my life sky-high?

Given the details she put in the book, could she have committed a murder? Or does she know the murderer?

What else is she capable of, then?

And what does she have in mind for me if she knows I stole her book?

"Connor."

I freeze among the streaming lines of students. They ripple around me like I'm a boulder in a river. Bulked in their winter coats, phones to their ears or in front of their faces. I look behind me in the direction I heard my name called.

It's Lance coming toward me. He's almost sixty and has been teaching creative writing at Commonwealth for nearly thirty years. When he was young, he published a number of poems, some even in prestigious journals around the country. But the well apparently ran dry a while ago. I'm not even sure he writes anymore. Lance's moods fluctuate like spring weather, and I never know which version of him I'll encounter. He may speak about something that occurred in his classroom in a self-aggrandizing way, or he may bemoan his own laziness and lack of focus. Every once in a while when I pass him in the hallway, he ignores me for no apparent reason. So I always approach him cautiously and follow the cues.

"You look a little ragged," he says when he reaches me, shaking my hand. We start walking side by side. Lance is shorter than I am by an inch or two, and he's grown a little bulkier through the middle with each passing year. He's never been married, never had a steady partner as far as I know, and even though they're good friends, Preston has told me he thinks Lance sits at home and drinks too much. On more than one occasion, I've smelled liquor on his breath early in the morning. At least once a year, he misses a few days due to the "flu" or a "nasty cold" that won't let him get out of bed, which I've grown to suspect is code for him being on a bender, a debilitating combination of alcohol and depression.

We've socialized more in the five years since Emily and Jake died. Two single men passing the time by going to a sports bar, eating wings, and watching basketball. I never wanted my life to go that way, but those are the cards that were slapped down on the table in front of me.

"Champagne," I say. "Gets me every time."

"I hear you. I've been trying to cut back on drinking. That's my New Year's resolution. One of them."

"What's the other?" I ask, not because I want to know or believe he'll follow through on any of them. I ask because it seems polite.

"To write more," he says. "I'm not getting any younger, and I just need to get some things finished. Get that old fire back. I've let that part of my life fall away. I feel sorry for myself. You know, with all the teaching I do and the committees . . . It's one thing to have helped so many young writers the way I have, but I need to think of myself."

It's a familiar litany, one Lance recites almost every day. We approach my office, and while he goes on—*and on*—about his workload, I start scanning student faces again, hoping not to see Madeline.

". . . besides, you've inspired me, Connor."

I tune in to Lance again. "How's that?"

"You wrote your book while you were teaching. Why can't I write a few poems? Right?"

"Sure. I'm glad to hear you say that."

"You must have written pretty fast, though," Lance says. "A book like that. A page-turner. A potboiler. A money shaker. I remember you and me commiserating over drinks just a short time before you got the book deal, and you were saying you'd been in a long dry spell with writing too. That was our bond: that we were both running on fumes. Something turned it around for you because that book came out of you." He snaps his fingers. "Like magic."

Every word that comes out of Lance's mouth is tinged with an archness, a hint that there's something behind the words that the listener may or may not understand. So I try not to make too much of this casual hallway conversation, but my mind starts to race away from me. Why is Lance asking me about my writing dry spell right after the book has come out? Right after Madeline showed up at my house?

"I guess I felt inspired," I say.

"Is that the secret? Just . . . inspiration?"

"I guess we all have to keep plugging away," I say.

"Yeah." And he laughs, as though I've said the funniest thing he's heard in a month. "We all have to keep plugging away, don't we?"

He claps me on the back and walks away.

CHAPTER TWENTY

I return home a little after five. On the way, I stopped by the bank and managed to get some information about a second mortgage in order to find money to pay off—or to *pay back*—Madeline. As conversations about money often do, this one overwhelmed me and made me realize I wouldn't be able to get my hands on a bunch of cash that quickly.

When I pull into the driveway, the sun is already disappearing, the winter dark descending. The snow flurries have stopped, and the skies are clear, which means an even colder night. Emily and I used to take turns cooking dinner, and I want to believe all I have to look forward to is going inside and making my not-so-famous spaghetti and meatballs. We'd pair it with a bottle of semi-cheap wine and watch Jake roll his eyes at us as we laughed at our not-so-clever jokes.

Instead, I psych myself up for walking Grendel and getting back inside, battening down. Maybe eat a turkey sandwich or make a frozen meal in the microwave. I haven't prepared the meatballs in five years.

But an unfamiliar car waits for me in the driveway when I pull behind the house.

"Shit."

Madeline?

But would she be so obvious? She came without a car the night before. It's too cold for the driver to wait around outside, so it isn't until I step out that I see it's Bowman. She climbs out and nods at me as I approach her, her hands tucked deep into the pockets of her coat.

"I hoped you'd be here soon," she says. Mercifully, the wind is calmer, sparing us the worst of the windchill effect. "I considered going up to Goodlaw, but then I thought that might be a little too embarrassing for you. Who wants a cop showing up at their place of employment?"

"Thank you for that," I say. "Is there something you need to ask me?"

"Oh, yes," she says. "A few somethings."

"Would you like to come inside?"

"I thought we'd talk down at the station," she says. "My car's running and warm. And I'll bring you back when we're finished."

"At the station? Is that necessary?"

"It is."

I try not to stutter. "Yeah, but I don't know—"

"It won't take long."

My eyes roam longingly to the back door of the house. Inside are warmth, sanctuary, calm.

"I have to let Grendel out," I say. "He's been alone all day."

"Go right ahead," Bowman says. "He might burst if you don't. I'll wait here."

Bowman stays rooted in place, watching me while I approach the door. I'm hoping like hell Grendel barks when my key goes in the lock. It wouldn't be the best look to have Madeline sitting inside the house waiting for me with Bowman standing in the driveway.

But Grendel barks, just like it's any other day, which it certainly isn't.

I toss my bag on the kitchen table. It takes no time at all to get the leash on Grendel and bring him back out the door into the cold. He's been holding his water for hours, so despite the cold weather, he's only too happy to get outside and find relief. And I think then what I've thought many times—if Emily and Jake were still alive, they'd be helping with Grendel. We always talked about getting a dog but never did, and I wish we had while they were alive. I wish they'd been able to enjoy having him around as much as I do. Emily and her family always had dogs when she was growing up, and she volunteered at the animal shelter here in Gatewood. Several times she dragged me along with her, and we always talked about adopting a dog someday. We just never did.

Grendel doesn't acknowledge Bowman at all. Once he's seen a person up close and spent a little time with them, he doesn't feel the need to bark at them. And once someone's been in the house a few times, he never barks at them again. Bowman could have been a snowman or a bush for all Grendel cares.

He hikes his leg and sends out a healthy stream that looks like it might peel a few layers of bark off the small tree he's aiming for. When that's finished, he sniffs around. I'm about to hurry him up since Bowman is waiting when the detective clears her throat.

"You walk him around the neighborhood here?"

"Sure."

Bowman keeps watching me, the sky turning red behind her. She looks like she expects me to say more.

"We go for a longer walk in the morning and then again at night. That's about all the excitement he can handle at his age."

Bowman blows on her hands and rubs them together. "You ever go to the dog park over by Gatewood South High School?"

"Sure. We used to go there."

"But you don't anymore?"

"Not really."

"Why's that?" Bowman asks.

I can't tell if she's asking just to pass the time while we watch my elderly dog decide if he has to piss again. And he probably does. Or if she's working up to something again. The paranoid part of my brain says Bowman has never had a casual, random conversation in her life.

"It's the other side of town," I say. "And Grendel's getting old. If I take him for a long walk, he gives me a look that says, 'Are you trying to kill me?'"

Bowman watches me. Face calm. Cheeks red from the cold.

She knows how much her silence induces people to talk. I know it too, and I know it's a ploy. But I fall for it.

"I used to go there when I first got Grendel, and when I was still . . . you know, a mess over my losses. I just wanted something to do to distract me, so the drive over and back didn't bother me. I have more going on now, a little more control of my life. So I prefer to just walk him here. It's more convenient."

"So you went over to the dog park when you were drinking more and not at your best emotionally or mentally. Is that what you're saying?"

It feels like she's putting words in my mouth, but I don't know what else to say. "That sounds about right. Sure."

"I see."

"Is there a reason you're curious about my dog-walking habits?"

Bowman points to Grendel. "It looks like his tank is empty."

Grendel is pulling against the leash, trying to drag me up the stairs and back into the house.

"Feed him or whatever you need to do," Bowman says. "Then come on back out. It's getting late."

CHAPTER TWENTY-ONE

Our ride to the station is about as awkward as it gets.

Bowman says nothing. The local public radio station plays the news—a series of disasters in China, Africa, America. Bowman keeps her eyes on the road. The headlights illuminate the road stained by salt, the traffic going against us streaming away from downtown. But the car is warm, and I follow Bowman's lead by keeping my mouth shut.

She pulls around to the back of the station, where marked and unmarked vehicles are scattered. I've been to the station once before. When Emily and Jake died, I came down to answer a few questions that the authorities in Maine needed to have cleared up. I walked in the front door, and when I gave my name, the detective handling the case locally—a woman who retired about a year ago—met me at the front door and treated me about as gently as anyone ever has. We sat in her office while I answered all of her questions.

Did your wife and son know how to swim?

Had they been kayaking before?

Why were they in Maine?

Did anyone want to hurt them?

I answered truthfully. But my mind was reeling then, like someone had placed electrodes on both sides of my head and left the juice on for too long. I probably shouldn't have been driving. I probably shouldn't have been allowed to shave myself. My mind swam with memories of them. Everything. Meeting Emily our senior year of college at Michigan. The three of us horseback riding at Mammoth Cave when Jake was nine. The endless hours he and I spent in the driveway shooting baskets.

When Madeline disappeared, Bowman came to my house. And while her questions then had been pointed, the story and the police interest quickly faded away. With no leads and no real evidence, Madeline's story moved to the back of everyone's minds.

I suspect this trip to the police station will be different.

Bowman leads me to a heavy metal door plastered with enough warnings to scare anybody off. She waves an ID card over the electronic lock and leads me through, still not speaking. We pass two uniformed cops who nod to Bowman but don't look at me. What must they think? That Bowman is bringing in yet another pedophile or drunk driver or embezzler?

We go down a short hallway and turn right, and Bowman opens the door to a small conference room. She points for me to go inside and then speaks for the first time since we were standing in the driveway. "Do you want something to drink? Coffee? A Coke?"

"I'm okay."

She leaves, closing the door. And I'm alone in the cold, windowless room. It has a small table, and there's a screen in the wall they can pull down for presentations. I have nothing to do, so I sit. And wait. Fifteen minutes later, Bowman comes back, offering no apology or explanation for keeping me there.

"Is something wrong, Detective?" I ask, trying but failing to keep the impatience out of my voice.

Bowman stands at the head of the table. She looks surprised to hear me speak. "You tell me. Is there?"

"I don't know why I'm here."

"I'm about to tell you." She sits down and slaps a steno pad onto the table. She clicks her pen open with an exaggerated flourish and looks at me. "I just need to follow up on our conversation from this morning. You don't mind, do you?"

"I don't seem to have any choice."

She affects a casual air, like we're two friends sitting in a coffee shop. "You can go if you want. Is that what you want to do? Leave?"

"I just want to know why I'm here."

Bowman taps the pen against the pad. She looks lost in thought, like I'm not here. Until she says, "You already kind of answered one of the questions I wanted to follow up on. When we were back at the house."

"I did?"

"I asked you about the dog park, and you admitted you used to take Grendel there."

"'Admitted,'" I say. "That's a strange word to use about my habits. I don't think I was *admitting* anything. I was telling you something fairly mundane I used to do with my dog."

The pen in her long fingers taps. *Tap tap tap.*

"Do I need a lawyer, Detective?" I ask.

"That's your right. Would you like to exercise it?"

"I'm just trying to understand why you care where I took my dog two or three years ago."

Bowman stops tapping and lifts her hand in the air. "So you took Grendel to the dog park. Did you always stay inside the dog park? Or did you sometimes walk him in the neighborhood around the dog park? I know some people do that. Maybe they get bored just standing there, watching the dogs run around. Maybe they want to get some exercise themselves. Did you ever do that? Walk Grendel around the neighborhood there?"

Again, it seems like an odd question. And I know Bowman is once again building to something.

"Yes, I did. When I first got Grendel, he didn't socialize well with other dogs. So I'd let him spend some time in the park with the other dogs, and when he'd had enough of that and started to get cranky, I'd put him on the leash and walk around the neighborhood. I work with a guy who lives a few blocks from the park, so I kind of knew that area.

Grendel never liked to walk very far. I do the same thing in my neighborhood now. He didn't really like the dog park or my attempts to get him to play well with others. So I gave up eventually."

"And this time you were going to the dog park . . . that was about two and a half years ago or so?"

"Yes."

"It would have been in the summer about two and a half years ago?"

"I can remember going there in the summer, yes. Summer and a little into the early fall. That was part of the appeal. The weather was nice. It was good for me to be outside. Grendel too."

"Got it." She pauses a moment, then says, "You see, Sophia Greenfield lived one block from the dog park. And you were going there during the time she died. So I need to know exactly where you used to walk when you went outside the park."

CHAPTER TWENTY-TWO

It's been so long, I'm not sure I can remember the exact route I followed.

And even if I did remember, I'm not sure I should tell Bowman. I'm not sure I should tell her anything. *Ever.*

But I didn't know Sophia Greenfield. And I didn't kill her.

"I'm going to try to remember," I say, "and after I tell you, I'm going to leave."

"You can leave before you tell me, if you want," Bowman says. "I already told you that."

"There's a street that runs parallel to the park," I say. "I'd start there. But I don't remember what it was called."

Bowman stands up. She goes over to a built-in cabinet beneath the projection screen. She opens a drawer, removes something, and comes back to the table. It's a map of Gatewood, and she unfolds it on the table between us. Her long index finger with a nail painted light pink lands on the dog park and then slides up a fraction of an inch.

"This street? On the north side of the park?"

I study the map in the bright light. "Yes. That's it. Cherokee Street. They're all named after Native American tribes, right?"

"Yes. Whoever built the neighborhood wasn't very woke. So you started on Cherokee. . . ."

"And we'd turn right on the next block." I point to the map. "Iroquois."

"And how long would you stay on Iroquois?"

"For a while. Three or four blocks. It dead-ends at that point. See? It dead-ends into Creek."

"So you're on Iroquois from the four hundred to the eight hundred block," Bowman says. "Let's stick to that. Sophia Greenfield lived at Five-oh-seven Iroquois. And you didn't know her? Could she have been a student of yours? She didn't get a degree from Commonwealth, but she took some classes there toward a master's. She never finished it."

"I don't think so," I say. "I can't promise you I remember every student after all these years. But I don't think so. I saw her picture online today. After you came to the house, I briefly read about her murder. I'm going to be honest with you, Detective, she looked a little familiar to me, but I haven't been able to place her in my mind. Did she spend time in the dog park? Maybe I saw her there."

"And you wrote a book with a freakishly detailed account of her murder." Bowman leans back in her chair and rubs her eyes. She tosses the pen onto the table. "Here's the problem I have, Connor. You spent time in her neighborhood. You wrote about her murder, although you claim it was a coincidence. She kind of looks familiar to you, but you don't remember from where. And a student of yours disappeared two years ago, and you were the last person to see her alive."

"Wait a minute," I say. And it's as if the room has turned upside down, done a loop de loop with me strapped into my chair and no way to get off the ride. "You can't start laying all that on me. You talked to me back then."

But Bowman is up and over at her magic drawer again. And I realize that she doesn't normally just keep stuff in there. She's planted these objects. She's planned this whole discussion. With props.

She brings back a thick manila folder stuffed with papers. She flips it open on the table and starts paging through, turning the documents over with crisp efficiency.

"I don't know what you're getting at, Detective." But even as I say it,

I should have known it was coming. Madeline. Sophia. The book. Except I know Madeline is alive. And I don't know Sophia at all.

Do I?

I run my mind back through the trips to the dog park. Admittedly I wasn't in the most social frame of mind back then. Yes, I talked to the other dog owners, made small talk about the weather, politics, the university. The dogs.

But I rarely learned names. Never made lasting connections. No one invited me out for a drink or a coffee or a meal. I'm sure I seemed closed off, shut down. And if I gave my name, people might have even recognized it. They might have known or heard about what happened to Emily and Jake, and then I'd no longer be the quiet guy at the dog park. I'd be the "poor man whose family died." I'd be set off by quotation marks, an object of curiosity and sympathy and even a little fear. After all, what do you say to a guy who lost his wife and son to the ocean? A guy who mopes around with his only companion, a wheezing, arthritic beagle-husky mix?

But there is something else.

There is the blue house that must have been on Iroquois. The blue house with the perfect lawn and the perfect yard. And the perfect couple inside . . .

There was something about them. . . .

"Here it is," Bowman says, poking the paper with force. "We interviewed Sophia Greenfield's husband, Zachary, quite extensively. He was the person who could really be Sophia's voice after she was gone. And do you know what he told us?" She taps the paper again. "He told us Sophia was nervous. Scared even. She said there was a guy who used to walk his dog on their street in the evening, and do you know what that guy used to do?"

The perfect blue house. The perfect yard.

The blond woman. The dark-haired man with the neatly trimmed beard.

And I would see them working in the yard, the two of them, laughing together. Or through the windows of the house. Watching TV as I walked by. Having a drink on the porch.

"She said he used to . . . watch them," I say.

"She told her husband she thought the man with the dog was behaving strangely," Bowman says. "Creeping around. Watching them. Watching *her*. And after she died, we all tried to find that man, but we couldn't." Bowman looks pleased. She smiles. "Spoiler alert, Connor. I think I just found him."

CHAPTER TWENTY-THREE

CONNOR
SUMMER, TWO AND A HALF YEARS AGO

I've always looked inside other people's windows.

When I was a kid, I used to ride my bike home from basketball practice on winter evenings, the cold air rushing against my face, my legs pumping faster in the growing darkness. I passed house after house in my neighborhood, the windows glowing with an internal light, the TVs playing, the families gathering in a kitchen or a dining room. Instead of watching the sidewalk in front of me, my eyes trailed across the lawns, hoping to catch a glimpse of what went on inside.

Why?

My parents divorced when I was six. My dad came around, most of the time, and he always sent the support payments for my sister and me. I always envied those kids with complete families, the ones I imagined talking and laughing around a bountiful table. I even fantasized about the father stepping in and telling one of the kids to finish their peas or not to talk so loud. I didn't care because the father was *there*, the family was *complete*.

I watched those houses go by, and even the blue TV glow looked like a beacon of warmth and love.

When Jake was born, I continued to look in windows. When I was on runs through our neighborhood or coming home from work, my eyes were still drawn to the light from inside other people's houses. They looked tranquil and safe and warm. . . .

Until one day I took the garbage out to the curb at our house. And when I turned around to walk back up the driveway, one of those moments occurred—they're rare, but they do happen—when I saw my life, my house, the way everybody else did. I saw the warm glow from the kitchen. I saw Emily holding Jake. I saw the TV glowing blue in the corner. And I understood that my life looked like those lives I'd been observing all those years. Why did I need to spy on others when my own life was the nest, the hearth, the cocoon?

After Emily and Jake were gone, I started looking again.

When Grendel came to live with me, I started taking him to the dog park specifically because it wasn't the same as walking through a neighborhood. There were no houses to peek into. And there would be other people to talk to. Real people, not silhouettes through a lighted window.

But Grendel's temperament and my own lack of interest in carrying out forced social interaction with strangers at the park drove me to walk through the subdivision where Sophia Greenfield lived as the sun went down and families and couples gathered at home for their evenings together. All over again I was that kid pedaling home from basketball practice, the one on the sidewalk but with his face pressed against the metaphoric glass, hoping some of the warmth and glow from inside the house would light a spark inside me.

I saw the blond woman the second time I walked Grendel through the neighborhood by the park.

It was a warm night in late June. Lightning bugs were just appearing. Everything blooming.

Grendel trudged along two steps ahead of me, the leash slack between us. He wasn't in a hurry. He was just happy to be away from everything else—dogs and people alike. I watched the houses we passed on Iroquois Street. Some were open and lighted. Some were quiet and dark. The houses were smaller over here, boxier, but just like in my neighborhood, the residents maintained their yards well. They cut the grass, planted flowers, picked up the kids' toys instead of leaving them scattered across the lawns.

Halfway up the block, a woman with blond hair, wearing a baseball cap pulled low, sat on her porch reading a book. She looked to be in her mid-twenties and wore denim shorts and white sneakers. A bottle of craft beer sat on the stoop next to her, and as I came closer, she sipped from the bottle and then turned a page. She looked up and caught my eye.

If we had lived in a big city, we would have been able to ignore each other. In Gatewood, strangers generally said hello to each other. Or at least waved. It wasn't about whether you would have an interaction. The question was always how much of one you would have.

The woman on the porch waved.

And I waved back.

And that might have been that. But as I passed her house, a car came along and pulled into the driveway. A guy about the same age as the blond woman climbed out, and when he did, the woman on the porch jumped up and put her book aside. Neither of them seemed to care that Grendel and I were walking by.

The guy dashed up the sidewalk, and the blond woman bounded over to him. They kissed and hugged. I have no idea how long it had been since they'd seen each other. It was possible it had only been hours. But they acted like only the two of them existed in the entire world.

I took the scene in subtly, trying not to be noticed. But the truth was, they had no idea Grendel or I existed. I went on with my walk, and the couple receded behind me. Grendel and I looped through the neighborhood as darkness fell, and we finally made it back to the car and started for home.

But I couldn't stop thinking about that couple.

How young they were. How attractive.

How joyous to see each other.

I knew—*I knew*—I'd be walking there again. Looking for them. Seeing them.

CHAPTER TWENTY-FOUR

For weeks and weeks, I watched for them. That whole summer.

Grendel and I walked up Iroquois Street almost every evening, rain or shine, hot or starting to get cool, and sometimes we saw one or both of the couple and many times we didn't. When we saw them, they were working in the yard together, cutting the grass or raking leaves. We saw them sitting on the porch, having a drink or reading. We saw them entertaining friends, a group of young people gathered around the dining room table. And we saw them together or alone inside the house, watching TV, eating, painting the dining room.

They were constantly working on the house. Landscaping, carpeting, gutters. Something was always being removed or installed, replaced or painted over. I never spoke to them, only exchanged a wave that first time. But I assumed they were newlyweds living in their first house, and so they attacked the project of being homeowners with the gusto only the young could generate. I imagined the trajectory of their lives— upward. Once that house on Iroquois was whipped into shape and beautiful, they would sell it and move to a larger home. Maybe a child would be born while they still lived there. Maybe they'd put that off and have their children later. Promotions at work, money socked away in a retirement account.

I thought of those early days with Emily and Jake. The little apartment we lived in while I was in graduate school. When Jake used to wake us up during the night, crying, I used to drag myself across the room to comfort him. And I worried I wouldn't be able to do it all—work, teach, write, provide. Be a parent. I thought of that time as a series of endless anxieties.

But I wish every day I could go back and live it all over.

I never once felt envy for that couple in the blue house. I never really wanted to be them.

But I did wonder what it was like *to be them.* To be at the start of it all, not to know what lies ahead. Not to carry the burden of knowing something precious had already been taken away. To see everything as possible.

To be so consumed by each other, to be so intensely possessed of love and desire that late nights and languid mornings were given over to fucking without the interruptions of children or exhaustion or aging. To be in every moment, physically and emotionally.

And maybe I looked too much. Maybe my gaze lingered too long on them. Maybe I seemed odd or off as I walked by. The lonely guy with his mutt.

On a dozen occasions, when loneliness and grief gripped me like a boa constrictor, I took Grendel for a walk in their neighborhood after midnight. Instead of going to the cemetery, I went over there, hoping for a glimpse of that couple. Usually their blinds were closed. Sometimes the house was already dark.

Once or twice, the curtains would still be open, the lights on. And I'd see them inside, watching TV or talking. And I'd take Grendel up and down the street a few times, comforted just by being close to them. I never knew if they saw me. If they looked out and saw the guy walking his dog aimlessly up and down the street. I assumed they never noticed me because everything was so good inside that house. . . .

But maybe they saw me and thought I was a nut.

I should have known something wasn't quite right with them. But I was so consumed by my assumptions about them, so taken by who and what I thought they were, I didn't take serious notice of the subtle changes in that house.

I should have noticed that I saw them together less. That frequently when I walked by, one or the other of them would be home, but not both. I should have noticed that the household projects that were formerly performed together were suddenly being performed separately. If I'd been closer to the house—and I never went closer than the sidewalk and so didn't see any real detail—I might have seen strained looks.

Instead the crack in their marriage shocked me.

On an early September night that was unseasonably hot, I walked Grendel up their street. The leaves hadn't come close to turning, but the kids were back in school. Real autumn loomed on the horizon.

It had been a few days since I'd seen anything in the couple's house. The blinds had been drawn, everything dark. I thought they might have gone away on a trip, and my mind conjured images of them in a tropical paradise, sipping drinks by the pool, snorkeling in blue water.

But the house was lit up. Every window glowed with bright light.

And the front door stood wide open. Not just the storm door, but the screen door as well.

As I approached, I heard them before I saw them. Voices raised, one male, one female. I thought someone had turned their TV up too loud. Or a car approached with the radio blasting. But the voices were not singing, the dialogue unscripted.

I saw them through the dining room window, facing each other. He spoke forcefully, poking his finger near her chest as he did. He moved closer and closer. And she refused to yield. She stood her ground, shaking her head. She gave it right back, poking with her own finger. He let her get it out, let her go on for a while.

I paused on the sidewalk directly in front of their front door. If they'd looked out the window, they would have seen me out there. The voices grew louder, and I felt like an intruder. A few words reached me, snatches of the fight. *Her . . . Did you do that to her? . . . I didn't . . . Not that* . . . I resolved to go on, to let them have their privacy, even as the fight I watched seriously dented the notions I'd been carrying about them. I tore myself away. I took a step to the left, moving up the street.

That's when he did it.

She continued to poke her finger at him, and he made a quick movement with his left arm, swiping it up and knocking her hand out of his face. He followed that up by taking a step forward. Threatening.

I decided. Almost before I knew what was happening, I was going up the steps, Grendel by my side. I reached the porch and went through the wide-open door and made a right turn toward the dining room. When I did, I saw the blond head disappearing into the kitchen, leaving her husband behind. He must have heard me because he spun around, his face still contorted by anger.

"Who the fuck are you?"

"Is she okay? I heard the yelling. I saw you swing at her."

"I didn't swing at her."

"Is she okay?" I asked again. "I'm calling the police. This isn't right."

Some of the anger drained from his face. He came back to himself. Tension went out of the muscles in his neck and shoulders. He straightened up, no longer in a defensive crouch that looked like a prelude to a fight.

He looked and sounded like a man trying to defuse.

"It's okay," he said. "We just had an argument, that's all. A misunderstanding. It happens, and that's all it was. Something between married people. Okay? Thank you for checking, but we're okay."

"I want to see her," I said. "I really want to know she's okay, or I'm calling the police."

"You can't just—" But he bit off his words, the muscles in his jaw clenching. "This is a matter between the two of us. My wife and me. And we're handling it."

"Hello?" I called out. "Hello? Are you okay back there? I need to know you're not hurt and that you feel safe. Otherwise, I'm going to call the police."

A long pause.

The guy stood before me, his breath coming in little huffs. His eyes looked like two dark pebbles. They were focused on me so hard, I thought they might give off heat.

"Honey?" he called. "Did you hear him?"

Another pause.

"I'm calling," I said. "I'm sorry, but I can't just walk away—"

"I'm okay." The voice sounded faint and muffled, but I heard it. She spoke again a moment later with more volume. "I'm really fine. We just had a fight. And it's okay. Really. You can leave. Thank you."

I hesitated. I thought about calling anyway. I didn't see the woman. I didn't lay eyes on her and *know* she was okay.

Maybe my illusions about them influenced me. Maybe I just felt like I'd stepped into the home of a stranger, and it wasn't my place to insert myself into their problems, even though adrenaline blasted through me, making my hands and legs shake.

Maybe I was just wrong.

But I gave Grendel's leash a gentle tug, and the two of us turned around and walked out of the house.

CHAPTER TWENTY-FIVE

CONNOR
PRESENT

"So you didn't call the police?" Bowman asks.

I don't say the words. I don't want to admit it.

I'm embarrassed.

Bowman goes on when she sees I'm not saying anything. "When Sophia was murdered, we looked into everything about her marriage. I can answer my own question—no one ever called nine-one-one and reported anything. There were no charges of domestic violence or even a domestic disturbance. No assaults or fights."

She pauses, studies me. Gives me a chance to say anything, which I don't.

"And we talked to all the neighbors. Sophia and Zachary lived there for a couple of years before the murder, and in all that time, the neighbors never heard anything. No arguments even. And you know how volatile young relationships can be."

"That doesn't mean they didn't happen," I say. "It sounded like he cheated on Sophia. They seemed to be discussing another woman."

"But you don't know. And you didn't call."

"If you're thinking of a way to make me feel worse, I'm not sure that's possible. Is Zachary a suspect? Has he been cleared?"

"It's an open case. Until we make an arrest, I consider everyone a possibility."

"But he's the husband. Isn't he *more* of a possibility?"

Bowman doesn't say anything else.

More than anyone, I know how things can change in a moment. I know how easy it is to start with a horrific event and then trace a chain of choices backward. If this didn't happen . . . If I'd done this instead of that . . . If I could do everything all over again . . .

But the universe refuses to grant us do-overs. Those happen only in romantic comedies in which the main character gets hit on the head and wakes up back in the past and gets a second chance to win the heart of the girl he overlooked in high school.

They don't happen in real life.

"Obviously, Detective, if I knew this woman was going to end up murdered, I would have done anything in my power to stop it. But she told me she was okay, and that's all I could go on. I wasn't at my best back then."

"You've said that."

"Are you telling me the husband is the prime suspect?" I ask. "If he was cheating and she caught him, maybe that led him to silence her. It's been two and a half years, and you haven't been able to make an arrest."

"But she thought you were behaving inappropriately," Bowman says. "She told her husband she saw the man with the dog lingering outside the house late at night. Sometimes after midnight. She thought that man was trying to look in the windows at them. At her, presumably. How is a woman supposed to feel about that? Do you see how this looks for you, Connor?"

"I told you I didn't mean them any harm. I was . . . curious. I was . . . floundering."

"Here's what I'd like to do, Dr. Nye. Just in the interest of covering all my bases." Bowman sounds reasonable and calm. We could be two coworkers shooting the breeze in the company break room, casually spinning out options for the project we're about to launch. "We took quite a bit of forensic evidence at the scene of Sophia's murder. Fingerprints. Hair samples. DNA. The whole nine yards, as my father used to say. If you'd just consent to some tests and provide some samples, then we could eliminate you from any further consideration in this matter."

Eliminate you from further consideration.

Bowman doesn't care about my not calling 911 when I saw Sophia and Zachary having a fight. She's still fixated on the details in the book and my time in Sophia's neighborhood.

She thought I was watching them, acting strangely.

And Bowman sure is hoping I was because she thinks she's going to catch a murderer.

"I'm not staying for this." I stand up. "You said I was free to go whenever I want, so I'd like to go." I realize I don't have a car. It would be much more dramatic if I could simply storm out of the police station and drive off. Less so if I need to call an Uber to take me away.

"That may have changed," Bowman says.

"What changed?"

"My flexibility on letting you go," she says. "As a matter of fact, I feel compelled to remind you of your Miranda rights before any further questioning occurs. I'd hate to have my investigation derailed because of a procedural error."

And she proceeds to recite them with me standing there. When she gets to the part about having the right to representation by an attorney, it dawns on me that I don't know an attorney. Certainly not one who could represent me in a criminal case. A moment of indecision paralyzes me. Then I know who I need to call, and I bring out my phone.

"Are you calling an attorney?" Bowman asks.

"Can I have some damn privacy? You can't just sit there and watch and listen to everything I do."

Bowman weighs her options for a moment while she looks at me like I'm a bug she wants to squash. Then she flips her manila folder shut and stands up with it in her left hand. "Are you saying you won't submit to being fingerprinted?"

"Not without talking to a lawyer," I say. "I want someone to talk to."

At the door she stops and turns back. She speaks more harshly than at any other time all day. "Okay, go ahead and call a lawyer. Then we can continue our conversation."

CHAPTER TWENTY-SIX

Preston knows everyone in Gatewood.

Preston the Politician.

He's the one I call from that conference room in the police station, asking for help with finding a lawyer. I give him a quick rundown of my situation, and he listens without losing his cool.

"I know just the person," he says. "Sit tight."

Bowman comes back once I'm off the phone, sticking her head in the open door.

"You decided to stick around? Does that mean you're willing to be fingerprinted?"

"I have a lawyer coming."

She clucks her tongue. "I told you you're free to go. Bringing a lawyer into things just makes them messy. I can call a judge and get a court order for fingerprints and DNA."

"I'm going to wait for the lawyer."

"Suit yourself."

Bowman leaves and makes me sit here and stare into space until that happens. During that time, my despair grows, and I begin to imagine myself on trial, in a jail cell, shipped off to prison. It's bad enough to live with the guilt over not calling 911 that late-summer night when I saw Sophia fighting with her husband. To imagine a life in prison for a crime I didn't commit . . .

I'm ready to tell Bowman the truth about the book. Everything hinges on that. If I simply admit I didn't write it, then they lose their main reason to suspect me of Sophia's murder. I'd lose just about everything else, but I'd have my freedom. And I've already lost everything once before. It can't be any worse.

Nothing ever could be.

But Preston told me to keep my mouth shut until the lawyer arrived. He emphasized that. *Keep your mouth shut. Don't even ask to use the bathroom.*

I listen to him. I don't speak. And Bowman seems to know what's going on because she doesn't say a word to me either. She comes back with a laptop and clicks and taps away, the two of us in the same room, each acting like the other isn't there.

Then the lawyer arrives—Diana Lukas. And once she's there, it's all out of my hands. She looks to be a few years younger than I am and wears a dark overcoat, her large hoop earrings glittering in the harsh light. She talks to Bowman like she knows her well, like the two of them are bickering, rivalrous siblings. I feel like I'm watching a performance they've both given more than once.

"Alicia, what are you trying to pull here?" Diana asks, not even bothering to say hello. Not even bothering to introduce herself to me. She has a large purse on her shoulder and holds an iPhone in her hand. "Do I have to remind you about the concept of due process?"

"Can we discuss this in the other room, Diana?" Bowman says, standing up. "I'm sure you have all kinds of crazy notions you want to throw at me. And maybe one or two of them will actually be connected to reality."

"Ah, yes. *I'm* the crazy woman disconnected from reality, right? If a male lawyer came in here, you'd be shaking his hand, telling him what a good old boy he is."

Bowman laughs. "You're trying to paint me as a big bad part of the big bad system? You know I'm a woman married to a woman in Kentucky, right?"

"That doesn't matter. You're part of the system by virtue of that badge you tote. The fact that you're married to a woman doesn't change that. But have it your way." She steps aside and makes a sweeping motion toward the door. Once Bowman goes out ahead of her, she turns to me and places her finger over her lips. "Not a solitary word, and I'll have you home in an hour or so."

"I have to pee."

"Cross your legs."

It takes longer than an hour. Seventy-five minutes later, Diana comes back into the conference room alone, closes the door, and tells me I'm free to go.

I have to pee so bad, my eyeballs are probably turning yellow. I'm not sure I understand what she's saying. I must look at her like I'm a visitor to a country where I don't understand the language.

"You can go home," she says slowly. "Bowman is getting the release form ready now. You didn't say anything important to her, did you?"

"I told the truth."

"Interesting strategy. These cops think they can pull off this bullshit and get you to give up DNA and fingerprints without a court order. Around here they fit you for the noose and build the gallows before they even know your name."

"Thank you," I say.

"No problem. Of course, you can't leave town without telling the police. And if you can bring me your passport tomorrow, that would really help."

"I'm not going anywhere."

She reaches over and squeezes my arm. "Damn right. We'll have to talk in more detail soon. But it's getting late, and my husband is in charge of putting our kids to bed since I'm not there." She shudders and rolls her eyes. "I love that man, but he's hopeless sometimes. Last time I was out this late, the kids ate ice cream for dinner and Popsicles for dessert."

"I don't know how to thank you."

"We're not out of the woods yet, so we'll hold off on naming the courthouse after me for a few more days."

Bowman comes in without knocking and hands Diana a piece of paper. She doesn't even look at me, just turns and goes.

"They hate it when their plans go awry," Diana says.

"Plans?"

"Her plans for the evening," she says. "She really hoped she could have you in a jail cell before the night was out."

CHAPTER TWENTY-SEVEN

Diana leads me out the front door of the station, and as if by magic, a car I recognize pulls up as we emerge into the bitter cold.

Diana turns to me, her dark coat open, and extends her hand. "Here's your ride, Connor. We'll be in touch."

I thank her, but she's already hustling away, and my words float off along with the puffs of my breath.

The driver's-side window of the car in front of me rolls down, and Preston leans out. "Get in, dummy. It's cold."

And I'm all too happy to do it. He pulls away while I'm buckling my seat belt.

"Thank you," I say. "For finding Diana and for picking me up. I could have called an Uber. I know it's after ten, and you have your family."

"I don't mind," he says. "I wanted to see how you were doing. What the fuck is going on? All this cloak-and-dagger shit."

The streets are dark and quiet. Everything feels hushed by the bitter cold. I ask him about the murder of Sophia Greenfield.

"Do you even remember that?" I ask.

"Sure," he says. "She was strangled in her car. I thought it was the husband. It usually is."

"Maybe not this time. The cops haven't arrested him."

Preston is shaking his head and not saying much. His hands grip the steering wheel tightly as the heat blows through the vents at our feet. I think he's angry at the injustice of it all.

"I'd still be there if it weren't for Diana. And you. I didn't want to have to call my sister in Michigan and tell her I was in jail."

He remains quiet as he makes the last turn, the one onto my street. I study his profile, watch his jaw clench tight.

He pulls into my driveway, stopping next to my car.

"What do you think?" I ask. "You haven't really said much."

He leaves the car on. The headlights shine against the garage door.

"It's a problem," he says through pressed lips.

"I know that."

"No," he says. "It's a problem at work. On campus. When you called me from the station, and after I got ahold of Diana, I checked in with Paul Armstrong in Human Resources."

"What for?"

He turns to face me. "Connor, we're kind of through the looking glass here. I've never had a member of the department become part of a murder probe before. I had to know what to do."

"What is there to do?" I ask. "What are you getting at?"

He sighs through his nose, his lips pursed tighter. "Connor, do you remember what we talked about this morning? About the changing attitudes on campus? They just can't have someone working there, going to classes and interacting with the students, who might be guilty of a murder."

"No one's charged me with anything. They were trying to rattle my cage with a lot of bullshit."

Preston's voice goes up. His voice never goes up. He never seems to lose his cool, but I can tell he's pissed right now. "And everyone's going to make that fine distinction when the news breaks about this? Right? That's what we all do so well these days as a culture—make fine distinctions when we hear something on the news."

"Are you firing me?"

"No. No one's firing anybody." He pauses, collecting his thoughts. "This isn't corporate America, where you can just run someone out of the building if you want. But you're being placed on administrative leave. Until we know how all of this is going to shake out, that's your status. With pay. But you can't come into Goodlaw, and you can't go near a classroom."

I smack my fist against the dashboard. "Are you kidding me?"

"Calm down, Connor. It's out of my hands. Paul made the call. And he talked to the president about it just to make sure."

"The president?"

"Yes. The university doesn't want any black eyes. Not now. Not with a capital fund-raising campaign under way."

The curtain has really been lifted now. And I see what's happening behind it. "Oh, a capital campaign? Fund-raising? I thought it was all about the students."

"It is. Of course. But it's about money too. You know that. We're practically begging the legislature in Frankfort to send us more, but all they've done is cut. To the bone. Do you think we need a bunch of politicians getting up and saying, 'Why should we give more money to higher ed when the professors murder people?'"

"That's insane."

"And it's about the reputation of our department and the work everyone is doing. We've all busted our butts to have the department in the right place. We can't lose that. You'll be hearing from Human Resources. They'll make you sign some forms."

I fumble for the door latch with my right hand. "I thought you'd go to bat for me."

Preston must have overridden the locks, because I can't get out. "Now hold it. Don't run off. You need to listen to me."

"I have been. And it hasn't helped."

But I stop trying to open the door—a fruitless gesture anyway. And since I'm trapped in the car, I decide to listen. I don't have a lot of allies, and it sounds like I might need more in the future.

"I have stuck my neck out for you," he says. "And you know that. Going all the way back to when Emily and Jake died."

I remain silent, a grudging admission that he's right.

"And if you want me to continue to do that, if you want me to try to go to the administration and go to bat for you, I have to know everything. And I mean *everything*. I need to know that nothing else is going to surprise me."

"I didn't kill Sophia Greenfield," I say. "I didn't even know her—" But I can't get those words all the way out of my mouth. I did know her. Or I thought I did. And I'd created a story for her, the way any author would. My story turned out to be wrong. Very, very wrong. "I mean, I didn't even know her name. I didn't really know who she was."

"What about Madeline?"

"What about her?"

"Is there anything with her that's going to bite me in the ass?" he asks.

"It's weird the way you bring that up."

"No, it's not weird that I want to keep all of us out of trouble. And run a department smoothly. How do you think the rest of the university will respond when they find out you might have killed a woman? How do you think the female faculty will respond? They've felt like their concerns have been taking a backseat for years. They have a stronger voice now. And I'm glad. We have a female provost now, in case you haven't noticed. The first time in the history of the university. It's a new world, and you don't want to be in the crosshairs."

"I didn't do anything. Why am I in the crosshairs?"

I'm shaking my head, disgusted. But my disgust is served with a heaping side of hypocrisy. I know a giant secret about Madeline, and in the confined space of the car, with the night getting late and the cold wind blowing outside, I almost tell Preston all of it. The book I stole and Madeline's reappearance. I desperately need a friend. . . .

But I can't blow everything up.

So I give him a piece of the puzzle.

"You know I might have been the last person to see her alive," I say.

"Sure."

"I don't really know what happened that night. I was drunk at Dubliners. And she walked me home. Part of the way or the whole way, I can't be sure."

I hesitate to say more.

But Preston pushes me. "Go on. What happened?"

"I don't know," I say. "I don't know what happened to her after that. She disappeared."

"Jesus, Connor."

"I know. I'm sick about it, Preston. I've thought about that night a lot over the last two years. If I was the last person to see her, then maybe I could have helped prevent whatever happened. I blew it."

"It's bad," he says.

"I know. I told you this so you wouldn't be blindsided. That's everything about her disappearance."

"I don't know what to say, Connor. Really."

"I'm trying to get this out in the open here. You know I need my job. You know it's the only real stability I have in my life. What would I do if I couldn't teach?"

"Yeah, I know."

"I need the money and the benefits."

"What about the book?" he asks. "You should have plenty of money."

"What is this with everybody thinking the damn book made me rich. It didn't, okay? It's not *The Da Vinci Code*."

Preston lets out another sigh, this one longer. And he turns away, looks at the dashboard display like he really needs to know how much gas is in the tank. "I've got to get home."

"So what are you going to do at work?" I ask. "Are you going to talk to Paul?"

"I'll do what I can tomorrow," he says, still not really looking at me. "But you stay away, you hear? Just lie low. And don't talk to anybody on campus. Especially students."

I push the door open, feel the blast of cold wind. I pull my coat tighter around me and reach back, extending my hand to Preston before I shut the door. "Thanks."

He mumbles his reply. "Sure." But he doesn't reach for my hand.

I shut the car door, and he backs out, the headlights sweeping over me in the driveway.

CHAPTER TWENTY-EIGHT

Grendel greets me with a series of barks.

I still step inside cautiously, like I think the place is laced with land mines. For all I know, Madeline is back, waiting for me. Ready to deal with me in whatever way she sees fit.

Maybe the same way she killed Sophia Greenfield.

I go through the house, moving quickly, checking every room and closet. I even go into the bathroom and pull the shower curtain back, but find nothing except grime. I let out a breath.

And I remind myself to get a dead bolt installed on that basement lock.

It feels like it's been three years since Bowman came to the door and started asking me about the book, but it was just that morning. I go back out to the kitchen, Grendel at my feet, sniffing my shoes and trying to make sense of the unfamiliar scents on me.

"That's what jail smells like," I say.

I haven't even taken my coat off. I'm hungry and tired, worn-out from being questioned by friend and foe alike. The bottle of Rowan's Creek remains on the counter. I never put it away after the night of the book launch. Its presence makes it just too easy.

I pour a healthy shot. I hope it will calm me.

I lift the glass toward Grendel, toasting him. "Buddy, I think you're my closest friend these days. Here's to you."

My soulful confession doesn't seem to move him, so I throw the shot back, enjoying the burn as it goes down. The warmth passes through me, and I take my coat off and hang it over a kitchen chair. Grendel yawns and shuffles back out to his perch in the living room.

No one likes to drink alone, but it appears I have no choice. I swallow another shot, and as that one burns through me with less intensity, I try to look ahead. Without the possibility of going to campus to teach, the days stretch ahead of me like a desert. It's true that in the days and weeks and months after Emily and Jake died, I did a horrible job as a professor. I showed up unprepared. I turned assignments back late or not at all. I took up space in the classroom but wasn't actually there.

But having someplace to go, having a routine and a purpose in my life, might have saved me. I shudder to think what I would have been doing with my time if I hadn't had a job to go to.

Those dark days nearly swallowed me up. Every day, just waking up felt like an ascent out of the depths of a deep, slippery pit. If I slid back in there again, I'm not sure I'd ever pull myself out. I study the floor, the cabinets, the familiar space. Everything menaces me. The bottle that could be turned into jagged, cutting shards. The knives in their block. The gas oven.

"No," I say. "No, no. Not that."

I summon willpower and push the bottle of Rowan's back across the counter into the corner. I grab a dish towel and drape it over the bottle.

"Okay," I say. "Eat something. Act like a normal human being and eat something."

I find some ham in the refrigerator. It smells okay, so I make a sandwich. My hands shake while I spread mayonnaise on the bread, but the act also feels reassuring. A normal thing in an abnormal time.

Before I can take a bite, someone knocks on the back door. I nearly jump out of my skin. And Grendel barks like we're being invaded by zombies.

I think about not answering. It's ten thirty. The curtains are drawn.

Maybe they don't know I'm inside. Maybe it's all a mistake. Wrong house.

But I'm acting the fool. Someone coming to the back door knows me. Preston?

I'm happy to toss the sandwich aside and go over and part the curtains on the window. My initial reaction is to say, "Shit."

It's Madeline, her arms crossed, shifting her weight from one foot to the other as she tries to stay warm. She looks small, like a child coming in from playing outside. Sometimes I see all my students this way. Small, young, vulnerable. Jake would be a college student now, and I feel the knife gouge in my heart just thinking about him and the future he'll never have.

But Madeline is here. On my stoop.

I pull back, wondering if she saw me.

Everything I learned at the police station about Sophia Greenfield's death comes back to me. And I knew her. At least in some way, I knew her. In my mind, I knew her much, much better. In my imagination, she'd grown to be larger than life.

And the only person who knows the details of Sophia's death, besides the cops, is Madeline.

She knocks again, her palm pounding against the door, rattling the glass.

"Come on, Connor. I'm freezing my ass off."

Of course she knows I'm here. She saw the lights, likely saw me through the window.

My phone is in my pocket. I can call Bowman, let her know what's going on. She could be here in minutes and haul Madeline away. I'd lose everything.

But I'd be done with Madeline. And Madeline seems more and more like a killer.

Who might be here, at my door, to do something to me. I stole from her. I took money that belonged to her.

"Connor?" she says. "Please? We need to talk."

Did she not do me in the night before only because Preston and Lance showed up and interrupted? Did they save my ass with their bottle of champagne and stupid jokes?

Has Madeline only spared me long enough to get the money she wants . . . and then . . . ?

I go across the room and take a steak knife out of a block on the counter. It's one of a set Emily and I received when we got married. I doubt the knife will do me any good. It's probably so dull it can only slice butter.

But it's something.

My mouth is dry as I walk over to the door. I slip the knife into my pants pocket, within easy reach. The only question—would I actually have the guts to use it even if I needed to?

I'm about to find out.

I yank the door open. Madeline looks up, blinking in the light that spills from the kitchen.

"It took you long enough," she says. "Do you know how cold it is?"

"Come on in, and yes, I do."

She blows past me, and when she gets inside, she stomps her feet and runs her hands up and down her arms. Grendel stops barking and goes over to her, but she's too busy trying to work warmth back into her body and she ignores him.

"I came by earlier and you weren't here. Were you out at Dubliners with the new crop of students?"

"I wish. I was with the police, learning all about Sophia Greenfield."

CHAPTER TWENTY-NINE

MADELINE
FALL, TWO AND A HALF YEARS AGO

Madeline walked two blocks from campus to the attic apartment she reached by climbing a rickety staircase in back. The metal contraption looked more like scaffolding than an actual conveyance for human beings, and footsteps shook it like it was about to decouple from the building and tip over into the yard.

She was taking a full load of classes, including a nearly impossible science requirement—Introduction to Biology—with a professor who wore an oversized beard sprinkled with crumbs and talked in a whisper. Madeline preferred to sit in the back of the room, but the guy spoke in such a low voice she moved to the front, squeezing in next to two basketball players who sprawled out in their desks like they were in their own living rooms.

Madeline should have skipped that day. She'd been sick to her stomach ever since hearing the news about Sophia two days earlier. Little eating, no sleeping. A friend from the studio Yoga for Life! had shared the news on Facebook, and when Madeline saw it, she literally sank to the floor, crumpling onto the shitty tiles in her kitchen like discarded clothes. She wanted to sleep somewhere else that night. Wanted to feel safe. She resorted to wedging a kitchen chair under the knob of the door to her apartment and kept a large cast-iron skillet next to her bed. Weaponized kitchenware. The best she could do.

She felt marginally safer in the early-fall daylight. She had gone to Biology only because there was a test, and Madeline never skipped tests or quizzes. She walked faster than normal, operating under the assumption that moving quickly would keep her from harm. Walk with a purpose. Act confident. When she made it inside, she planned to collapse into bed, pull the covers over her face, and maybe never come out. And keep the skillet nearby.

Or maybe it was time to move on. Try a new place. Avoid the trouble that seemed to be swirling around her.

As she approached her building, she saw someone standing at the bottom of the fire escape. A woman, middle-aged or older, in a white shirt and tan pants, her bobbed hair mostly gray. She smiled when she saw Madeline, like she recognized her. And Madeline froze about twenty feet away, uncertain if she should proceed.

The woman lifted something that glinted in the midday sun. Something gold.

"Madeline, I'm Detective Wallace with the Gatewood Police. I was hoping I could ask you a few questions."

Madeline stayed rooted in place. She felt like one of those stupid animals, a deer or an opossum, that thought if it stayed still long enough and didn't move, a predator would attack something else. Even though this woman bore no resemblance to a predator, Madeline hoped she didn't have to talk to her. Cops had put her on edge ever since her childhood. A cop showing up unannounced never led to anything good. They'd shown up once when she was four and taken her mom away for leaving the scene of an accident. Later, much later, she learned her mom had been drunk and had hit a parked car. Madeline went to live with her grandparents for a time after that. Her mom was in jail—she had to go somewhere.

And more than once the cops came because of one of her mom's boy-friends. Madeline called them herself once when one of the guys shoved her mom against the dishwasher. But the guy told the cops it was an accident, and her mom refused to press charges, and Madeline never looked at the police the same way again since they didn't seem to care.

The woman came closer, still holding her badge up. Maybe she thought she could hypnotize Madeline with it. "You do know why I'm here, right?"

Madeline decided to move. Otherwise the woman might think she was an idiot. So Madeline nodded. Her hand started up, reaching for her eyebrow.

No, she thought. *No.*

She scratched her nose instead.

"It's about Sophia Greenfield," Wallace said. "We're trying to talk to everyone who knew her in any way. And I understand the two of you attended the same yoga studio. Do you think I could just ask you a few questions?"

The cop looked friendly, more like a grandma than a detective. Madeline knew cops liked to pretend to be one thing when they were really something else.

Madeline ran through excuses in her mind, reasons to get away from the cop, but nothing plausible popped into her head.

She tried her best.

"Well," she said, "it's a lot of steps up to my apartment."

Wallace turned her head, took in the three-story climb on the ancient stairs. "I'm deceptively fit. I do yoga too. I think I can handle it. Unless you want to talk somewhere else. We could go down to the station in my car. But that's a lot less friendly." The woman smiled again, took a step toward Madeline. "I'm not here to get you in any trouble, Madeline. I'm just here to find out what happened to Sophia. It's possible you don't know anything useful. And if you don't, then I'll just leave. But the sun is hot, and you have those books you probably want to put down."

Wallace nodded toward the metal stairs, raising her eyebrows. She looked like she was suggesting something fun. An adventure. A day at the park. Not questions about a woman who'd been murdered.

But Madeline hadn't talked about Sophia with anyone. Maybe she needed to. At least some parts of it.

"Okay," Madeline said. "Let's go."

CHAPTER THIRTY

Wallace complimented the skylight but nothing else. Madeline trusted her more because she didn't try to come up with some bullshit about what a homey apartment it was. Madeline knew it was a dump, crappy even by student standards. But it was all she could afford without mortgaging her entire future. As things stood, she'd be paying off loans until the end of time.

And she'd be paying off those loans while trying to make it as a writer.

Poverty much?

Wallace settled on a chair Madeline had rescued from the Salvation Army store. A five-dollar special. She'd asked the guy downstairs—the one who frequently played music so loud her own windows shook—to help her pick it up, and together they'd wedged it into the trunk of his car. He'd carried it up by himself, and clearly thought he was going to get something more in return than the cup of tea Madeline gave him. She knew she'd disappointed him, but Madeline had enough trouble in her life without getting entangled with a neighbor. Her mom, who wasn't good for much, taught her that: *Maddy girl, don't shit where you eat.*

Thanks, Mom.

Madeline sat in the other chair, which had remained in the apartment after the previous tenant moved out. Madeline had thrown a sheet over it before she sat in it the first time, hoping to cover it up and eventually forget about the multiple unidentified stains on the upholstery.

Wallace smiled. "I know this is hard. It's always difficult when a young person dies senselessly."

It wasn't a question. Madeline knew she was supposed to look sad, to nod her head and bite her lip. So she did.

"You knew Sophia from Yoga for Life! How long had you been seeing her there?"

"I guess a few months. I started going at the beginning of the summer. I only go once a week. On Tuesday evening they have a pay-what-you-want class, so I go then. I usually put in a dollar. I feel cheap, but it's all I can afford."

"Sure. That's student life. Did you ever socialize with Sophia? Outside of the yoga studio?"

Without meaning to, Madeline looked at the door and then back at Wallace. If asked why her eyes made that dart across the room, Madeline would refer back to her childhood, to the times the police came and asked her questions about her mother or, perhaps, one of her mother's boyfriends. Madeline felt certain one of those boyfriends—and she couldn't name the guy or even picture him in her head anymore—gave her the advice never to enter a room without knowing how to get out. The cops, he said, liked to cover all the exits, but if you tried hard enough, you could always find a window, a trash chute, an exhaust vent. . . .

So much worthwhile wisdom from her childhood. She felt certain most of her classmates at Commonwealth had grown up in very different worlds from the one she had grown up in. She tried to embrace the difference, tried to see herself as unique. She knew she'd absorbed it all, knew it was part of who she was. A college education didn't bleach it all out of her.

"You're not in any trouble, Madeline," Wallace said. "This is fairly routine. And I'm not even the lead investigator on the case. I'm just helping out."

Madeline knew there was only one door. And if she went out a window, it was a three-story drop to the yard below. She took her life in her hands enough just by going up and down the rickety stairs every day.

"We went to get coffee sometimes," Madeline said. "Just to talk after yoga. And I saw her out at a concert once. And we talked there."

Madeline had noticed Sophia a month before they ever spoke. Sophia looked older than Madeline by a few years and wore a wedding ring on her left hand. Sophia's body looked like it was chiseled out of rock, like it would take several good-sized men to be able to push her over. And maybe not even then. Madeline had once stood behind her at yoga and marveled at how gracefully she did every move, her blond hair in a long braid down her back. More than once, Madeline had opted to do child's pose instead of something particularly difficult the instructor presented. But not Sophia. She had done everything, never missing a beat. Strength, beauty, and poise had radiated from her as if they came from a glowing core.

"What did you talk about?" Wallace asked.

Madeline knew she couldn't tell Wallace everything they'd talked about. She couldn't say any names, not in a town as small as Gatewood, a place where everyone seemed to know everybody else three times over. And Wallace was here to talk about Sophia's life. Not Madeline's.

"I guess I just told her some of my problems," she said. "Mostly we talked about school. My future plans. My writing. I'm working on a thesis, and it's kind of . . . Well, one of the characters is based on Sophia."

"Is it finished? Can I see it?"

"Oh, no. Not even close. In fact, I might . . . I might trash it and start over. It isn't very good."

"How did Sophia feel about you writing about her?"

"When I first told her, I guess she thought it was a little weird. But once I explained it, she didn't seem to mind. She was really supportive. And Sophia gave me good advice. She listened, and, you know, she was a little older, so she saw things the way my friends couldn't."

Friends. Madeline didn't have a lot of friends. She had talked to

Sophia in a more real way than to any of them. Sophia just seemed to invite that kind of openness.

"Did she ever talk about her own life?" Wallace asked.

Madeline didn't know if the relief showed on her face or not, but she felt it. A wave passed through her, and despite the awful circumstances of Sophia's death and the nausea she still felt over it, she didn't want to talk about her own life, which was nowhere near as orderly and straightforward as the animal taxonomy she was learning about that semester.

Madeline thought about her answer. She wanted to be clear and, since she could, honest with the cops. "She talked about her job more than anything else. The one at the nonprofit. How they helped kids with literacy, which I thought was awesome since I'm an English major. And she talked about her house. I guess she'd just bought one and was fixing it up. It sounded like it needed a lot of work."

"Did she talk about her husband?"

Madeline scanned through her memories of her conversations with Sophia and decided she didn't have anything to lie about. "She didn't."

"Never?"

"Never."

Wallace remained quiet and still. If the conversation between them came down to a waiting game, it was obvious to Madeline that Wallace would win. She looked like a guru, a Zen master, someone content to sit on that crappy-ass chair for hours at a time until Madeline said something, anything she could use. She looked perfectly at ease in the cramped attic apartment, not bothered by the stuffy air, the scattered books, the dirty laundry spilling out of the lone closet.

But Madeline held the line. If Wallace wanted to know what had happened at the party, she could ask. And if she wasn't going to ask, Madeline wasn't going to offer. And nothing really happened anyway. And how on earth could any of it be related to Sophia being murdered?

Could it?

Wallace broke the spell by asking, "Did Sophia ever say anything was wrong in her life?"

"To be perfectly honest, Detective, we mostly talked about me. Maybe I went on too much about my own issues."

"She was a good friend, then."

Madeline didn't use the word "friend" lightly. Did it apply to Sophia? Was Madeline nauseated by her death and sleeping with the skillet next to her bed just because a woman had been murdered in Gatewood? Or was she feeling so distraught because she had known the person and cared about her?

She decided there was something real there. A real sense of loss. A real pain that stabbed her in the side and wouldn't stop.

Like when her dad died when she was three. Aortic aneurysm when he was only twenty-nine. *Twenty-nine.* Who did that fucking happen to? It was like winning the world's worst lottery. And Madeline reminded herself at least once a week not to dwell on her dad's death, not to think about the alternate timeline that could have been her life. A life where she grew up with him, in a normal house, and her mom was happy.

Was all of that too much to ask?

Don't think about it.

"Yes, she was a good friend." Madeline looked down at her stained threadbare carpet. "Is it true what they said online? That someone strangled her in her car?"

"It's true," Wallace said.

Something rose in Madeline's throat, the feeling that came right before she threw up. She lifted her hand to her mouth and was about to run for the bathroom when the feeling started to pass.

"Are you okay?" Wallace asked.

"I think so."

"Do you want me to get you some water?"

"I'm okay," Madeline said. "It's just . . . How could someone get so close to another human being and kill them? It seems so—"

"Personal?"

"Yes. I was going to say 'intimate.'"

"Strangulation is a very personal, intimate way to kill someone. But it doesn't mean the killer knew Sophia. Some killers just like doing their business a certain way. It gives them a sense of control to put their hands on their victims. Especially if the victim's a woman."

"That's so sick."

"Or a killer may use another item to strangle a victim. Sometimes that gives them the thrill they're after."

"Is that what happened?"

Wallace shrugged and stayed quiet.

Madeline felt tears rising inside of her, stinging her eyes. She pressed her lips tight, tried to hold it together.

But Wallace was no dummy. She saw it. She saw how upset Madeline was.

"I'm sorry to bring all this up," Wallace said. "Do you have someone you can talk to about this? Another friend? Or your parents?"

Madeline wiped her eyes, choked back more of the tears. "I'm okay."

"You may think that, Madeline. But we all need people to talk to. I know on campus they have counselors. And you can just go in and talk to someone, and they don't charge you anything. It's all confidential."

"I've heard about those services."

"You might want to try it. Okay?"

"Okay. I might talk to one of my professors. He listens to me."

"That's good," Wallace said. "Just don't keep it bottled up."

"You really don't know who did this?" Madeline asked.

Wallace took her time answering. "It's early in the investigation. Sometimes it takes a while to sort everything out. But we're definitely trying. I can promise you that." Wallace pushed herself out of the chair and, as she did, reached into her pocket, bringing out a business card. "If you think of anything else, you can call me here."

Madeline stood up and took the card. Her hands were damp with sweat and stuck to the thick paper. "I saw the funeral is in a couple of days. I wanted to go, but it's down in Tennessee. And I'm in school. . . ."

"You don't have to go to the funeral to remember your friend," Wallace said. She sounded so wise, handing out the kind of help Madeline thought a mother should have been dispensing.

"I was going to send a card to her parents."

"I think they'd appreciate that. Just let me know if you want to talk about anything else. I mean, if those other avenues don't work on campus." Wallace paused at the door. "This lock," she said. "You might want to call your landlord and have it fixed. It's not in the greatest shape."

"Are you saying that because there's a killer on the loose?"

"I'm saying that because you're a woman."

CHAPTER THIRTY-ONE

CONNOR
PRESENT

Madeline keeps her coat on.

For a quick moment, I'm reminded of past winter days, the rare times it really snowed here in Gatewood, and Emily and I zipped Jake into a jacket, took him to Harmon Hill near campus, and went sledding. Even in winter, the days with him felt like they'd last forever. Red-cheeked, snotty-nosed days. Emily making hot chocolate on the stove when we got home. The three of us watching a movie together while darkness fell outside.

Now I'm in my kitchen, the same kitchen Jake went in and out of for most of his childhood, and I'm facing another young person. And I'm shaking inside, my blood cold, my organs quivering.

In the classroom, in my office, I'm always in control. I stand before the students with authority and command, which rarely gets questioned.

But Madeline has flipped the script on me. She holds the upper hand.

She unnerves me. Scares me.

What is she here for tonight?

"Why don't you take your coat off?" I ask.

"I'm fine," she says. "Do you have any more of that bourbon you gave me yesterday?"

"No."

"You don't?"

"I don't think it's a good idea for you to be here," I say, keeping my voice more level than I feel. "The police are questioning me. They might be watching me for all I know. And you're . . . you're kind of wanted, aren't you?"

"'Wanted,'" she says. "Now that's an interesting word. It can mean a lot of things. Does a parent *want* their child more than they want to be with someone else? Does a lover *want* their partner? Do the police *want* someone?"

"You seem pretty agitated."

"I'm probably being followed."

"By whom?" I ask.

"'By whom'?' Ugh, you professors. Someone who is pissed about the book. You should watch out too."

"You need to tell me what's going on, Madeline. What about the book? Why do you know things about Sophia's murder that only the killer could know? What's your connection to her death?"

"Whoa, now. Easy there, Chief." She holds her gloved hands out in front of her, like she wants to push me away. She stares at me through the owlish glasses, the cold light of calculation burning there. "So the cops put all of this in your mind, right? How did they come up with that? Or did you tell them you saw me?"

"I don't have to tell you any of this," I say.

"Tell me, Connor. What do the cops know?"

"Did you think I'd just give you your money and you'd leave town, and then I'd be left holding the bag for what you wrote in the book?"

Madeline takes a couple of steps toward the table, pulls a chair out, and sits.

I feel just a little relieved when she's off her feet.

"Yeah," she says, "I did kind of assume that. Do you have the money?"

"No. It's not that easy to get your hands on a bunch of money. More important, what do you know about this murder?"

"Okay. When I wrote the book, I didn't think anyone would make the connection with Sophia's murder. But then after I turned it in to you, I realized that might not be the case. And I panicked. Do you remember? I wanted the book back?"

"I do. Was someone pressuring you?"

She ignores my question. "And then when you were going to publish it . . . well, I still hoped it would be okay. You said most books don't sell a lot."

"Not unless a writer has really good fortune."

"And then one of those people who read the book you published—and I wrote—would have to know the details of the crime, right?" She shifts in her seat, and when she speaks again, she sounds knowing, like she's asking a question she may already have the answer to. "Maybe someone you know read the book? Who is it? Or did you admit the whole damn thing? The plagiarism and everything? Did you cave that easily?"

I'm shaking my head, trying to slow down her train of thought.

"I didn't need to. We got incredibly lucky," I say. I regret throwing the towel over the bourbon. My mouth craves a taste, but I resist. "And when I say 'lucky,' I'm being sarcastic. We have a cop here in Gatewood who loves to read thrillers. And guess which one she bought right away. So now I'm the guy they're looking at."

"Fuck," Madeline says, thumping the table with her gloved hand. "I really didn't think that would happen. But I didn't even imagine the book was going to be published. I mean, that part of it is on you. You're the idiot who submitted it. Remember, I wanted to take it back as soon as I turned it in."

"Okay, I understand you didn't expect it to be published. When you were gone, you figured that was the end of it." I shake my head. "Madeline, if I'd known you were alive, I never would have done it. Forget the cops and all of this. I didn't want to steal from you. I hope you know that now."

She studies me and then she nods. "I can believe that. But once you published it and got paid, that's when I decided to make the best of it. These are all unintended consequences. But so what? You wrote a book. I mean, *I* wrote a book, and they think *you* wrote it. Big deal. You wrote about a murder. People do that all the time."

She reaches down, and I flinch. My hand goes to my pants pocket where I can feel the presence of the knife against my thigh.

"Jumpy much?" she asks, pulling out a tissue and wiping her nose. "I'm the one who should be nervous. I'm the one being followed."

"Followed by—"

"Do you think I'm here to knock you off?"

"How would I know? Madeline, you wrote about details of that murder. Only the cops and the killer can know those things."

She blows her nose, and it makes a surprisingly loud sound in the small kitchen. She stuffs the balled-up tissue back into her pocket.

"Did you even know Sophia?" she asks.

"Not at all," I say. "But I used to walk Grendel by her house." I consider how much I can tell her, how much she needs to know. But I'm in so deep, I might as well share. "I saw her and her husband through the windows of their house. I watched them sometimes."

Madeline makes a face like she swallowed a fishhook. "Ugh. Creepy."

"Not creepy," I say. "It wasn't like that. . . . I know it doesn't look right. Just forget it."

But Madeline is looking up at me, her eyes wide behind the owlish glasses. The light reflects off the lenses. "Go on," she says. "I think I know where you're going with this. Maybe it's healthier than hanging out at a grave in the middle of the night. I don't know."

"Did I tell you I do that?"

"You did."

I check her face for any sign of judgment or mockery, but neither is there. She looks attentive, genuine. Curious. Just like she always did in class when I held her attention. I could so easily hold an entire roomful's attention on my very best days. And how very good that always felt to me.

I tell her what I saw in Sophia and her husband. How appealing it was to see a young couple so different from the way I was at that point in my life.

"They were my opposites," I say. "Like in a comic book or a science fiction movie where the hero has an evil double who is the exact opposite of him in every way, except they look the same. That's what I thought when I watched Sophia and her husband. They were everything I had been and never would be again."

Madeline nods. She takes off her wool winter hat, and the red hair flops across her shoulders and face. She brushes loose strands away, clearing her vision. "I used to do the same thing. Not with Sophia, but with families when I was a kid. I think I told you my dad died when I was three."

"You mentioned it the other night."

"I also told you that night at Dubliners. That last night. You were so trashed, you probably don't remember. After Dad was gone, my mom went through a series of guys. Some were okay. Most were shits. It wasn't good. Not at all. I ran away a couple of times. That was my way of coping. Not really a plan . . . Then I discovered reading and writing." She slides her gloves off and reaches up for her eyebrow. "I've got to stop doing this." She puts her hands down, under the table, shifting her weight so she can sit on them and prevent the nervous tic. "I'd go to my friends' houses and just marvel at what it was like. Two parents in the house. Everything working. Nobody screaming. Nobody drunk or on drugs. No one pushing anyone around. Who would have thought the most everyday things would be the most miraculous? Food on the table, someone to help with homework. A man in the house who wasn't a total shit."

She brings her hands out, starts to lift one to her forehead again, then closes it into a fist.

"No," she says. "Stop."

I go to the bottle of Rowan's and whip the towel off. I pour her a shot and bring it to the table, setting it down in front of her. I pull out a chair for myself and sit across from her.

"I thought that was gone."

"I lied."

She eyes the shot. "Are you going to make me drink alone?"

"I'm cutting back," I say.

She shrugs, slams the shot. She smacks her lips. "I needed that." She reaches over and pats my hand. "Thanks. You know, Connor, I always thought you were really decent. All the students did. Really."

I look at her hand on mine. Her hand is small, the skin red and raw. The nails bitten.

"Madeline, do you know who killed Sophia?"

For two seconds, she keeps her hand on mine. Then she pulls it back as if she's been bitten by a venomous snake.

"Don't ask me that."

"Was it her husband? Zachary? Is he the one following you? Let me tell you something I saw one of those nights I walked by their house."

"I don't want to hear this shit," she says. "You don't know what you're into. And it's coming after me too. I don't feel safe."

"Then you should go to the police."

"Drop it, Connor."

"You know what? You're right. If you go to the police, they might charge you for the time and effort they spent searching. They do that sometimes. If you fake your disappearance, you can face charges."

"Quit snowing me. What were you going to say about Zach and Sophia?"

"Listen, they got in a fight, Sophia and Zachary. They were screaming at each other. They seemed to be arguing over a woman, like he'd had an affair."

She watches me, wary. Her eyes shine with a feral intensity, ready to dash if the threat grows too great.

"And then he got aggressive with her," I say. "He knocked her hand away. It looked like things were going to get physical between them, so I intervened."

"He's a fucking bastard, then, isn't he? A fucking pig. There's a lot of that going around, I might add."

"Madeline, if you know who killed her, if you know it's Zachary, you need to tell the police. We can call them right now, and they can come over and hear what you have to say."

"So they can charge me with faking my disappearance like you said? Fine me? Haven't you been listening? I don't have any money."

She pulls all the way back and knocks the chair over when she stands.

"Madeline, you need to listen—"

"No, you need to. You don't really know what's going on. I guarantee you don't."

"If you don't tell them what you know, then I'm going down for it. I got suspended at work because of this."

Her eyes narrow. "Who suspended you?"

"The university. Dr. White had to report the investigation to Human Resources. It's university policy. I can't go to campus or talk to students."

Madeline throws her hands up in the air. "Oh, did they? Dr. White did? Wonderful. He's a fucking prince, isn't he?"

"I'm pissed at him too, but it's out of his hands."

"He came here last night. That's who pulled in. I watched, you know. I watched you all standing in here, drinking champagne and yukking it up. They think *you* wrote the book, all those English professors with their fancy degrees and easy lives. You all have it made, clapping one another on the back and celebrating your success. While I stand in the cold."

"Do you think our lives are that easy?"

She's moved across the kitchen and stands in a corner near the refrigerator, hands on hips. "Just give me the money. Give me the money and we're square."

"What do you need it for?" I ask. "Can't you work . . . do something?"

"Not that it matters, since the money is mine, but do you know what it's like to try to get a job when you're considered a missing person? Always looking over your shoulder? Always starting from scratch? Always worried someone will recognize me? I don't have a degree. I left without that because I had to. Do you think you can get a decent job when you don't have a degree or real references or any work experience? Have you ever tried to do that?"

"No, of course not."

"No, you haven't. I've watched my mom do that. Work shit jobs, never get ahead. Always just a little underwater, always running to stand still. One step forward and two back. Or else you depend on some asshole guy to bring home a paycheck. And if the guy does bring home the money, then he thinks he owns you. He can take whatever he wants whenever he wants it. Maybe he can knock you around a little bit."

"I'm sorry—"

"And these days there are a lot of guys who can't even be bothered to have a job. They might be more likely to have the cops trailing them home than it is they'll have a paycheck. It's women who are carrying all the water. But maybe that's always been the case." She shakes her head, her hair flopping from one side to the other. "It's a shit life. I can tell you that. Like eating dirt every day and trying to be grateful for it. Well, I'm not doing that."

"If you'd stayed in school—"

"Bullshit, Connor. Bullshit. Don't act like it's all so easy. I've thought and I've thought about the right thing to do. I've thought about staying, and I've thought about going. But it's not like you just wave a magic wand and have a great life."

"You know, I haven't had a great life either. I'd give up the book, the job, all of it, to have my family back. But I can't get that."

"Don't play the sob-story card," she says. "Everybody has one. Some worse than others."

"Madeline, if you're in danger . . . if someone wants to hurt you . . ."

"I've gone back and forth. I really have. There are people in this town, people who may have done bad things. I'd like to see them go down. I really would."

"If you want to do the right thing, Madeline, I can help you."

"That's rich, coming from you. What are you going to do about the money?"

Her words land with a finality. They ring through the small kitchen like metal against stone.

I try to think of anything else I can say, but there's nothing.

"I told you it's going to take time. I just started looking into it. I may not be able to get anything."

She looks disappointed. Not because the money isn't there. It's something else. It looks like she's disappointed *in me*, like she held out hope I'd deliver and now I can't.

Like she expected more of me. As her teacher. Her mentor.

As a person.

"And that's it?" she asks.

"That's it. I'm sorry. But if I can help you another—"

"Save it." She comes back to the table, dodges the fallen chair, and picks up her gloves and hat. "I have no choice now. I'm going to the university tomorrow. I'm telling them who really wrote the book."

"Madeline, the world, all of it, is much more complicated—"

She looks up, her eyes flaring. "Oh, really. Really? You're going to tell me about the world. Please."

"You have no proof of what you're asserting," I say, sounding very much like the professor I am. "If you go in and tell them I stole your book, they're not going to believe you. Whose word are they going to take? Yours? Or mine?"

"Because you burned my manuscript, right?" Some of the heat goes out of her eyes. They look more like banked coals than a blazing fire. "That's the way it always is for women, isn't it? Who gets to be believed? And who doesn't?"

"I'm sorry," I say. "I can't tell you that enough. I said there might be more money from the book down the road. It's all yours. I don't care about that."

She stuffs the hat and gloves into her coat pockets. She comes toward me, and I stand up, keeping my hand near my pants pocket. And the knife.

But she goes past me, over to the counter, and takes the bottle of Rowan's. She pulls the cork and tilts the bottle, guzzling a more-than-healthy shot. She brings the bottle down but doesn't put it on the counter. She holds on to it.

"Good-bye, Connor."

I start to say good-bye, and I feel a twinge of relief passing through me. Madeline is turned to the side, half of her body obscured from my sight.

I can see only one of her hands, the one closest to me.

The one not holding the bottle.

Like a dancer, she spins toward me, and I see the bottle arcing toward the side of my head as she turns.

I duck. I lift my arm.

But none of it is fast enough, and I don't even feel the pain of the blow as the darkness descends. I realize I'm fading as I hit the floor, as I hear Grendel scampering into the kitchen, barking and barking. . . .

PART II

CHAPTER THIRTY-TWO

REBECCA
PRESENT

Rebecca makes it to class right at the wire.

She hates to be tardy, but she woke up late this morning, reluctant to emerge from beneath the warmth of the covers, leave the house, and trudge the three blocks in the freezing air to reach the bus stop.

But she did it.

Except then the bus arrived late, and by the time it dropped her off near Goodlaw, she was way behind and ran through the wide first-floor hallway, dodging around her fellow students, the cleaning people, and the professors to make it to class on time. Dr. Nye hated it when students came late. Some of them strolled in almost ten minutes after class started, and when they did, he always sighed, acting like they'd done him a grievous injury.

Rebecca makes it on time every day. And she wants to keep that streak intact. With Nye eventually reading her thesis and deciding if she could graduate with honors or not, she didn't want to risk irritating him.

But when she goes through the door into Goodlaw Hall room 117, she sees not Nye standing at the front of the room where he's always perched, looking over his notes, his brow furrowed like he isn't quite certain he can pull off teaching what he has to teach. Instead, she sees

Dr. White and Dr. Hoffman. The two men stand off to the side, their heads leaned in toward each other, whispering in low voices. The students who are already in the room sit in silence at their places, looking like obedient kids from a posh boarding school instead of the ragtag batch of creative writing majors they are. Normally before class they lean over toward one another, telling jokes, showing one another videos, laughing and joking and complaining about anything they could think of.

Rebecca wonders what the hell is going on and tries to slide into her desk unobtrusively. Once, when she was nine, her parents went out and the usual babysitter was sick with mono. Her parents called her mom's great-aunt Sylvia, who must have been eighty-five years old, and she came over and sat with Rebecca while her parents were gone. That's what it feels like to have White and Hoffman standing at the front of the class and not Nye. No one knows how to act, so they stare straight ahead like mannequins.

Except for the two frat boys next to Rebecca, the ones who always look right through her. They start whispering to each other. The one closest to her says to his friend, "Do you remember when Hoffman told that girl to add more details about her breasts to her poem?"

"Dude, she was pissed," the other one says.

Rebecca takes out the book of short stories they're reading, wondering if they're still going to have a quiz, but Dr. White clears his throat and steps forward. He rubs his hands together, his forearms exposed by the perfectly rolled-up sleeves. Rebecca has never taken a class with White, but she's heard he's difficult. Very, very difficult.

"Okay," White says. "I'm here because we have an announcement to make. As you can see, Dr. Nye isn't in class today, and I'm sorry to tell you he won't be for the foreseeable future. He's dealing with a personal problem, unrelated to his work at the university, and so your class will be taught by Dr. Hoffman for the rest of the term. As I'm sure you know, Dr. Hoffman is an excellent poet and teacher, and you're in very capable hands going forward."

White gestures toward Hoffman, who smiles and nods to the students like he's a game show contestant.

The guy next to Rebecca mutters under his breath, "God, not Hoffman."

The guy next to him says, "I thought I'd never have to see him again. I don't even care if he does cancel class every time he's hungover."

"Excuse me," White says, looking over at them.

Rebecca stiffens in her seat. She hates to think she'd be lumped in with the guys who can't keep their mouths shut.

But she knew Hoffman. Just a little. She'd been to that party at his house a couple of years ago, the one where she first met Madeline. The one with the thing that happened in the alley. And she remembers Hoffman having too much to drink and insulting her home county.

He did kind of seem like a jerk. But now he's teaching her class.

Where the hell is Nye?

"If you have any questions," White says, "feel free to ask, and I'll try to answer them."

Rebecca hates to have a one-track mind. She hates that her first thought isn't about what might be wrong with Dr. Nye—illness, injury, accident—but instead goes right to her own problems. Who is going to direct her thesis if Nye isn't here?

But she can't help it.

She starts to lift her hand and ask, but White barely takes a breath between asking for questions and cutting them off. He doesn't even look at Rebecca.

"Okay, then," he says. "I'll hand this over to Dr. Hoffman."

And White breezes out of the room so fast, it looks like his shirt is on fire.

And then Hoffman steps forward and sits on the desk. Despite the cold he wears a short-sleeve button-down Hawaiian shirt and light-weight blue pants made for summer.

"I took a cursory glance at Dr. Nye's syllabus before I came down here," Hoffman says, "and I found the whole document to be both pre-scriptive and restrictive, so I thought we'd branch out in some other directions. Which reminds me of the professor I had at Yale who refused to assign letter grades. Let me tell you a little story about her. . . ."

CHAPTER THIRTY-THREE

Hoffman starts to talk, and the student on Rebecca's left, a woman she sometimes talks to before class and who always smells like patchouli and has an elaborate tattoo on her right hand, leans over and says, "He's an amazing professor. I learned so much about writing from him. I think he's a mad genius. He gave me so many useful suggestions for my poems. He thinks I should go to graduate school."

Hoffman has a deep, resonant voice. He sounds smart. And he has a big vocabulary, using words Rebecca has heard but isn't sure she understands.

Rebecca isn't sure who to believe—the students who hate him or the one who loves him.

After ten minutes, Rebecca realizes Hoffman isn't going to stop anytime soon. And she can find no connection between the story he's telling and the subject of the class, which is short story writing.

So Rebecca stops listening. Her eyes lose their focus, and she stares straight ahead. Her mind wanders, and she finds herself thinking of Madeline O'Brien. Ever since the night of Nye's talk at the library, Rebecca has replayed the scene of the woman in the back of the room with the red hair, the one who tugged on her eyebrows. Rebecca wouldn't say she knew Madeline well. They took one class together when Rebecca was a sophomore and Madeline was a senior, and while they rarely spoke to each other, Rebecca admired the way Madeline conducted herself. Professor Richter taught the class, and Rebecca thought she was brilliant, but Madeline spoke up frequently and didn't shy away from openly disagreeing on matters both big and small. Rebecca never disagreed. She rarely participated. She liked to listen and write down her notes and absorb the discussion.

Hoffman finishes his story fifty minutes later and dismisses everyone.

Rebecca's classmates appear to have been lulled into a stupor by the lengthy story, and they gather their things and shuffle away, yawning like sleepy children. Rebecca grabs her things and jumps out of her seat. She follows Hoffman out of the classroom.

"Dr. Hoffman?"

He turns, smiling. "Hello."

"I wanted to ask you a question," Rebecca says. "If you don't mind. If you have a minute."

"Sure. Come along. I always have time for an eager writer."

He leads her down the long hallway, his pace languid, his legs propelling him forward as he says hello to nearly every student or faculty member he passes. When they reach his office, he pushes the door open and pauses. He looks around and lifts a giant stack of papers and books off one chair and points to it, indicating that Rebecca should sit there. Hoffman clears off another chair, and Rebecca wonders how the man sits at his desk if both chairs in the space are covered with crap.

"That was a great class, wasn't it?" Hoffman says.

It sounds like a rhetorical question, but he watches Rebecca expectantly, as though he requires an answer.

"Yes, it was," she says. "Awesome."

"One of my favorite stories," Hoffman says, leaning back, the chair squeaking. He folds his hands across his stomach and crosses one sneakered foot across the other. "I never tire of sharing it with my students. And they always seem to enjoy it. Now, what's on your mind?"

"Well, I know you're taking over for Dr. Nye, and I guess we don't exactly know when he's coming back."

"I think it's safe to say he'll be gone for a while," Hoffman says.

"Oh. Okay. Since he's going to be gone for a while—"

"You see—what's your name?"

"Rebecca Knox."

"Have we met before?" he asks.

Rebecca isn't sure what to say. "I kind of went to a party at your house a couple of years ago."

"Kind of? How can you 'kind of' attend a party?"

"Well, I was there. Yes. My friend invited me."

"You see, Rebecca Knox, Dr. Nye has been having some personal issues for a few years now. I'm sure you've heard about them."

"I guess I know about his wife dying and stuff."

"Right. Everyone seems to know about his new book, the one that I guess you can buy in some of the finer retail establishments and grocery stores all over Gatewood. The one he toiled laboriously on for . . . what? Three weeks or so before he published it? I thought it sounded familiar when he discussed it at the library, but most of those thrillers sound the same. I don't read them. Well, things have been kind of unstable for our friend Connor for a while. And now he finds himself in the middle of something that doesn't look good at all. I'm not really at liberty to say more than I already have."

Hoffman remains slightly reclined in his chair, his thumbs moving over and over each other in tiny loops. Rebecca tries to make up her mind about him. He seems to talk just to hear himself talk. She wonders how much more interesting he would be if he talked about something relevant to her.

"Okay," she says. "I see. So can Dr. Nye still direct my thesis?"

"Oh, no. He won't be working with any students anymore. Not at all. He's already faced the wrong kind of scrutiny once. And this latest incident isn't going to look any good either."

"There was an incident?" Rebecca asks.

"Do you remember Madeline O'Brien?" Hoffman asks.

A sizzle of electricity shoots up Rebecca's spine. She stiffens in the hard wooden seat. "I know who that is."

"Well, our friend Dr. Nye was the last person to see Madeline alive. Did you know that? This is all a matter of public record, of course. Not that you students follow the news. But it never looks good to be the last person to see someone alive."

Rebecca flashes to Madeline—if that was actually her—in the back of the library. Is Rebecca now the last one to have seen Madeline?

Or was Nye right—Rebecca was just seeing what she wanted to see?

"And now," Hoffman says, "well, let's just say . . . the wicket's getting stickier."

Rebecca isn't sure what Hoffman means. She isn't even sure she knows what language he is speaking, although he's trying to hint at something about Dr. Nye and the reason he's absent from class. And maybe he's trying to say it has something to do with Madeline and her disappearance. Hoffman is wrong about something—Rebecca followed the news about Madeline closely when she disappeared, had gone to the trouble of buying herself a canister of pepper spray and taken a self-defense class at the university health center. But nothing else happened in town, and before too long, the police and the media stopped talking about Madeline.

Rebecca remembers that Hoffman was at the reading at the library. Had he seen Madeline too? Whatever he is trying to convey, he looks pleased to be saying it, and his thumbs continue their perpetual motion against his belly.

"Is something going on with Madeline's case?" Rebecca asks.

"Madeline?" He says the name like he's never heard it. Like he hadn't just brought her up a minute earlier. "I don't know anything about that. She was an excellent student. Very talented. In so many ways. But that's all I know."

"Okay," Rebecca says. "So Dr. Nye isn't directing my thesis anymore. I just met with him about it yesterday. Is he okay? I mean, should I be doing something for him?"

"Can you bake a cake with a file in it?"

"What's that?"

"He can take care of himself," Hoffman says. "He can use all his royalties to hire a good lawyer. But if you're worried about your thesis, I can direct it for you."

Rebecca feels relief replace some of the rigidness in her spine. "Really?"

"Sure. It's all about the students. What kind of thesis is it?"

"I'm writing a series of linked short stories," Rebecca says. "It's the same character during a few different periods in her life."

"Fascinating," Hoffman says. "But poetry tends to be my strong suit. Have you ever written any?"

"Not for a long time. I don't really—"

"If I were you, and you want to work with me, I'd seriously think about writing some poems. Maybe you can write them in various forms about this character you've dreamed up. I'm sure your fiction is delightful, but under the guidance of Dr. Nye, it might tend toward the commercial and the jejune. But if you stretched yourself and wrote some poetry, that would really be something. The thing I really feel I excel at is taking a student's work and enhancing it. Providing advice, help with form and structure and language. Finding the right concrete detail for the right moment. Do you see what I'm saying?"

"I guess. . . ."

"Madeline was a student who was equally adept at poetry and prose. Were you close to her?" Hoffman asks.

"Not close. We took one class together. . . ."

"Such a shame," Hoffman says. "I think about her from time to time. Has she been on your mind lately?"

"Well, in a sense . . ."

Rebecca told Nye about thinking she saw Madeline. She'd thought about telling her roommate or one of her other friends, but how weird would she sound mentioning the eyebrow thing when that was the only real "evidence" she had?

But then Hoffman leans forward and stops twiddling his thumbs and acts like he is all receptive to whatever Rebecca has to say about Madeline, so why not get his opinion too? He is obviously a weirdo but also smart. And he's been teaching at Commonwealth for so long he knows all the ins and outs.

She'd tried with Nye, and he wasn't interested.

Could Hoffman be just weird enough to care?

"Okay," Rebecca says, taking a deep breath before she plunges in. "You know the other night at Dr. Nye's reading? You were there too. There was this person in the back of the room with red hair. . . ."

CHAPTER THIRTY-FOUR

CONNOR
PRESENT

Something wet and cold against my face.

Wet and cold. Wet and cold.

Like someone's running a washcloth over me.

"Emily?"

For a moment, I see her. The deep brown eyes. The auburn hair.

This is the way she woke me up on thousands of mornings. A kiss on my cheek . . .

So much better than an alarm clock.

The cool sensation stops. My eyelids flutter. Bright light comes through, spearing me in the face. Like a dam bursting, pain rushes through my head. It's localized on the right side, and I tentatively reach up. My right arm has been pressed beneath my body, and it's asleep and feels like a club. My hand gets the pins-and-needles treatment, which hurts almost as bad as my head. I flex, trying to work circulation through.

"Ugh."

When my hand starts to feel normal, I reach again. I touch the side of my head and pull my hand away, examining my fingers.

Dry. No blood. Just a knot.

I look around. Is anyone here?

I see no one, feel a little relief.

Grendel's nails clack against the linoleum. He licks my face again, his way of telling me he wants to be fed. He wants water. He wants to pee. Somewhere on the list is him asking if I'm okay.

"I'm fine," I say to him, but the words make me wince.

I sit up, lean back against the counter. The night before comes back. Madeline's visit. My inability to give her the money she wants that I don't have. Her threats to go public with my plagiarism.

I worried she carried a gun or a knife. Her weapon of choice was the deadliest of all—bourbon. The bottle sits on its side on the floor across the room, some of its contents dribbled out on the tile. I pat the side of my pants, searching for the knife. I feel lucky I didn't fall on it and stab myself.

But there's nothing in my pocket. No knife. I check the floor around me as well.

Nothing.

Has Madeline taken it?

Fragments of the night dance in my mind, like images viewed through a curtain. Someone stood over me. Someone checked my pockets.

The back door hung wide open, the cold air blowing in.

Someone said my name.

Wasn't it a man's voice? Was Madeline alone?

"I'm going to stand, Grendel."

He wags his tail, encouraging me. Everyone needs a cheerleader in their life.

I look over. The back door is closed. Wasn't it open at one point?

I push against the tile with both hands, bend my knees. I move slowly, getting my feet under me. So far, so good . . . I straighten up. When I'm all the way up, the room tilts, sliding to the left like I'm in a fun house.

"Crap."

I steady myself against the counter, take a few deep breaths. In a moment, the room stops spinning. I see my abandoned sandwich, which looks even more unappealing in the harsh morning light.

"I'm okay," I say. "It's okay."

Grendel's tail wags. He comes over, nuzzles against my leg. I know he's hungry. I know he has to pee.

"I see you there," I say. "And I know what you're thinking. But this isn't because I was drinking bourbon. This is because someone hit me with a bourbon bottle. You saw it, didn't you? Thanks for protecting me, by the way."

I feel capable of moving around. I should see a doctor, but how would I explain why I'm there? *You see, my former student whose book I stole and who might have murdered someone . . .*

"All right," I say. "Let's go for a walk, and then I'll feed you."

I decide to change my shoes before we go. I'm still wearing what I wore the day before, what I wore all day at work and while at the police station. And I have to pee, probably as much as Grendel does.

I take a step into the hallway, heading for the bathroom. The linen closet door is open, the towels and sheets and spare soap spread all over the floor.

"What the . . . ?"

I step back and look out into the living room. The couch cushions are thrown around, the books dumped off the shelves. The coat closet by the front door stands open, the bin of gloves and hats emptied, its contents flung across the carpet like there's been an earthquake.

"Oh, shit."

Madeline didn't just hit and run. She hit and ransacked.

And I think I know exactly what she was looking for.

I go down the hall to our spare room, the one I used as an office when Jake was little and I needed to lock myself away to attempt to get any work done. Each step jars my head, makes the pain throb. The office is a cluttered mess. Overflowing with books, stacks of old student papers. Everything I should have been dealing with for the past five years but haven't.

It's also where—

The desk drawers hang open, gaping like the mouths of dead fish. The closet door stands wide, having vomited its papers all over the worn carpet. Inside the closet is a chest, one Emily received from her grandmother as a wedding present. It's stuffed with old quilts, Emily's baby book, and her First Communion outfit. A lock of hair from when she was two.

And underneath all of that, hidden in a place I thought no one would ever bother to look . . .

The chest lid is closed. The lock broke a year after we were married, but is it possible Madeline passed it by?

I fling the lid open, look inside. Everything is there, everything in its place. Unlike the rest of the house, the chest appears to be untouched.

My heart sinks. Why put this one spot back in order unless you wanted to send a message, a giant middle finger to me?

I dig to the bottom, moving aside the musty heirlooms. In a matter of seconds, my hand scrapes against the bottom of the chest, my nails hitting the cedar. I move the pile one way and then the other.

I could sit here all day, moving shit around. But I know.

I know for damn sure.

Madeline found her handwritten manuscript.

She took it back.

CHAPTER THIRTY-FIVE

A couple of hours pass. And nothing happens. No doom lands on me as a result of Madeline having the book. I walk Grendel, looking over my shoulder the whole time, expecting Preston to show up and fire me. Or my publisher to call, saying I'm ruined.

My head thumps, but nothing happens.

Maybe Madeline fears her own exposure. Maybe she plans to come back to try to pressure me one more time.

Maybe she has something more diabolical and dangerous in mind.

Maybe I'm driving myself crazy over nothing.

And I *am* driving myself crazy. I pace the house. I check my phone.

If Madeline isn't going to blow the lid off things on the publishing side—at least not yet—that means the biggest threat to me remains the police. They think I'm a killer because they think I wrote the book. They know I was lingering outside the Greenfields' house. And they know I wandered around the neighborhood where she lived. That I watched them so much, Sophia thought there was something wrong with me. And maybe there was . . . but I was watching their normalcy. Nothing else.

Is it possible there's a way to take some of the heat off with the police?

"I'm going out, boy," I say. I grab my keys and my coat and head for the car.

It's easy for me to find the little blue house north of the dog park.

It helps that Bowman gave me a refresher the night before, but even without it, I'd remember. For those months over two years ago when I walked Grendel there, hoping for a glimpse of the couple I now know as Zachary and Sophia Greenfield, that house and the street—those people—loomed larger in my mind than anything in my own life. I don't think it's overstating things to say they kept me going and gave me something to look forward to during the grayest time.

They gave me hope.

I park on Iroquois, a few doors down from the Greenfields'. It occurs to me as I lock the car and walk up the familiar sidewalk that Zachary may not live here anymore. Would he want to remain in the house that held so many memories of his late wife? He's a young guy. He may be off in another part of the country.

But then I look at myself. I'm in the same house I shared with Emily and Jake. Why? Inertia, for one. Who wants to move? But when my family died, many people asked me if I planned to sell, to find a place not so haunted by their memories. My response was the opposite. I cherish the memories—the familiar scents and squeaks of that home. And those details keep Emily and Jake alive for me. My house is like a time capsule, sealing in the things I hold most dear. I can't let it go.

As I mount the steps to the Greenfields' wooden porch, I check out the yard. It's not as pristine as I remember, not as well manicured and cared for, and that makes complete sense to me. If someone were to look at before and after photos of my house, they'd see how much things slipped once Emily was gone and my interest and energy flagged. Zachary must have been the same way, a guy who realized how much harder it is to maintain a life when half of yourself is gone.

My heart flips one way and then the other as I ring the bell. Bowman refused to say that Zachary was cleared of his wife's murder. It's possible he's the killer. But if he is, what's taking the cops so long to close the deal? I told Bowman about the fight. Might they turn their eyes back to Zachary now? Had anyone else ever been a suspect? Was I a fool for coming to his house?

The blinds are drawn behind the large front window. Brittle stalks of long-dead flowers remain in a window box, quivering in the cold wind. It's almost ten, and Zach is likely to be at work. But I have to try something. Anything.

I wait. The wind kicks up, freezing the tips of my ears, and I keep my hands in my coat pockets. My head thumps dully, a steady but not excruciating presence. A reminder of Madeline's wild swing. I wait some more, then ring the bell again.

I think it's a lost cause until the lock starts rattling, the sound just reaching me above the wind. The door swings open and I'm face-to-face with Zachary for the first time since that night I stepped in between him and his wife.

He stares at me across the threshold, searching for recognition that isn't quite there. He looks the same but without a beard. Maybe a few flecks of gray in his dark hair.

How do I start? Where?

"Can I help you?" he asks, still searching my face.

"I'm sorry to bother you," I say. "I'm not sure if you—"

His eyes shift. Something brightens there. Or maybe it flares. I can't be sure. But I see the change. He knows who I am.

"What do *you* want?" he asks, his voice sharper.

"I want to talk."

"About what?"

"I think you remember me, right?"

"I do," he says. "It's been a while, and I do. You're the creep who used to come by here with your dog."

"No, I'm the guy who stopped you from fighting with your wife."

"Oh, yeah. Well, I'm not interested in relitigating the past. Whatever you're here for, you're way too late. Just like the cops, just like everybody else. Get lost."

He steps back and shoves the door toward my face.

I make the only move I can and stick my foot out. I place the sole against the bottom of the door, blocking its progress. Zachary's brow wrinkles. He bites down on his lower lip and applies more pressure to the door, as if through sheer application of strength he can knock me out of the doorframe and out of his life. And he probably can. He's younger than I am. Stronger.

But I do what I can.

"Zachary, wait. Just wait."

He pushes harder.

"Sophia," I say. "I want to talk to you about Sophia."

It's like I said the magic word. He stops trying to push me away.

"Why are you talking about her?"

"The cops suspect me because I used to walk by here," I say. "And she told you about me. But I think there's someone else they should be looking into. Can I come in and explain?"

"You can talk out there," he says. "I know you were walking by the house. I know the cops tried to find you."

"Zachary, it's cold. Look, you're barefoot. Can we just talk inside? For a few minutes?"

He watches me, appraising me like he's the emperor and I'm the gladiator awaiting the thumbs-up or thumbs-down. Then he takes a step back, flinging the door open.

"Make it fast," he says. "I work at home, so you're interrupting me at my office."

CHAPTER THIRTY-SIX

The last time—the only time—I'd been in the house was when I stepped between Zachary and Sophia, interrupting their argument. And guilt strikes my heart like a burning brand. If I'd called the police then, if I'd reported what I'd witnessed, would Sophia be alive?

Had I added my name to a never-ending list of those who turned away when something could have been prevented?

Zachary closes the door, blocking out the faint sunlight. He stands between me and the door, hands on hips. He doesn't invite me to sit. I study him, trying to decide if he looks like a murderer. How would I know? Do *I* look like one? Does Madeline?

"I need your help," I say.

"I don't see what I can do for you— Wait. You mentioned another suspect. If you just—"

"You know I interrupted that fight—or argument—between you and your wife."

He sighs. "Isn't it great to always be judged by your worst moment?"

"I'm in trouble with the police about that," I say. "Your wife's murder."

"You should have been a suspect all along. . . . Wait a minute. Is this why Detective Bowman called me this morning? She said she wants to come over and ask me about something relating to Sophia's case. Is it *you* she wants to ask about?"

"When is Bowman coming over?"

Zach's face darkens. He takes a step back to look at me more carefully.

"Are you a *new* suspect? Let me tell you something—if you laid a hand on Sophia—"

"Wait." I don't know exactly how to proceed. The thumping in my head returns, doing its best to drown out my powers of logic and reason.

"Why should I wait?" he asks. "You killed my wife—"

"I didn't." I decide to come clean. "Okay. Your wife told you a man was watching her before she died. Someone who walked by with his dog and—I don't know—looked at her. Looked in the house."

"How do you know Sophia thought that?" he asks.

"Bowman told me. Yesterday."

"Why?" Zachary cocks his head, curious now. Listening. "Why is Bowman stirring up the pot again? Did something happen?"

"That night I came in, the way I heard and saw your fight . . . I was walking by with my dog. I *always* walked by here. I used to see the two of you together." It seems foolish to try to explain to this guy why I noticed them. I sense he's not feeling very patient and won't want to hear a litany of my downward emotional spiral. "It was a misunderstanding. I wasn't a creeper. I wasn't anything but . . . curious."

Zachary sounds disbelieving. "And the cops want to arrest you for being curious? Is that what you're saying? Just over two years later you're going to get arrested for curiosity. You're not making any sense to me. And I'm out of patience for things that don't make sense when it comes to Sophia's murder—"

"You never told the police about the fight you had with Sophia," I say. "The one I interrupted. They have no record of it, no witnesses but me. And they're not exactly fans of mine right now. They think I made it all up to cast blame on you and away from me."

Zach takes a couple of steps away and plops into a wooden chair. His body is slack and loose, like he's ready to collapse. He shakes his head and looks a lot older than he really is. He looks broken.

"I don't think you know what this has been like. My wife was murdered. Do you understand that? *Murdered?*"

"I'm sorry. I am."

"And then for weeks and months after I buried my wife, the cops were asking me questions. Checking my financial records, talking to all of our friends. Calling my mom at work. They asked the most personal questions. Am I a cheater? Am I abusive? Did I owe somebody money for a gambling debt? Or was I being blackmailed by an unhappy lover?" He shakes his head again, his eyes blinking rapidly. "And you want me to rip *that* scab off? Everybody in town, everybody I work with, they all look at me like I'm guilty. That's why I switched to working at home. That's why I can't see most of our old friends."

"I'm sorry to hear that, Zach," I say.

"I don't even know who you are."

"Okay, maybe this was a mistake. My coming by. I was just . . . I'm trying to figure out what's going on too."

"Join the club." He points to the door. "You can see yourself out—" Then his arm falls limply to his side. "Wait a minute," he says. "I thought you wanted to talk about *another* suspect. That's what you said when I let you in. That's the *only* reason I opened the door for you. And I've heard my fair share of whacked-out theories about the case. People call me on the phone. I have an unlisted number, but they find me. They message me. Everyone in this town thinks they know who killed Sophia, but none of them has been right. What are you bringing to the party?"

"I think there might be someone they haven't thought of," I say. "Someone who might know more about this than either of us."

"Okay, you've got my attention, friend. Who? A name. Say a name."

"Madeline O'Brien," I say.

If I'd stuck Zachary with an electric cattle prod, he likely wouldn't have jerked around any faster.

"Madeline," he said. "What the fuck are you bringing her up for?"

CHAPTER THIRTY-SEVEN

Zachary jumps out of the chair and comes toward me, taking several quick steps across the room.

Maybe I'm gun-shy from the blow Madeline delivered, or maybe my instinct for self-preservation is at an all-time high, but I move back, lifting my hands in the air between us.

"Look, just hold on," I say.

"Why are you asking me about *her*? She's dead."

"She's *missing*," I say. "There's no proof she's dead." I think about the night before. Whoever went through my pockets. A male voice saying my name. Was it Zach? "You haven't seen her, have you?"

"She's been dead for two years, and you're asking if I've seen her. What are you smoking?"

"But you did know her?"

"Sophia knew her. A little. They went to yoga at the same place and used to talk." He shrugs, almost too casual. "I met Madeline once. Maybe twice. I'm not really sure. When she disappeared, the cops came and talked to me about that as well. I could tell they wanted to add her disappearance to my shopping list. Might as well, right?"

"Were she and Sophia friends?" I ask. "Good friends?"

Zachary's demeanor cools. He no longer looks like he plans to charge through me like he's the angry bull and I'm the red cloth. But something hums beneath the surface of the guy's body, as if every one of his nerves and cells jangles with potential lethal energy. I threw

Madeline's name out, hoping to strike a nerve. It looks like I've hit more than one.

"Why should I tell you anything?" he asks. "Why shouldn't I just call the police?"

"Maybe we can help each other. By sharing what we know."

"I can't trust anybody in this town."

"You don't have to trust me. Just . . . give me a few more minutes. Okay? How well did Madeline and Sophia know each other?"

He stares at me for a long time. And I think he's going to go ahead and send me packing. Instead, he says, "Sophia knew a lot of people. Everywhere she went, she met somebody new. That's why the cops had to cast such a wide net to figure out who killed her. She came in contact with so many people." He pauses, lifting a hand to his forehead. He rubs the flesh there as if he's easing a sharp pain. "I have to tell you, man, I don't know how this became my life. Talking about my wife being murdered. Talking about suspects. Like I'm in the middle of a fucking TV show. I just want them to solve the crime so it all goes away. So I feel . . . peace."

"Did Sophia talk about Madeline a lot?" I ask.

Zachary drops his hand from his forehead so it again hangs limply at his side. "You have to understand something. Sophia was a sucker for a hard-luck case. She was always befriending someone, always talking to someone about their troubles. She had this instinct . . . a vibe she gave off, and others just responded to it. Like a tuning fork. Or a divining rod. She'd go to the grocery store to buy milk or the post office for a stamp, and she'd be gone for an hour or more. When she'd come home, I'd ask what happened. 'Oh, the woman in line behind me started talking about her daughter's drug abuse, so we had coffee.' *That* happened all the time. For all I know, that's why she got killed. And I told the cops that. Somebody probably took advantage of her kindness."

"Could it have been Madeline?"

"If Madeline had any problems, Sophia would have talked to her about them. I can guarantee you that."

"Do you know what Madeline's problems were?"

"I think they talked about Madeline's classes. Life in general, I guess. You've really thrown me for a loop today. I've been trying to move on. To . . . get past all of this. And now . . ."

"I'm sorry," I say. "I know how that is."

"Sophia not only was on the lookout for hard-luck cases, but she really saw herself as a protector of younger women. She took women under her wing at work. The interns from the university, the kids who just graduated and were working their first jobs. That's who they could afford to hire at a literacy nonprofit. She wanted to be the big sister to the whole world."

"That's not a bad quality."

"No." He purses his lips. "I was a philosophy minor in college. At Commonwealth. When Sophia was killed, I started looking at the books I'd kept. I've been reading Marcus Aurelius. You know, the Stoic?"

"Sure."

"It's helped me accept what happened to her. Or at least try to. It's helped me stay calm. I struggle with that sometimes. I'm trying to deal with stuff from my childhood. I get . . . Well, every day is a battle to do that. To make sense of where my life is."

"I understand."

"You married?" he asks.

"Widowed."

"Shit. Then you get it. You really do."

"Can I ask you something else, Zach? And I'm sorry to be so pushy."

"Go ahead. It's good not to feel so alone all the time."

"Okay," I say. "So you know that night you and Sophia were arguing, and I came in here. It seemed like you were arguing over another woman."

Zachary freezes in place. His body is still. "I don't know what you're getting at."

I think of the book. *Madeline's book.* The relationship between the two women—Sarah and Lilly. Things get difficult between them when Sarah's husband starts to hit on Lilly. And when Lilly tells Sarah, Sarah ends up dead.

If so many of the details of the murder are true to life . . . then maybe the details of the relationships between the three characters are true to life too.

"You and Sophia and Madeline . . . you were all friends, right?"

"*They* were friends."

"But you all knew one another. And you and Sophia had that fight. And I'm just wondering . . . I mean, maybe you and Madeline . . ."

Zach's body stiffens. "Are you saying what I think you're saying?"

"Look, relationships can get complicated. Especially when we're young."

Zach shakes his head again. And he looks at me with a combination of pity and disgust.

"I don't think Marcus Aurelius has a chapter about this," he says. He walks over to the door and pulls it open, letting in the cold air again. "You'd better go before my Stoicism wears off completely. And don't ever come back, or I can't be held responsible for how I'll respond to you."

I wish I'd kept my mouth shut. I wish I'd never come.

I do what Zach wants and walk out the door, which he forcefully slams behind me.

CHAPTER THIRTY-EIGHT

MADELINE
SUMMER, TWO AND A HALF YEARS AGO

She wanted to go out.

Alone.

She wanted to *be alone*. But not by herself.

She understood the difference.

Madeline worked her usual Friday night shift at the grocery store. She'd been working there the past two years, almost forty hours a week to try to pay for school. And even working that many hours couldn't pay for it all, which meant she still had loans. Thousands and thousands of dollars of loans. She started out bagging groceries, and then the manager came along one day five months earlier and told her she was being transferred. To the deli. The manager needed someone over there, and she thought Madeline would be perfect for it.

"You're fast and efficient," the manager said. She was about fifty, with three kids and two grandchildren and a husband she helped support even though they were divorced. "And you have brains, unlike most people I've tried over there."

Madeline went along with the change because it came with a fifteen-cent-an-hour raise. But she hated the work. Slicing meat, then weighing it. Trying to tell the difference between something called "pickle loaf" and something called "olive loaf." Customers forgetting to take a number and then trying to cut the line. The perpetual fear of the meat slicer taking off the tips of her fingers, leaving her unable to write. Going home every night smelling like a butcher shop.

The hairnet.

But it was a job. And it was money. It really embarrassed her only when a professor came in. Like Dr. Nye, who showed up once and ordered a half pound of cheese and a pound of ham. He looked so sad, and she imagined him sitting alone in his house eating ham-and-cheese sandwiches and missing his family.

She wanted to go home with him and try to make him feel better. Talk to him. Or make him a real meal, even though Madeline didn't cook and struggled to boil water for instant mac and cheese.

That Friday night in August, when the students were just starting to come back to town en masse, she showered and changed at home and then headed to the Owl's Nest, the concert venue downtown. Live music every night of the week. And dollar beers. PBR or something like it, but she didn't care at all. A local band that had kind of made it, the Sharpshooters, was playing. They'd been on *Jimmy Kimmel* once, and that had been a big deal. Then the lead singer left and they never went on TV again, but they still played around Gatewood with a new singer, and everybody turned out like they were Vampire Weekend or Cage the Elephant. Madeline wondered what it was like to be so close to achieving a dream only to see it all fall apart. Was it better to have that little taste than nothing at all? She thought about these things when she wrote. And lately she'd been writing and writing, trying to get her thesis going and not having much luck.

At the Owl's Nest, she danced in the middle of the crowd. Alone. The music pounded, and bodies pressed against her. She held her breath for a while, then let it go. No one groped her. No one spilled a drink on her shoes. She counted herself lucky. She usually ended up with both happening at the Owl's Nest. A hand or two squeezing her ass. Cheap beer on her pants and shoes. At the end of the night, going home feeling and smelling like the floor.

Someone bumped against her. She ignored it. Kept dancing.

Go away, she thought. *Just go away and leave me alone.*

The heat made her hair stick to her neck. She peeled it away, kept dancing.

The person tapped her on the shoulder.

Shit.

She offered a glance, a sideways look she hoped conveyed no interest. Better yet, she hoped the glance conveyed contempt. Disdain. Disinterest.

When she saw who it was, she smiled.

"Oh, my God. Sophia."

"Hey, girl."

They hugged on the dance floor. Sophia's blond hair hung loose, brushed across Madeline's face. Even in the cramped space amid the sweaty bodies and spilled beer, Sophia's hair smelled like a forest of lavender.

"Are you here with friends?" Sophia asked.

"Just me."

"Cool. I was about to go outside. Do you want to come?" She leaned in. "I want to smoke. And I don't want Zach to know."

"Sure."

Sophia took Madeline by the hand and started pressing through the crowd. It was always easier to get out than to come in. People moved out of the way when someone left, and then moved forward themselves, hoping to find that small pocket of space just vacated.

Sophia led them through the double glass doors and into the parking lot, the night air warm but better than the sauna inside the club. The sweat on Madeline's body evaporated, the hairs on her arms standing up. They moved to the side of the building, to the parking lot, where a scattering of people stood around, smoking and drinking and talking.

They weren't supposed to bring beers outside, but everybody did. If a cop cruised by, everyone threw their beers into the bushes. At a dollar a pop, they were easy to replace.

Sophia dug in the pocket of her jeans and brought out a crumpled pack of Camel Lights. Madeline felt disappointed. When Sophia had said "smoke," Madeline thought she'd meant weed, and her hopes rose. She couldn't afford to buy it herself, but if someone offered . . .

Sophia struck a match and lit a cigarette behind her cupped hand. She blew out a plume of smoke.

"Can you believe I'm using matches? I'm like my papaw when he used to sit on the porch. Do you want one?"

"I'm cool."

"You're smart. This is a terrible habit. Imagine what the people at Yoga for Life! would think if they saw me smoking."

"I won't tell on you if you don't tell on me for eating one of those chemical-filled frozen burritos at work tonight."

"I love that kind of shit," Sophia said. "I'd eat them every day if I could."

Sophia held the cigarette between the first two fingers on her right hand. The wind blew a strand of hair across her face, and she shook it away, the gesture effortless. Like everything Sophia did.

"You're here with Zach?"

"And some friends. He ran into some guys he knows. He didn't want to come. He's kind of a homebody. And there's a baseball game on or something. But I wanted to go out. A long week of work. Who wants to sit home?"

"Right. I agree. That's why I'm here. I just wanted to get out and be around other people and listen to good music."

"I hear you. Are things better with your mom?"

Madeline looked at the ground, kicked a shard of glass from a broken beer bottle away with the toe of her boot. Her hand went up for her eyebrow, got all the way there before she stopped it. "I haven't heard much this week. When she has a new boyfriend—and she always has a new boyfriend—I don't get as many calls. She reaches out only after the boyfriend is gone, and she's alone. I'm her therapist."

"Kind of like I am for you, right?"

The remark stung a little. Madeline felt her face flush.

"Hey, I'm just fucking around," Sophia said. "I like talking to you. I'm living vicariously through you. It makes me feel like I'm a college kid again and not an old lady."

"An old lady of twenty-seven?"

"That *sounds* old."

"Well, my mom must be fine because I'm not hearing from her," Madeline said. "I always swore I'd never be like her, never depend so much on a man to make me feel good. I want to stay focused on me. On school and writing."

"That's the spirit." Sophia dropped the cigarette on the ground and crushed it beneath her sneaker. "It sounds like you're doing well in school. And writing a thesis."

"Can I tell you something strange?" Madeline asked. "I hope you don't think I'm a freak."

Madeline rarely cared what others thought of her. She tried her best to stay out of the kind of drama her fellow students seemed to be absorbed in. She hated the way her mother judged her own worth based on how a man felt about her. And yet . . . Sophia brought out something different in Madeline. When Madeline talked to her, she wanted to believe Sophia thought the best of her, that she looked at Madeline as more than a dumb kid or a hanger-on. She wanted to do and say things that impressed Sophia. Madeline wondered if that's what it was like to have a big sister, someone you emulated and tried to impress. Someone who laid down tracks you could put your own feet in.

"I would never think that," Sophia said. "But I will light another while we're out here. You sure you don't want one?"

"I'm good."

"See. You're smarter than me." She shook another cigarette out of the crumpled pack and struck a match. "Go on. Tell me your freakiest shit."

Madeline crossed her arms in front of her chest. Her face flushed again. "You know how I'm writing my thesis?"

"Yeah."

Madeline shivered as the wind blew. "I'm kind of basing the main character on you."

"You are?" Sophia's eyebrows went up, and her big green eyes opened wide, catching the floodlights on the side of the club.

"Is that too weird?" Madeline asked.

"Really? Why me?"

"Writers sometimes draw on something true from their own lives. That's the way I understand it. There's a character based on me too. It's about the friendship between the two women. Honestly, I'm having trouble getting the story going. There's not much happening yet."

"They could rob a bank. Go on a crime spree. Or maybe they become spies."

Madeline laughed. "I need some ideas like that. Something dramatic. Are you sure it isn't weird?"

"No," Sophia said. "I'm flattered. Seriously. I dated this guy my freshman year who wanted to photograph me. At first I thought it was cool. Then I found out he was photographing a lot of girls. It was a way to get us to take our tops off." She stuck out her tongue. "No, I'm flattered. Seriously. What's this woman like? Is she smart? And pretty? And sensitive?"

"All of the above."

"Then all I care about is getting to read it when you're done."

"Okay. I don't know if I'll ever finish it. It's just kind of me writing and writing without getting anywhere. A lot of character stuff."

"You're warming up," Sophia said.

"And you have to be honest when you do read it. If you don't like it . . ."

"I'll like it."

"I'll be finished at the end of the year. My favorite professor is my thesis adviser, and you know, I really want him to like it too. He's been such a huge influence and a mentor."

"That's the dude you mentioned once after yoga?"

"Maybe I did. He's a real writer. He published a book."

"That's cool. It matters that people believe in your talent that way. We all need that."

A guy popped his head around the corner of the building. Brown hair, neatly trimmed beard. His eyes were dark brown, like small stones embedded in his face.

"Sophia?" he said.

He didn't wait for an answer but walked right up to them.

Sophia's mouth formed a small O, and she opened her fingers, letting the cigarette drop to the ground, where it sparked. She turned and said, "Hey, babe. Ready to dance?"

The guy came and stood with his hands on his hips. He looked at the ground, looked at Madeline, back to the ground.

"Really? I thought you quit."

"It's just one."

"Look, I'm ready to go home," he said. He studied the smoking cigarette and shook his head. "It looks like you are too. It's getting late."

"This is my friend Madeline. The one I told you about. The one from yoga."

"Are you ready?" he asked. He ignored Madeline.

"I wanted to go back in," Sophia said. "Do you want to go home without me? I can Uber."

He took a step closer. He glanced once at Madeline and then back to Sophia. "Don't you think we should go together?"

Sophia started to say something back to him but cut the words off. Instead, she said, "Okay, babe. We can go."

"I don't want you going home alone after what you told me earlier."

"Okay," Sophia said. "Sure." Sophia shrugged as she turned to Madeline. "Do you need a ride?"

"I'm good."

"Be safe, okay?" She hugged her, pulling Madeline tight, a whiff of cigarette smoke cutting through the lavender.

"Are you okay?" Madeline asked.

"Right as rain," she said. "There's just a creep in our neighborhood. He's kind of watching us. He comes around late at night and walks up and down the street with his dog. Zach's right."

"Gross."

"It's fine," Sophia said. "Maybe he's harmless. But who can tell these days? Something for your book, right? See you at yoga next week?"

"Yes."

Sophia blew a kiss in Madeline's direction and started walking with Zach, taking his hand.

Madeline watched them go, a little envious. And Madeline looked away only when Zach turned back, checking her out over his shoulder, his look lingering longer than seemed right.

CHAPTER THIRTY-NINE

REBECCA
PRESENT

Rebecca goes to one more class after she leaves Hoffman's office—World History II—and while she sits through that lecture on Henry VIII, she starts to worry that she shouldn't have said anything about thinking she'd seen Madeline at the library. Especially to Hoffman.

Once she'd mentioned it, his interest perked up in a weird way, and he showed more enthusiasm in talking to her about Madeline than he had about her thesis. The discussion of her own work seemed more like an excuse for him to ramble on and on about things *he* wanted to talk about—just like he had in Nye's class—but when the conversation turned to Madeline and the possibility she was back in town, Hoffman asked question after question. And actually appeared to be listening to the answers.

It now seems silly to think she worried he'd be dismissive of her concerns, like Nye was. Hoffman kept the conversation going for almost twenty minutes, and it felt like he was playing the role of detective, as he wanted to know everything Rebecca knew about Madeline.

Rebecca admitted she didn't know much. They weren't such great friends. But Hoffman pushed.

"Maybe she had her heart broken by someone and left."

"She never mentioned any guys to me," Rebecca said.

Hoffman nodded, like he wanted her to say more. She wasn't sure what she could have said. But Hoffman looked so eager to hear, she went on.

"Madeline was kind of secretive about her life," she said. "Once before Christmas break the year she disappeared, I asked if she was looking forward to going home. I know I was. I couldn't wait to be in my parents' house with good food and plenty of hot water. But Madeline said no. I thought she was kidding, and I laughed. But she looked really pissed at me for laughing and said, 'No, I really don't want to go home. I'm staying in Gatewood as much as I can.'" Rebecca shrugged. "She said it in a way that made it clear she didn't want any follow-up questions."

"Interesting," Hoffman said.

And Rebecca thought that would be the end of it.

But he went on and said, "So maybe she had a guy here in town she wanted to spend time with. Do you think *that's* possible?"

It's strange—Rebecca knows about the guy at the party. And the party was at Hoffman's house. But Madeline swore her to secrecy about that. Rebecca considered breaking the promise, and would have if Madeline were dead. But since Madeline might be here . . . and since Hoffman might be freaked out if she mentioned something that went wrong at his house, she kept her mouth shut.

When Rebecca finally left his office, she felt a little off-balance. She wasn't really sure if Hoffman had interrogated her out of genuine concern for a former student in trouble or for some other reason. Two years had passed since Madeline disappeared—did Hoffman think he was going to solve the case by asking about Madeline's love life when the cops must have already dug into all of that?

After World History—and the stories about Henry VIII slicing off the heads of his wives, stories her professor told with a sly smile on his face—Rebecca heads to her job at the public library downtown. She spends four hours there, shelving books off a cart, which she thinks is just about the best job a writer could have. She rolls the cart into the far reaches of the library, picks up a book, and if it strikes her interest, she stands around, paging through it, seeing if it's a book she might want to check out and read on her own someday.

Someday when she has money to buy all the books she wants.

Someday when she has all the time in the world to read on her own.

Rebecca waits for the bus at six when her library shift ends. The wind blows straight into her face, and she turns her head to the side as she waits on the brightly lit sidewalk. Mercifully, the bus arrives quickly, and she steps into the warmth. The bus is never full, and it's only five blocks to her apartment, but she refuses to walk once the sun goes down. Not since Madeline disappeared. Rebecca looks back at some of the times she's walked or jogged in the dark and wonders what she was thinking. She always assumed a place like Gatewood was safe, that nothing that bad could ever happen here. Clearly she'd been way wrong. She still carries in her left coat pocket the pepper spray she bought.

She trudges up to the second-floor apartment she shares with her roommate, Mikaila. As she goes up the steps, Rebecca hopes against hope Mikaila isn't home. Or if Mikaila is here, that she is alone. Mikaila and her boyfriend, Steven, have been spending more and more time in the apartment, sprawled out on the couch watching Netflix, or giggling—*loudly*—in Mikaila's bedroom. Rebecca wants to ask but never does why they don't spend their time at Steven's place since he lives alone near campus.

But Rebecca hears them giggling through the door before her key even goes into the lock, and when she steps inside, Mikaila—her bare legs intertwined with Steven's on the couch—shivers in an exaggerated fashion.

"Oh, God," she says. "It's awful outside."

"Sorry," Rebecca says. "But that's the only way I can get inside. Through the door."

"It's just so cold. Isn't it, babe?" Mikaila leans over and kisses Steven, who is staring at the TV screen.

"You could try wearing pants," Rebecca says, her voice too low for Mikaila to hear. Rebecca keeps her coat on and starts down the hall to her bedroom, looking forward to nothing more than putting on her noise-canceling headphones and starting to read for class.

But Mikaila's voice stops her. "Oh, hey, Becca?"

Rebecca hates it when Mikaila calls her Becca. She likes it only when her mother calls her that—not anyone else. But she's given up on correcting Mikaila.

"What?"

"There's a package on your desk. It was sitting outside the door when I got home."

"Okay. Thanks."

"It's weird." She leans over and kisses Steven again. "There's, like, no postage on it or anything. It's just a fat envelope. Were you expecting something?"

"I don't know."

"Okay, cool."

Steven finally looks away from the TV and returns Mikaila's kisses, so Rebecca takes that as her cue to leave. She feels relief when she steps into her room and shuts the door behind her. She drops her bag and peels off her coat. She kicks one boot off as she picks the package up from her desk.

A giant yellow envelope sealed at the top with a strip of packing tape. Across the front, in Sharpie, someone has scrawled Rebecca's name. But she doesn't recognize the writing. It feels like a stack of papers inside. She slips her index finger under the flap and rips. It takes a few tries to get the tape and sealed flap open, but she finally does.

She tips the envelope to the side and a stack of papers slides out.

Rebecca kicks off her other boot while she turns the stack right side up.

Handwritten pages. Pen on paper. Hundreds and hundreds of pages of a handwritten manuscript that matches the writing on the front of the envelope. The first page reads "Chapter One," like it's a novel. No title. No author name. She flips through the pages but doesn't recognize anything.

Has a classmate sent it? A friend?

What the hell is it doing here?

CHAPTER FORTY

CONNOR
PRESENT

The phone starts to ring just after eleven.

I've made sure every door is locked, every window slammed tight.

I'm up, trying to distract myself with the Ken Burns Civil War documentary, which is running continuously on the university's PBS station. I've seen it before. Twice. But it draws me in, takes my mind off the craziness of the day. And since I don't have to teach for the time being, it doesn't matter how late I stay up. Preston e-mailed me earlier and told me Lance was taking over my fiction-writing class, which makes me feel bad for the students. Lance's attendance can be spotty, and he is easily distracted. And he has a polarizing effect on the students. About half see him as a lovable, dedicated eccentric who changes their lives by spending a great deal of time with them as they revise their work. The other half despise him for being a self-centered blowhard.

I don't recognize the number on the ID screen. I know I should let it go, ignore it, but I can't. So while the Battle of Antietam rages on my television, I answer the call.

"Connor? This is Diana Lukas."

I sit up straighter when she says her name. My lawyer, the one Preston told me to call.

"Diana," I say, "why are you calling so late?"

I lean forward, use the remote to mute the sounds of gunshots and cannon fire on the TV.

"Connor, we have a problem. I need you to listen, okay?"

"I'm listening."

"You've really stepped in it, and it's going to come and bite you in the ass."

"What is, Diana?"

She takes a deep breath, then starts. "I have a friend on the police force here in Gatewood. And I got a call from him just a few minutes ago. Connor, did you pay a social visit to Zach Greenfield earlier today?"

Her words don't really surprise me. What did I expect to happen if I went around to the home of a murder suspect or person of interest or whatever he is and started asking him questions? Did I think the police would be happy?

"Did you hear me, Connor?"

"Yes, I did. I just—"

"Why did you do that?" Diana asks.

"I was going to say . . . I thought he might know something about all of this. And I thought he might be able to help me out."

"Help you out? Connor, you have a doctorate, right?"

"Yes."

"Is it in stupidity? Is that what you studied?"

I feel slapped. More than that—my head buzzes as though I've been smacked with a two-by-four.

"Okay, Diana. So I fucked up. But I'm a person of interest or whatever in a murder case, and I kind of want to know what's really going on."

"That's my job. You're supposed to listen to me and do what I say. And I'll keep your nuts out of the fire. Do you understand?"

"I do."

"Good. Well, you're up against it now. Detective Bowman wants to come and talk to you again. I put her off briefly, but she's not going to let go of this."

"Shit."

"Connor, if the cops come to your house or call you, just shut up and don't do anything. Except call me. I'll be there before they really start asking you anything. Okay? Did you hear me? Just shut your damn mouth and wait for me."

"Okay."

"Do you have friends you can call? Family?"

"I have a sister in Michigan, but I'm not going to bother her. I'm fine."

"If you say so . . ."

"Diana, none of this can be real. Can it?"

But I'm talking into the void.

"Diana? Diana?"

She's gone.

And I feel completely alone.

CHAPTER FORTY-ONE

I tell myself I'm doing this for Grendel. If the police come at some point and haul me away, bring me to the station and question me all night, who will take care of my dog?

But really, I know why I'm doing it.

I'm scared.

The police already think I know more about Sophia's death than I should, so what are they going to think now that I've gone and tried to talk to her husband?

I grab Grendel's leash, a bag of his food, and a box of his treats.

"Come on, boy. We're going on a visit."

I'm not even sure it's going to work. I worry about running into the cops as we go out the back door into the freezing night. When I'm out here, my body freezes. But not from the weather.

What if the person who killed Sophia is now looking for me?

What if it's Zach, and he's decided to take revenge another way?

The night is so quiet, it's like I'm the last man on earth.

No one to call to for help. No one to defend me.

If there's a killer lurking in the darkness . . .

Or maybe it's Madeline waiting . . . ready to gong me again. . . .

The atmosphere feels brittle and sharp. It's like the very air has edges that poke and prod my skin. Grendel climbs into the backseat, tail wagging. He loves going in the car, but he must be wondering what the hell I'm doing so late.

I slam the driver's door shut and engage the locks. I breathe a little easier as I start the car.

I back out of the driveway, looking both ways up and down the street. No flashing lights, no sirens. I'm slipping away.

It's a ten-minute drive to Preston's house. I don't even bother to text or call. His kids will be asleep, but I know he stays awake working most nights when the house is quiet. He gets by on less sleep than I do and bounces out of bed early in the morning, heading to the gym before he works a full day on campus.

The streets are quiet, most houses dark. While I drive, I also think about Madeline, out there in the world with that manuscript that incriminates me. I always liked her as a student, and I believed she liked me. I remember her coming to my office to discuss a story she wrote. Even coming to my house a couple of nights ago, sitting in my living room, so calmly laying out what she wanted me to do.

I've always felt paternal toward my students, even before I lost Jake. Since his death, that feeling has swelled, filling me with an intense appreciation for the kids in my classes. Their wit and talent, their anxieties and insecurities. Their striving. Jake would be one of them now, attending a college, going to classes, making new friends. Even stumbling and falling as he tried new things.

I have to slow down, wipe tears from my eyes. I simply can't process or accept that I'm a suspect in the eyes of the police.

I can't.

I pull into Preston's neighborhood, which is just outside downtown. Mostly ranches built after World War II, back when not everything looked the same: low, sleek houses with large windows and big yards. I pull into his driveway and feel relief when I see the light on in his office near the back of the house. I text him, telling him I'm here with Grendel.

He writes back immediately and comes to the front door, waving me in.

I grab Grendel by the leash, along with his supplies, and go up the walk. Preston lets me into the living room, where a single lamp glows, casting a warm light over the space. The furniture is modern and spare, but the room still feels inviting. Maybe it's something about the lives being lived here—a family, children. A refuge against everything.

Preston speaks in a low voice. "Kelly and the kids are asleep. What is going on that you're over here this late?"

Grendel loves Preston and his family. Even though he hasn't lived with them for a while, he remembers them. I've occasionally brought him over to run around the yard with Preston's kids. Even his daughter who is supposed to be allergic enjoys playing with Grendel, which confirmed my belief it was a story meant to make it easier for me to accept the gift. She'd throw a ball over and over, giggling when he brought it back to her, slobbering on her tiny hands. And she'd stick her face right into his fur, showing no side effects.

Preston bends down and pets Grendel while I start to talk.

"You're going to want to hear what's going on," I say.

"Okay," he says, still petting the dog, but his eyes trail up to meet mine. He must detect something in my voice, my manner, that tells him something is really wrong.

"I mean it, Preston. I'm in real trouble."

He remains in place, bent over Grendel, but the muscles in his arms tense. His jaw looks set.

I wish I knew a better way to tell him, some words that wouldn't embarrass me or make him think I've lost my mind.

I just say it.

When I tell him about talking to Zach and the police finding out about it, he slowly straightens up, his mouth partway open, his eyes watching me like I'm a crazy person.

"Why did you go harass that guy, Connor?" he says.

"I wasn't trying to harass him, Preston. I'm sorry."

"You're not making any sense, Connor. None at all. Are you saying you went to the home of a murder victim's husband and threatened him?"

"I didn't threaten him. I wanted to talk to him because of what the police think about Sophia and me. But now he's told them, and it makes me look very bad."

"You're damn right it does." Preston runs his hand through his hair, looks up at the ceiling. "This is all wrong."

"It's true, Preston. I hate to be the guy to bring this news so late at night. In the middle of your family's lives." I look around the calm space, let my eyes drift down the hallway to where his kids peacefully sleep. I feel like a barbarian intruder, carrying the insanity of the outside world into this sanctuary.

I explain about the call from Diana.

"They might come and question me more at any point," I say. "I couldn't think clearly. I couldn't stand the thought I'd be locked up and might never get out. I didn't want Grendel to be abandoned in the house. What if they really start to think I'm guilty of her murder?"

"Okay, okay." He wipes his eyes, once with each hand. "Holy shit, Connor. Damn."

"I know."

"Okay," Preston says, ever the voice of reason. He uses this voice in meetings, calming passions and moderating arguments. He uses this voice and then moves everyone toward a consensus. Mostly we call him "Preston the Politician." We also call him "Preston the Peacemaker." And that's what I desperately need right now. Peace. "This is all coming at me pretty fast, Connor. I was back there working on something a few minutes ago. Honestly, I was working on my novel because your success and advice motivated me to keep doing it, and now you're telling me you're more deeply entangled in this murder. Are you sure you really understand all this?"

"I do, Preston. I do." I notice my voice rising, so I dial it down. I take a few deep breaths, trying to channel some of Preston's calm. I try, but

I can't get there. Not with everything that's going on. "It's for real, Preston. And there's even more that I can't tell you about quickly. It stems from the book and from things that happened years ago."

"Your book? You know I haven't read it yet, Conner. I just—"

"Yes, my book. And Madeline. And this murder."

"Whoa, whoa." Preston takes a step toward me, his hands signaling for a time-out. Even Grendel looks up at me like I'm losing my grip. "Why don't you sit down? And you can tell me exactly what you want me to do for you. Right now there's a gushing waterfall of information cascading on my head."

I don't sit, but I start to talk. "I don't know what you can do. I don't. But I couldn't just let myself be led away by the police. I knew you'd take care of Grendel, and then I thought you might have some advice and some ideas. You always do. And you could talk me off the ledge and tell me where to go to get away from all of this."

"Okay, okay." He points to the couch. "Why don't you sit? Really. Sit."

Like a small child being guided by an adult, I obey. I plop onto the couch.

"I'm going to go out and get us a drink. We both need it now. Okay?"

"Okay."

He starts for the kitchen, but I reach up and place my hand on his arm.

"Thanks," I say. "Really."

"Sure." He watches me for a moment. "Are you sure you wouldn't rather just go in and talk to the cops? You have a lawyer. Let her protect you. If you didn't hurt this woman, just tell them what you know and be done with it."

His words make sense. They do. But I'm not ready to listen.

"Have you ever been in the police station that way?" I ask. "I was there yesterday being questioned. I felt trapped, like I'd never get out. And I've been there for other stuff, as you know. When Emily and Jake died. It's just . . . I feel the walls closing in when I'm there. I don't think they want to let me out, Preston."

"But you could clear it up. Get out from under this."

"Not yet, okay? Just . . . let me think."

"Okay, bud."

My hand is still on his arm, and he gives me a reassuring squeeze.

"Sit tight while I check on the kids and then get us a drink. Okay?"

"Sure. Okay."

"Then we'll figure out the next step."

He pulls away and leaves the room.

I finally let out a breath I feel I've been holding forever.

CHAPTER FORTY-TWO

CONNOR
FALL, THREE YEARS AGO

I dreaded that date.

More than anything in my life—I dreaded that date.

The year before, the first time I faced the terrible anniversary of Emily's and Jacob's deaths, I fell completely apart. I canceled my classes, and I sat in the house, head in my hands, drinking and crying all day. Friends called and texted, but I ignored them all and stewed in my own misery, eventually passing out on the couch around seven o'clock.

I decided not to do the same thing that second year.

I attended my classes as usual. I went in clean and sober, shaved and showered, looking like the picture of health and contentment. I still received calls and texts during the day from friends and family—not as many but some—and I responded to them all with a simple "Thanks!"

At the end of the day, I sat in my office alone. Most of Goodlaw was empty—students and faculty gone for the evening. I was afraid.

I didn't want to go home. I didn't want to face the empty house I knew waited for me. The house still held nearly every artifact of Emily's and Jacob's lives. Pictures. Clothes. Emily's painting supplies in the basement. Jacob's soccer equipment in his room. Going home meant entering that museum of grief, that monument to everything I'd lost.

I started thinking of ways I could sleep in my office. Move some of the furniture to the edges, use my messenger bag or coat as a pillow. Peaceful oblivion on the floor of Goodlaw Hall. I expected to find the sounds of the overnight cleaning people comforting. The sweeping of brooms and the rustle of trash bags proof I wasn't spending the night alone.

But around five thirty, Preston came to the door.

He looked as fresh as he had when he'd entered the building in the morning. Every hair in place. His shirt unwrinkled.

"Good," he said. "You're still here."

"I am. Just . . . catching up on some things."

He stepped inside, closer to my desk. "I thought we could do something. Dinner. Drinks. Rebuild a car engine. You know, man stuff."

"Oh. I just . . ."

"Connor, I know what day it is. You shouldn't be alone. And Kelly gave me permission for a boys' night out."

It took me a moment to answer. I hated everyone knowing. I hated having everything on display, especially the most terrible, brutal thing that ever happened to me. But I recognized I was no longer in a position not to ask for help. The previous anniversary proved that to me—and I didn't want a replay.

So I agreed to go.

Preston drove, and we went to several bars. At every stop, I drank and drank, while Preston bought the shots and the beers. He egged me on, never allowed me to have a moment when my mind drifted to the kinds of thoughts I'd been trying to avoid the entire day. Eventually, the rooms we were in started tilting. I remembered being on a Tilt-A-Whirl once when I was five, and the way the world spun for hours once I stepped off the ride. So much so, I ended up vomiting on my father's shoes.

That's what the night with Preston turned into.

Near one o'clock we pulled up behind my house, and Preston led me inside, one of my arms draped over his shoulders, most of my weight resting on him. He guided me to the bedroom and let me flop onto the bed, one hundred and seventy pounds of dead, drunk weight.

He tugged my shoes off, stood by while I fumbled with my belt. Then he came back with a glass of water and Tylenol.

"Take this," he said. "Then go to sleep. For a long time. You don't have any classes tomorrow."

"That sounds terrible."

"What does? Not going to campus with a hangover?"

"Not teaching," I said. "That's terrible." I rolled over, fumbled on the nightstand for the Tylenol. I managed to pick one up but knocked the other onto the floor. Preston bent and picked it up for me.

"I'm not following you," Preston said. "Maybe you're just drunk."

"No," I said. "No. I mean, I am. But I'm trying to say something." I tossed the Tylenol back and held on to the glass of water long enough to chase them down. When I'd swallowed, I thumped back against my pillow. "You know what I'm saying. My students . . . you all, my colleagues . . . I need to *see* you. You all distract me. I socialize with you. At school. Outside of school . . . like tonight."

"You're saying . . . I see." Preston nods. "You need the social interaction that comes on campus. It helps you cope."

"It does. I need you people. That's why I go out drinking with my students. I never did that when Emily was alive. And Jake. But now . . . I mean . . . all our old friends have kids and wives. They don't know what to say to me. You know? But the students don't always know about my family, so it feels like a clean slate in a way."

"I hear you," Preston said.

I could tell he wanted to keep the pity off his face, but even in my drunken state, I saw it there. Loud and clear.

"Thanks, Preston," I said. "You're a good friend. And boss."

"Thank you," he said. "I'll let you sleep."

But he didn't go. He stood next to my bed, looking down at me as my eyelids fluttered. I managed to keep them open while he stayed there.

"What?" I asked.

"You need to be careful of that," he said. "You don't want to be like some people who take that kind of thing too far. You can be a mentor to your students. Maybe a kind of friend. But . . . you have to be careful."

"Careful, boss?"

"Let's talk another time." He reached down and patted my leg. "Go to sleep."

"Careful? Like . . . don't get too *involved*."

Preston nodded. "We've had some colleagues do that. People I respect. And like. Friends of ours. Don't let your vulnerability lead to that. Being a professor can be a lonely life. The students are right there, young and beautiful."

"Who?" I asked. "Who's doing it?"

Preston shook his head. "No time for gossip. Remember, loyalty matters. A lot. That's how I can protect you all. Go to sleep, okay?"

"Who?"

Preston turned his back to me, but at the bedroom door he looked back over his shoulder. "Our poetic friend might be doing that. And he needs to be careful."

"Lance?"

"I know he has his low moments, but I can only do so much to protect him. Good night."

"Is that who you mean? Come on, Preston the Politician, tell me."

But Preston was gone.

CHAPTER FORTY-THREE

CONNOR
PRESENT

Preston comes back into his living room, carrying two glasses and a bottle of Four Roses.

He puts the glasses on the coffee table in front of me and pours two healthy shots.

"Here you go," he says. "This will steady you."

"I'm trying to cut back, but I think you're right."

He puts the bottle down, and we both pick up our glasses. Preston remains standing as we drink. The bourbon feels good. Warmth and a sliver of calm do spread through me.

"Do you remember that time you and I went out on the second anniversary?" I ask. "The night you had to basically carry me in to my bed?"

"Sure. You were pretty blotto. With good reason, I might add."

"You said something about Lance that night, and we've never really talked about it. But it came back to me now. Plus the other day you were warning me about the new atmosphere on campus."

"Lance gets too close to the students," Preston says. "He's an excellent teacher. I should have been more discreet. Usually I am."

"That's true, but—"

"Besides, you have to think about *this* now. A lot. You were with

Madeline that night she disappeared, and you don't really remember what happened between the two of you. So you say. That's going to come back at you if you're a suspect in another death." Preston drains his glass. He looks like a weight is pressing down on him, pushing his head and shoulders lower. "I can't even believe this is going on."

He wipes his eyes again. And that's Preston. Cool and collected. But also likely to choke up when a student or a faculty member achieves a great success. Or when one of his daughters makes a drawing for him. Or on Kelly's fortieth birthday, when he made a loving toast to her. When I told him about my book deal, he hugged me tight. I thought he'd never let go.

"I know," I say. "I'm sorry I dragged it to your door."

"Let's deal with the problem at hand, which is landing on you pretty hard."

"Okay, you're right. My problems." I haven't finished my drink, but even the small amount I've swallowed loosens my tongue. And Preston's a good friend. A rock in the storm. "If I told you something about the book, something I think I need to get out . . ."

"Of course you can," he says. "Look, I'm sorry I haven't read it yet. When you went up for tenure, you only had the contract. And it just came out . . . I mean, I bought one, but it's tough to find the time."

"I know my colleagues won't read the novel. We know the dirty little secret of academia—we don't read one another's work. For a variety of reasons."

"I will, though. Kelly wants to read it too. Just . . . Look, I didn't eat enough for dinner, and this is hitting me. I'm going to get some cheese and crackers for us. I'll be right back."

I want to keep talking, but I stop as he leaves the room. I stare into my glass and then finish it. Grendel watches me, his eyes dark pools above his graying muzzle. My future looks like a narrowing tunnel, shrinking to a pinpoint of light.

"It's just one," I say.

The bottle tempts me, but I resist. So I sit and wait, deciding whether I should go ahead and tell Preston about who really wrote the book or not. He'd listen. He'd know what to do.

But he'd follow the rules. He'd report me to the administration and that would be that for my academic career, which is already on the ropes.

But should I really be worrying about myself so much?

I hear voices in the kitchen. Preston talking to someone.

I figure it's Kelly, and maybe we woke her up. I haven't seen her in weeks, so I put my glass down and get up to say hello. I'll apologize if we woke her up. Maybe I can tell them both about the book, have more than Preston's thoughts on everything I face.

The house is hushed except for the voices in the kitchen. When I get closer, I hear it's only one voice. Through the entryway, I see Preston at the counter, hunched over, one finger plugged into his ear, the other holding his phone.

"He's here now," he says. "I can keep him here if you hurry over."

"Who are you talking to?"

Preston spins toward me. His face flushes, and he ends the call with one poke of the red button. "Keep your voice down. The kids."

"Was that the police?" I ask. And I know I'm not keeping my voice down. No way.

"Connor, I called them for your own good. You need to talk to them. You need to clear this up. It will be better for everyone to get this over with. I can call Diana too. Think about it—"

"I *have* thought about it. I can do my own thinking."

"If you tell them everything, it's going to be so much better. Isn't that what Diana told you to do?"

He takes a step toward me, his hands out asking for calm. He looks like an animal trainer approaching a spooked tiger. One that might bite his head off.

"Connor, I'm only trying to help you. You know that."

"Goddamn it. Are they coming now?"

Preston nods. "They're coming."

"Shit."

I look around. The kitchen feels small. And getting smaller. I feel a choking sensation in my throat, something cutting off my air. I start backing up.

"I'm going," I say.

"Don't, Connor. Stay. Talk to them. You're in a world of trouble now."

"No thanks to you." I turn to go, heading for the front of the house. Grendel lifts his head when I come into the room. Preston follows me, ready to say more.

At the door I turn back. "Stay away from me." I pull it open, feel the cold air. "And do me a favor. At least take care of Grendel for me. That's the least you can do."

CHAPTER FORTY-FOUR

The cemetery is quiet.

And I figure no one will look for me here. I come here often when I need a place that's quiet, when I need a place to stop and sit still.

Emily and I were married for just over seventeen years. We never once discussed funeral or burial plans for each other. And we certainly never contemplated the possibility of our son dying. We thought we had years and years together. Endless years. So when the time came and I faced that awful decision on my own, I made the best choices I could in the midst of my confused grief.

The city of Gatewood maintains an old cemetery outside of downtown. Some of the first settlers to the town were buried there, and for many years no new burials occurred because it was full. Not long before Emily and Jake died, a city surveyor went to work there and discovered a number of unused plots, which were then made available for the public to buy. Do I consider it good fortune that I was able to take advantage of that surveyor's ingenuity and purchase three plots on a gently sloping hill overlooking the river?

I park on the narrow road near the gate to the cemetery, where the tree has grown against the fence, and get out of the car. In the weeks and months after Emily and Jake died, I'd wake during the night and come out here, sitting on their graves in the pitch dark, kept company only by the night birds and the skittering skunks and opossums.

I know Preston is right.

I know I should go to the police and explain what I wanted from Zach.

I know I should call Diana and let her protect me. And explain that I didn't write the book.

I will.

But it's not his choice when to do it. It's mine.

I'm happy to be able to stretch my legs. I squeeze through the fence—thankful that of all the things I've done, I've at least managed to stay trim—and head in the direction of the familiar headstone with one name chiseled across the top: NYE. I know that below Emily's and Jake's names, as well as their dates of birth and—exact same—dates of death, an empty space remains for me to be added.

For the first six months after they died, I couldn't come out here without completely losing control of my emotions. For the next year or year and a half, it was hit-and-miss. Sometimes I sobbed. Sometimes I felt like shit. Sometimes I managed to summon a happy memory—Jake's first bike ride, a trip we all took to the Grand Canyon, Emily's thirtieth birthday party—and I would drive away from the cemetery feeling better.

The past few years I've found the visits mostly comforting. I always thought the notion of burying someone, of paying a ton of money to put someone in the ground with a rock over their head, was silly. But when it happened to my family, I got it.

The wind has eased. I checked the weather earlier and saw we're in for a warming spell. I can already feel the temperature climbing a bit, and I hope like hell it continues, because I didn't move to southern Kentucky expecting to be cold all winter.

I stop about thirty yards from our headstone and see its outline at the top of the little hill. I wait while my eyes slowly adjust to the dark. I'm about to move forward when I notice a lump to my left, about twenty feet away.

I squint. It looks like a large animal—a dog? a deer?—has curled up and gone to sleep. But the animal doesn't stir as I approach, hasn't dashed away as I would expect.

Maybe it's simply part of the landscaping. The maintenance crew takes good care of the property, and from time to time they plant new grass or a tree.

My heart thumps a steady beat. My fingertips are cold. Stinging.

"Scat," I say. If it's an animal, it will go.

But the lump remains, still and steady. I feel like a child, spooked by a pile of clothes in the corner of my bedroom. For weeks after Emily and Jake died, I slept with every light on in the house, trying to bring myself comfort and security. I imagine my early-rising neighbors saw them and knew what I was doing. A grown man sleeping with all the lights on.

Speaking of light . . .

I slide my phone out of my back pocket. I activate the flashlight, which illuminates a bright cone around me. It shows the brown grass, scattered twigs, a fake flower petal blown here off someone's bouquet.

I move forward slowly. I lift the phone, shifting the light away from my feet toward the lump in front of me. At the edge of the cone, I see a pile of debris. Twigs and leaves that the landscaping crew has gathered from around the cemetery grounds and mounded until they can come and cart them away.

I almost laugh out loud.

I spooked myself over a pile of yard waste. That's how on edge I am.

My breathing starts to calm, and I lower the phone. But as I lower it, I see something—

No, I think. *No. I'm imagining things again.*

But I lift the phone and aim the light at the edge of the pile of debris. And I see my mind hasn't been playing tricks on me. It's really there. . . .

A brown boot and, above it, a ragged cuff at the end of a pant leg. Sticking out of the pile.

My heart goes into a higher gear.

My hand trembles, and I concentrate to hold the phone. A homeless person? Someone seeking refuge in the cemetery?

I will myself forward, taking two more steps.

"Hey," I say. "Hey! Wake up! Get up!"

But the pile doesn't move. The person—*body*—doesn't move.

I bend down, use my free hand to move the debris aside. I work faster and faster, moving frantically.

I aim the light and see more. A red winter coat thrown open. A torso. The sweater wet and sticky with blood. I brush more aside. Revealing more.

I run the light up the body—because that's all it can be, given the amount of blood. *A body.*

The light catches the red hair, the owlish glasses.

I recoil, stumble backward, and fall onto my ass on the little hillside. "Oh, God, oh, God. Fuck fuck fuck."

CHAPTER FORTY-FIVE

I pass the light over Madeline and nearly drop it when it reaches her face, shows her unseeing eyes behind the glasses.

"Oh, God."

I extend my hand, place it against her neck. The skin is cold and not just because of the temperature in the air. She's gone.

I move the light down her body to the large bloodstain. I see no weapon, but it looks like she's been stabbed.

And why did this happen here?

What was Madeline doing here?

Someone killed her here and tried to hide the body.

My mind can't grasp any answers. I lift the phone. I need to call someone, need to report this to the police. I'm about to dial when I stop myself.

I can't do it while I'm here. Not unless I want to be arrested. And accused of her murder.

I'm likely to be accused anyway, given the location of her body. Given the suspicion that has already fallen on me about Sophia. I'll call the police—but only as I'm driving away.

But before I stand up to go, I lean forward over Madeline's body, looking for the manuscript she took from my house. The manuscript that can blow up my life.

I shine the light over her coat and on the ground around her. I don't see it. I even risk patting her jacket, avoiding the sticky blood, hoping to feel that lump of papers. I hunch over and look around, my phone light guiding me. But I don't see it. And I don't want to stay.

Which means whoever killed her—*Zach?*—has the manuscript now. "Shit."

I push myself to my feet and back away, down the hill. And I move as quickly as I can through the darkened cemetery. I squeeze back through the fence and climb into the car.

I drive away and find a pay phone, where I anonymously report what I've seen.

CHAPTER FORTY-SIX

REBECCA
PRESENT

The alarm rings at seven thirty. Rebecca bolts up like someone stuck her with a pin.

She fumbles around on the nightstand, trying to find her phone, trying to shut it off. It feels like the alarm is inside her head, emanating from a place deep inside her skull. It's so loud, it hurts.

"Stop, stop."

Someone thumps against the wall from Mikaila's room. It has to be Mikaila, since Steven is usually too polite to do something like that. Mikaila is the nervy one, the type to say something.

Rebecca grabs the phone, shuts the noise off. Sweet relief. She feels like her eardrums have been punctured, like blood must be cascading down the sides of her head.

"Stop being overly dramatic," she says to herself.

She checks the phone. Seven thirty-one. *Ugh.*

The bed is a mess, papers spread all over the sheets and comforter. Last night, Rebecca started reading the manuscript that landed on her doorstep, the one with no name or return address. The one about the two women who are friends—and then the friendship is threatened because one woman might be cheating with the other woman's husband. While it isn't exactly her style—she prefers Jane Austen or maybe Dickens over contemporary novels—the pages flew by faster than she could turn them. It felt like the book was covered with glue and the pages stuck to her hands, leaving her unable to put it aside. She read and read until she fell asleep with the book covering her like a blanket. She slept like homeless people who covered themselves with newspapers in order to stay warm. She barely stirred during the night, didn't even get up to pee.

But duty calls. In addition to her job at the library, she also tutors at the writing center one morning a week, and it's this morning. She needs to dress and get to campus, and she dreads the thought of the January cold that is unseasonable for Kentucky and seems to be eternal.

No time for a shower, so she brushes her teeth and then pulls her hair back into a ponytail and splashes what passes for hot water in their apartment onto her face. When she emerges from the bathroom, Mikaila's lithe body is leaning against the wall of the hallway, her mouth open in a tremendous feline yawn.

"Becca, you know I'm a light sleeper and a really sensitive person. If I don't sleep enough, my anxiety really goes into overdrive. We have to do something about that alarm. You set it too loud."

"I'm sorry. I'll remember tonight."

"Steven and I are so tired. We were watching a documentary about nine eleven last night. Did you know the government set charges inside the Pentagon? That's why it exploded. It was totally an inside job."

"Um . . . well . . ."

"The shit these professors don't teach us."

"Can I ask you something, Mikaila? You know that package I got yesterday, the one on the porch with my name on it?"

"What? Oh, yeah. That. What was it? Did you order something?"

"It's a book."

"Oh. Snooze."

"Did you see the person who left it here?" Rebecca asks.

Mikaila yawns again, her T-shirt riding up, exposing her navel. She closes her eyes like she might fall asleep leaning against the wall.

"Mikaila?"

"I don't know, Becca. So many questions so early in the morning."

"So you didn't see anyone?"

She sighs. "I don't know. I told you the package was already sitting there when we walked up. It could have been there all day. I had a really early class at eleven yesterday, so I was gone for a while."

"Okay. Thanks."

Mikaila reaches out and starts moving Rebecca's hair around. "You'd be so pretty with a better haircut, Becca. Maybe some bolder color? Liven up this brown. I can take you to the place I go. It's only, like, two hundred dollars."

"Two hundred?"

"Oh, and yeah . . . Steven's going to be staying here for a few days. He forgot to pay his heating bill, so the landlord shut it off. Can you believe that? So there's no heat at his place. You don't mind if he crashes here."

Mikaila slips into the bathroom without waiting for a response.

Rebecca doesn't have time to offer one. She's running late. And she knows Mikaila wouldn't listen anyway. She dresses in her room—jeans, a sweatshirt, boots. She thinks about bringing the pages of the book with her to read on the bus or during any downtime she has at the writing center, but decides against it. She fears losing some of the pages, since they were just floating around loose, and she could look forward to reading more when she comes home this evening. As she pulls on her coat and steps out into the cold, she pictures the scene playing itself out in reverse in seven hours or so. Rebecca entering the apartment, heading to her room, slipping under the covers, and then reading the rest. Mikaila and Steven could swing from the chandeliers for all she cares, so long as she holds a good book in her hands. And this one is very, very good. . . .

And the more she thinks about the book, the more familiar it sounds. The bus rumbles toward campus and the low set of buildings—

none more than three stories high—that makes up Gatewood's downtown. The air brakes hiss at every stop, the door letting in a rush of cold air as passengers climb on and off. That book—the one from the porch. It kind of sounds like the one Dr. Nye wrote and talked about at the library a few nights ago.

At his book launch, Nye told the crowd he wasn't going to read from the book. He said he found that boring, and he hoped he wouldn't test the audience's patience or put them all to sleep. People laughed, but Rebecca agreed. A few times a year, the English Department brought poets and fiction writers to campus to give readings, and some of them read in such a monotone voice, they killed the energy and mood in the room faster than a gas leak. When Nye said he wouldn't read, Rebecca didn't laugh, but inside, she breathed a sigh of relief. She would have hated to see a professor she liked give a disastrous performance onstage.

But Nye talked about the book. He summarized the plot and told the crowd what had inspired it and how long it took him to write it, all the nerdy shoptalk Rebecca loves to hear. And the book he described sounded a lot like the one that landed on her doorstep. In Nye's book and in the handwritten one she is reading, a young woman gets murdered in a town very much like Gatewood. Rebecca thought it was just a coincidence. After all, she doesn't read a lot of thrillers, but she spends a lot of time in bookstores and online. She knows how many books these days tell stories of women getting knocked off in various gruesome ways by various people—boyfriends, husbands, lovers, doctors, therapists, serial killers. Just like the books she prefers always seem to deal with an inheritance or a will or a lost love, thrillers plow their own fertile and murderous ground over and over. But this one isn't just a thriller. It's about the friendship between the two women, the way they confide in each other. And help each other. Until the man starts to ruin everything . . .

Nye said in class once that every writer has only one story to tell—and if they're lucky and have a career, they get to tell it over and over.

Was that as true of Jane Austen as the mysterious author of the book on her stoop?

The bus rattles up College Street. It's close to full, students packed in next to one another in their bulky coats, trying to text and scroll through their phones with gloves on. The bus stops a block from campus, at the edge of downtown, and Rebecca stands up, tugging her bag over her shoulder. She knows she shouldn't do it, she knows she needs to hustle, but she also knows she won't survive the day without coffee. And she has just enough time to run into Troy's and grab something she can bring into the writing center with her. Troy's is a little pricey but also locally owned. Sometimes she thinks she works in the writing center so she can buy Troy's coffee on the way in.

She exits by the rear door, stepping down onto the sidewalk, which is stained by the rock salt that has been thrown everywhere. She hates winter because it's just so dirty. Everything stained and gray and cold. She turns left, starting for Troy's, when she hears her name.

She looks back toward the bus. Has she forgotten something? Her wallet? Her keys? She's done it before and then had to pay for new credit cards, a new student ID, a new key. But no one on the bus knows her name, and a quick check of her pockets tells her everything feels like it's in place.

She hears her name again. She looks around.

People pass back and forth in front of her. Not just students but also faculty and people on their way to jobs downtown—lawyers, cops, business owners.

Is she hearing things? Thinking she's heard her name twice when she hasn't?

Then there is no mistaking it—someone almost shouts her name. "Rebecca."

She jerks her head to the right. An alley runs along the side of Troy's, leading to the small parking lot in back. Someone stands there in the entrance to the alley, and when she looks that way, he beckons her over.

"Come on," he says. "Over here."

And it all seems so weird because she's just been thinking about him and his book and his talk at the library.

And she doesn't have time to wonder why Dr. Nye is calling to her like he doesn't want anyone to know he's in the alley next to Troy's.

CHAPTER FORTY-SEVEN

CONNOR
PRESENT

Rebecca finally hears me and starts over, even though she looks suspicious.

She wears a wool hat pulled low on her forehead, and her eyes look out from under it like she thinks I might bite. I step back, relieved to be out of the exposed opening to the alley.

"Dr. Nye? Is everything okay?"

I'm far enough back so no one walking by can see me. The kid looks at me like I'm nuts, but I also benefit from teaching in an English Department. Everyone seems eccentric or odd or flat-out crazy—the students grow used to it and at most roll their eyes behind our backs when we behave like lunatics.

"Everything's . . . okay," I say. "I didn't want to talk in Troy's. It's so crowded this time of morning."

"Did you want to talk to me?" she asks, pointing at her chest with a gloved hand.

"I do," I say.

"Did you know I'd be here?"

"I figured a lot of people pass through Troy's in the morning. And you always have a Troy's cup with you in class. Do you have a minute?"

"Well, I'm on my way—"

"It'll be quick."

She half shrugs, accepts she's stuck talking to me. Maybe out of pity, maybe out of simple curiosity. She steps forward, close enough to hear me over the passing cars and chattering pedestrians.

Rebecca looks me over, letting her eyes trail from the top of my head on down. I must look like hell. I spent the rest of the night driving around after I called the police, stopping a couple of times at twenty-four-hour fast-food drive-throughs for a hamburger or a cup of coffee. Around four o'clock, my eyelids grew as heavy as manhole covers, and I drove out behind the football stadium at the far edge of campus, back to where the parking lot meets a stand of trees. I found a spot there and closed my eyes, locking the doors in case the same person who killed Madeline was following me. I managed to fall asleep in the driver's seat for a couple of hours, then woke up with a sore neck and a full bladder, but the sleep helped. I intend to get in touch with Diana, allow her to help me. But I need Rebecca to do something for me as well.

I came downtown, then parked behind Troy's as the sun came up. I'd met Rebecca here for coffee a few times as she began her thesis. I frequently meet students here because it's close to campus and because most of them pass through here at one time or another, especially the creative writing types who see it as part of their essential selves to hang out in coffee shops and brood over their laptops.

"I need to talk to you about Madeline O'Brien," I say, cringing inside. I know news may not have reached the students yet. It may not have reached anyone this early in the morning. But with social media, it may have started to spread. "Have you heard anything about her?"

"You mean since I told you I thought she was at your reading? No, I haven't. Why?"

Shit.

I've become the bearer of bad news, the messenger with nothing at all good to share. A medieval rider on a pale horse.

"Okay, Rebecca." I clear my throat, trying to force the right words out. "I found out very early this morning that Madeline is dead. Someone murdered her."

The whites of Rebecca's eyes appear to double in size. She lifts her gloved hand to her chest, placing it there like she's about to recite the Pledge of Allegiance. She looks right at me, but I don't think she's seeing me.

"I'm sorry, Rebecca. I'm sorry to be the one to have to tell you that news."

"She's dead?"

"Yes, she is." I wait a beat, watch Rebecca carefully, looking for signs that she's going to fall over or cry or lose her composure in any way. But she doesn't. She remains upright, even with her face blank. "Are you okay? Do you want me to go inside and get you some water or something?"

She shakes her head ever so slightly, her hand still pressed to her chest.

"Would you like me to drive you home?" I ask. "I saw you got off the bus."

"I'm okay," she says. She starts nodding. "I am. I'm just . . . really shocked."

"I know."

"Does this mean that really was Madeline at your reading the other night?" she asks.

"Yes, it does. And the police are going to be trying to figure out why she was here and who might have wanted to hurt her."

"I thought someone hurt her when she disappeared. I thought she was already . . . you know, dead. That's why I didn't believe it at first when I thought I saw her at the library."

"You were right about that. And I was kind of dismissive when you told me you saw her, but I shouldn't have been."

"That's okay. It's pretty fucking weird."

"It is."

Rebecca seems to be coming back to herself. Color returns to her face, and her eyes focus on mine for the first time since I told her the news.

"That's why I wanted to talk to you today, if I could. I wondered if you'd had any other contact with Madeline since that night. I know you were kind of friends and both writing majors, so I thought maybe she tried to talk to you or reach out to you."

But Rebecca is shaking her head. "No, she hasn't. Like I told you, she was at the library, but then she left before I could talk to her. I was kind of freaked by seeing her. I mean, I wanted to go up and get closer and see if it was Madeline, but then a part of me didn't. I don't believe in ghosts—I really don't—but seeing that person there just freaked me out. I was scared."

"That's understandable."

"Yeah, sure."

"It's even more complicated because another woman was murdered before Madeline disappeared. And the police are trying to make connections between the two crimes. It looks like Madeline knew the first woman who was killed."

"Who was that?" Rebecca asks.

"Her name was Sophia Greenfield. I guess she and Madeline went to yoga together and were friends."

"Oh, yeah. My mom read about it and called me when it happened. She was totally freaked out. Then she talked about making me come home, but I wanted to stay. So I signed up for a self-defense class and bought pepper spray to make her happy. I don't think the murder was on campus. . . ."

Her gaze grows unfocused again. She appears to be slipping away, and I step forward, worried that she's having a delayed reaction to the news about Madeline, that it's just now sinking in and she's going to collapse to the ground.

Or . . . she knows something else, and Sophia's name triggered it.

"Rebecca?"

"I'm okay," she says. "I'm fine."

"Are you sure?"

"Yes."

"What's the matter?" I ask. "Do you know Sophia?"

"No, I don't. Not directly."

"Then what's the matter? You looked like you were going to faint."

"I think I knew who Sophia was. I saw her at a party once. And I definitely remember her husband."

CHAPTER FORTY-EIGHT

REBECCA
SUMMER, TWO AND A HALF YEARS AGO

Rebecca wasn't a big partier.

She rarely went to parties, preferring to spend her time with the friends she'd made in the dorm or her classes. Movies in someone's room or at the theater. Game nights at the local bookstore. Writing in Troy's with coffee and a laptop. Sometimes with a friend who also liked to write, and sometimes alone.

But she wasn't a prude. She drank on occasion. Freshman year, her friend Monique got ahold of a bottle of Wild Turkey, and a small group of women did shots in Rebecca's room until the floor started to swirl like a planet, and Rebecca woke up in a chair with the empty bottle and a bunch of red Solo cups scattered on the floor. Her head pounded, and she nearly ran out of the cafeteria to vomit when she tried to eat cereal, but she and her friends had a story to laugh about and a bunch of inside jokes to share, just as they'd shared the bottle.

And then there was Kent, the guy who had lived one floor below her freshman year. They met in the second-floor study lounge one night, when Rebecca was reading *Gulliver's Travels* in a chair by the window and Kent was sprawled across one of the couches scrolling through his phone, his books and laptop on the floor by his feet untouched. They started talking after a while. And talking led to kissing. And periodically throughout the semester, they texted each other and then met in one or the other's room to fool around. And Rebecca loved every minute of it until Kent dropped out of school at the semester break because he hadn't gone to class in two months and his GPA was just above zero.

So she knew how to have a good time. She just didn't like parties. People pushing against one another, yelling and screaming. The music always too loud, the beer always gone, and the liquor disgusting.

But she showed up at that party sophomore year because a professor threw it. Dr. Hoffman. And while she'd never taken his class, she was a creative writing major and knew someday she might end up with him as a professor. And Monique—who was also a creative writing major and a sophomore—said Hoffman occasionally threw these parties for students and it was a good way to meet people.

"Besides," Monique said, "your boy, Kent, left a few months ago, and you need someone to take his place."

And Rebecca remembered her mother telling her once that when she was in college—a thousand years ago and in another state, but Rebecca liked hearing the stories about her mom anyway—her professors used to have students over for dinner or parties, and it was one of the best memories she had of her time in school.

So Rebecca went with Monique. Hoffman lived in a small house about ten minutes from campus, and Rebecca didn't know the area well but remembered looking out the window as Monique drove them in her SUV and noticed a dog park on the way. Rebecca wished she'd been able to bring her pug with her to school, but she couldn't do that in the dorm, and her mom would never let her anyway, since she'd basically become obsessed with taking care of Toby. Rebecca couldn't ever take him away from her.

Rebecca expected a professor's house to be kind of fancy, with a lot of dark wood paneling and antique furniture and bookshelves, and Hoffman's place had the bookshelves but not much else. His furniture was kind of ragged, and some of the walls needed to be repainted. At first, Rebecca saw Hoffman only from a distance. But the bathtub was filled with cans of beer on ice, so she and Monique each took one and wandered around together—a pack of two—looking for people to talk to. Monique made friends in three seconds flat, but Rebecca mostly looked at the bookshelves, curious to know what an English professor would have in his house. She recognized some of the authors but not others. A lot were just names she'd heard but hadn't read—Baldwin, Carver, Morrison, Lahiri. Would she ever read everything she wanted and needed to read?

She was thinking that when she bumped into another student, one who seemed to be doing the same thing.

"This must be where the writers gather," the woman said. "Or the socially awkward."

Relief flowed through Rebecca. She wasn't going to just stand around alone. She had found one person to talk to. And apparently someone who had something in common with her.

The woman said her name was Madeline. And she was also a creative writing major.

"Do you know Dr. Hoffman?" Rebecca asked.

"I'm in his class now. He's okay." Madeline wrinkled her nose. "He has moments of being a really good professor and mentor. But other times he's just kind of . . . not there."

"I'm no good at poetry anyway." Rebecca switched her beer can from one hand to the other, relieving the cold, which was starting to hurt. "I'm kind of surprised a professor is having us all here drinking. It seems like a lot of people are underage. Including me."

"Hoffman doesn't care. He's not exactly a rules kind of guy. You'll find that out if you get to know him better. Or take his class."

"I guess college really is a different world." Rebecca laughed a little.

"It is." Madeline looked past Rebecca's shoulder and nodded. She kind of rolled her eyes. "Oh, I have to go. My friend is leaving."

"Oh, yeah. That's cool."

"Maybe we'll take a class together soon. Or I'll see you at one of the open mics they have in the department."

"Yeah, I need to come and read at one of them." Rebecca said this even though the thought of reading her work at an open mic sounded overwhelming.

"You do."

Madeline went off, leaving Rebecca alone again by the bookshelves. She took a quick glance around, hoping to see Monique. She caught a glimpse of Madeline heading to the door, walking alongside a woman with blond hair. Very pretty.

Beautiful, in fact.

CHAPTER FORTY-NINE

Rebecca wandered around the party for a while. She finished one beer and opened another. Monique seemed to have disappeared, likely with a guy. Or possibly a woman. Monique said she liked to check all the boxes. Rebecca thought that seemed like the kind of thing you should say if you're in college, but she wasn't ready to say it about herself yet.

Rebecca drank her beer and felt a tingly buzz along her hairline. She liked the feeling, and it probably allowed her to stay around at the party longer than she would have without it. Liquid courage, her dad called it. He sometimes threw back a shot before a conference call with his boss. He said it took the edge off.

"You appear to be a lost freshman."

She looked up, and Dr. Hoffman was speaking to her. He wore a Commonwealth U sweatshirt, and she saw a dark stain—coffee or chocolate—near the giant white "C." He held a beer, and his eyes looked red and seemed to be seeing nothing while looking right at her, like the kids in her high school who used to get high before they came into the building in the morning.

"I'm actually a sophomore."

"Well, you're among friends here. This is your tribe if you're an English major."

"Cool. I am."

"Some people are smoking out back if you want to join in," Hoffman said, grinning like an elf. "I bought the stuff, so tell them I sent you. Do you know Isaac? He's a creative writing major. He can't get enough."

"Okay. I've never done that before."

"You haven't? Oh, wow, you really are a babe in the woods. What shitkicker county did you come from?"

Shitkicker?

"Hart County."

"Get out there and smoke," he said. "Start your education tonight."

And he walked away from her like they'd never spoken.

Rebecca considered her options. She suddenly felt weird about being at the party. Maybe she didn't belong there. Maybe she wasn't in her tribe.

Maybe she didn't have a tribe. And she belonged back in Hart County like so many of her high school classmates who didn't go to college and never planned to leave.

Despite the nearly two beers, her rational mind still functioned. She told herself she was thinking silly thoughts. She knew Monique, and Monique was an English major, and the two of them were close.

Did she just need to loosen up a little? Get outside of herself like she had that night with the Wild Turkey? Like she used to do with Kent? Monique had pushed her to come to the party because she wanted Rebecca to meet a guy. Could she meet one sharing a bowl or two? Would this Isaac guy be the next Kent?

Her brain lost its ability to override her feet because Rebecca was moving before she knew it. She went out the sliding-glass door onto the small patio, lit by a floodlight that made it seem like they were standing on the moon. The patio was cracked, and little weeds poked through all over. A warm night, early September, still feeling like summer. Three guys stood at the edge of the patio, one of them holding a bong, another a lighter. The guy with the bong in his hands was coughing like a consumption patient in a Victorian novel. He saw Rebecca but couldn't do anything to stop hacking.

He held the bong out toward her.

"Go ahead," the guy with the lighter said. "Hoffman bought it. And Isaac can't get his shit together now."

She recognized the smell from high school parties. Sweet and inviting.

She put her beer on a window ledge and took the bong in her hands and looked at the guy with the lighter. His eyes were glassier than Hoffman's, and he wobbled a little, like he might tip over.

"I just inhale when you light it," she said. "And then I hold it in as long as I can. Right?"

"You seem to have the basics down," he said, flicking the lighter with his thumb.

What the hell? Rebecca thought. *It's college.*

She took what seemed like a reasonable hit, but the guy with the lighter said, "Easy now."

The smoke burned her throat and then her lungs. She thought her chest was going to explode. She held the smoke for about two seconds, and then it all came flying out when she started to cough.

"All right," the guy with the lighter said. "That'll get you there."

Even Isaac, the coughing guy, started to laugh as he collected himself. "She'll fit in just fine around here."

Rebecca reached for her beer, happy to have the cool liquid. She took a large swallow, which soothed and burned at the same time.

The tingling along her scalp increased in intensity, a telegraph wire transmitting under her skin. Dots and dashes and urgent messages.

She took another long drink of the beer. It felt like her lungs were sunburned.

"Want more?" the guy asked.

She shook her head, drank more beer, stepping away from the three guys and out into the yard itself.

She heard the voice then.

"Stop it."

Rebecca thought it came from behind her, one of the guys laughing and jostling for the next turn at the bong. But it was a woman's voice. And it came from in front of her.

Rebecca walked that way, still holding the beer, even though she'd drunk it down to where just the brackish stuff sloshed around, like in the bottom of a boat. Ahead of her, she saw an alley where a few cars were parked, the only illumination coming from a lone streetlight.

"I'm not joking. Stop it."

"Come on."

As Rebecca approached, she saw a guy and a girl near one of the cars, their bodies partially in the shadows. The woman's back was pushed up against the car, and the guy faced her, his hands on her hips, his head leaning in close for a kiss.

But the woman turned away.

Madeline. It was Madeline. And a guy with a beard.

Rebecca hesitated for a moment. The party waited behind her. As the tingling increased along her scalp, so did her heart rate. Blood rushed in her ears, like the ocean in a seashell.

But she didn't like what Madeline was saying to that guy. Didn't like that she'd already said it twice and his hands were still on her.

"Will you please? You're married."

"Easy."

The guy's hands slid from Madeline's hips to up under her shirt, exposing some of the flesh above Madeline's jeans.

"Hey," Rebecca said. As soon as she said it, she knew she hadn't been loud enough. So she tried again. "Hey."

Both heads turned, and the guy stepped back. He fixed his eyes on Rebecca, and while he didn't say anything, she could see the contempt in the look, the sense that he couldn't believe someone had dared speak to him that way. Especially someone like Rebecca.

A woman.

Madeline straightened her shirt and used the interruption to slide away from the guy and walk out of the alley, heading toward Rebecca and the house.

When she reached Rebecca, she said, "Let's go. He's drunk."

"Are you okay?"

"I'm good. Thank you. You really helped me out."

They started walking toward the house together, through the yard, where the grass was mostly dead, and toward the patio, where the three guys were still standing. One of the guys looked up, the one named Isaac. He waved.

"Madeline?" he said. "Want some?"

Madeline just waved and then she put her hand out, stopping Rebecca twenty feet short of the patio.

Rebecca looked back, worried the guy from the alley would be following them. But he was nowhere in sight, which relieved her to no end.

"Seriously," Madeline said. "Thank you."

"Are you really okay?"

"I am." She looked like she was trying to get her breathing under control, like she had been underwater too long. "He's just . . . I can handle him. Okay?"

"Who was that guy?"

"His name's Zach Greenfield. He's just someone I know."

"Do you want me to call the police?"

"No, don't do that," she said. "I don't know him that well. And he's drunk."

"That's not an excuse. Ever."

"I know. But look. Do me a favor? I've seen these kinds of guys before. Don't say anything to anyone. He has a wife, and we're kind of friends. And I wouldn't want Sophia—her—to know anything about this. Because it's . . . I just wouldn't want her to know. Okay?"

"That's the blond woman. The one who was with you earlier."

"She wasn't feeling well and went home. Yes. Can I count on you to keep this quiet?"

Rebecca didn't like the secrecy, didn't like going along, covering up that kind of behavior by a guy. But she barely knew Madeline, barely knew anyone in her major yet, and she didn't want to do anything that might hurt the way people saw her.

Besides, Madeline seemed to have it under control. She gave off the aura of being the kind of person who had everything under control.

"Okay, sure," Rebecca said.

"Thank you. That really means a lot to me. It's good to know someone like you has my back. It really is."

"Yeah. Of course."

"Great. Come on, let's get you another beer."

CHAPTER FIFTY

CONNOR
PRESENT

Rebecca mostly tells her story to me in a matter-of-fact way. But at certain points, her voice quavers.

She always gets past those wobbles, manages to get back on track and maintain her composure. But her voice tells me all I need to know about how tough it is for her to share this.

When she finishes, she shivers. And I assume it's not from the cold that swirls around the alley.

My mind bounces back to my encounter with Zach in his house. He acted like he had a vague, passing acquaintance with Madeline. Either it was more, and he wanted to avoid admitting it, or he really didn't know her that well—and the night in the alley behind Lance's house was a drunken attempted assault he's forgotten or written off as nothing.

"I don't want to get anyone in trouble," Rebecca says. "I told you about that party at Dr. Hoffman's house, and you know, he's taking over your class for you. So I don't want it to get back to him I was talking about him."

"I know about the parties he has for students," I say. "We all do."

I remember what Preston said about Lance that night a few years ago when he'd taken me out to get drunk. Did he just mean the parties or something else?

"Rebecca, I know how tough it is for you to talk about this kind of thing. I can see that on your face. And I know it's weird for me to just come up to you this way on the street. I get it. But I think we need to do something more with this information than just keep it to ourselves."

"I told the cops about it when Sophia died. My mom made me call them."

"What did they say?"

"They took my statement over the phone. And they seemed really interested in anything I knew about that guy. Sophia's husband. I thought they were going to arrest him, but I never heard anything else. I don't want to get all tangled up in this again. I mean, I'm still a student here, and I don't want Dr. Hoffman pissed at me because I talked about his party. And I don't want that dude, Sophia's husband, mad at me either. He might be dangerous."

"Rebecca—"

"I've got to go, Dr. Nye."

"Rebecca. Just wait. Just wait for a minute."

Mercifully, she stays. If she hadn't, I'd be faced with the prospect of either letting her go or else running out in the street, following along behind her while everyone downtown watches me.

She looks impatient, but she waits. Her upper teeth rest on her lower lip.

"There are a lot of people whose lives are being affected by what happened to Madeline. The police are investigating me."

Her eyes widen when I say this.

"Did you know I was probably the last person to see Madeline alive when she first disappeared?"

"I heard that. Yes. But people say a lot of shit around a school. You can't tell what's the truth and what's just nonsense people are saying to get attention. It really sucks."

"I know. Everybody talks shit. It's not just students. Did the police get back in touch with you when Madeline disappeared?"

"They asked me a few questions."

"They had to, right? I know they came and talked to me and all of her professors."

Her chin quivers, but she rights the ship. She folds her arms across her chest. The skin on her cheeks looks red and raw. "I wasn't good friends with Madeline, so I didn't know much. But I told the cops about the thing at the party. They acted all interested again, but I don't know what they did about it."

I tell her about the night I heard Sophia and Zach fighting, and how I went into their house and saw the trouble but didn't notify the authorities.

"I hate myself for not calling the police. I really do," I say. And when I say it, my face grows hot with shame at the memory. "If I'd called the police then, maybe Sophia would be alive. And maybe Madeline would be too. Do you see why I feel it's so important for you to tell what you know now?"

"I already told it to them. And they didn't care. They didn't do anything, so that means they don't care."

"Why do you say that? Did something happen to you?"

She looks to my right, her eyes trailing over the well-worn and stained bricks that make up the side of Troy's. Out on the street, brakes squeal as someone avoids an accident, but neither Rebecca nor I flinch.

"I have a friend. I knew her freshman year in the dorm. She wasn't an English major. She didn't stick around here long enough to declare a major at all. But she had a professor in one of her Psychology classes who started harassing her. First he'd ask her to come to his office. Then he wanted to meet for coffee. Here." She points to the building, as though it's to blame. "Then he wanted her to come to his house."

"That should never happen, Rebecca. Never."

"No, it shouldn't. That's why she reported the guy to the head of his department. But the head of the department blamed her. He said she was spreading gossip. It's funny, isn't it? It's always gossip when a woman wants to talk about something." She looks behind her once and then faces forward. "Then the professor, the one who was harassing her, he started coming down on her in class. Giving her lower grades. Not even giving some papers back. It all got to be too much for her. And she left Commonwealth. She transferred and really doesn't talk to any of us anymore."

"That's a terrible thing to happen to a student. The very thought of it disgusts me. It would disgust any right-thinking person. And I want you to know the university is changing. They're taking claims made by women more seriously. The culture is different. That kind of thing that happened in the past shouldn't happen anymore. I know that. Our department head, Dr. White, he's committed to that. I promise you. And what I'm asking you to do is to go to the police. To help them solve a crime."

"Cops don't take women seriously either. It's all the same."

"These cops *want* to solve these crimes. I know because I've been in the station with them. I've had them coming to my house. You need to remind them of the thing with Zach and Madeline. They have a lot of information to sift through."

She reaches back and pulls her phone out of her jeans pocket. She checks the time. "I'm going to be late to the writing center. I'm already late. I barely had time to get a coffee in Troy's. And now . . ."

"The police can write you a note," I say. "Or call the writing center."

She stares at her phone as if I'm not here. Her teeth clamp down on her bottom lip again. Doubt creeps in. I think I'm losing her. She's going to turn and go and never tell the cops what she knows.

And I'll be the guy they want to arrest.

"Are you going to go with me?" she asks.

"I can't really do that, Rebecca. It's not good for me to go there."

"Why not?"

"I'm going in to talk to them soon."

She still stares at the phone, but the corners of her mouth turn down.

"I don't know about going there alone. I've never been in a police station. That just seems like too much—"

"Rebecca, I'll call the detective in charge of the case. Her name is Alicia Bowman. She's decent. She'll treat you well. And maybe you'll feel like they're taking you more seriously because the cop is a woman. Do you know where the station is?"

She shakes her head. "I've never been there."

"It's two blocks that way. Over on Kentucky Street." I point east. "It's right on the corner. You can practically see it from here."

She remains rooted in place, staring at me. She's looking to me for answers, and I'm not sure I have any. I just hope she can summon the courage to make that two-block walk.

"I'm going to call my mom on the way. I want to know what she thinks."

"You should do that. Absolutely."

She heaves a big sigh, the motion lifting her heavy jacket up and down. "Okay."

"Thank you, Rebecca. Really. Thank you so much."

She stands in place a moment, and I see everything wavering, ready to tip over out of my control. But then Rebecca turns and starts out of the alley. And I hold my breath, hoping she's really on her way to do what I need her to do.

CHAPTER FIFTY-ONE

I head the other way, back toward the parking lot behind Troy's, where I've left my car.

I slide my phone out of my pocket, ready to dial Bowman. Someone enters the alley at the far end, and I'm not really paying attention until they say my name.

I lift my thumb off the CALL button.

It's my colleague Carrie Richter. The one who went out of her way to tell me she didn't like the kind of book I wrote. She's carrying a canvas shopping bag and wearing an oversized winter coat and earmuffs, which she pulls off when she sees me. She smiles but looks guarded. I wonder if news of Madeline's death has begun to circulate online or on campus.

"Hi, Carrie."

"Connor. How are you?"

She asks me that question the way one would ask the elderly or a small child. It's the way people spoke to me for months after Emily and Jake died.

"I'm okay. How are you?"

"Preston e-mailed the whole department saying you had to take a leave of absence. I'm sorry to hear that."

"Oh, right. Thank you." I have no idea if Preston gave any more details. I doubt he mentioned my being a murder suspect, but I don't know. He was eager to get me to talk to the cops. I know that. "Well, I just needed some time to work some things out."

"Sure, of course."

"I need to go—"

"Is this an illness, Connor? Or some kind of personal situation? I thought maybe your book was doing so well that you were quitting teaching altogether. It would be . . . unusual to do that so early in the term with so much time left to go, but I thought that might be the reason."

When she fishes for information, Carrie isn't subtle. Most academics aren't. They want to know if someone else is getting something they aren't—grants, raises, office space—and they want to know it now. And I can guarantee whatever I tell Carrie will be all over the department by late afternoon.

"Just a personal issue," I say. "I hope to be back soon."

"Are you getting paid during this time? Do you know Larry Hood over in Music? He had to take a leave when he got divorced, and they paid him. I thought that was excessive, given the state budget cuts, but nobody asked my opinion. I know Preston's always concerned about our 'image.'" She makes an air quote with her free hand. "Of course, we all know his motivation, right? Preston the Politician. He wants to get promoted to dean. And between you, me, and the brick wall, I'm sure he'll get it, too. Being a good-looking white man with a picture-perfect family. They still value all that, despite all the strides we women are supposedly making and—"

"Carrie, I'm late for something right now. But it was good seeing you."

"Oh, yeah. Sure. I have so much to do, I can't even see straight. I'm going to grade here in Troy's all day."

"Oh, wait," I say.

Carrie stops, looks back. Her face is expectant.

"I was just wondering about something," I say. "Do you remember we talked about Sophia Greenfield the other day?"

"I do."

"Is there anything else that stood out to you about her?"

Carrie's face grows suspicious, like she's the night watchman and I'm the guy casing the place she's guarding. "Why are you asking me about that?"

"I'm just curious. Because . . ." I don't mention Madeline. "Just curious. I'm sorry."

"I don't know anything except Sophia's death was a tragedy, Connor. I don't know what else I can say."

"You're right. I'm sorry." I wave at her. "We'll talk soon."

I go down the alley next to Troy's, not looking back.

When I reach the parking lot and my car, I get inside and call the police station right away. I ask for Bowman, expecting her to be unavailable, but my name must be the magic word because when I mention it, I'm connected. And Bowman comes on the line quickly, greeting me like we're old friends.

"Connor. So glad you decided to call. It doesn't look good that we haven't talked to you yet."

"I just want to tell you something important."

"Again, maybe face-to-face would be the best. Where are you right now?"

"Far away," I say. "In another state."

"Now that's not good either, Connor—"

"Can you just listen for a minute?"

I tell her about Rebecca. That she has information about the case, specifically about Zach Greenfield and Madeline. And she's coming in to the station right now and should be there any moment.

"She's nervous about going in there and talking to the cops," I say. "So handle her with kid gloves. She hasn't done anything wrong."

"I deal with students all the time in this town," Bowman says. "I'm on it. And thanks for the heads-up. Now, let's talk about you, Connor. Are you sure you don't want to come in and clear things up on your end? We still have some stickiness relating to Madeline's death. It's odd her body was found so close to your family's graves, isn't it? Like someone had killed her there and then tried to cover it up. Did you know she was still alive, Connor? Had you seen her back here in town?"

"I'm going to go now—"

"It's possible someone has seen the two of you together. Or knows she was with you. Again, it's better to get things out in the open."

I don't know if she's bluffing. Or if she really does know something about Madeline's visits to my house.

I don't want to find out. Not now.

"Good-bye, Detective."

I end the call.

But before I can start the car and get out of here, someone knocks against the passenger-side window, and I jump so high, I nearly hit my head on the ceiling of the car.

CHAPTER FIFTY-TWO

I can see only a portion of a person outside the window. A torso. A zipped-up winter coat.

My insides turn to water. It's Bowman. She traced the call somehow to find my location. And now I'm going into the police station and never coming out.

My rational mind wrestles for control of my brain. The midsection outside the window wears a beat-up coat, one that was new about fifteen years ago. Nothing like Bowman would wear. And the body is broader, heavier than Bowman's trim figure.

The person bends down, knocks again. Waves for me to open the door.

It's Lance.

"Shit," I say. Relieved.

I undo the locks, and he pulls the door open, slipping inside along with a blast of cold air.

"You looked like you'd gone to another world there for a minute," he says. He's wearing the checked Ivy cap he always wears outside when the weather is cold. "Are you okay?"

"I've been better."

He rubs his hands together. "Are you going to turn this thing on? It has heat, you know."

I do what he says and start the engine. The heat comes out cold at first, and I shiver. I smell whiskey on Lance. Not an unusual occurrence. On many a morning in the English Department, he smells like booze before nine o'clock. I've always given him the benefit of the doubt and told myself it was likely left over from the night before. I've always suspected he drinks at home, sinks into a funk, and then fails to bathe before coming to campus. But I'm never sure if I'm correct.

The car starts to warm. A little.

"Preston called me early this morning," Lance says, shaking his head and still rubbing his hands together. He hasn't shaved, and his stubble is a mixture of gray and black on his pockmarked face. "He told me about Madeline. The news is starting to spread. It really has me struggling. It's depressing, horribly so. What a shit show. It makes me wonder what anything is worth. Things are so . . . futile. So hopeless." He stares at the glove box, his eyes wide and disbelieving. "I don't even know what to say about it. It's rare that words fail me, but they do."

"What else did Preston say?"

I want to ask a more pointed question—did he mention calling the police on me? But I don't.

"He said you were likely to be a suspect of some kind," Lance says matter-of-factly. "I mean, I know you were the last one to see her before she disappeared and now there's something bigger brewing. I have my own theory on it, of course."

"Oh, you do?"

"Sure." He stops rubbing his hands together.

"Are you going to share with the class?"

He sniffles, rubs his hand across his nose. "That night your book was launched, and Preston and I came over to the house. Madeline was there, right? She was the one you were drinking with before we showed up, and she split out the back door when she saw us coming. It wouldn't have looked good for anybody if we'd seen her there with you. I mean, she was supposed to be missing."

"Where did you come up with that craziness?"

"It makes sense. You were probably involved with her before she disappeared. And so when she came back to town, she must have come to see you. I'm right, aren't I?"

Lance looks pleased with himself. I can imagine him in the classroom, pinning some underprepared, immature student to the wall with the same glee.

"You're talking about my life, Lance. My freedom."

"I have to do right by her. I have to tell the police she was at your house that night."

"I know she was at *your* house," I say.

"What?"

"Before she disappeared. When you had one of your famous parties. She was there. Right?"

"She might have been. I don't keep a guest list."

"Do you keep track of what happens to those students when they're at your house? Besides the underage drinking?"

Lance's lips part. I see his teeth, which aren't in the greatest shape. Slightly gray with silver fillings in the back. Finally, he makes a disgusted grunt. "I'm really disappointed in you, Connor. That's soooo conventional. I would have expected it from other people in the department, but not you. You're going to worry about college students drinking at my house when they're underage? Really? Why is that? Because they don't drink underage in their dorms or at other house parties?" He shakes his head like I'm vermin that has crawled into the vehicle. "Whatever is going on with this Madeline stuff has really knocked you off your game. I defended you to Preston. I did. But I'll go now."

As he reaches for the door handle, I say, "You let Zach Greenfield into your party. He's almost thirty. Was that good for the students? Was it good for Madeline?"

He stops moving. "Why are you asking me about Zach?"

"He tried to assault Madeline at your house. Did you know that?"

"That's not true."

"How do you know?"

"It wouldn't have happened. I know Zach. He's a friend of mine. He lives in the neighborhood. Just because his wife was killed and everyone blamed him, you're piling this on top as well. He's a good guy. Okay?"

"I think you're blind, Lance. You're blinded by whatever friendship you have with Zach. He's going to be in trouble with the police soon, and then all of this is going to come out. You might want to make sure some of the shrapnel doesn't hit you."

"You're the one who's blind, Connor. You've been blinded by all this creeping morality. What an adult over the age of eighteen does with their body is up to them. Whatever Madeline did or didn't do was her choice. You can't go all nanny state on her."

"We're supposed to look out for these kids."

"Is that what you were doing the night Madeline disappeared?" he says. "I know all about it, Connor. The drunken walk home. Back to your house."

"Preston shouldn't have told you—"

"Glass houses, Connor. Glass houses."

He pushes the door open and leaves.

CHAPTER FIFTY-THREE

Diana keeps an office downtown, only five blocks from the police station. I go straight there from Troy's and park in the lot next to the redbrick Colonial building, and when I step out into the cold sunshine, I wish I had a hoodie to cover my face. I feel exposed as I walk to the front door, like someone expecting to be hit by a sniper.

When I get inside, into the carpeted and freshly painted waiting area, I give my name to the receptionist, who doesn't even blink before she calls back and tells Diana I'm here. In the flesh.

It takes about three seconds for Diana to appear, holding the door between the waiting area and the suite of offices open and pointing behind her. "Come on back, champ. It's about time you showed up."

I go down the hall, my steps hushed by the thick carpet. I feel dirty and unkempt, having spent the night in my car. And when I wasn't in the car, I was crawling around on the ground in the cemetery, discovering a murdered woman. I see the open door of Diana's office on the right and go in. She comes in behind me and we both sit.

"You're a hard man to find," she says, scooting toward her desk.

"Gatewood isn't huge, but it's not hard to hide. For a while."

"You have a doctorate, right?"

"I know, I know, but it's not in stupidity. I couldn't just sit around, Diana. And I helped the case. I sent Rebecca Knox to the police. She's there now. She knows Zach assaulted Madeline."

"What are you talking about?" she asks.

242

So I tell her. About Madeline and Zach at the party. Diana listens without taking a note, but she nods along as I talk.

When I'm finished, she says, "She'll make a compelling witness. And unlike some people in this room, it sounds like she does what she's told. Her story about Zach's assault on Madeline at the party dovetails nicely with yours about the fight you witnessed between the lovebirds. And it's possible the fight you saw grew out of the incident at the party. The timing lines up well."

"So you're saying the police are going to think it's less likely I just made it up?"

"They're going to want to talk to our friend Zach if he's still around. I'm assuming that was you who anonymously called in about Madeline's body."

"It was. I went there for some quiet—"

"I assume you go there a lot. How many people know you do that?"

"A lot. My friends. Some people I work with. My sister knows, and so do Emily's brother and mom."

"Your students?"

I see where she's going. "Do you mean did I ever mention it to Madeline? I think I did."

"So a lot of people know you make these nocturnal visits. You weren't at home, so if someone went to your house looking for you late at night, they might assume you were in the cemetery. Right?"

"You could say that. But I didn't—"

Diana holds her hand up, silencing me. "Hey, I get it. But the fact is she was dead there. Murdered. It doesn't look good for you right now, so we need to get out ahead of this. If a lot of people knew you went there, then we start to raise doubts. Is there anything else you need to tell me now? I assume you didn't just come by to visit. And I can't help you unless I know it all. I'm your lawyer. I'm working for you."

I let out a deep breath. It feels like it comes from my shoes and out of my mouth. "And all of this is confidential? I can tell you anything?"

"It is. You tell me, and then together we decide what to do. Is there something you want to come clean about? Confession is good for the soul. And it might keep your buns out of jail."

"Okay, I didn't kill anybody."

"That's a good start."

I let out another breath. "I'm sick about what I did do, Diana. It's the . . . it's the worst, most embarrassing thing. As a writer. As a teacher. I just . . . I fucked up royally. And I can never make it up to Madeline now that she's gone."

"You look kind of green around the gills. Do you need water?"

I shake my head. "No, let me get this out. I have to, okay? It's overdue."

"Go for it."

"It's okay if you think the worst of me once I tell you."

"Just spill it, Connor. I guarantee you I've heard worse."

So I tell her the truth about the book. The tenure deadline and my grief. Madeline's disappearance after turning in the handwritten thesis. The book getting published and Madeline coming back. All of it.

When I finish, I don't really feel relief. I feel dirty because I relived it all. My dishonesty. My theft.

Diana shows nothing on her face. Her only movement is tapping her fingers against the top of the desk.

"I'll say this—you did fuck up."

"Thanks," I say.

"It's okay, Connor. It's not fatal. You'll take a public scalding, but you kind of have that coming."

"Sure. So you see . . . I didn't know those details about the murder. Madeline did."

"Or whoever told them to Madeline," Diana says. "It could be the actual killer. Or it could be a cop or someone else close to the case."

"Zach. He knew Madeline. We know he assaulted one woman. And fought aggressively with Sophia."

"I'm going to call Bowman and tell her we want to talk. Are you okay with that?"

I nod. "Sure. Yes, of course."

Diana flips her glasses down and picks up the phone on her desk. While she's waiting for someone to answer, I stare at the floor. Madeline will never see the book in print with her name on it. She'll never see *any* book in print with her name on it. And she should have and would have. I'm the only one who can try to make that happen—

"When will she be finished?" Diana says into the phone. "Will you have her call me as soon as she is? I have someone who needs to talk to her. . . . Yes, she'll know the matter to which I'm referring. It's the only matter she and I are talking about right now. . . . And can you ask her for one more favor? Tell her to call the dogs off my client Connor Nye. He's going to wait at his house, and he doesn't need to be arrested. I'm going to bring him in. . . . No, I don't think I'm Detective Bowman's boss. I'm just someone who wants to engage in mutual respect with her. If she backs off my client until he's ready to talk, I'll bring him in. I promise. . . . Just tell her, okay? Bye."

Diana slams the phone down so hard, I jump. She takes her glasses off and shakes her head.

"Can you believe that shit? I've been practicing law in this town for twenty years, and they want to give me the runaround. Some rookie cop answering the phone . . ."

"Is everything okay?" I ask.

"It is. Don't worry. Bowman is with a witness. Probably that student you sent her way. When she's done, she'll call, and we can go in. Or she may just come to your house. We'll see."

"What am I supposed to do?"

"Go home and wait. I bought you a little time to make sure you have your story ready. Just tell her what you told me when the time comes. I'm trying to keep you from getting hauled away like a common criminal. You're a plagiarizer, not a danger to society."

"Diana, what exactly happened to Madeline?"

Diana takes a moment to answer. "They're saying she was stabbed."

"Oh, God," I say. "I just . . . I don't even know what to say. It's horrifying."

"It's a lovely world, isn't it?"

"That young woman . . ."

Her death seems personal. Angry and personal. Just like Sophia's murder over two years ago in a dark parking lot. Sophia died alone and in terror as well.

"Who the fuck is doing this to these young women? Is it Zach?"

"I wish I knew," she says.

"What else did they find?" But then I remember—the knife. It was missing from my pocket when Madeline was gone in the morning. And she died of a stab wound.

If the cops found that—

"Shit," I say. "There's a knife missing from my house. The night Madeline came in and hit me with the bottle, it went missing."

"Was there someone else in your house?" she asks. "Besides Madeline?"

I tell her I think someone else—a man?—stood over me while I was out of it. That the door I thought was left open was then closed. . . .

"You didn't see this man?" she asks.

"No, I was groggy. It felt like a dream."

"But the knife is gone?" she asks. "For real?"

"For real. We got them as a wedding present. And one is gone. I had it out because . . . I was afraid of Madeline."

"That makes things a little stickier," she says. "But the truth will set you free." She knocks her fist against the desktop. "We hope. I'll call you when Bowman is ready. If there are any cops outside your door when you get home, call me."

"Okay."

"Connor, if you ran anywhere besides home now, it would look bad. Very, very bad. And I don't take well to looking bad."

"I've been gone all night. I don't want to go anywhere."

"That's a boy."

CHAPTER FIFTY-FOUR

MADELINE
SUMMER, TWO AND A HALF YEARS AGO

Madeline skipped yoga the week after the party.

She knew if she went, Sophia would be there. And they'd talk.

And if they talked, Madeline didn't want to have to lie. So she skipped.

She hated to do it. Hated to give up everything that wasn't the endless cycle of work and school. But she spent the early evening reading for class, a story by her friend Isaac in which a man from earth travels through a wormhole in space to another planet where all the males have died. He must repopulate that planet. He called the story "Adam's Curse," which was the best thing about it. The guy downstairs started in with his music, the thumping bass lines. It made it tough for Madeline to concentrate, but she didn't mind. She wanted to be distracted from the terrible story.

Sophia texted just after seven.

Missed you at class. What's up?

Madeline felt breathless when she read the message. She decided to ignore it, claim she was in the shower or with a study group or that her phone had died. Anything not to talk to Sophia.

No, it wasn't talking to Sophia that was the problem. It was the inevitable *lie* she'd have to tell Sophia that was the problem. Madeline hated lying, especially to someone who had been so good to her. Minutes passed. Five. Ten.

Madeline allowed herself to feel relief, felt the air come back into her lungs. Sophia gave up. She let it go and moved on with her life. Next week, Madeline would think of something else. A pulled muscle, a sick grandparent. She'd take the whole thing a week at a time.

But then her phone dinged again.

Do you have time to talk? I was hoping we could.

Everything changed then. It sounded like Sophia needed something—a helping hand. A sympathetic ear. And she specifically directed her request at Madeline. Not one of her many other friends. Not to her husband. To Madeline. She sounded like she wanted to talk *to Madeline.*

And how could Madeline ignore her if she needed her? Not when Sophia always listened to her troubles.

Madeline tried to keep breathing, tried to reach back and remember things she'd learned in yoga next to Sophia. *What a week to skip the class that calms me down.*

Okay, she thought. *Okay.* She wrote back:

Hey! Studying. But I've got a few minutes if you need to talk.

The response came immediately: Great. Where do u live?

Madeline sent the address—up the rickety stairs at the back, try not to fall down—and then paced around the apartment, hands on hips. Breathing, breathing.

She couldn't know. How would she? And if she knew, that meant Zach had told her. And if Zach had told her, then why would Sophia need to talk to Madeline at all? Her problem wasn't with Madeline. Her problem was with Zach. Her husband. The pig.

But what if Zach had shifted the blame to Madeline? Told a tale about Madeline being the aggressor? And Sophia was coming over to tell her to stay the fuck away from her man?

Her mom had received those visits and calls before. Angry women pounding on the door or confronting her in the grocery store parking lot. Her mother yelling back until a vein shaped like a Y popped out on her forehead.

She should just leave. Just get out of the apartment and avoid Sophia. Wasn't that the best way to deal with it?

No, she told herself. *Running isn't always the way.*

"Shit," Madeline said. "Shit, shit, shit. Why is this my life?"

Three minutes after Madeline sent the address, Sophia knocked on the door. Madeline knew she was coming but jumped anyway, like a scared little kid. And she felt like one compared to Sophia. She felt like she'd been caught doing something and was about to get punished.

But, she reminded herself, she hadn't done anything. *Zach had.*

Sophia smiled when Madeline opened the door, the light from the one bulb above the door casting her face in a pale glow. But her smile lacked the wattage it usually had. Madeline hated clichés, desperately fought to keep them out of her own writing, but she'd always thought it about Sophia—that she had a smile that could light up a room. . . .

The blond hair, the big eyes. The incandescent smile. Sophia made Madeline feel warm every time she saw her. But the glow was dimmed that night, like something had gone out of it.

Sophia came in and looked around. Madeline apologized for the rickety stairs, the crappy apartment, the pathetic lighting on the landing. "The place is kind of a dump."

"Don't apologize for that," Sophia said. "It kind of makes me nostalgic for college. Good times, you know? Simpler times."

"You went to Vanderbilt, right?"

"I did. My mom's a lawyer with a really big firm. She's done well. Privilege, I know."

"I wasn't saying that," Madeline said, although she had thought it. What would it be like to go to a school like Vanderbilt? And have your parents pay? And graduate with no debt so you could maybe buy a house or a car or take a vacation? But she didn't really know if that was the case with Sophia. Madeline was doing what she always did—making a character biography of everybody she met. "I'm sorry. Do you want something? I think I have some tea. Maybe a little coffee. I don't cook much."

"It's cool," Sophia said, taking a seat in the recliner. "I won't be long. And I'm sorry to just barge in when you're studying."

"That's okay. I could use a break. Some of the guys write these stories for class. . . . I think they all believe our society is going to be taken over by sexy robots."

Sophia's hair was in the braid she always wore to yoga. Her oversized Commonwealth U sweatshirt hid most of her body. Madeline wondered if the sweatshirt belonged to Zach. Sophia crossed one leg over the other and jangled her foot in the air. She seemed nervous, not her usual calm self. And that made Madeline freaked. Madeline wished she did have something to drink. A cheap beer. Some shitty wine. Anything.

"I'm sorry to bring all this up, Madeline," Sophia said. "I've just been wondering if everything went okay at the party after I left." She looked down at her lap, played with the strap on her purse. She kept her eyes down when she said, "I know Zach and I talked to you when you first showed up. We only went because Lance invited us. We know a few Commonwealth graduates, people closer to our age who were going to be there. And Zach plays golf with Lance and hangs out with him sometimes. Lance likes to brag about these parties he has for students and recent graduates. And I know how Zach is. He has his issues, growing up without a dad. I saw the way he looked at you. It was the same way he looked that first night you met him at the Owl's Nest." She lifted her eyes then, fixed them on Madeline. They were watery. "So . . ."

She let the word hang in the air between them. Madeline thought everything hung on that word. An entire friendship. An entire marriage.

"Sophia, I don't know what you've heard—"

"I haven't *heard* anything. I could tell by the way Zach looked at you, by other things he's done since we've been married. By the way he talked about you when he came home. And then you didn't come to yoga when you always do. . . ." She shook her head. "I should have stayed at the party, but I wasn't feeling well. I'd eaten something that didn't agree with me. But now I wish I'd been there. It would have made everything so much easier." She started to play with the purse strap again. "You can just tell me, okay? We're friends. We've talked about a lot of things. Please, tell me."

"Zach had a lot to drink that night. He must not have been himself."

"Just tell me, Madeline."

Madeline shifted in her seat. If there'd been a way out, a magic portal through the floor or ceiling, she would have taken it.

But things like that existed only in stories. Like the kind Isaac wrote. Not in her actual life, which had suddenly become very, very real.

"I don't want you to hate me."

"I won't."

Sophia said the words quickly. Madeline tried to believe her. Wanted very much to believe her.

And Madeline refused to lie and make it better.

So she told Sophia what had happened. How she had been talking to Rebecca by the bookshelves, and then she saw Sophia leaving, and she wanted to say good-bye. And Madeline didn't really mind going outside since the house was getting hot and Hoffman was getting drunker and drunker. After saying good-bye to Sophia, Madeline got waylaid on the patio by Isaac and the stoner guys. Madeline talked to them but refused to smoke since she wanted to stay in command of her faculties. She grabbed a beer and started walking, hoping to be alone for a minute and look at the stars. But as she went through the backyard, someone called her name.

"Madeline."

She knew who it was without looking, without turning.

And looking back, she wished she'd just kept on going. She could have claimed she hadn't heard and dashed away, back out to the street where she'd parked her car. Left.

But she hated to be rude, especially to Sophia's husband. She considered Sophia a friend—a pretty good friend, all things considered—and even if the guy was kind of acting like a creep, maybe she could just talk for a minute and then keep right on going.

But things like that happened fast. She knew. She'd seen it before. With her mom. With other friends. *Things happened fast.*

She considered herself smart, streetwise even. More so than the spoiled kids she went to school with. She kept her guard up, always watched three hundred and sixty degrees around. She'd learned that from her mother.

But Zach moved quickly. And before she knew it, he'd maneuvered himself between her and the alley, guiding her with his body until she was against a car. He leaned in, his eyes glassy in the shadowy light.

"I just want a kiss," he said.

His hands landed on her hips. Then started sliding up.

She pushed them away once. And then again.

"Just a kiss," he said.

"You're married. What about Sophia?"

"It's just a kiss."

There was Mace in her purse, which she'd never have been able to get out. She'd dropped the beer can, so her hands were free to fight back. If only Hoffman had bought bottles, she could swing one. . . .

Then Zach's hands were under her shirt, moving up. She tried to push them away, but he was faster. Stronger. She saw Sophia's face in her mind.

Her friend. Her loving, caring friend.

And then someone called her name. A woman.

"Madeline?"

And it was enough to make Zach step back, even to distract him so Madeline could slip past him and away from the car. In the dark, Madeline squinted to see who it was. A familiar face, kind of. Someone she'd just been talking to inside.

Rebecca. The quiet girl from the bookshelves. The one who looked scared and a little out of place.

"Hey," Madeline said. And started toward her.

And as she walked away, she heard Zach muttering to himself. Only one word reached her ears that she understood.

"Bitch," he said.

She told Sophia everything. She told her friend everything because what was the point of hiding it? Sophia seemed to suspect already. And she certainly deserved to know.

She didn't tell Sophia that she'd started working it into the plot of her novel. Sophia might remember that Madeline had been casting around for a plot, starting and restarting, but now she thought she'd discovered what her book could be about. Two friends, and the husband of one of them started showing an unhealthy interest in the other. Driving a wedge between the two women.

"I'm sorry, Sophia," Madeline said. "I didn't mean for any of it to happen."

Sophia didn't cry, but she did sniffle. She gathered her purse and stood up. Normally she hugged Madeline every time she left her, but that time she didn't. She just stood up and started for the door, turning her back to Madeline.

And Madeline didn't know what to say, didn't know if she should reach out or follow her, but decided to just let her go.

And that was what Sophia did. She went right through the door, slamming it shut behind her.

And Madeline assumed she was never going to see her friend again.

CHAPTER FIFTY-FIVE

CONNOR
PRESENT

Despite Diana's—and Bowman's—promise, I expect to see cops waiting for me at the house.

If they're there, I tell myself, I'll take my medicine.

But I see nothing and no one as I pull up. And I feel relieved to have a few minutes alone to gather my thoughts.

Inside, the house feels as lonely as the cemetery without Grendel here.

I once again make a circuit, checking every door and window. I peek into every closet.

I'm tired of being freaked in my own house. And everywhere I go.

I think about going to Preston's house and bringing Grendel back home, but what if I'm stuck in the police station a long, long time? I know Grendel is well taken care of. It's best to leave him where he is.

Once I know the place is secure, I go to the kitchen and check the knives. There is one missing from the block on the counter. And it isn't in a drawer or the dishwasher.

Or anywhere.

The house is still turned upside down from Madeline searching for the manuscript. I make a halfhearted attempt to clean. As I do it, the task feels Sisyphean. Will the cops just be in here later tearing the place up again, looking for evidence to use against me?

Looking for that knife?

No matter. I clean up. I try to be useful. And distract myself.

I go down the hall to my office. That is the biggest mess. I already had too many old student papers and stories piling up around the edges of the room. Emily used to make me toss them when a year had passed. I've grown completely lax at doing that. I'm not sure I've gone through the papers and tossed the old ones out in five years. And when Madeline went tearing through the house, looking for her manuscript, she did a number in here. Papers are strewn everywhere. It looks like a tornado hit.

I begin on my desk, start pushing the piles of papers into stacks. I've been digging through piles for ten minutes when something catches my eye.

Some typewritten pages, about ten of them—a short story.

And it's called "My Best Friend's Murder: A Brief Sequel," and there's no date on it.

But I know who wrote it. Who else could be the author?

And she must have left it here for me to find the night she knocked me out and stole the novel manuscript.

I start reading. And it's excellent, just like her thesis. Just like everything she wrote. I fall into the story immediately. It's about a young woman returning to the town where she attended college after an extended absence. The description of the town is dead-on for Gatewood, and I'm flipping to the second page when I hear something at the front of the house and look up.

I listen.

And I miss Grendel because he would have let me know if it's something to worry about or not. But he's at Preston's house, and I'm alone.

I keep listening, and the house grows quiet. I'm imagining things.

I'm jumpy because of everything that's going on. I turn back to the story—

And I hear it again. A rattling noise, like the wind blowing a branch against the side of the house. Except there's no wind, and the only tree that ever grew close to our house had to be cut down before Emily died.

Could it be Diana? Did she come this quickly?

I allow my hopes to rise. Maybe she came to give me good news? Maybe they decided I didn't have to go to the police at all.

But then why wouldn't Diana just call?

Or did the cops show up?

I put the story down and go out to the front of the house. I half expect to see Grendel perched on the couch, his snout pressed against the window in order to decide whether he should be alarmed or not. When I look outside, the porch, bathed in the glow of the light by the door, is empty. No one walks by. There aren't even any cars.

I let out a long-held breath. Maybe someone was here a minute ago. A kid, a salesperson.

Maybe the neighbors slammed their car doors.

I turn to go back to the office and the story when I hear the rattling sound again. And this time it's coming from the kitchen. The back door?

I head that way, stepping onto the dirty linoleum. My scalp feels cold. The spot where Madeline smacked me with the bottle starts to ache again. A flashback. But everything here looks fine.

The back door is locked and secure. There's no one on the back stoop, no one in the driveway.

But then I hear a noise coming from the basement. Footsteps up the stairs. Madeline came in that way the first night she was in here. Someone else is doing the same thing now.

But the door from the basement to the kitchen is locked.

I bolted it.

But it hits me how flimsy that door is. How old. How thin. The footsteps stop. I sense someone on the other side. The door explodes into the kitchen. Wood flies toward me. Someone has kicked it open. Shattered it, busted the lock. Zach Greenfield is in my kitchen, his eyes blazing with anger.

CHAPTER FIFTY-SIX

I retreat, moving toward the back door as fast as I can.

But Zach's faster than I am. He's across the kitchen in two long strides and has my shirt in his hands. He spins to his right, yanking me away from the door. His strength and my body weight propel me. The room swirls around me, like I'm on an out-of-control merry-go-round. I hit the table, and he lets me go.

I'm unable to stop. I go over the table and fall on the other side, crashing against the floor. I scramble to get back to my feet, the cells in my body lit up with adrenaline like an overloaded circuit board.

But Zach is here above me, and before I can get to my feet, he knocks me back down, looming over me.

I don't have my phone. Or anything like a weapon.

If I'd only packed a knife as I had when Madeline was here.

And Zach is younger and stronger than I am.

"You killed her," he says. His voice is raw and husky. His eyes glazed and red. He looks like something forged in a furnace of anger.

"I didn't even know your wife, Zach. You have to believe that."

"Sophia saw you walking by the house. You watched her. You came by like you were walking your dog, but you were really watching her."

"I was watching both of you." I wish I could retract the words as soon as I say them. Zach isn't in a state of mind to hear a nuanced description of my grief. Or to understand the reasons a man would watch another couple going about their mundane lives. "I had no reason to kill anybody. And I promise you, I didn't."

"It was Madeline," he says. A wave of whiskey-tainted breath comes off him. "It started with her. I know you were the last one to see her before she left. And I know that's a bad look for a college professor. It's not that uncommon for professors to get involved with their students. I'm sure you and Madeline were doing it."

"You're crazy. There was nothing like that."

"And Madeline told Sophia during one of their post-yoga bitch sessions, so you killed Sophia to silence her."

"I didn't. I didn't know your wife except to see her from the street. Jesus, Zach, you have to know none of this is close to true. It isn't."

Zach goes on, ignoring me. "And that must have spooked Madeline for a while. But then what happened? Did it all get to be too much for her? Did she finally just have enough of whatever was going on between the two of you and run away? She let everyone think she was dead. You must have thought she was dead too, right? Or did you always suspect she'd come back into your life?"

"I thought she was dead, just like everybody else. I can promise you that."

"What happened when she came back?" Zach asks. "Did she threaten to finally expose you? Had she worked up the nerve to do that?"

My elbows ache where they touch the tile. Zach towers over me, but his certainty and anger strike a deeper chord within me—a chord of injustice. He accuses me in my own home, asserts his right to come in and attempt to dominate me.

"You're out of your mind," I say. "You're the one who attacked Madeline at a party. Did you follow her when she got back to town? Kill her at the cemetery? You're the one they should be after."

His face changes. The anger wanes, only to be replaced by confusion. He drops his chin, flexes his hands like they're weapons he's keeping loose and ready.

"How do you—" He stops himself. He snorts. "That girl from the university. Is she one of your students?"

"You got physical with Sophia. You assaulted Madeline. You're the guy with a reason to hurt them both."

"Okay, so I got a little handsy with Madeline. I had too much to drink. It happens. I probably had too much today."

"Do you have the book?"

"The what?"

I roll to the side, and he stumbles. I use the opportunity to kick with my right foot, which connects with his left knee, causing it to buckle.

Zach grunts, his face contorted by pain. I kick out again, but this time I strike only a glancing blow. He recovers his balance and shakes off the pain. I hoped the kick would incapacitate him, but he keeps coming. And with greater fury.

He swings at me once and then twice. He connects with the side of my head. I try to cover, to get my head out of the way of his blows. But he manages to pin my left arm and swings away again and again.

For a moment, I'm able to turn my head, avoid taking the blows directly. But he keeps swinging. And connecting more and more.

And then it's like I'm walking down a dark hallway, and the sides are narrowing until there's only a faint circle of light far ahead of me.

And even that starts to dim.

I think the blows stop.

Or maybe I just can't feel them anymore.

Whichever it is, the light goes out. . . .

PART III

CHAPTER FIFTY-SEVEN

MADELINE
SPRING, TWO YEARS EARLIER

For three blocks, Madeline walked behind Dr. Nye.

For a drunk guy, he walked awfully fast. It was a cool night, late March and just starting to feel like spring. Heavy rain had fallen earlier, gushing through the gutters and down the sidewalks, but everything was finally clear. Stars shined above, and a quarter moon sat directly overhead. The night smelled like rich earth and growing things.

Madeline was buzzed too. Three—*or was it four?*—drinks at Dubliners, and she felt it. But the walk would sober her up. She still needed to study when she got home, still needed to get ready for tomorrow's classes.

So why was she spending valuable time making sure a grown man made it home okay?

Because she cared about him.

And she still wanted to ask his advice.

In class, Nye treated everybody the same. She could tell, watching him, that he didn't want to play favorites, didn't want to tip his hand too much about which stories students wrote were good and which ones were terrible. That was the thing she admired about Nye—he even treated the terrible writers like their work possessed some value. A couple of weeks earlier, the class had read Isaac's latest story, a hot mess full of grammar errors and impossible plots resolved by ridiculous coincidences. Nye sat in front of the room while the rest of the class voiced their critiques. He nodded like a wise man, like one of those bearded figures in cartoons who sat on top of a mountain and told other people the meaning of life.

Madeline expected him to join in, to take Isaac to task for his piss-poor grammar and sexy robots that resolved the plot by taking off their shirts. But Nye let the class have its say, and then he stepped in and complimented Isaac on one description that occurred on the third page of the story. When he did that, Madeline looked at her copy of Isaac's story and saw she'd noted the same thing. That one description was the best thing in the story—and Nye made sure to point it out. He tried to compliment everyone, whether they deserved it or not.

Madeline picked up her pace. Nye seemed to be moving faster, even with the alcohol. Or maybe because of its effects. He looked determined to get home in record time. Maybe he needed to piss. Or puke.

Maybe he thought she was a stalker, although he hadn't looked back once.

What had he heard about her?

Madeline knew Nye was friends with Dr. White and Dr. Hoffman. Not only did she occasionally see the men talking in the hallways of Goodlaw—sometimes all three of them, sometimes just two of them—but she'd seen them out in town a couple of times as well. Drinking at Dubliners together, the three of them at a table in the corner, pints of beer in front of them. Once at a bluegrass concert on campus. They seemed like good friends. And both Preston and Lance spoke about Dr. Nye when he wasn't around.

But there was a difference in the way they each spoke about him. Dr. White was always complimentary—he talked about Nye's book of short stories or his teaching, pumping him up to the students and telling everyone how lucky they were to have him on faculty at Commonwealth. Lance Hoffman was different. Sure, he talked about Dr. Nye and praised his teaching, but Lance always did it with a little smirk on his face. Madeline didn't think it was anything personal between Lance and Nye—Lance pretty much talked about everyone with a smirk on his face. Students, faculty, administrators, politicians, writers. They all got the smirk.

And Madeline had intentionally not told Nye that Hoffman was helping with the thesis. Her Honors College adviser—an older professor with a white beard and dirty glasses—told her that she had to work with the thesis director first. Only the director.

"You can show the thesis to the rest of the committee when the director says it's okay," he said. And she listened. And wondered how he could see her through the dirty glasses.

Madeline felt guilty going to Hoffman for help, like she was cheating. But Nye was pretty out of it, and Hoffman was eager to jump in and advise. And he did it pretty well.

Nye made a beeline for a small house with a light burning on the back porch. The road went uphill a little there as it approached the house, and finally he seemed to be slowing down. Madeline made up some ground but then thought it might be best to back off, to just let him go on inside on his own. If her goal had been to make sure he got inside his house okay, she could stop and watch from a distance and then turn and be on her way. Maybe it was the wrong time to talk to him. Maybe she was overreacting about the thesis. Maybe no one else would read it or come to the defense.

But did Madeline want to take that risk?

No matter what she decided about the thesis, she was certain it was the wrong time to ask.

Nye didn't need to know she was behind him. He didn't need to wonder if she was some kind of freaky stalker.

Just as she decided to turn and go home, Nye stumbled.

He didn't fall, but he came close. And once he righted himself and regained his balance, he stood on the side of the road, a block from his house, and looked utterly and completely lost. Madeline wondered if he felt sick. Maybe he was going to vomit right on the sidewalk.

He wobbled again, lifted his hand to his head.

"Shit," she said. And rushed forward.

When she reached his side, he looked like he was about to tip completely over, so she placed her hands on his arm, trying to steady him. For a moment, she thought he was going to fall down. And take her with him. But then he found his equilibrium, blinked his eyes a few times in the darkness, and threw his shoulders back.

"I'm okay," he said. "Thank you."

He said that first, then turned to look at her. His eyes blinked a few times again.

"Oh, Madeline. I thought you were just a passing stranger."

"I wanted to make sure you were okay."

"Do you live around here?"

"My apartment is closer to campus."

"Oh." He looked puzzled and then appeared to give up on trying to figure it out. "Well, thanks."

Madeline kept her hands on his left arm. Just in case. "Why don't I just walk with you to your door?"

"Were we talking about your thesis?" he asked.

"Some. But it's okay—"

"No. I know we were just talking about my family at the bar, weren't we? I mean, that was you, wasn't it?"

"It was."

"Oh, boy. When I think of them dying too much, I tend to indulge. And I think of them all the time. . . ." He stared into the distance like he expected something to materialize out of the darkness. "My son, Jake, he'd be college age now. I always wonder what he would have been like as he got older. Would he be a writer?" He turned to her. "Would he date a girl like you?"

"I'm sure he was a great kid."

"He was." He stood there for a moment, still staring at her. "I'm going to go. You don't have to worry about me. I'm fine. I can tell."

"If you're sure."

He stared at her, his eyes suddenly sharply focused. "Are you sure? Are you okay? You seem like you have something on your mind. Is it the thesis?"

"Yes. But look, just forget it. It's late, and I'm probably overreacting, like you said."

"If you don't feel comfortable with it, just come inside and get it. Take it back and think about it."

Madeline thought about it. She really thought about it.

And almost did take it back.

But it was late. And maybe she was overreacting.

And maybe Madeline hoped Connor would read it. And . . . would he have some advice about what had been happening with her and Sophia?

Would he be able to do something about it?

Would he piece it together and help?

"No," Madeline said, "I want you to keep it. I want you to read it. And . . ."

Connor wobbled a little. "And what?"

"If I'm not here at some point . . . if I drop out or something—"

"Drop out? Why would you—"

"If I'm not here, then you'll understand why. Okay? It's not because I don't want to be in college. I love school. I love Commonwealth. And I want to graduate. It's just sometimes . . . you have to move on. Okay?"

She started to pull away. Her hand slid along his arm and then, as she backed up, he clasped it.

"Madeline, wait."

He held on for a moment, maybe just to make sure he was really okay. But then he squeezed her hand, and their hands remained that way for a moment until he finally eased away, his body moving up the sidewalk toward his house.

Only then did she let go.

He looked back once and said over his shoulder, "Be careful getting home. It's late. I'd drive you but . . ."

"I'm good, Dr. Nye. Thank you."

CHAPTER FIFTY-EIGHT

CONNOR
PRESENT

When my eyes open, I'm on the couch.

A woman in a white uniform shirt and black pants, with her dark hair pulled off her face, is staring at me, a penlight in her hand. She moves it first one way and then the other, asking me to follow it with my eyes.

I do. And she corrects me.

"Without moving your head."

So I do that, and she clicks the penlight off.

"Are you feeling nauseated?"

"No."

"Any vision troubles?"

"No. Can I ask what happened?"

"Neck pain? Chest pain?"

"No."

She steps out of the way and I come face-to-face with Bowman. She stands with hands on hips, examining me like she's a doctor. "Feeling all right, Connor?"

"I think so. What happened?"

"Do you remember anything?" she asks.

My mouth is dry. My lips feel like baked desert. "I got a visit from

Zach Greenfield. And he tried to pound some sense into me with his fists. Why did he stop?"

Bowman looks to her right. Diana is standing there, a phone pressed to her ear. When she sees me looking, she lowers the phone. "I'll let you know when to keep your mouth shut."

"You came in and scared him off?" I ask. "Thanks."

"She didn't scare him off," Bowman says. "She held him at gunpoint and called us."

"Gunpoint?"

Diana pats her purse. "I have my concealed carry. Do you think I'm going to work as a lawyer and not carry a piece?"

"So Zach's been arrested?" I ask.

"He's in custody," Bowman says. "Assault. Breaking and entering." She shrugs. "We'll see what else we can add to his tab."

I reach up and rub the back of my neck. I didn't lie when I told the paramedic it didn't hurt. But it feels stiff. And I can feel pain spreading through the side of my head where Zach hit me. Fortunately, Madeline hit me on the other side with the bourbon bottle, so everything is equalized now. Both sides hurt.

"So it's over," I say. "Now you know Zach is capable of violence. He's going to prison, right?"

Bowman laughs a little. "Not so fast, friendo. What did Zach say when he was here?"

I look to Diana, who has the phone to her ear again. She nods, telling me I can answer her question.

"He admitted assaulting Madeline that night," I say. "The way Rebecca Knox described it. Of course, he didn't exactly see it as an assault. I think he said he got a little 'handsy.'"

"Ugh."

Bowman and I both look at Diana when she makes the noise. She continues with her phone call, but she's shaking her head over Zach's choice of words.

"He actually thinks I killed his wife," I say. "And Madeline. He was pretty inflamed, so he wanted to take it out on me. Or drag me in to be arrested." I try to go back to summon as many details as I can. "I think he'd been drinking. His eyes were glazed. And I smelled it on him when he got close to me."

"He'd had a few too many," Bowman says. "That didn't help his judgment."

"It never does," I say. "But he was so angry. It seems like he was really wound up. Was it just the booze and feeling like he was being wrongly pursued?"

"What do you mean?" Bowman asks.

"I don't know. Why come here now? Why attack instead of run?"

"Some people are fighters," Bowman says. "When backed into a corner, they claw and slash. He knew we had new evidence in his wife's case, that we'd been talking to you. I have to keep him abreast of developments up to a point."

Diana asks Bowman, "Did you all find out who Madeline was dating back then? Anybody?"

Bowman hesitates a moment, like she isn't sure she should share such sensitive information. But she relents. "We didn't find evidence she was romantically involved with anyone. If she was, she kept it hidden. Madeline didn't have a ton of close friends. She didn't text or use social media a lot. She didn't have a lot of money. She worked a job outside of school. She may not have had a big social life."

"She didn't seem to have a great family," I say.

"What about colleagues of yours?" Bowman asks. "Now, that party was at whose house? Someone you teach with, right? Hoffman? Is that the name?"

"What are you asking me?"

"Was Madeline involved with one of your colleagues?"

"I didn't know anything about that."

But as soon as the words are out of my mouth, I remember what Preston said that night years ago. In this very house. He hinted that Lance was crossing the line in some way with his students. But isn't it likely Preston just meant the parties? I never thought it was a good idea for Lance to do it. And I never went despite being invited. The risk was too great. If one kid drank too much and wrecked their car going home . . .

But Lance is an adult, and I can't stop him from doing what he wants to do. Preston is the only one who might be able to put a halt to it. Instead, he called the cops on me.

"I know Lance has the parties," I say. "But that's all I know. Zach's the one we know assaulted two women. His wife and Madeline."

Bowman runs her shoe over the carpet. Back and forth. "There's also the matter of a murder scene that happens to be located in the vicinity of your family's graves. It points directly to—"

"That's enough, Detective," Diana says. "That's enough. My client was all set to come down to the station today and talk to you. And he was going to answer your questions under my watchful eye. But my client has been attacked and is quite shaken up."

"Quite shaken? He seems okay."

"He's *very* shaken," Diana says. "I can tell by looking at him he's not himself."

I sense Diana is exaggerating, playing for time. But to help her along, I slump in my seat, trying to look more out of it than I am.

Diana goes on. "And you have another man in custody who has assaulted your two victims. Any evidence you claim to have found on Madeline's body could have been put there by someone else to frame my client. I told you there was someone in this house who could have taken a knife from my client's kitchen."

"But your client just said Zach Greenfield is denying killing Madeline or his wife."

"You're right, Alicia. Murderers always tell the truth. They never try to shift the blame onto someone else. Has anyone come forward who saw my client with Madeline?"

Bowman remains silent. She looks as contemplative as a monk.

"Everyone in town has access to that cemetery," Diana says. "Even when it's locked. I walk my dog there. Everybody walks their dogs there. Or they jog. Or they bird-watch. That fence is like Swiss cheese. Just because a grave in the area says 'Nye' doesn't mean he did it."

"We'd like to go ahead and search this house," Bowman says. "Maybe there's more evidence here that can help us."

"You can search," Diana says, "as soon as you have a warrant. My client doesn't need his rights violated any more than they already have been. That's assuming the guy down at the station, the one who has already displayed violent tendencies and a predilection for breaking into my client's home, isn't the source of any other evidence you might be searching for."

"You're lucky, Diana. I do need to get down to the station and talk to Mr. Greenfield."

"As taxpayers, we all appreciate your dedication to your job."

"This isn't over, though," Bowman says. "Where's the passport?"

Diana looks at me.

"It's in my office. Top drawer on the left. I can get it—"

"You sit," Diana says. She goes to retrieve it and comes back. "Here you go."

"And he can't go anywhere else," Bowman says to Diana as if I'm not here. "Not out of the city. At all."

"He'll be here."

Bowman smacks the passport against her palm.

"We'll be talking soon, Dr. Nye," she says as she goes. "Very soon."

Once Bowman and the paramedics are gone, I look at Diana. She sits down in the chair across from me, her purse in her lap.

"What gives?" I ask. "I thought you wanted me to tell her every-thing?"

"I want you to tell her everything that's relevant. Maybe the author-ship of the book isn't at this point. Or maybe you want to take a little time to decide if you really want to admit to that. You were under duress before—and now. Do you still want to do it?"

My head is throbbing. And so is my heart. But I'm not really under duress. Not about this issue. Not in the way Diana suggests.

"I do, Diana. I just want to be finished with my part in this mess. I want a clean break. And if they figure out Zach did all this, then I can help them wrap it up."

"Fair enough." She stands up from the chair. "I'll arrange it with Bowman. Once she's done with Zach, I'll get you there."

"Thanks, Diana."

"Stay out of trouble in the meantime, okay?"

"I promise."

CHAPTER FIFTY-NINE

REBECCA
PRESENT

Rebecca returns home at the end of the day. Ordinarily she rides the bus, a slow, rattling trip from campus back to her apartment.

But not tonight. Not after everything that's happened.

Not after working, after classes.

Not after spending the morning at the police station.

Not after finding out someone murdered Madeline. Someone who is still out there.

Her mom told her—*ordered her*—to take an Uber home. Mom insisted on paying, and while it felt a little weird to get in the car with a stranger driving after hearing the news about Madeline, it felt way better than walking to and from the bus stop in the freezing cold with the sun and the daylight slipping away. That—and her conversation with Dr. Nye—made her think of the other woman who was murdered two years ago, the woman she saw at the party.

With Madeline.

Was it possible the two were related?

When she walks into the apartment, Rebecca immediately locks the door and latches the chain. Mikaila and Steven are not on the couch. Rebecca saw their cars parked out front and assumed they'd be home. Strangely, she looked forward to seeing them, if only because she didn't want to be alone after her hellish day. So when she goes inside and sees the empty couch, the blank TV screen, her heart sinks a little. Wouldn't it feel good to see those two morons?

She goes to the kitchen and opens the refrigerator. She finds some leftover pizza, two slices from a frozen one she baked two nights earlier. It's a miracle it's still here, since Mikaila tends to graze through anything Rebecca leaves behind.

Before she sits down to eat the cold pizza, Rebecca remembers the manuscript. She goes to her room and retrieves a stack of the pages. In the chaos of the day she's forgotten about the book, but now that things are quiet again and she can hear herself think, she remembers how much she was enjoying it the night before.

Reading. *For fun.* Such a much-needed luxury.

When she leaves her room, she passes Mikaila's. She hears giggling through the closed door.

"Baby, come on," Mikaila says.

"Just for a few minutes."

"Steven. No."

And more giggling.

At least someone is having fun. At least it isn't happening on the couch, a piece of furniture Rebecca's mom bought for the apartment at the beginning of the semester.

And she's happy they're here. Company. A pack.

Rebecca sits down with her pizza and a glass of water and starts to read. It takes just a few sentences to fall back into the world of the book. She's a third of the way through, and even though the town isn't called Gatewood, all the descriptions totally match. And the writing is so vivid, it makes Rebecca uneasy because the book is clearly building up to a woman being murdered. The character is leaving work alone, late at night. And the character—*Sarah*—has the uneasy feeling someone is watching her.

As she reads, Rebecca feels something tingling along her spine. The apartment is warm—Mikaila likes to turn the thermostat up—but despite that, Rebecca gets a shivering feeling in the center of her body. She spent the morning telling the police about Madeline and the party—the guy with her out in the alley, his hands slithering up Madeline's shirt after his wife was gone. Even when Madeline tried to stop him.

And is Rebecca nuts or does the description of the woman in the book who is about to be killed sound a lot like the woman from the party? Blond hair. Big bright eyes. Married. The guy who might be about to kill her—her husband—has brown hair and a beard. A lot like the creep from the party.

And in real life, that woman is dead. Murdered. Six months before Madeline disappeared. That's what Nye told her in the alley.

So whoever wrote this book based it on the murder?

So why did the author send it to her?

In the book, the woman is in her car, turning the key to start the engine. And just before she does, she hears something in the backseat.

Maybe it's the wind.

Maybe it's outside.

Maybe it's her mind playing tricks.

She turns around to look—

"Boo!"

Rebecca screams, knocks over her glass of water, dumping its contents everywhere. Then the glass rolls off the end of the table and shatters against the linoleum floor. Rebecca springs from her chair, spinning as she does, turning to face her attacker. Ready to fight or flee.

"Oh, my God, Becca. Are you okay?"

Rebecca stands with her back to the refrigerator. Her hands are out in front of her, both of them clenched into fists. Her dad taught her how to do that when she was little, how to get into a fighting stance and throw a punch.

She's ready to do that now, the chill in her spine growing hot. The water cascading off the table and onto the floor like a mini waterfall.

She sees Mikaila before her, her mouth wide open, a shocked look on her face. She's wearing the same shorts and T-shirt she always wears around the apartment, and she lifts her hand to her mouth, covering it even as she speaks.

"Chill, Becca. It was just a joke." She holds up a beer bottle with her other hand. "I pressed this against your neck, just trying to irritate you. My God, you totally overreacted."

Rebecca wants to go ahead and punch Mikaila anyway, even though she isn't a threat. She wants to punch her because Mikaila is acting like Rebecca is the one behaving strangely when it's her who's doing the wrong thing, sneaking up on someone who's had a long, shitty day hearing about murder and spousal abuse and kidnapping.

"Jesus, Mikaila. What the fuck is wrong with you?"

All of a sudden, Steven is here, just behind Mikaila. "Easy, babe."

"With me?" Mikaila asks. "What's wrong with me?"

"You can't just sneak up on somebody like that. You scared the shit out of me. And I broke a glass."

"It was a joke, Becca. Lighten up."

"And stop calling me Becca. It's *Rebecca*."

Mikaila's mouth opens again. She gasps like she's offended. Or hurt. Or both.

"I've tried to be your friend, Becca—*Rebecca*. But I don't have to deal with this shit." She turns, her hair flying out and surrounding her head like a halo. "Come on, Steven. Let's go back to our room."

"Hold on, babe."

Mikaila stops mid-storm-off. She stands in the middle of the living room, turning back, hands on hips. She looks like she's pretending to be a fashion model, all the way down to the pouty look on her face.

"What?" Mikaila asks without losing the pout.

"I need to say something to Rebecca," Steven says.

And Rebecca remains tense. What could Steven have to say to her? The two of them rarely speak, and while he seems like a decent enough guy, she also has to wonder what he sees in Mikaila beyond the way she looks. If that's all there is, aren't there a thousand other girls he could pursue in this town who might look just as good without being as shallow?

And then she worries that Steven is about to go off on her—take Mikaila's side and turn the whole apartment into a war zone. Two against one, even though one isn't paying any rent.

Would Rebecca have to move out and find a new place to live?

But then Steven says, "I heard you ask Mikaila about that package we found on the porch. The one in the big envelope?"

Rebecca feels like she ran five miles. Her breathing is just coming back to normal. "What about it?"

"You asked if we saw who left it here," he says. "And Mikaila was ahead of me because I was carrying both of our bags and our food from the car. But I looked over to the side of the building—you know, over where people wash their cars when the weather's warm? Anyway, there was a woman standing there, peeking her head around the side of the building. And it was like she was watching us come home. And when Mikaila got to the top of the stairs and picked up the envelope, the woman pulled her head back and disappeared out of sight."

"For real?" Rebecca asks.

"For real."

"What did she look like?" Rebecca asks. But she thinks she knows the answer.

"I don't know. All I saw were big glasses. And red hair. Really bright red hair."

CHAPTER SIXTY

Rebecca's hands shake as she sweeps up the broken glass with the little broom and dustpan they keep under the sink. She soaks up the water with a towel. She hopes the mundane task will ground her, make her racing mind calm down some.

So Madeline came back to town, went to Dr. Nye's reading, and then left a manuscript on Rebecca's doorstep before she was murdered?

Why?

Rebecca goes back to her bedroom for her phone, which she plugged in to charge. She needs to call her mom, to talk to someone who can make some sense of everything that's going on. She's already called home five times today, including once before she went into the police station and then again on the way out. Her mom has a way of making everything sound manageable. She told Rebecca just to tell the police the truth, to leave nothing out, and so she did. And before they hung up the second time, her mom said she and Dad would come visit during the upcoming weekend, take her out to dinner. Or if Rebecca preferred, she could come home, sleep in her old room. Rebecca likes the sound of that idea the best—get out of Gatewood for a couple of days.

After all—isn't there someone on the loose who killed Madeline?

She's about to make the call when their doorbell rings, and Rebecca jumps again.

Could the police be coming by to ask her more questions? They said they might.

Steven sticks his head out of Mikaila's bedroom doorway. Rebecca refuses to think of it as "their" room. Not unless he starts paying rent, and she doesn't see that happening.

"Was that the door?" Steven asks.

"Did you guys order food?" Rebecca asks.

"Nope."

"Are you expecting someone?"

Mikaila has done that a few times—invited people over without telling Rebecca. She'd come home from work or class or studying and there'd be six or eight people in the living room, drinking beer or passing around a joint. And Mikaila would say, "Hey, everybody, this is my super-chill roommate, Becca. I love you, Becca Boo!" And Rebecca would have to stand there and smile and act like it was cool to have a bunch of people she didn't know in the living room on a Tuesday night.

"No," Steven says. "We're just hanging out."

"Will you answer the door, then?" Rebecca asks. "I mean, since you're a guy and everything. And just . . ."

"Just what?"

"Just say I'm not home."

"Sure." But he doesn't leave. He stands before Rebecca, his head cocked to one side. "You seem pretty tense tonight. A guy in one of my classes said a former student got murdered. Did you hear that too?"

"Yeah, I did. And I knew her."

His eyebrows rise. "You knew her? Oh, shit. I'm sorry. You know, Mikaila doesn't know. She doesn't pay attention to anything like that. She wouldn't have snuck up on you that way if she knew."

"It's okay," I say. "I'm not really mad at her."

"I'll handle whoever's at the door," he says. Steven is wearing a pair of gym shorts and nothing else. He's broad-shouldered and has so much hair on his torso, it looks like he's wearing a sweater. But Rebecca has to admit she feels a lot safer having him in the apartment and is glad he's spending the night. "I'll tell them to get lost. And my dad has a few guns. I can get one and bring it back tomorrow. And protect you guys."

"Just answer the door. Okay?"

He strolls across the living room, arms swinging at his sides. Rebecca steps back into the hallway, out of sight of the front door. She tells herself it's likely a mistake. There's so much turnover in these off-campus apartments that it's not unusual for someone to knock on the wrong door, looking for a friend who used to live there. Or maybe one of Mikaila's drinking companions decided to show up. Even that sounds good to Rebecca. As far as she is concerned, Mikaila can have everybody over, the whole gang. And they can sit in the living room all night if they want.

Anything so she's not alone.

Rebecca hears the door open. And Steven's muffled voice.

"I'm not sure if she's able to talk to anyone right now," he says. "I have to check."

It's someone for her? No one ever just drops in on her. No one she knows drops in at all. They text first. It's not 1993.

Rebecca hears the door close and then Steven is back. He jerks his thumb over his shoulder toward the door. And he's wearing a little half smile on his face.

"Rebecca, it's for you. The dude says he's one of your professors, and he needs to talk to you about something important."

Rebecca thinks Steven is kidding around, playing another joke on her. But Steven isn't the kind of person to do that, unlike Mikaila. And she isn't even sure Steven could think of something this weird—a professor showing up on her doorstep. She remembers fiction-writing class with Dr. Nye. He always says the weirder the detail, the more likely it is to ring true with the reader. And what could be weirder than a professor coming to her apartment unannounced at night?

"Who is it?" she asks. "What's his name?"

Steven looks stumped for a moment, like he already forgot the name. Then he snaps his fingers. "Hoffbrau? No. Hoffman. Lance Hoffman."

CHAPTER SIXTY-ONE

"You look totally freaked out," Steven says. "Do you want me to tell him you're not home or something?"

"No, that's okay. It's just so weird to have my professor at my door. And he didn't say what it's about?"

"No." Steven shrugs. "Maybe it's some shit from class. Like he forgot to give you an assignment or something."

"He can just e-mail us all. Or use Blackboard."

"That's true." Steven rubs his chin. "Maybe it's about that student who died. You said you knew her. Did he?"

His guess makes as much sense as anything. Rebecca saw Madeline at Hoffman's house. Madeline was an English major. Is that why Hoffman is here? Are they getting in touch personally with every student to reassure them? To calm them down or give them counseling?

"Do you want me to get rid of him?" Steven asks.

"No," Rebecca says. "I'll go talk to him. He's going to direct my thesis now. Maybe it's about that."

"Sure. Just yell if you need something. Mikaila's watching Netflix, and I have Psych homework. Okay? But I'm listening."

"Thanks, Steven."

Rebecca walks across the living room to the closed front door. Could Steven have misunderstood who is waiting out there hoping to speak to her?

She takes a deep breath on her side of the door and pulls it open.

Hoffman is on the landing, wearing a heavy green parka that looks like it came from an army surplus store. He smiles when he sees her, his hands clasped together in front of his body.

"Rebecca. I'm so sorry to barge in on you like this and at this late hour. Do you have just a moment to talk to me? Your boyfriend didn't seem certain if you were home or not."

"He's not my boyfriend," she says as if that matters. "He's my room-mate's boyfriend."

"Ah, I see. Well . . . time for a quick chat?"

"Sure. I guess. Come in."

Hoffman hesitates. He looks past Rebecca into the apartment. "Well, I'd rather . . . Can you get a coat and step out here? I was hoping to speak privately. And you seem to have company."

Rebecca feels her heart jump into a higher gear. If he wants to talk outside, it must be something personal, right? If he wants to reassure her about Madeline's death, why not come inside and do it?

Can she say no to a professor, even on her own doorstep? Does she want to risk pissing him off when he's about to direct her thesis?

"Okay," she says. "Let me get my coat."

It takes her a minute to walk to her room, grab her coat, and come back out. On her way, Steven sticks his head out of the bedroom again. "Everything okay?"

"I think so. I'm just going outside with him for a minute."

Mikaila's voice comes through the partially open door. "I'm sorry about pranking you, Rebecca. I mean it."

Steven raises his eyebrows, the look saying, *See, she isn't as bad as you think.*

"Thanks, Mikaila," Rebecca says. "It's fine."

"What does your professor want?" she asks, still a disembodied voice. "Extra credit?" She giggles.

"I'll tell her what's going on," Steven says. "About your friend."

"See you in a few, Steven," Rebecca says, and goes through the living room and outside onto the small landing. She pulls the door shut behind her. "Okay. What's the matter, Dr. Hoffman?"

Hoffman looks around, glances at the door. "Why don't we go down the stairs? We can talk more privately in the parking lot."

Rebecca looks back at the closed door and then out at Hoffman. It's dark near the building, just a few streetlights brightening the parking lot below.

"We don't have to get in my car," Hoffman says. "But we can talk and not worry about anyone hearing. You know, little pitchers have big ears."

Rebecca doesn't know what Hoffman is talking about. Pitchers and ears?

Is that from a poem?

Hoffman starts down the steps without hearing Rebecca's response. She feels she has no choice but to follow him. The wooden stairs squeak as they both go down, and when they reach the bottom, Hoffman moves out into the parking lot and stands near the halo cast by one of the streetlights. He rubs his hands together. He isn't wearing gloves or a hat.

"Well," he says, "I'm glad I found you at home."

"How did you know where I live?".

"Oh, that. It's in the university database. I have access to that. We all do."

"Okay. I guess."

"I wouldn't have come over if I didn't think this was important."

"Is this about my thesis?" she asks. "Or is it about all the stuff going on? You know, the stuff about Madeline."

Hoffman blows on his hands. "That's it," he says. "Madeline." He shakes his head, his lips pursed tight. "Such a terrible loss. You indicated in my office that you knew her. Isn't that right?"

"I knew her, yeah. We took a class together."

"Well, I'm sorry for your loss. This is a shock to everyone in the department. She was a bright light. And so young. Alas, she's now the townsman of a stiller town."

Rebecca rarely knew what Hoffman was talking about, but she remembers that poem from high school. "A. E. Housman, right?"

Hoffman's face brightens. "Wow, good for you. See, we'll make a poet out of you yet." He rubs his hands together again. "Since it's so cold, I'll try to cut to the chase. I know you saw something at my house a couple of years ago, something that you may feel inclined to talk to the police about."

Something she doesn't even understand moves Rebecca half a step back toward the apartment building.

It must also show on her face because Hoffman says, "You probably talked to them already, right? As I'm sure you're aware, Gatewood is something of a backwater, the kind of place great ideas go to die. But it also means it's a place where everybody knows everybody else. And it's clear you're involved in this because you were friends with Madeline and you were at my house that night when a certain unfortunate incident may or may not have taken place. It made me look bad, and it made my friend look bad."

Hoffman takes a step toward her.

Rebecca tries not to but can't help moving back again.

When Hoffman shifts forward, his head moves in front of the streetlight behind him, casting his face in shadow.

"What I want you to understand is that things aren't always what they seem," he says. "It's easy to look at a situation and to see only one part of the picture. And when you're young, like you are, you may not understand all the subtle nuances and complexities inherent in the situation. Are you following what I'm saying?"

"I only told the police what I saw. That's it."

"But see, that's the problem. It's like when I help a student with a story or a poem. I provide them with a detail or an idea for the plot, and then students think it's something I've really experienced. When what

I'm doing is brainstorming. The police get ahold of one sliver of information, and they're simply not creative enough to understand it or where it came from. They're not writers like us. From their limited perspective, they can see only trouble. And then they try to destroy someone's life. A good man. Do you understand?"

"They weren't interested at all in the underage drinking or the pot smoking, Dr. Hoffman. They didn't even care."

Hoffman laughs. But it isn't a real laugh. It's a sound that indicates contempt, like Rebecca is so small and insignificant she can't possibly get anything right. "See, that's the kind of thing I'm talking about. That narrow focus on the simplest things. I don't care what the police think of my parties. Let them come and try to do something to me about it."

Rebecca takes another step back. And then another. "Like I said, I only told them what I saw with Madeline—"

"Madeline was a troubled girl. From a troubled home. Look at the way she behaved. Faking her disappearance, making the police do all that work. Scaring her mother. What kind of person does those things? Someone who isn't right. Someone with problems."

"I don't know what you want me to do. I already talked to the police."

"I want you to understand that it's always dangerous to talk about things that are more complex than you understand. That people can get hurt when the wrong things are said. Even if you talk about one person, it can reflect poorly on another person as well. There's a ripple effect. Do you know anything else about Madeline? Anything else about what she might have been doing back here in town?"

Hoffman looks taller than he is. He seems to be looking down on her, waiting for an answer.

"I don't know anything about that."

"You're sure?"

"I am."

"You didn't see her since she's been back? Outside of the thing at the library."

"No, I haven't."

"Good, good. It's best that we keep some things to ourselves. And I really am looking forward to working with you on your thesis. You've dodged the bullet on working with Dr. Nye, I think. You know he was the last person to see Madeline before she disappeared two years ago. And I wouldn't be surprised if his name came up with this recent unpleasantness. That's really what I'm worried about. I was just talking to a friend of mine about this earlier, as we had some drinks. How does Dr. Nye's behavior affect the students? Or others in the community? Would you want to work on a thesis with someone like that? I've had to jump in and help on other theses when he dropped the ball. I've had to clean up his messes behind his back. And try not to bruise his pride, which, I suspect, is fragile as glass. For all we know, Rebecca, we're going to find out that Dr. Nye is the person we should all be concerned about. And afraid of. Not my friend."

"I just want to get my thesis finished."

"And you will. I think it's going to be a good one, don't you? And we all want to make sure you pass it and are able to graduate in May. Right?"

"I definitely want to."

"Good."

Hoffman takes two steps forward, closing the distance between them, and reaches out with his right hand, placing it on Rebecca's shoulder. It feels heavy, like a weight. He's about to say something else when Rebecca hears the door open behind and above her.

"Rebecca?"

She turns and looks.

It's Mikaila, out on the landing in her T-shirt and shorts, her long hair lifted by the breeze.

"Are you coming back in?" she asks. "We want to finish that movie we were watching."

"I'm coming," Rebecca says. "I'm coming right now."

She slips out from underneath Hoffman's hand and backs toward the stairs.

"Thanks for coming by, Dr. Hoffman. I guess . . . in class . . . I'll see you there."

"Of course," he says.

But he remains at the bottom of the steps, looking up, watching her disappear back into the apartment alongside Mikaila.

CHAPTER SIXTY-TWO

CONNOR
PRESENT

Diana calls that night and tells me Bowman is still tied up with Zach.

"Sit tight," she says. "It may be tomorrow morning before you get her undivided attention."

After I hang up, I go into the kitchen and find the remains of my smashed door still scattered everywhere. I need to clean that mess up, but I go past it, impressed by the amount of force Zach was able to deliver with just one solid kick.

I take the rickety stairs down to the basement and cross the room to the door leading to the outside. The one lacking a dead bolt that everyone and their brother has been using as a portal to my world.

It smells musty down here. The air is cool. Around the edges of the room, boxes and boxes of old crap are stacked, waiting for someone to go through it and toss it out.

I give Zach credit—he didn't need to smash this door down. He must have used a credit card or knife to get past the tiny lock. He even closed the door behind him when he came in.

I spend little time in the basement unless it's to do laundry. I look around and see an old kitchen chair, one with a broken rung underneath. It's been down here hoping to be fixed since before Emily and

Jake died, so I take it over to the door and wedge it under the knob. It fits well and has a purpose again for the first time in years.

But I'm not sure the chair alone will keep anyone out. I look some more and find a cinder block. I'm not sure why it's here. I think it came with the house. When I pick it up, my fingers sink into the cobwebs inside it like cotton candy. I place the cinder block on top of the chair, hoping to make it harder for anyone else to come in. And I make a mental note to call a locksmith.

I wipe the cobwebs off on my pant leg and turn to go. When I reach the bottom of the stairs, I stop. I see across the room some boxes that hold items from Jake's room. Clothes. Books. Toys he played with when he was little.

Just like the broken chair, they've been down here for years, waiting for me to deal with them. And I haven't wanted to. I couldn't bring myself to take the job on, and I always told myself I was too busy with other things.

There's a lot of crap from the past I haven't dealt with.

Maybe it's time.

I go through the house and make sure everything is locked before I head back to my office and pick up Madeline's story again and start reading. I sit on the end of the leather couch we inherited from Emily's parents when they moved into a smaller home. I flip on the lamp, which casts a soft glow over a small portion of the room. I almost feel at ease and try to imagine I'm back in the past, reading a student story in the comfort of my warm home. And maybe Emily and Jake are out in the kitchen, working on his homework.

But I know none of this is true.

I'm in a new reality.

And this is confirmed for me when I turn to the third page of Madeline's story.

The protagonist is entering the campus where she used to go to school, a campus that looks a lot like Commonwealth's. And when she walks through the gates on the east side of campus, she passes a brand-new alumni center, one named after a graduate of the university who went on to serve for decades on the state supreme court. He bequeathed the university a crap ton of money for the alumni center, and it was built so fast, everyone joked the university was acting like they were afraid the judge was going to change his mind in the great beyond.

It's a state-of-the-art Georgian building, redbrick with huge columns.

I look up from the page.

A minor detail about the landscape. Something I might enjoy and then move on from in any other story.

Except . . .

The alumni center wasn't built or named until after Madeline disappeared. It wasn't here when she was a student.

Which means the story *was* written since she disappeared. And was left on my desk for me to discover.

Now.

It's Madeline trying to tell me something. To tell everyone something.

I go back to reading, my eyes moving over the words as fast as they can.

CHAPTER SIXTY-THREE

MADELINE
FALL, TWO AND A HALF YEARS EARLIER

Madeline sat in Troy's facing the door. She'd splurged when she'd arrived, even though her budget was limited. If she was being honest with herself, she'd hoped Dr. Hoffman would be there first. And he would offer to buy her a coffee, maybe even a muffin or a scone.

But Hoffman was frequently late—to class, to conferences—so when she came into Troy's and didn't see him . . . and she smelled the rich roasted coffee. The scones fresh out of the oven. She broke down and ordered.

And while she waited at the small table, two bites of the scone already gone, she marveled at how much better the coffee tasted there than the cheap stuff she bought in a giant can at the grocery store. She bought the same brand her grandparents used to drink, and she worried she'd made a huge mistake by indulging in the good stuff at Troy's. She might never be able to go back to drinking the crap in her apartment.

Hoffman showed up fifteen minutes late, his messenger bag slung over his shoulder. He waved to her, a smile affixed to his face, and he went and placed an order at the counter, chatting with the barista as if he had all the time in the world. When it was ready, he carried the drink over to the table and sat down across from Madeline.

"I'm so sorry I'm late," he said. "A couple of students came by. Freshmen. And they think they're going to fail my class. Which they are. Anyway, they delayed me. But I'm here now."

"That's okay," Madeline said because what could she say? Should she scold her sixty-year-old professor for being late? Reach across the table and slap his hand like the nuns who had taught her grandmother? She'd given Hoffman the beginning chapters of her thesis. She hoped he wasn't going to bring the party up. Madeline wanted to forget about it, not have it linger in her life. Sophia was already pissed, and they were probably no longer friends. She didn't need any other trouble, especially at school. "I've just been enjoying my coffee. I don't let myself do this too much."

"It's tough on a student budget, isn't it? Of course, they don't pay the professors much more these days. We're living in austere, draconian times."

They made more small talk after that. Hoffman lamented the political climate in the country—and on campus. And he claimed he must have been born in the wrong time because he longed for an era when things on campus were looser and freer.

"No one is engaged these days," he said. "Not the students. Not even the faculty."

Madeline listened. She'd learned it was best to let him go on and on during a one-on-one meeting. At some point, sometimes after thirty minutes or so, he slowed down his verbal waterfall and let her say something.

And many times Hoffman even said something interesting. He once told her a story about driving across the country with a group of friends the summer he finished high school. He made the trip sound so romantic, so adventurous, and as Madeline listened, she became aware of how rarely she'd traveled, of how little of the world she'd seen. Somehow it seemed as though her professors had all done so much and traveled so far. Europe. Asia. Australia.

New York. California.

She'd never been farther than a trip to Florida with her grandparents when she was five. It rained a lot, and they never entered the gates of Disney World because her grandfather said it was too expensive. Instead, they camped in a state park, and Madeline climbed on a rusty jungle gym with some kids from Georgia whose parents watched them all play while pounding beers.

Madeline wanted to see more. To do more.

True to form, Hoffman ran out of steam. "So about the beginning of this thesis."

"Thanks for reading it."

He waved his hand over the table, a king dispensing favors. "Anything to help. I know Dr. Nye can be . . . distracted sometimes. He's had a difficult time. And our department chair, Dr. White, asked me to assist in any way I can, so since I was already the second reader, I thought maybe I could take a more active role in the project. Let's not tell Dr. Nye, since it isn't really protocol for me to step in this way. We don't want to step on any toes. But I may have a different set of literary insights than he would."

"Any insights at all would be appreciated. You're right. Dr. Nye has been . . . kind of distracted."

Hoffman pulled the pages—handwritten—out of his bag and tossed them onto the table. He pointed to them. "I see this story building to some act of violence. You're not there yet, but you seem to be moving in that direction. I guess I'm wondering why you wanted to tell a story like this in the first place."

Madeline cleared her throat. Her coffee was almost finished. She was down to the bottom of the paper cup, and the liquid was lukewarm. "It's not autobiographical. But it is loosely based on something that's happening to a friend of mine." She went for her eyebrow and couldn't stop herself. She gave it a good tug, felt one of the little hairs pull free with that satisfying pop. If Hoffman knew Zach and Sophia, might he recognize them in the book? "She's having trouble with her husband.

Or at least I think she is. See, I don't really know, but I'm imagining where it could go. Some of it's real, and some of it isn't."

"That's my point," Hoffman said. "I think I can tell when you're on sure footing with your details. And then other times, it feels like you're grasping. For example, all the details about Lilly's family life and childhood. Her father dying, her mother having a succession of men. The protagonist searching for a father figure elsewhere. Her grandfather. Her soccer coach. That all feels very real." He drank his own coffee, scratched his nose. "I suppose those details are . . . autobiographical from your friend's life."

Madeline felt her face flush. She swallowed the lukewarm—practically cold—liquid in the bottom of her cup, hoping to obscure her face. "Yes. Autobiographical."

"But the stuff about what's going on in the marriage between the couple," he said. "The way they interact. The kinds of things they fight about. It feels . . ."

"Forced?"

"Inauthentic."

If Hoffman had thrown hot coffee in her face, it wouldn't have burned more. What an awful word for an author to hear about their writing.

Inauthentic.

But she couldn't deny it. When she wrote those parts, it felt forced, like she was struggling up a steep hill with a heavy pack on her back. She strained her imagination but just couldn't get it to go where it needed to go. At times like those, she wanted to throw her pen across the room and burn the whole manuscript.

How did anybody do this for a living?

How did anybody do this at all?

"Maybe I should abandon this," she said, hating to admit defeat. It ripped at the very fiber of who she was. But she didn't know if she had enough time, energy, or knowledge to go on. "Maybe I should write poetry instead. I have those poems from your class."

She expected Hoffman to burst with joy. And he did.

A mile-wide smile split his face. "You don't know how much that does my heart good."

Madeline was glad to see him happy. And she tried to cover her own disappointment over admitting she might not be able to write a novel for her thesis project by forcing a smile across her face. She probably looked ill.

Then Hoffman did something unexpected.

He reached under the table and placed his hand on her knee. And he left the hand there for a moment that drew out longer than Madeline imagined it could, his fingers against the denim.

Right when Madeline was about to look around, to see if anyone else was watching, he pulled his hand back.

"I want you to write that novel, Madeline. I think you have the ability to do it." His smile lost none of its intensity. And even though his teeth looked a little gray and uncared-for, there was something charming about how much he wanted to help her. "And I have some ideas for how you're going to get there."

CHAPTER SIXTY-FOUR

Hoffman's behavior in Troy's shook Madeline.

She went home that night, back to the little apartment on the third floor, the one at the top of the rickety staircase, and replayed the conversation in the coffee shop. She realized everything about it had been pretty normal. Hoffman had acted like he always did—a little out of it, a little condescending, but ultimately supportive. When he told her he wanted her to go ahead and write the novel and not poems, her heart flipped like someone had shocked her with jumper cables.

She was so thrilled for that split second.

But she couldn't ignore the hand on her knee. The lingering hand.

As she drove home from Troy's, she tried to cast the interaction in a different light. Maybe Hoffman touched all his students that way, male and female. Maybe he was trying to be encouraging, like her female soccer coach, who used to smack all the players on the butt as they ran laps around the field.

Maybe Hoffman saw through to who she really was—a smart kid, dreaming of a life as a writer, but who was scared to death the dream would disappear like a puff of smoke. Like all the things her mother talked about doing but never did. And maybe Hoffman wanted to reassure her.

Madeline sat in her shitty chair in her apartment, the one with the sheet over the ugly stains, staring at the wall. She looked at the chipped plaster, the dirty paint. *No,* she thought. *I know what he wants. It's what Zach wanted at the party.*

It's what Mom says all men want. All the time.

Madeline weighed her options. Hoffman wasn't even her thesis director—Nye was. So did she even have to keep meeting with him? But Nye was so hard to pin down, so hard to get to pay attention. When they met and discussed her plans, his eyes wandered off away from her face. He'd stare at the rows of books on the shelves in his office, or out the window at the people walking by. She knew he'd lost his family somehow, knew the guy was in some kind of excruciating emotional pain, but he needed to do his job just a little, right?

Should she ask Dr. White, the head of the department, for advice?

She'd heard from other students that he was approachable, that they could talk to him, and he'd be understanding, nodding along as the students shared their problems and then giving them a few reasonable options to make things better. He seemed a little full of himself. He liked to roll up his shirtsleeves and show off his muscular arms. He was in good shape, obviously went to the gym a lot.

White and Hoffman and Nye were all friends. They hung out together sometimes, and if she complained to White, wouldn't it get back to Hoffman like a spreading virus? And hadn't Hoffman asked her to be discreet about letting Nye know he was helping with the thesis?

Madeline dropped her head into her hands, an overly dramatic gesture no one would see. Her head still buzzed a little from the good coffee at Troy's. And she was hungry. She stood up from the chair and trudged out to the tiny kitchen, where she pulled open the freezer door. Slim pickings. A package of hot dogs and two frozen burritos. She wished like hell she had some ice cream, wanted to see some materialize right there out of the mist in the freezer.

She slammed the door.

Madeline knew who she wanted to talk to. There was only one person in town, one person in her life, she trusted enough to share a real secret with.

Unfortunately, that person likely hated her. And would never speak to her again.

"How the fuck did everything get so fucked up?" She knew she was frustrated when she was using "fuck" as more than one part of speech.

She took out her phone. No texts, no nothing from Sophia since the night almost two weeks ago when she had come to her apartment and asked about her husband. And Madeline told the truth. And Sophia stormed out.

She thought about everything else Sophia had done for her—listened, gave advice, acted like the big sister Madeline had never had. Would Sophia ever get over it?

Did Madeline have anything to lose by asking?

She spent fifteen minutes composing the text. She spent as much time on that as she did on a page of one of her short stories. And despite all the time she spent, the message ended up being short and direct.

> I'm so sorry about what happened. But I'd love to talk. Have a problem.

Five minutes passed. Then ten.

Madeline gave up pretty quickly. Sophia was done with her, and the response would never come. Madeline went to the freezer and took out one of the burritos, ripped off the wrapper, and tossed it in the microwave.

"If my life is going in the crapper, my health might as well go along with it."

She pushed the START button as her phone dinged.

She checked Sophia's message. It was also very short. But it said so much:

U okay?

Madeline hated to admit when things were wrong. She hated to admit she couldn't handle things. She hated to need anyone for anything. That was why she was working her way through school. That was why she had signed the student loan papers herself.

It wasn't her way to say she needed help.

But with Sophia . . . it felt different. It felt okay to say it.

So she did:

No. I'm not.

Are U home?

All night.

Five minutes later:

I'll be there in fifteen.

CHAPTER SIXTY-FIVE

It was awkward.

When Sophia knocked, Madeline thought about not letting her in, pretending like she wasn't there and just blowing the whole thing off. If she did that, her friendship with Sophia would most definitely be over. Not because of what had happened with Zach but because Sophia would have no choice but to think of Madeline as the biggest freak ever to live. Invite her over and then refuse to let her in . . .

Madeline stood on her side of the front door while Sophia knocked again on the other. Madeline's hand went up to her eyebrow and pulled. Once and then twice before a tiny hair came out. She needed to open the door before her eyebrows were gone, so she did.

Sophia stood there, looking as naturally beautiful as ever, even though she wore a pair of denim shorts, a hoodie, and green Chuck Taylors that almost matched her eyes. Madeline backed up, and Sophia came in. When the door was closed, Sophia held her arms out, and she folded Madeline in a big hug.

"I'm so sorry about the other night," Madeline said. "You know, I mean, I'd never . . ."

"I know."

Sophia dropped her purse next to the sheet-covered chair and sat down.

"I think I'm out of wine. And I had only cheap shit anyway."

"Don't worry about it."

"I might have some tea bags my mom gave me," Madeline said.

"I'm good, Madeline. Just sit."

So Madeline did. And she sat on her hands, like she sometimes did, to keep them from going up to pluck at her eyebrows.

The two women sat across from each other. And Madeline was so nervous, so scared. She just wanted things to be normal with Sophia.

"I'm so sorry," she said. "I didn't want any of that to happen. And I didn't want you to find out."

Sophia shook her head. "It's not your fault. I would never blame a woman for a man doing something like that. I know who Zach is, and I know the kinds of things he does when he drinks." Sophia's jaw was set firmly, like it'd been carved into the side of a mountain. "We talked about it. Very thoroughly."

"I'm sorry. Really, I am."

"You need to stop apologizing for things you didn't do," Sophia said.

It sounded to Madeline like ancient wisdom, like something someone wiser had said to Sophia, and now she was passing it on to Madeline. And someday Madeline might be smart enough or old enough to hand it on to another woman who needed help.

"Thanks for coming over," she said.

"When a friend's in trouble . . . Besides, I don't get the feeling you share much with many people. Maybe I'm just special."

"Maybe you are. Maybe that's why I'm writing a book based on you. And me. Our friendship."

Sophia smiled for the first time since she came in. And Madeline started to think things really were going to be all right between the two of them.

"What's on your mind?" Sophia asked. "Writer's block? Do you want to study me so you can write more of your thesis?"

"I wish. But it's kind of related." Madeline pressed down on her hands with greater force. "I think you know Lance Hoffman, right? He's one of my professors at Commonwealth."

Sophia rolled her eyes. "He's not *my* friend. Zach knows him. They met playing golf at that course called Crosswinds. And we don't live too far from his house. You really don't have to apologize about that night. We can just move on."

"It's not really about that night. And I'm sorry to even refer to it. But it's just . . . I gave Hoffman some of my thesis. My director is another professor, but he's a little out of it right now. His wife and kid died in an accident, and he's kind of slow to respond. But Hoffman is fast to get back to me, and he's doing me the favor of helping out. He likes to talk to students and meet with them."

"He *does* like spending time with students," Sophia said, rolling her eyes again. "You can see that from his parties. I don't want to go to any more of them."

"Yeah . . ."

Madeline shifted her weight in the chair. She really wanted to pull her hand out and pluck her eyebrow. She really, *really* wanted to.

"What is it?" Sophia asked. And from the way she asked, Madeline thought Sophia knew what she was about to say. She knew why Madeline had called and what she needed help with.

"I just had a meeting with Dr. Hoffman, to talk about my thesis. And I'm not sure what to do about what happened."

CHAPTER SIXTY-SIX

REBECCA
PRESENT

Rebecca reads late into the night, finishing the manuscript that landed at her door.

Madeline's manuscript.

She still feels shaken by Dr. Hoffman's unexpected visit.

She replays the conversation in the parking lot over and over, trying her best to make sense of what exactly he was saying. She draws on the lessons she learned at the beginning of the semester in Dr. Nye's class, before he stopped teaching and started lurking in the alley outside Troy's.

Subtext. He taught them that word. Subtext. When someone says one thing, but there's a deeper meaning buried underneath.

And what's buried underneath Hoffman's request that Rebecca not tell the police anything else?

He seemed to be saying that Zach wasn't as bad as Rebecca thought he was. And that Nye was the real bad guy.

And beneath it all was a threat, right? For sure. He pretty much came out and said her ability to pass her thesis defense hinged on keeping her mouth shut.

Did guys just stick together no matter what? Was it some kind of man code of conduct?

Despite being buried under several layers of blankets, including a quilt her grandmother had made her before she went off to college, Rebecca shivers. She feels better than ever, knowing Steven and Mikaila are in the bedroom right next door. Steven went around and made sure the door and all the windows were locked, and he even offered to sleep on the couch so no one could get past him. Mikaila whined over that option, and Rebecca agreed it seemed unnecessary as long as the dead bolt and the chain were engaged on the front door. And Rebecca couldn't very well deprive Mikaila of time snuggled with her boyfriend after she came out and helped save her from Hoffman.

And how exactly did Mikaila know the right thing to do? How did she have the smarts to extract Rebecca from a difficult situation? Mikaila may lack common sense, and may seem totally self-absorbed, but she could be a good friend when she wanted. And when Rebecca came back in and thanked her, Mikaila simply said, "Hey, we ladies need to stick together against the creeps of the world."

And speaking of creeps—there is Madeline's book.

It tells the story of a woman in her twenties being murdered in a town that sounds exactly like Gatewood. And the woman who gets murdered has a creepy husband who likes to slime around with the woman's friends. And the guy even gets violently angry sometimes, which makes Rebecca shiver all over again when she reads that part of the book.

And as she nears the end, she realizes the creepy, domineering husband kills his wife. And then he decides to come after his wife's friend, forcing her to run for her life. . . .

The shivers won't stop.

And it all feels so familiar, so real, that it almost seems like Rebecca might have read the book before. But she knows that's not true.

Madeline wrote the book and passed it off to her.

Rebecca turns what appears to be the last page of the book.

Except . . .

There are more pages. But they're typed. They look so different from the rest of the book, which is handwritten on yellowed and crinkly paper, like it's been sitting around for a while in a closet or on a shelf. These other pages, the typed ones, are clean and crisp. New.

Did Madeline write something else and include it?

It says at the top: "My Best Friend's Murder: A Sequel."

Rebecca knows *My Best Friend's Murder* is the name of Dr. Nye's book. So did Madeline write a sequel to that? And why?

She starts reading this new story or whatever it is, and it's about a woman returning to the town where she went to college, and the town is also an exact match for Gatewood. And the campus an exact match for Commonwealth, just like in the novel.

But the character is back in town to confront a professor who has sexually harassed her.

And the description of that professor sounds very, very familiar . . .

Dr. Nye always said the purpose of art is to make us feel less alone.

By reading Madeline's story, Rebecca knows she's not the only one to have had an uncomfortable encounter with Dr. Hoffman.

She knows she's not alone.

CHAPTER SIXTY-SEVEN

CONNOR
PRESENT

I jog up the steps to the main entrance of Goodlaw Hall. It's a cold morning, my breath frosting as I climb. But the sky is clearer than it has been, promising the possibility the day will be warmer. When I reach the top of the stone stairs, my phone rings. It's Diana.

I stop and answer the call.

"Where are you now?" Diana asks. "I'm at your house. Bowman is ready to talk to you, and I said I'd bring you in."

"I had to come to campus real quick. It's important. I might have figured something out."

"Connor, this isn't the time to flake out. If you want to tell your—"

"I'll call you when I know for sure. Okay? I might need Bowman and I might not."

"Connor—"

I hang up and pass through the breezeway, two sets of double glass doors. I know exactly where I'm going. In my right hand, folded into a cylinder shape, is Madeline's short story, the one I finished reading last night. The one I read over and over again, late into the night, making sure I understood what it was really saying. I turn left past Preston's office, where the door is wide open, and I see him sitting inside but I don't bother to stop. Or allow him to stop me. I keep going down the long hallway to the familiar classroom where I always teach.

Where Lance has taken over.

As I approach the room, I hear his voice. Deep. Commanding.

Even wise.

He's talking about the president, bemoaning budget cuts to higher education. How he's going to tie that to fiction writing, I have no idea. How he ties anything he talks about to creative writing, I never know.

I always close the door to my classroom. Lance keeps his wide open. Everyone and anyone can hear. He loves to think all the world is his audience.

I stop in the doorway. It takes him a moment to look over and see me. When he does, his face shows surprise, and he stops his monologue. But then the composure quickly returns, and he smiles at me in a sly way.

"Well, well, class, it looks like we have an unexpected visitor this morning."

The students realize Lance is looking toward the door, so they follow his gaze toward me.

Lance goes on. "Late of Commonwealth University. Late of the Gatewood city jail. Clearly, you miss the limelight of being in the classroom, Dr. Nye."

"Lance, I think we need to talk."

He has his hands folded on top of the desk, and he shrugs. "I have office hours after this class. Why don't you wait for me down there, and then I can finish imparting the wisdom of the ages to these eager young minds?"

The students, faces I know so well, turn to look at me. Ordinarily, they're sleepy and a little dazed this early in the morning. But my appearance and my request to talk to Lance have them wide-awake and confused. And as I look at them and they look back at me, I realize I've been out drinking with more than one of them. And I feel embarrassed by the thought. I may not be as bad as Lance and his parties, but I'm on the continuum. I could use grief as an excuse, grief that made me turn to my students for companionship. But that's all it is—an excuse. And I need to get my life on a different track, if I get the chance.

The students don't all keep their eyes on me. Many of them turn back to Lance, waiting to see what he's going to say or do next.

"Class, you may not all be aware of it, but Dr. Nye certainly is. He's currently suspended from the university, pending an investigation into some of his off-campus activities. He's really not allowed to be here in any capacity." He looks at me now but addresses his remarks to the students. "I'd hate to have to call the campus police on an esteemed colleague of mine, one I admire so much. But if he doesn't leave the premises, I'll have no choice."

"We can talk about this right now, Lance." I unroll the paper tube. "This story written by Madeline O'Brien."

When I say her name, a ripple of recognition passes through the room. Some of the students gasp, and others begin to whisper. They've heard by now that a former student has been found dead. Murdered. I can only imagine the kinds of rumors swirling on social media and in the dorms and the bars and everywhere else students congregate.

Lance pushes back from the desk, and a cloud passes across his face. The smug certainty drains away, and he presses his lips together into a wire-thin line.

"We don't have time for this, Connor."

"Let me read this last part," I say. "The part that gets really interesting is here at the end when Madeline says—"

"That's enough." Lance stands up from the desk. He looks small at the front of the room, surrounded by students whose faces are now all frozen in expressions of disbelief. "I'm sorry Dr. Nye isn't able to contain himself and has to come back and interrupt our work today. He's never quite been the devotee of teaching that I am. You all have a reading assignment for today, don't you?"

Twenty heads nod in unison.

"Well, why don't you review that while I talk to my former colleague? We'll see if we can't get him to leave quietly and allow us to get back to the work at hand."

Lance starts my way, so I back out into the hall and wait for him.

CHAPTER SIXTY-EIGHT

MADELINE
WINTER, TWO YEARS EARLIER

Madeline's book took an even darker turn once Sophia was dead.

Hoffman had been right when he first read the early chapters of her thesis—Madeline planned on the story building up to some act of violence. And when she experienced Zach's behavior at the party, she started to have an idea of which way the story could go.

But could it simply be about a man killing his wife?

When she was ten, a woman in her hometown, someone her mother knew a little, had been found murdered in her home. Beaten to death. For days, the police looked for the killer, and they seemed to have no idea who it was. Long before they made an arrest, Madeline's mother had looked at her and said: *Maddy girl, it's always the husband.*

And she'd been right.

So what would make her story different?

Weeks and then months had passed since Sophia's death. Madeline stumbled through her life like a zombie, like she was so deeply sedated she didn't even notice what was going on around her. She sleepwalked across campus, going to her classes. She worked at the grocery store but barely talked to anyone.

She came home in the evenings, always jamming the chair under the doorknob, and stared at the blank pages she needed to fill with words.

Nothing came.

Her mind drifted away from the task at hand. She spent an inordinate amount of time on social media, refreshing Twitter feeds from local journalists and the police department, hoping to get some new information about Sophia's death.

But the news grew stale. No new leads, they said. Zach was being questioned, his life being turned upside down. But he maintained his innocence. And no arrests were made.

Madeline thought about calling the tip line set up in the wake of Sophia's death and telling them about the party. The way Zach had touched her. The way he had looked at her the first time they met outside the Owl's Nest. The way he had seemed to be ordering Sophia home.

But . . .

What did any of that mean? A guy could be a creep and not a killer. Look at the guys her mom had brought home. Nearly every one a creep. Some of them criminals. A few even violent. Had any of them been murderers?

She remembered the last time she spoke to Sophia, right there in her apartment. She'd told Sophia everything about Hoffman—about him putting his hand on her knee and appearing to suggest that something more go on between them while he directed her thesis. Madeline watched Sophia's face flush red. Even the tips of her ears turned the crimson color of a winter sunset.

"That is such fucking bullshit," she said. "Hoffman? Really?"

"I'm not naive, Sophia. I've seen my mom deal with this stuff all her life. I know men always gave her that kind of shit. Comments about her looks. Even outright assault. Pinching. Grabbing. She ate that shit for years because she needed to work. I guess I thought it would be different in college."

Sophia laughed, and it was one of the few times she sounded bitter or cynical. "It's not different anywhere, Madeline. No way."

Once Sophia said it, Madeline felt like a fool. Why did she think Commonwealth would be different from the rest of the world? Why did she think anyplace would be different? Wherever there were men, there were creeps. . . .

"I want to be done with him," Madeline said. "But he's involved with my thesis now. He has a lot of power over me."

Sophia shook her head. "No, you don't have to avoid him. You have to report him. That's the only way it stops. You shouldn't have to change your life because Hoffman is such a creep. He needs to learn how to be appropriate with students. Every institution has a way to report these things. You just tell someone in an important position, and they have to deal with it. I know this from working at our nonprofit. It's the law. If they don't do anything once you've reported it, they can face charges."

"But if I tell . . . I'd have to give my name. And then Hoffman would know. And everyone at the school would know. All the other professors. I'm not sure that's the best way to handle this."

Madeline already regretted dragging Sophia into the middle of the mess. She didn't want to go to anyone and report anything. She wanted to handle everything quietly and smoothly, without making a big mess—for herself or anyone else. After Zach had come on to her that way at the party, Madeline told Rebecca to keep it quiet. Not because Madeline felt she'd done anything wrong but because she wanted to handle it as quietly as possible. She hated attention, hated having anyone know what she was thinking or feeling.

She trusted Sophia—but she wanted Sophia's help in just quietly avoiding Hoffman and making the whole thing go away. Not to fan the flames until the whole campus knew.

"I'm sorry this is so awkward," Madeline said. "I don't want you to have to think about the stuff with Zach. He was drunk—"

"You don't have to apologize for that either. Zach was wrong. And he knew he was wrong. He was drunk, yes, but that's not an excuse either." She looked away for a moment, her right hand clenching and unclenching. "He and I are reaching a decision about our lives as well. But it's very different when a person with that kind of power harasses someone."

"I don't want to make a big stink," Madeline said. "I just thought you might know a way I could quietly extricate myself. That's the way I've always handled things. I don't really like to confront that much. I'd just, you know, like to quietly slip away from the whole thing."

"You can't. You just can't. You have a duty to all the other women who are going to come after you. All the other students."

"Okay, okay." Madeline knew Sophia was right, knew she was saying what any other good friend would say. But things were easier for Sophia. Better. She had a job and protection there. Hoffman could ruin her life. Fail her thesis. Make sure she didn't graduate. "Just give me time to think about this. I don't . . . I have to prepare myself for what might happen."

They left it at that. Sophia went home, but she made Madeline promise to text her if she needed to talk about anything.

Anything.

And Madeline felt better having told Sophia. Having told someone.

Maybe that was enough—just getting it out. Just saying the words to someone who listened and understood. Was that why people went to therapy? Just to be heard?

But that was the last time she saw Sophia. A week later, she heard—on Facebook—that Sophia had been found dead. Murdered in the parking lot of her office. She'd worked late, preparing for a fund-raiser. She was supposed to have a meeting, and when she didn't come home and didn't answer texts, Zach went to look for her. And found her strangled to death in her car.

And at the beginning of the new semester, in the late January cold—as she still lived her life in the fog of disbelief and grief—Hoffman reached out to her. He said he had some new ideas about her thesis. Could they get together and talk about them?

CHAPTER SIXTY-NINE

CONNOR
PRESENT

I pull the door to the classroom closed behind us when we step into the hallway.

It's empty and quiet out here. Muted voices come from behind other classroom doors, and a few students congregate at the far end of the hall, standing in a little circle, looking at something on one of their phones.

"Connor, you are way out of line coming in here like this. I'm not sure what you're thinking. I know this has been hard on you, being suspended and under suspicion this way, but you can't let your judgment get away from you like this. It's best if you just turn around and go right now. If you walk back out of here, everybody will forget it. I'll tell the students it was a misunderstanding. And Preston doesn't even have to know."

"Preston saw me coming in. He'll probably be here in a minute. I hope he is."

"I don't think you can count on Preston's help with this one. He's going to want to keep his hands clean."

"Madeline," I say. "You were sexually harassing Madeline. Before she disappeared. You insisted on helping her with her thesis because you thought I was overburdened and off my game. That's when it started. Right?"

"This is sad, Connor. I guess this is grief over your family being transferred to grief over Madeline. That is, if you're not the one who killed her."

I hold the story in the air between us. "You harassed her. You took advantage of your position on the thesis committee to keep her coming around. You dangled favors in front of her. Like a computer. It's really classic predatory behavior. And she put it all down here in this story before she died."

"That's a short story you're holding in your hand?"

"It is."

"Fiction? You're using a work of fiction to justify all of this?" Some of his perpetual condescension returns in the form of a half smirk. "You can't even believe that. You can't base that kind of accusation on a stupid story." He shakes his head, full of disappointment and disgust. "Just go, Connor. Take your sorry ass out of here and get back to what's left of your life."

"She wrote it down, and she signed her name at the end. It's like her last will and testament. She explains how your behavior led up to her disappearance. That she felt threatened by you because she revealed what you knew about Sophia's murder in her thesis. Yes, it's fiction, but that's how young fiction writers express themselves. With stories. That's the way Madeline communicates with the world. Or do you have an explanation that contradicts what she said in here?"

"I can deny it. And I will. How did you end up with that?"

I ignore his question. "Would you like to go down the hall to Preston's office? We can explain all of this to him. And he can sort it out. For all we know, there's more to the story. He wants me to go to the police. I'm sure he'd want the same for you. And maybe it's a misunderstanding. Right?"

Lance takes a step toward me. He lowers his voice and speaks in a conspiratorial whisper, one meant to convey that he and I aren't that different. That we're a couple of guys who understand each other and wouldn't do anything foolish to harm the other. Not if we could help it.

"Connor, you're being narrow here. And warped by the reactionary politics of this whole backwater state. *You* were with Madeline that last night before she disappeared. We all know that. We're all adults here. Not children. What happened to Madeline is terrible, but we don't know what she was mixed up in. Her family life was awful. She wasn't like us. She wasn't as . . . refined. She carried a lot of baggage along with her. It doesn't have to be our baggage." He comes closer and pats me on the upper arm and then flicks the papers in my hand with a dismissive index finger. "Let's just let this all go. Okay? It's not worth ending anyone's career over."

I step back, out of his reach. "She talks about writing her thesis in here. The way you helped her. Isn't that true, Lance? You helped her with her thesis. A lot."

But Lance is shaking his head. And now he's backing away. "I had to because you were AWOL."

"It's not just about the harassment, Lance. It's about the book. The book you were helping her with. The details in the book *you* gave her . . ."

His face is ashen. But it looks like I've reached him in some way.

He starts to nod, as though he agrees with me.

"Lance, we all have things we have to admit to. None of us is coming out of this unscathed."

I take a step in the direction of Preston's office. Then another.

I hold my hand out, indicating he should follow.

"Seriously, Lance. This story makes you look bad. Really bad. But if there's something you can explain . . ."

He says, "I have to tell the students I'll be . . . I'm stepping out. . . ."

"Do that," I say. "I'm going to get Preston."

I get twenty feet down the hall before I turn and look back. Lance has opened the door of the classroom, but he doesn't go in. When he sees me look back, he starts the other way.

Running.

CHAPTER SEVENTY

MADELINE
WINTER, TWO YEARS EARLIER

She agreed to meet at Troy's again.

Madeline tried to think of ways to get out of it, tried to think of excuses—including using Sophia's death and her own continuing depression—that Hoffman would believe and have to respect. But it had been four months since Sophia died, and she wondered if the statute of limitations had expired on using a friend's death as a reason to avoid people.

And whether Hoffman knew it or not, he pressed the buttons that always worked with Madeline—he wanted to talk about school. And he wanted to talk about writing. And Madeline couldn't say no.

In his e-mails setting up the meeting, Hoffman even dangled something that made Madeline more curious than anything else.

> Been thinking about your handwritten thesis over holiday break,
> as I read it more. While the quill-and-ink approach worked for
> Austen, Dumas, Tolstoy, I may have a solution to bring you into the
> 21st century.

Dear God, Madeline thought. *How I'd love to be writing in the twenty-first century.*

She remembered growing up and going to school with shoes that were a little off from what the other kids wore. Clothes that were never quite as new. Internet access that was always spotty. Her mom always telling her to suck it up and quit whining about it.

She hated to be that kid. Hated to be dragging along at the tail end of the parade.

She'd spent three years of her college career living on hot dogs and frozen burritos and store-brand peanut butter spread on stale crackers.

Yes, she thought. *I'd love a solution.*

And maybe she'd overreacted to Hoffman's behavior at Troy's the last time, his hand resting on her knee.

Would a creep touch her in such a public place where half the professors in the university sat to grade papers and informally hold office hours?

She told herself not to be so naive. Her mom once told her, *Maddy girl, it's a man's world. You have to do what you have to do.*

So Madeline vowed to do that and nothing else.

When she entered Troy's that day, Hoffman was already there. Bright and early, sitting at a table with the pages of her manuscript in front of him. And when she stepped to the counter to order a coffee—figuring that if she was going to get through the meeting, she needed and deserved some good caffeine—Hoffman popped up and paid for her order.

She thanked him, and when they sat down across from each other, she noticed that Hoffman appeared to have lost his usual energy, some of the smirking condescension he normally displayed. He looked a little like his puppy had just died.

He jumped right in.

"I feel like I owe you an apology before we begin talking about your thesis," he said.

Madeline sipped her coffee. Blazing hot and rich. She loved it that way. She couldn't get that black gold flowing out of the cheap coffeemaker in her apartment, the one she had bought at Goodwill for five dollars.

She remained quiet. Listening. Nervous.

Heart thumping from more than caffeine.

"The last time we were here, at the beginning of the last semester, and we talked about your thesis, I think I . . . I think I may have given you the wrong impression. Sometimes I get a little carried away when I talk to students, and I believe I reached out and placed my hand on your knee. I hope that gesture didn't make you uncomfortable."

He paused and seemed to be waiting for an answer.

So Madeline gave him one. "It was a little surprising. Yes."

"Well, I'm sorry about that. And I understand if you don't want me to have any more involvement in your thesis. It wasn't my intention to make you feel uncomfortable. I've given you space for these last months because of what I did. I worried . . . well, I worried you wouldn't want to have anything to do with me. I was just trying to help you while Dr. Nye was incapacitated. And I've tried to give you some space and not contact you during the rest of the fall semester, in the hope you would see I wasn't trying to hurt you or crowd you. But I wanted to apologize the whole time. So I'm doing it today. It's late, but I'm doing it."

Around them, people talked. The machines steamed and hissed behind the counter.

Hoffman looked expectant. The dynamic between them had shifted. She was judge and jury. He the accused, hoping for mercy.

You have to do what you have to do.

"It's okay," she said, shrugging it off. "Don't worry about it."

"Really?" Hoffman's face brightened. "Are you sure?"

"Yeah, it's okay. Forget about it."

"Thank you for understanding," he said. "My students are kind of my life. I don't have any children. And I'm not married, so I tend to pour myself into what I do at the university. That's why I haven't written as much poetry over the last few years. And maybe that's why I don't always know what's appropriate."

"Appropriate"? That was the word Sophia used when Madeline had told her about Hoffman.

Madeline looked down as the steam from the coffee rose past her face. Sophia. She was all Madeline could think of. Sophia had known Hoffman—a little. And Zach knew him better. Had Sophia said something to Hoffman about touching Madeline? Was that why he'd apologized?

Or had he been in a funk because of Sophia's death? Maybe they shared that shock and grief.

She wanted to know.

"Did someone . . . did—"

"Did what?"

She decided to let all of it go. To keep Sophia's name out of it. And to do whatever Hoffman needed her to do in order to complete her thesis and graduate with honors. No one in her family even had a college degree, let alone one with honors. And no one in the family would really care about the extra designation on her diploma, but she would. And wouldn't it be good to stay and finish something for once? To see it all through and suppress the impulse to run?

"It's good," Madeline said. "It's all good. Thanks."

"Okay. Thank you for understanding." He pointed to the manuscript on the table. "Shall we?"

"Sure. You said something about bringing me into the twenty-first century. Are you saying my writing feels old-fashioned? I never thought that would be a criticism."

"No, no. Not that." Madeline noticed Hoffman hadn't written anything in the margins. "I have an old computer, a desktop, one I haven't used in years. You see, my eyesight is getting to be so bad, I struggle to read. And while your handwriting is perfectly neat and clear, I'm just not used to reading it. My eyes start to hurt after an hour or so."

"I'm sorry, Dr. Hoffman. My computer died, and I just couldn't afford a new one. And I don't want to go to the lab really late at night. And I have to work."

He waved her off. "It's okay. I understand. I went to college with a Smith Corona and two extra ribbons. I understand the technology problems."

Madeline wasn't sure what he meant by Smith or Corona—she often didn't understand his allusions—and she was too mortified to ask for clarification.

"I can let you use my old computer," he said. "It's a bulky thing. Kind of heavy. But you'd be welcome to use it in order to finish the thesis. And any other work you had until you graduated. Maybe even beyond. It's just collecting dust on my table. . . ."

Madeline hadn't cried when she learned Sophia was dead. She'd wanted to, but she just couldn't get it out. Madeline couldn't remember the last time she'd cried—and certainly not the last time she'd cried in front of another person. In a public place.

But she wanted to cry in Troy's. Because of the offer of the computer.

Something she never would have been able to afford without going deeper into debt.

She stared at the tabletop, felt Hoffman's eyes on her. She drank coffee. A long, hot swallow. And wiped at her left eye, hoping it just looked like she had an itch.

For once, she didn't feel like pulling her eyebrows out.

"Thank you, Dr. Hoffman," she said. "That's incredibly generous. My study environment isn't great because my neighbor makes a lot of noise, and I have to work at the grocery store—"

"It's fine. Like I said, it's not in use. And a writer as talented as you should have the best equipment. We can figure out a way for you to pick it up before we leave." He pointed at the thesis again. "Now, as for this, I was thinking about the murder you seem to be heading for in the story. You haven't really figured out where it's going to occur, have you?"

"No. I thought maybe I'd change it to the kitchen . . . because she likes to cook for her husband."

Hoffman nodded, scratched at his chin. "Or maybe . . . and I'm just riffing a little bit here, trying out ideas. But you have this murder happening in a parking lot, which is maybe influenced by certain events in real life. But it's not very vivid. Didn't Dr. Nye ever talk to you about the importance of details? Vivid three-dimensional details."

"Well, yes—"

"Think about how important that crime scene is to the advancement of your plot. . . ."

CHAPTER SEVENTY-ONE

CONNOR
PRESENT

"Shit," I say.

Lance quickens his pace, heading down the hall toward a set of double doors that lead to a staircase.

I follow, going past the open door of the classroom. When I go by, some of the students are standing, coming over to see out into the hallway.

"Stay in there," I say.

But they ignore me. And as I go down the hall, I can hear them coming out behind me. I take a quick look back and see a couple emerging, their faces wide with curiosity.

Lance busts through the double doors, pushing with both hands and swinging them open. By the time I get there, the doors have swung back and then out into the staircase again, and I have to dodge them to avoid getting caught in between.

I see Lance going up.

"Lance. Wait."

But he keeps going, moving quickly. So I go up, following in his wake.

After one flight, I start to puff. Adrenaline does only so much to keep me moving, and I slow. Lance, despite being almost twenty years older than I am, keeps moving at a steady pace. I try to guess where he's going. Above us are offices—the History Department and then Philosophy.

Above those departments is the cupola bell tower that makes Goodlaw stand out above and beyond the rest of campus.

But why would he be going there?

No matter. I huff and puff and keep going. The phone vibrates in my pocket. I ignore it, figuring it's Diana again.

"Lance. Wait."

He doesn't slow. He goes past the next floor and the floor after that. Which means he has his sights set on the bell tower.

I've been up there only once. A few years ago, the giant solar eclipse passed over us, and Preston got his hands on the keys and allowed a few of us to go up and observe from on high. But it's supposed to be kept locked to prevent drunken students from dangling over the edge or throwing water balloons at passersby.

I reach the third floor and hear the door to the bell tower open above me. Either it's been left open, or Lance has a key.

I stop for a moment, try to catch my breath. After a few gasping heaves, I will myself forward and go up the last flight. Since it's rare for anyone to come up here, the steps are dirtier, the air mustier. But I can feel a cold draft as I go higher, meaning Lance left the door open behind him.

Then I worry he's done something rash.

I finally get there, and the heavy rusted metal door stands wide. I can see the giant bell, the arched cupola surrounding it, and, beyond that, a sweeping view of the surrounding area. The campus buildings give way to the town and then the countryside. Bare trees, rolling hills. It's beautiful, even in winter.

But I don't know why I'm here.

"Lance?"

Something scrapes across the way, on the far side of the bell. I see

Lance, standing over there, about fifteen feet away, with his hands resting on the metal railing that rings the cupola platform.

It's cold up here. The wind picks up and lifts my hair.

"What are you doing up here?" I ask. "It's too cold. Come down and talk to Preston."

"Preston doesn't care. You know who he's looking out for. He can't help me."

"Then come down and talk to somebody. A counselor or a lawyer. Whatever you need. Just don't stand up here. You're right at the edge, and it's dangerous."

I'm still in the doorway, but I take a step out into the tower itself. I immediately feel the vertiginous drop on all sides of me. I see students walking by below us, cars passing on the street. My head whirls, and I reach out, bracing myself against the railing.

"This will ruin me, Connor." His voice reaches me over the wind. "You're trying to ruin me."

"I'm not trying to do anything but get to the truth." I'm still holding the story, so I wave it around. "Madeline is telling her side here. I'm giving it to the police and the university. We have to listen to it. We have an obligation."

"You sound like Preston. All his talk about needing to listen to women. All of that crap."

"He's right. Don't you agree?"

"He's a great talker."

"Lance, if you harassed a student, then you just need to come clean about it. You're going to face the music with Human Resources. And I don't know about the stuff with Sophia and the book that Madeline wrote about it, but it's not worth this . . . being up here. . . . It's dangerous. Just come down. Explain it."

"Coming down is more dangerous," he says.

"Are you saying Madeline is telling the truth in this story? Downstairs you said not to believe it. Did Zach tell you these things that went into the book? If he killed Sophia, he would know."

Lance looks away from me and over the railing. A few students have gathered below us, looking up. Enjoying the show. I see one of them has a phone out, taking video.

"It's so much more complicated than you even know," he says.

CHAPTER SEVENTY-TWO

MADELINE
WINTER, TWO YEARS EARLIER

A couple of weeks passed after their last meeting in Troy's, and Madeline hadn't heard from Hoffman again.

In Troy's, he gave her a number of interesting suggestions about how to improve the book and move the plot forward toward its conclusion, and Madeline left the coffee shop that cold afternoon buzzing from the caffeine and overly excited about returning to work on her thesis.

She also wanted to get her hands on that computer—the one Hoffman had offered to let her use. But when their meeting ended, Hoffman stood up without saying anything else about it. He started talking to a student at another table, and he and Madeline made no plans for how to get the computer to her.

She thought he'd bring it up again. By e-mail. In the hallways of Goodlaw.

But she didn't see him or talk to him.

And Madeline knew how forgetful Hoffman was. Late, scattered, disorganized. Maybe he was still giving her space, keeping his distance. Leaving the ball in her court.

She'd almost cried when he offered the computer. She reached the point weeks later when she wanted to cry again because it wasn't going to happen. She worked her way up to letting it go, writing it off. It was one of those things people said in the moment but they don't really mean. Just a gesture, like when someone asks how you are doing but doesn't really want to hear the answer.

But Hoffman had been so helpful with the thesis. And he'd seemed so willing to hand the computer over. Eager even. And Madeline couldn't stop picturing herself sitting in her apartment, typing away. With her headphones on to block out the neighbor's music. After all, even once a draft of the thesis was complete, she'd have to type the whole thing again for the Honors College. How was she going to do that in a computer lab in the middle of the night?

So she e-mailed him on a rare night off from the grocery store, gently asking if she might still be able to get her hands on that computer he had mentioned. And if he'd already given it to someone else, she understood.

Hoffman wrote back immediately. As if he was sitting at his computer, waiting for her to write:

> My apologies, Madeline. The computer is yours. I'd deliver it to a neutral location right now, but I'm in my cups and shouldn't drive. (I've had a DUI before, sorry to say.) I can bring it to campus another day. Or you are welcome to come to the house and pick it up. Do you remember where I live?

She thought "in his cups" meant he was drunk. Right? Was it something from Shakespeare?

Did she want to wait? Did she want to waste the evening she had off work and not write?

She could stick to pen . . . and feel like the kid showing up to school in the off-brand shoes with the haircut given by her mother over the kitchen sink. . . .

It was the kind of thing she might ask Sophia about.

But couldn't.

I'll be there in about fifteen minutes. If that's okay.

When she arrived at his house, Hoffman opened the door. He stepped way back when he let her in, acting as though Madeline were carrying some kind of highly contagious germ that might leap over to him if they came within five feet of each other. He held a drink in his hand, amber liquid in a short glass. No ice. His eyes looked watery and red. His hair was mussed, like he'd been asleep.

With the hand that held the glass, he pointed across the room to a small table with a computer on top. "There it is. Nothing fancy, but it works. I kept up with the updates. Mostly. No printer, but you can do that on campus anytime. Right?"

"Yes. Thank you."

Hoffman stood with the door open. Things grew a little awkward. Madeline didn't know if she was just supposed to walk over, unhook the computer from the wall, and go. Or did she need to wait for him to say something else?

"I have been thinking about the book a little more," he said. His words sounded a little sloppy, a little slurred. How much had he had to drink? "I do that sometimes. Discuss a student's work with them, and then other thoughts occur to me later that I forgot to share. If I don't write them down right away, I forget. Like most everything." He points to the door. "I'm going to close this for a second."

Madeline started to say he didn't have to, but it wasn't her house. And were they going to stand at the front door with it wide open and have a conversation?

She tried not to let her eyes trail to the rear of the house, to the yard and the alley beyond, where Zach had placed his hands on her like she was a piece of meat. She hadn't seen or heard anything from him or about him since Sophia's death four months earlier. Just that he was a "person of interest" in her case but hadn't been charged or arrested.

Every time she saw that phrase online—"person of interest"—in relation to Zach, she shivered. Were the hands that ran up her body and under her shirt the hands of a killer?

"I had some ideas about the behavior of the husband character," Hoffman said.

It was like he'd read her mind. Did Hoffman know who everybody in the book was? Zach and Sophia? Would everyone?

Was that what it was like when you were a writer? Your innermost thoughts got shared with the whole world? And anyone who wanted could examine them and draw their own conclusions about you and the people around you?

Hoffman walked across the room. His bare feet shuffled, and the steps seemed to require more effort than they should. He went to the couch and slumped down onto it, the drink still in his hand. He rubbed his eyes, and when he took his hand away, the lids drooped.

On the coffee table in front of him, she saw pages of her manuscript. The ones he hadn't read yet when they met at Troy's. Ones he promised to give back just as soon as he made it through them.

"I told you I'd indulged a little," he said. "Maybe more than a little. Let me just tell you this, and then you can take that machine out of here."

Madeline stood with her arms crossed, her car keys still in her hand. She'd seen Hoffman drunk and high at the party, but him sitting on his own couch that way, on a weeknight, barefoot and sleepy, made him seem particularly pathetic. Was that the way he spent most of his evenings? And maybe all of his weekends too? Drowsy from booze, slipping away after reading the ten thousandth student poem or story of his career?

"This husband character," he said, scratching his head. "What's his name?"

"Trevor."

Hoffman snapped his fingers. "That's it."

Madeline found her hand going up to her eye and stopped the tic.

But she wasn't sure how long she could hold it off while she was in that house.

"He needs to be more sympathetic," Hoffman said. "The problem is, you paint him as an unmitigated jackass. And he may be that. But you have to allow the reader to feel some empathy for him. No character is all good or all bad. Did Dr. Nye teach you to write in such cartoonish ways? Or are you just trying to turn a man into an easy target? It's easy to do but doesn't make for good literature." Hoffman finished what remained in his glass and set it on the floor by his feet. He yawned, covering his mouth. "Give us something about him we can relate to. Does he collect stamps? Have a dog? Did his dad leave the family when he was young? Who knows? That can mess a person up. Just a little of that so we have a fuller picture of the guy. He can still be the killer, but give him a redeeming quality too. We all have them. Even I have them. I wouldn't want to be depicted in such a one-dimensional way."

As soon as he said it, Madeline understood what he meant. She hadn't shown another side of Trevor, mainly because she hadn't wanted to. She'd based him on Zach, and she hated Zach. So why not take out on the character what she couldn't do in real life?

But she remembered something Dr. Nye said once: *As a writer, you have to understand all of your characters so the reader can understand them.*

She needed to understand Trevor—not Zach—better in order to write about him more effectively.

"That makes sense," she said. "I can definitely do that."

Hoffman made no response. His breathing was deep. He was snoring on the couch, his head lolled back so far, it looked like it might fall off.

Madeline looked at the computer, looked at the pages on the coffee table. She listened to the snorting breaths coming out of Hoffman's nose. She turned, and on the pass-through window from the kitchen to the living room, she saw a bottle of Four Roses bourbon. Almost empty.

How much had he had that night?

Did he need help?

If Hoffman drank that much every night, he'd probably be okay. But how did she know?

She went closer, picking up the pages. She saw a few notes, written in red ink and a pinched script. Just a few notes, and she knew she'd have to rewrite those pages so Nye didn't see them.

She sat in a chair turned perpendicular to the couch, her eyes on Hoffman until she was sure he was still breathing. Then she started to read.

CHAPTER SEVENTY-THREE

CONNOR
PRESENT

I take another tentative step toward Lance. I reach out for the railing next to me to steady myself.

I hate being up here. So high. So cold. I want to turn and go back inside.

I want to walk away.

But Lance can't be left alone.

"What's more complicated?" I ask. "Tell me."

Lance turns to face me, and his back is against the railing.

I risk another glance down. A police car, lights flashing, pulls up in front of the building. In the distance, I hear a siren. A fire engine turns onto the street that fronts Goodlaw and heads our way. Maybe Diana called Bowman anyway, told the cops to get to Goodlaw.

I want Preston to appear, either behind me or on the ground. Lance might listen to him. Preston might be the only one Lance would listen to.

But Lance remains silent, watching me. I have to keep him talking.

"According to this story, which she wrote after she came back to town, Madeline wanted to expose *you*. The character of the professor is described exactly like you. He has your mannerisms, your clothes."

"You're quite the detective."

"Lance, none of us is perfect. I shouldn't have been drinking with my students as much as I was. I was out with Madeline's class the night she disappeared. Maybe if I'd been clearheaded, I could have helped her. Look, I need to admit my mistakes, and you can come down and admit what you did. We'll both face the music."

"Drinking with students is nothing. Madeline thought *I* killed Sophia," he says.

"I know. The story says that too."

"It's because of her thesis," he says. When he says those words, he seems calmer, like he's on steadier ground. "Madeline and I worked on that book together. I had to carry her through that project because you weren't there for the students."

"You're right about that."

"I just started reading your book last night, Connor." He laughs, a sound that cuts through the wind and the shouts that reach us from below. People are trying to get our attention. A cop with a megaphone calls up.

We ignore them.

"I hate thrillers," he says. "And I couldn't stand that you published that book and made all that money."

"It wasn't a lot of money. I promise."

"More than I'll ever make writing poetry." He looks down, makes a slashing motion across his throat, trying to silence the cop. "I don't even write anymore. I don't write anything. But you published that book. And I told myself I wasn't going to read it or anything about it. I refused to. At the library that night . . . I went to the bathroom while you were talking. But you know, finally . . . I couldn't resist. I wanted to know what you'd written, what the big deal was. So I started it . . . and lo and behold, it was awfully damn familiar. Awfully familiar."

His words have a strange effect on me. I feel a weight lift off my shoulders.

He knows. Somebody besides Diana and Madeline finally knows. . . .

"So tell everyone, Lance. Go down and tell Preston. I'm ready to tell the police and my publisher anyway. I'll be ruined. Okay? Won't that make you happy? We can be ruined together."

"I wish I could do that, Connor. I'd like nothing more than to see your career ended."

"We're colleagues, Lance. We're even kind of supposed to be friends."

"We're not friends." He leans back against the railing. "And I'm not coming down and going to jail."

CHAPTER SEVENTY-FOUR

MADELINE
WINTER, TWO YEARS EARLIER

Madeline sat in the chair, reading Hoffman's notes on her pages while he snored on the couch.

From time to time he stirred. His body shifted. Or one of his snorting inhalations reached a crescendo, almost waking him up. But he stayed passed out, head tilted back in that awkward pose. She could tell his neck was going to feel like shit when he finally woke up.

His comments inspired her. Again.

They were detailed. Rich.

Vivid.

They made her want to get back to work. To write. To make the book better.

She stood up and went to the computer, turning it on. It made a low grinding noise as it started, and she pulled up a chair and sat, waiting for everything to load and open.

When it was ready, she started typing, revising the most recent chapter she'd written based on Hoffman's notes. When he woke up and was out of his stupor, she could take the computer home and keep going.

And going and going.

She'd write so much faster with the computer in her apartment.

She started typing. And she lost herself in the work. She wasn't sure how much time had passed. Thirty minutes? Forty-five? She made it through one chapter. And then was on to the next.

She couldn't say how long he stood behind her.

Seconds? Minutes?

She didn't know he was there until his hand slid over her shoulder and landed on her breast, cupping it.

Madeline spun one way and jerked her body the other.

"Whoa, whoa," Hoffman said, standing over her. He lifted both hands in the air. "Just checking in on you."

He backed up two steps but remained between her and the door.

Madeline immediately looked at the door. For an exit.

The back door, the one that led out to the patio, where students smoked during his parties, was closed and covered by a curtain. Probably locked. And if she ran over there and had to fumble with the lock in order to get out, it would be too late.

And Hoffman's body, which was short and squat, stood between her and the front door. She didn't think Hoffman looked especially strong or powerful, but she thought he would be strong enough to stop her.

"Stop it," she said, not caring how harsh she sounded.

"Madeline, don't be like that. None of this has to be like that. We're connecting here."

"I'm going to go," she said. "And I want you to let me go." She pointed past him. "Out that door. The one I came in."

But Hoffman didn't move. He placed his hands on his hips and seemed to be anchoring himself into place, as if he expected her to charge at him and try to knock him down.

Which she might have to do. And she didn't think that would work.

She started to sweat. Sticky beads popping out on her forehead. Her breath came in small gulps.

"Madeline, I was just . . . Look, I feel close to you. We can be close to each other. And I had another idea for the book. I wanted to tell you. Why don't you stay and reconsider, and then we can talk some more?"

Madeline's hands shook. Her eyes made a quick dash around the room, looking for a weapon. A fireplace poker, a bookend. A baseball bat or a hammer.

But she saw nothing. Just the computer. She wanted it. Wanted to use it to rewrite her novel. But she couldn't take it from Hoffman.

And she couldn't carry it out the door alone. She had to let it go. She'd e-mailed her file to herself, so she needed to go. She needed to go because Hoffman was a pig. And tying strings to her acceptance of the computer. Terrible, terrible strings.

Just run.

Just go for it.

"I'm leaving now," she said, trying to sound as firm and confident as possible. She thought she'd pulled it off.

"Where are you going?"

"I'm going home. I need to work on this . . . and I don't want you touching me. Ever."

"Oh, Madeline." He remained in the rigid, solid position between her and the door. He showed no inclination to move. "I'm disappointed in you. I thought we really understood each other. I thought we could have fun. And work on your thesis, which I think I've made quite a bit better with my insights. Are you going to run off like a scared little girl?"

"I'm not a little girl. And I don't want anything else from you."

"What about the computer? My generous offer?"

"I don't need it. I'll . . . figure something else out."

"And handwrite your way through your last semester of college? That will surely impress everyone."

"Are you going to let me leave?" she asked. "I'll scream."

Then Hoffman laughed. He shook his head dismissively, and he laughed. A low chuckle, the kind of thing someone would do when a child acted foolish or immature.

"Oh, Madeline. And you say you're not a little girl?"

He took a step toward her.

Madeline tensed. Her hands clenched into fists.

Hoffman laughed again and walked past her, heading out to the kitchen. He opened a cabinet and started whistling.

Madeline dashed for the front of the house and grabbed the door-knob like it was a lifeline. She worried it was locked, that she'd be trapped inside still. But the knob turned, and she pulled the door open, felt the cool air from the outside rushing against her face.

"Wait."

Madeline hated herself for looking back. But she did.

Hoffman stayed in the kitchen, looking out. He made no attempt at coming closer.

"I'll give you a lovely parting gift," he said. "A freebie. And you can always remember who helped you more with the creation of your book than anyone else. The murder weapon in the book. Make it something personal, something that means a great deal to Sarah. A vintage scarf. A family heirloom. Something handed down to her, something she treasured. That will have the biggest kick for the reader."

Madeline stayed rooted in place for a moment. The detail he gave was so weird, so specific—it seemed like he was conjuring it from memory and not from imagination.

And what was it Dr. Nye always said—if a detail was weird and specific enough, the reader would believe it was true?

Madeline knew Sophia had been strangled in her car outside work. Everybody knew that. She'd pictured the crime in her head many times—and when she slept, it emerged in her dreams—and she always saw thick hands grasping Sophia, squeezing the life out of her.

But sometimes she thought about what Detective Wallace had told her—maybe the killer got his thrills by using a piece of clothing instead of his hands?

So was Hoffman just summoning a specific detail out of thin air?

Madeline hoped so. But the detail came to him so quickly, so effortlessly, and he seemed so . . . gleeful about sharing it. So much like the very mention of the detail of the scarf served as a triumph for him.

"I'm leaving—"

But Hoffman went on. And as he talked, the look on his face became distant. Almost . . . haunted? Like he was really seeing what he described. "Madeline, you can almost imagine the body slumped over to the right against the steering wheel. And the hands . . . her hands . . . the right resting on the seat. With the palm facing up. The left . . . let's say the left hand was hanging limply at her side. The middle nail on that left hand, cracked. Painted red but broken from the struggle with her assailant." His gaze focused again. "Ghastly, really. Terribly vivid if you describe it right."

The air from the outside felt colder than the temperature. It reached inside and chilled her bones.

She shivered.

And went out without closing the door behind her.

CHAPTER SEVENTY-FIVE

CONNOR
PRESENT

The cop speaks to us again through the megaphone.

"Is everybody all right? Does anybody up there need medical attention?"

Lance makes the throat-slash gesture again.

More students and faculty members have gathered on the lawn. They all look up, like we're the eclipse. Or maybe like we're animals in the zoo about to put on a spectacular show.

"You should talk to a lawyer, Lance. Maybe there's something you can work out. A plea, whatever."

He's looking down, ignoring me. Some of the students are from my class, the one Lance was just teaching. And they wave.

Where the hell is Preston?

But I don't see him.

My phone vibrates again. I take it out and check. Now it's a text from Diana. She's telling me the police want to search my house. They want to know if the knife that killed Madeline came from my kitchen.

I hold the phone up. "Lance, the murder weapon. They think it came from my house. The knife. I had it in my pocket one night when Madeline hit me with a bottle. But when I came to, the knife was gone. They think the killer used it on Madeline the next night when she was murdered in the cemetery. But the only person I know who was in the house with me that night *was* Madeline. Why would she take the knife out of my house? What would that do for her?"

"She was crazy," Lance says.

"Were *you* following her?" I ask. "I thought it was Zach. I kind of hope it was Zach. But maybe . . . Grendel didn't bark at whoever was in the house, which means he was familiar with the person. Did you come into the house while I was out on the floor? Did you take the knife because you were looking for a chance to frame me?"

"So what if I did, Connor?"

"And the night I found Madeline's body . . . that was the night I brought Grendel to Preston's house, the night after you must have taken the knife. Maybe Madeline came looking for me again while I was out. And I didn't go home right away that night after I dropped Grendel off. I drove around for a while and ended up at the cemetery . . . and maybe you were looking for her at my house again. Did you come across her and kill her that night?"

"I knew Madeline wanted to expose me," Lance says. "Why else would she come back to town that way? She was going to do the same to you, wasn't she? About the book? She wanted to take us all down. I hadn't seen or heard from her in two years. I kind of assumed she'd moved on to another life . . . but then she came back. . . ."

"We all failed her, Lance. Clearly."

Lance swings one leg over the railing, onto the narrow ledge surrounding the bell tower. I can hear the gasps from the crowd below.

"What about these things she wrote about you and Sophia? How did you know the details of Sophia's murder?"

He swings his other leg over to the sound of more gasps. He keeps two hands on the railing, the only thing holding him in place. His back is to the void, the open air four floors down to the ground.

I feel shaky. Unsteady. Like I might fall over. The height.

Lance's refusal to answer or explain.

"What was your connection to Sophia?" I ask.

"You know how I am. I had to be the big shot, had to run my mouth and give Madeline the best details for her book. I drank. I talked. And I'll be honest, Connor—I wanted to make you look bad. I wanted to be seen as the better teacher, the one the students came to when they really needed help. That's why I moved in and worked with Madeline on that thesis. That's why I told her every great detail I could think of."

"Because you hated me."

"I hated being eclipsed by you," he says. "Younger. More successful. I regretted telling her so much. My problems with drinking bit me in the ass. I tried to talk to her, to get the thesis back. . . . I had no choice once I'd said so much."

"How did you *know* the details you gave her? Did Zach tell you? I know you were friends. Is that it? Zach killed Sophia and told you what happened? And you gave it to Madeline for the book? If that's it—"

"Whatever you want to believe, Connor. Zach's my friend. I hated seeing him dragged through the mud when Sophia died. Friends have to stick together. They do. People have problems we may not see or know about."

"But what happened to Sophia was horrible."

"I knew she wanted to pursue a harassment claim against me on Madeline's behalf. I'd have lost everything, Connor. And I don't have that much. Without my job . . . my students . . . I haven't written a word in years. I don't think I can anymore. If Madeline or Sophia came forward about what Madeline perceived as harassment, there'd be nothing for me. . . ."

"Lance, come down."

He lifts one hand from the railing. He wobbles on the ledge.

I take two quick steps across the landing, reaching for him.

But I'm too late.

He lets go with the other hand and falls backward, his body bouncing once off the side of the building and then flying out into open space.

I watch from the railing as his body spins once and then heads directly for the ground.

The crowd below gasps. And screams.

And they spread out.

And I watch as Lance lands on the sidewalk among them all, his body hitting with a sickening splat I hear all the way up in the bell tower.

CHAPTER SEVENTY-SIX

MADELINE

SPRING, TWO YEARS EARLIER

Madeline hated walking alone. At night.

Ever since Sophia's murder, she'd tried not to go anywhere alone after dark. She wasn't crazy about walking around alone during daylight either. She frequently looked over her shoulder or changed direction to avoid anyone who looked suspicious.

No, she corrected herself—*to avoid any* man *who looked suspicious.*

But that night she had no choice. She had followed Nye home because she thought he needed help. And he pretty clearly did. If she hadn't followed along behind him, he might have been lying in the street, passed out, sprawled out over the curb and the gutter until someone else saw him.

If they saw him in time . . .

Nye wasn't in good shape. Not at all. But she'd left the thesis with him because she wanted him to read it. And if he read it and saw those details about the murder of "Sarah," and if he was able to piece it together, maybe he'd know what to do about Zach. He could tell her it was nothing to worry about, not to let her imagination run wild.

And Nye was somebody the police would listen to and trust if it came to talking to them about it. . . .

Madeline felt a weight lift from her shoulders when she saw her car in the glow of a streetlight a block away. The car meant safety. Warmth.

Yes, even freedom. It was a piece of shit, nine years old, with bad wipers and crappy tires. But it ran. It could take her just about anywhere she needed to go.

It could take her home, where she could wedge the chair under the door, grab her frying pan, retreat into her thoughts, and look forward to the future. Whatever it might hold.

"Madeline."

She froze. She held her keys in her right hand. But hadn't stuck them through her fingers the way her mother had taught her when she was in high school. *Maddy girl, those keys are a weapon you're always carrying. Go right for the eyes if you have to.*

Madeline turned and looked to the right, in the direction of the voice. *Is this going to be Zach?*

Instead Dr. Hoffman emerged from between two buildings and walked toward her in his slumped, shuffling gait. He wore a winter coat too bulky for the warming weather. And he looked older than ever before, like he was weighed down by something heavy.

What in the name of God does he want? Madeline didn't feel like dealing with his bullshit again. . . .

As he approached, she looked at the car. She could dash right for it, run around to the driver's side, and get the key in. . . . But was all of that worth it? Hoffman held all the power. Eventually he'd get close to her again. If she tried to report him, he could damage her reputation at school. Bad-mouth her to the other professors.

Call her a liar.

"I'm just on my way home," she said, feeling compelled to offer some kind of explanation. But it sounded weak in the darkness.

Hoffman kept coming, almost reaching her, his hands stuffed deep in his pockets.

"We have a problem, Madeline," he said, sounding very sad. Looking like a whipped dog. "I've been trying to reach you for two days. You won't answer my e-mails asking for a meeting. I couldn't find you in Goodlaw. It's like you're avoiding me."

"I won't tell anyone about . . . what happened at your house the other night. It was just a misunderstanding. That's all. I shouldn't have come over, and you were drinking."

For a moment, Hoffman looked confused. Like they were having two different conversations. Then his face cleared. "Oh, I'm not talking about our little misunderstanding. Those kinds of things happen between teachers and students. That's not my concern."

"Then . . . I'm sorry. . . . What are we talking about?"

"Your book," he said, standing at the edge of the streetlight's glow. "Those details I provided to you. I got carried away. I got fanciful. And I spoke as though I had some understanding and insight into things I really don't know a lot about. Talking like a big shot takes me away from myself, from my own depressive thoughts."

As so often happened with Hoffman, Madeline found herself lost, unable to follow exactly what he was talking about. And why.

"I think that's okay," she said. "It's just fiction. You were helping me write the book."

Hoffman looked to his left, in the direction Madeline had just come from. The direction of Dr. Nye's house. "You were with Connor. A post-class drink, I presume. Of course, he invited only the kids who are over twenty-one, right? He's quite the rule follower."

"He got home okay. I made sure."

"I bet you did. Let me ask you—did you show Dr. Nye the thesis pages? With those details I provided?"

Madeline hesitated. She wasn't sure which answer was the correct one. Which answer would cause the least trouble for everyone. For Nye. For herself.

"It's fiction, Dr. Hoffman. I wrote fiction. And I never told Dr. Nye you were helping me. That's what you told me to do."

Hoffman looked even more deflated. "So you *did* use those details. And turned them in to Dr. Nye." His head turned in the direction of Dr. Nye's house again. "Is he okay?"

"He is. He's fine."

"Maybe we need to talk further, Madeline," Hoffman said. "In private. I have a problem when I drink, as I did the other night. . . . I talk a lot, and then I regret it. Sometimes, like now, I regret what I say quite a lot. And some of those things I said, those imaginative details about the murder weapon and the crime scene and the body I provided, they might prove hurtful."

"Hurtful? You mean, Dr. Nye will be hurt because you helped me more than he did?"

"Can we forget about Connor for a second?"

His voice rose in volume and became sharp. Madeline saw that something else was on his mind, something more urgent.

"Okay," she said.

"I know you're friends with Sophia, right?"

"Yes. I am. Was."

"And what happened to her is terrible. A tragedy. But it's also led to a lot of misunderstanding. If those details I told you get out, then there will be more misunderstanding. Even by people you know and are connected to."

"I did use those things you told me because they were so good. They made the book better just like you said. They were vivid and real. You were right when you said the perfect details make the book more powerful."

"Of course I was right about that," he said. "But those details are going to cast certain people in a bad light."

"Oh . . ."

Zach appeared in Madeline's mind. Again. The hands that touched her at Hoffman's house . . . were they the same hands that . . . ?

"A thesis is a public document. The defense is a public event. Everyone will know about it. And people will get hurt. And that's not good."

"I don't want anyone else to get hurt," she said.

"Anyone else? See, that's it. Someone will get hurt by this thesis. Anyone who reads it will think the worst."

Madeline's mouth felt dry. Her head started to hurt. It was the beer. And she hadn't eaten.

And her heart raced more and more as the conversation went on.

"We're talking about Zach? That people will think the worst of Zach if these details get out? I know you and he are friends. And he's a suspect. Is that why you're worried about this? About him?"

It became Hoffman's turn to look confused. "Zach?"

Madeline said it before she could stop herself. "Yes, Zach. Is he the one who told you those details? I mean, everyone thinks he did it."

"Everyone does think he's guilty, don't they?"

"Pretty much," Madeline said. "But I can get the thesis back if—"

"You're right, Madeline. Those details I gave you will make a lot of people look bad. It will cast guilt on more people than just Zach. And they will cause a lot of problems." Hoffman took a step closer, crowding her. "You've found yourself in the middle of this quite by accident, haven't you?"

More people than Zach?

He couldn't mean Connor. Connor seemed to know nothing.

Hoffman meant himself. *He* knew the details. *He* was involved somehow. And *he* wanted Madeline to keep her mouth shut about what she knew.

"I think I should go. . . ."

"That's a great idea," Hoffman said. "Why don't we pursue this conversation further back at your apartment? I figure you don't want to come to my house again. But if I'm not mistaken, you live just a few blocks on the other side of downtown? Near campus? We could go back there and sort this out. It's very important that we do. A number of people are involved, and I think once you hear what I have to say and how important it is, you'll understand. I mean, you'll have to."

Madeline backed up, taking a step toward her car. "Sure, I think I do understand."

"I thought you would. So I'll see you there? That's One-oh-nine Fourteenth Street, right? Apartment three?"

Madeline nodded. She struggled to find any words.

Hoffman's posture stiffened like some of the weight had been lifted from him.

Madeline backed up and got into her car. Hoffman stood there on the sidewalk. He gave her a thumbs-up and turned and walked away, no doubt heading for his car. And then for her apartment.

Madeline shivered. She wished she had worn a heavier coat.

She wished she lived in the tropics, someplace she would never get cold again.

She started the car, knowing she couldn't go home. She couldn't go where Hoffman might find her.

PART IV

CHAPTER SEVENTY-SEVEN

REBECCA
PRESENT

Rebecca sits on the steps on the side of Goodlaw Hall.

She has her head resting in her hands, her backpack by her feet. She sits alone, the concrete cold beneath her. She can feel it through her jeans. But she has her coat open, her hat stuffed in her pocket.

She tries very hard not to remember seeing what she just saw.

Like the rest of the class—the rest of the building, really—she went outside and looked up. She saw Dr. Nye and Dr. Hoffman in the bell tower talking to each other. Dr. Nye held some papers in his hand, and he seemed to be trying to get Hoffman to come in. Twice he waved his arms that way, as if he was saying, *Come on, come on. It's okay.*

But Hoffman climbed over the railing and put his feet on the ledge.

And when Rebecca saw that, she felt her stomach drop, like she was about to throw up. She lifted her hand to her mouth, ready to turn away and vomit.

And then Hoffman let go, stepping back into thin air, four stories above the ground.

He bounced once off the top of the building, and then his body tumbled in space like an insane acrobat. . . .

She turned away before he hit the ground.

But she heard the noise. Heard the screams and the gasps and the sirens—

She shakes her head, as if that could make the memory go away. Forever.

She knows it won't. She knows she'll be seeing that for the rest of her life. She hasn't even called her mom yet, but needs to. It will be on the news. On Twitter. It likely already is, the videos students took being posted and hashtagged so the whole world can see Dr. Hoffman's death. It will trend before the day is out.

She feels sick again. She swallows hard, trying to get some saliva into her mouth.

"Are you okay?"

She looks up when she hears a voice.

"Dr. White."

The head of the English Department is standing in front of her. He's not wearing a coat despite the cold. And his face is drained of color. Pretty much like everyone else's.

She doesn't know him very well, hasn't taken any of his classes. She really only knows how he acted that day he came into Nye's class to tell everyone Hoffman was taking over. And that day he acted like he didn't want to answer any questions at all.

He looks concerned today. His eyebrows are raised, and he's offering her a tentative smile, one meant to make her feel like it's okay to talk to him.

"Are you doing okay?" he asks. "Would you like to go inside?"

"I feel better out here, actually. It's cold, but . . . I like it here."

"Sure."

And he just stands there in front of her like he doesn't have anywhere else to be. Rebecca can hear voices from the front of the building, where the police and the other first responders are cleaning up the mess and asking everybody questions. Where they're taking Hoffman's body off the ground and loading it into an ambulance . . . or a hearse or whatever it is. Students pass occasionally, all of them looking shocked, their hands covering their mouths, their phones out as they call and text friends.

"You're in Dr. Hoffman's class right now, aren't you?" he asks.

"Well, really, it's Nye's class. But then it was Hoffman's."

And now . . .

Would there be anyone to teach the class? What the fuck was going on?

"Right," White says. "I remember seeing you in there the other day. I guess I was wondering. . . . Has Dr. Hoffman been acting strange recently? Has he said or done anything that would make you think he was having problems?"

Rebecca almost laughs. Everything Hoffman did was strange. His long-winded stories, his political rants. His clothes.

But then she thinks about the question seriously and sees what White might be fishing for. Rebecca remembers going to talk to Hoffman about her thesis and how interested he was in talking about Madeline. Then Dr. Nye pulled her into the alley by Troy's and wanted to talk about Madeline and that guy at the party and sent her to tell the police all about it.

And last night . . . just over twelve hours ago . . . Hoffman showed up at her house and seemed to be warning her about saying anything else about Madeline.

Is that what Nye and Hoffman were arguing about?

Is that why they went up on the roof together?

Because of Madeline?

Madeline—who dropped that manuscript off on Rebecca's porch.

With the story at the end about the professor who looked and sounded just like Hoffman.

Rebecca never lies. She hates to do it. Even when she was a kid and did something stupid like steal a cookie or get into her mom's makeup without permission, she always confessed. She never made up a story or blamed someone else.

But she has no idea what's going on right now. No idea how she ended up in the middle of these bizarre events. And White is standing over her, his face less friendly than when he first showed up. Now it's eager, like he thinks she knows something, and he just needs her to admit it to him. And she hasn't even talked to the police or her parents or Dr. Nye. . . .

"No," she says, deciding not to mention Hoffman's visit the night before. "I mean, he's kind of a weird guy. But . . . that was just the way he acted in class. You know? Kind of . . . eccentric? But he didn't really say anything else. I've been in his class only a few days."

White leans farther forward, looming over her a little like he's a tree and she's in his shade. "So he didn't do or say anything unusual, inside or outside of class? See, I have to talk to the police because I'm the department head. And they're going to want to know what the students were thinking or seeing about Dr. Hoffman and Dr. Nye. So you would know very well. Are you sure there's nothing else to say?"

"I don't think so."

"Because it's *very* important—"

"Dr. White?"

Both Rebecca and Dr. White turn and look. A police officer stands about twenty feet away, and when they look, he walks toward them.

"Are you Dr. White?" he asks.

"Yes, I am."

"We've been trying to find you," he says.

Dr. White straightens up, and his jaw sets firmly. "I was in a meeting in another building. And then I stopped here to help this student, who is obviously upset. We do have an obligation to help the students."

"Sure," the cop says. "But our lead, Detective Bowman, needs to talk to you as soon as possible. If you could . . ."

The cop waves his hand, as if to say: *That means right now.*

Dr. White sighs. He looks down at Rebecca and says, "We'll be in touch, Rebecca. Just let me know if I can do anything to help."

Rebecca just nods and watches him go with the cop.

And she realizes she feels relief once he's gone.

CHAPTER SEVENTY-EIGHT

CONNOR
PRESENT

A cop comes into the classroom where they've been talking to me.

Questioning me.

It's not a room I've ever taught in before. Not in all my years here.

They must have brought me here because it's empty and kind of out of the way.

The uniformed cop comes over to Bowman and whispers to her. I'm not meant to hear, but I do. He tells Bowman he's found Dr. White, the department chair.

"Where was he?" she asks.

I'm wondering the same thing. He saw me come into Goodlaw, heading for Lance's classroom. . . .

"He had a meeting in another building. And then I found him talking to a student over on the side. The kid looked kind of green around the gills."

"No doubt," Bowman says. "She just watched a professor take a header off the bell tower. Okay, I'll talk to him in a minute."

The cop leaves, and Bowman turns back to me. She has the story Madeline left in my house on the desk in front of her. Another uniformed cop stands to the side with a notebook in his hand, writing down what I say. And Diana stands near me, keeping an eye on the conversation. So far, she's let me answer every question they've asked.

"Just to regroup, Dr. Nye," Bowman says, "it's Madeline O'Brien who actually wrote the book you published. *My Best Friend's Murder.* The book is really, really good, by the way. She wrote it, and you passed it off as your own work. And the reason the details in that book line up so closely with the details of Sophia Greenfield's murder is because Lance Hoffman coached Madeline while she wrote the book and gave her details about the murder weapon and the crime scene, which she included in the manuscript. The ones that were never made public. And he admitted all this on the roof before he stepped out into thin air."

"Lance knew what happened to Sophia. He knew what happened in that car. He was motivated to silence Madeline and Sophia."

"And he admitted to killing both women? Madeline and Sophia?"

"No, he didn't. But he didn't deny it either."

"Why not just admit it if you were going to jump off the building?"

"Why jump off the building if you didn't do it?" I ask.

"Good point," Diana says.

Bowman taps the papers in front of her. "And this tipped you off. This story Madeline left in your house after she beaned you with the bourbon bottle."

"It's a story about a young woman coming back to the town where she went to college in order to confront a professor who not only sexually harassed her but who also knew very specific details of the murder of her friend. And the description of the college and the town and the professor match real life here exactly. It's Gatewood and Commonwealth and Lance. To a tee. She spelled it out. So she came back to confront me, but also to confront Lance and leave this story behind. And Lance killed her over it. Madeline said she thought someone was following her. Lance knew I went to the cemetery, and so did Madeline. The night Madeline was killed, I wasn't home. Maybe she went looking for me. At my house and then at the cemetery. If Lance was following her, he ended up there as well."

"Madeline told you she was being followed?"

"Yes. You see, Madeline was acting skittish. That night when I was knocked out . . . someone came into the house after Madeline left. A man. He stood over me. The door was open . . . and then it was closed when I woke up. I assumed it was Zach. Grendel always barks if he doesn't know somebody, but he didn't bark that night. At least not enough to wake me up. So maybe it wasn't Zach in the house. Maybe it was Lance, and he found her the next night and killed her."

Bowman scratches her chin. One side of her mouth goes up. "Let me ask you something—why didn't Madeline just tell the police herself? Or the administration? Why communicate with a short story?"

"She was a writer. And a good one. That was the way she expressed herself. Fiction writers do that."

"Why give it to you? Why not to us?"

"She didn't think people in authority would believe her. Her experience in life had been that women aren't listened to. And I didn't help things much. I told her she might get in trouble for faking her disappearance. Resources were expended in looking for her. I know cops don't like that."

"We don't. We used some manpower looking for her. I don't know if she would have faced any charges for it, but we would have expressed our displeasure with her, that's for sure."

Diana speaks up. "Alicia, you know you can't place that heavy burden on a young woman. To have the courage and maturity to go to the police or the university administration. She'd be terrified. Be realistic."

Bowman crosses her arms. "Why did Hoffman kill Sophia in the first place? I mean, say your theory is correct. I can see why he kills Madeline, if she's coming back to hold his feet to the fire. Madeline threatened everything in his life with any accusation of sexual harassment she would make, even from two years ago. Hoffman could have lost his job. He could have been publicly embarrassed. And that's not getting into an accusation of murder. So maybe he tried to get Madeline to go away. Maybe he was following her. Maybe he followed her to the cemetery that night. Things didn't go his way, so he killed her. I can see that happening, as sick as it is. But why kill Sophia? What did she have to do with it?"

"Isn't it obvious?" I say.

"No," Bowman says. "Enlighten me."

"Lance and Zach were friends. If Zach killed Sophia, as a lot of people suspect, then maybe he told Lance those details."

"So we're back to blaming everything on Zach again?"

"Why not? He's the husband."

"We've been investigating him for over two years," she says. "If we had something to get the guy with, we would."

"So maybe this is it," I say.

"But this story implicates Hoffman. Not Zach," Bowman says.

"Okay, maybe Madeline told Sophia about the harassment and she tried to confront Lance about it. Sophia knew Lance and lived near him. Maybe Sophia stood up for Madeline and paid the price at Lance's hands."

Bowman taps the pages again. But her thoughts seem to be on things beyond those words in front of her. She gets a funny look on her face, kind of like she just remembered a good joke.

"Here's the thing, Connor. You submitted this book and published it. With all the details of Sophia's murder in it. You stood up in front of the library and also did all those interviews claiming the book was yours. And now that the authorship of the book makes you look like a murderer, you're saying you didn't really write it. Madeline did. And the two people who are able to back *that* claim up—Madeline and Hoffman—are now dead. And when I ask for proof from you that Madeline wrote the book, you say she stole the manuscript from your house. And there was only one copy in her handwriting. And Madeline's body was found hidden near your family's graves." She shrugs, and when she lowers her hands, they both thump against the top of the desk. "It's awfully damn convenient that you want me to believe you didn't write that book *now*. I mean . . . you sat right in front of me and *signed* a copy. Who does that?"

She's right. Who does that?

I can't give her a good answer. I never will. But my stupidity and dishonesty have doubled back on me, swinging around like a boomerang that flies back and hits the thrower in the face.

"I'm sorry," I say. "I fucked up."

"Somebody did. Bigly."

"Are you charging my client with something, Alicia?" Diana asks. "He's told you everything he knows. And I don't think plagiarism falls under the purview of the police."

"It doesn't," she says. "The university and the literary world will sort that mess out. I intend to look into whether or not you can be charged for stealing a manuscript. We'll see about that."

"So we're free to go?" Diana asks.

She scoops the papers—Madeline's new story—into a neat stack and pushes herself out of the desk. She hands the papers off to the uniformed cop, who slips them into a leather case.

"I have to talk to your boss," Bowman says. "Dr. White. And I'm sure the university police will be involved in that discussion as well. We always try to keep things cordial and open between the university and the city. I know I still have your passport. You can go home, but you need to stay there. I'll be talking to you again."

She stops at the door and looks back.

"A book signed by a plagiarist," she says. "Do you think that makes it more valuable? Or less?"

"The same," I say. "Most authors' signatures are hardly worth anything."

CHAPTER SEVENTY-NINE

CONNOR
PRESENT

Someone rings my doorbell just after six.

No one has called or texted all day since I came home from campus after talking to the police. I manage not to drink, even though I desperately want to. I'm desperate to do anything that would erase from my mind the image of Lance falling.

But I can't. It's in here forever.

I assume it's Bowman coming to ask more questions. Possibly to take me away forever.

Grendel is still at Preston's house, and I miss his barking. I feel very alone, not having him at his post in the front of the house watching the porch and the street.

When I look outside, though, I see Rebecca Knox clutching a large envelope to her chest. She wears a wool hat pulled down low on her forehead and a bulky winter coat. A car sits at the curb, lights on, exhaust puffing out of the tailpipe. Someone is in the driver's seat, but I can't tell who.

I pull the door open and hold it for Rebecca.

"I'm sorry, Dr. Nye. I know I'm just showing up here like a freak."

"That's okay. Do you want to come in out of the cold?"

"Just for a minute. My mom's waiting for me."

She comes in, and I close the door. She stands in the middle of the living room with the envelope still clutched to her chest.

"Do you want to sit?" I ask.

"This will be fast. I'm going home. Maybe for the rest of the semester. After what happened today . . . Well, the university says I can take as much time as I want. And I can finish the year long-distance if I want."

"I'm sorry you had to see that. I know it was disturbing."

"Yeah. The thing is . . . I *want* to come back. Maybe in a couple of weeks. I like being in class and stuff. And I'm graduating, so I don't want to miss anything. Like my friends. Even my roommate's pretty okay."

"I hope you do come back. But take your time. There's no hurry."

"Yeah. You're right."

"Did you have a question about class or something?" I ask. "I don't know who's going to be teaching it now. And I'm sorry about all the chaos."

"No, not that. And I hope you don't mind. . . . I looked your address up online. But I couldn't find your phone number or I would have called first."

"That's okay. It's nice to have company."

Rebecca shrugs a little with the package in her hand. Then she extends it, holding it out to me in two gloved hands. "I think this is yours."

Before she says anything else, I know what she's handing me. I reach out and take it, my hands shaking. It feels heavy, substantial.

Important.

"Madeline left it for me. And I thought you'd want to have it back."

CHAPTER EIGHTY

REBECCA
PRESENT

Nye takes the envelope.

He stares at it kind of like it's a lost treasure. Or a newborn baby.

"Madeline gave this to you? When? Why?"

"She left it on my porch. Right before she died. And I guess I'm not really sure why she gave it to me, except that she kind of knew me because we hung out at a party once." Rebecca has thought about this a lot over the past couple of days. And especially since this morning. But she can't reach any strong conclusions about it. "We kind of bonded over something that happened that night, something that kind of relates to the book. Or . . . maybe she didn't have anyone else to give it to."

"Why are you bringing it to me?" Nye asks. "Did she say to do that?"

Rebecca feels her cheeks get warm. She reaches up and unbuttons her coat, wishes she could take it off. But she doesn't want to stay long, doesn't want to keep Mom waiting. They have a two-hour drive ahead, and it's already dark. Mom doesn't like driving at night, and Rebecca doesn't want to add to her stress by taking forever with Dr. Nye. It already took long enough packing her clothes and things in the apartment while Mikaila followed her around, telling her how much she was going to miss her. She was practically crying.

It's weird, but Rebecca thinks she'll miss Mikaila. And Steven too.

"I didn't buy your book that night at the library. I forgot my credit card, and I didn't really think I liked to read thrillers, even though you wrote it." When she starts talking, Nye's shoulders sag. He looks disappointed. Kind of sad. And Rebecca doesn't want to pile on, so she tries to make it quick. "When this book showed up on my doorstep, I started reading it, and it was really good. I mean, it's smart. Not just a thriller. It's about the characters too. And their friendship and how they care for each other even though they're kind of from different walks of life. But it kind of reminded me of what you were saying about your book at the library. At first, I thought maybe they were just generally the same. I mean, how many different ways can an author murder somebody? You always said in class there are only seven plots, right?"

"I did say that."

"But I went out this afternoon to Target, and I bought a copy of your book and started reading it. That's when I saw. It's the exact same book, basically. I mean, the published one is all cleaned up with no typos, and some of the details are a little different. But it's the same book. And this is Madeline's handwriting." Rebecca points to the envelope. "I once went to a workshop the English Club gave, and shared one of my stories. Madeline was there that night, and she marked my manuscript up. I put that old story of mine in the envelope here, so you can see it. So I know *this* book was written by her. It's like proof or whatever."

Nye's grip tightens on the envelope. He's shaking his head, and Rebecca wonders what he's going to say. Is he going to have some story about how she can't be right about who wrote the book? Will he try to smooth everything over and lie like Hoffman?

Instead, he says, "I'm sorry about this, Rebecca. When I did this, I wasn't at my best. That's just an excuse, but it's the only thing I can say."

"I know," Rebecca says. "I know about your family and all of that. I just want you to know that I didn't say anything to anybody about it. Not to the police or my mom or my roommate. Nothing. And I didn't copy it or scan it or take any pictures. I wanted to give it to you and let you decide. It's not my choice to make."

"That's really thoughtful of you, Rebecca."

She turns and goes to the door but stops and looks back. Nye is still standing in the living room, looking down at the envelope.

"Can I say something else, Dr. Nye?"

He looks up. "Sure. Anything you want."

"I still think you're a great professor. My favorite, really. You really do seem to care about the students. And our writing and stuff. I hope you come back and teach the class again. I was really sorry when you got replaced. And I want you to direct my thesis, if you can."

Nye looks really moved, almost like he might cry.

But he doesn't, and Rebecca is glad about that. The day's been weird enough as it is.

"Thanks, Rebecca."

"You're welcome."

She steps through the door and hurries across the yard to the waiting car, excited to be inside its warmth and heading home with Mom.

CHAPTER EIGHTY-ONE

CONNOR
PRESENT

The manuscript sits on my coffee table.

For nearly an hour after Rebecca leaves, I stare at the fat pile of papers.

Only a handful of people know the truth—as far as I can tell. Madeline and Lance.

And Rebecca.

Madeline and Lance are gone. Rebecca says she won't tell, and I take her at her word.

Diana knows, but she's my lawyer.

I've told Bowman the truth, but she seemed less concerned with that than with everything else. And I understand. She's a cop. Not a literary critic.

"What a fucked-up day," I say to no one. I don't even have Grendel around to pretend to listen to me. And that's the reality that really sets in for me now. After everything, I'm still alone. I'm still a guy with a dog and a book I didn't write and a job I've managed to hold on to by cheating and not much else.

It all seems kind of pointless.

The front doorbell rings. I barely jump. I figure it's Bowman or a reporter or who knows who else. I decide to ignore it even though the lights are on, and anyone who comes to the window and peeks in can see me sitting here on the couch.

They must have done that because someone knocks lightly against the glass.

"Go away," I say. I doubt they can hear me, but it's all I've got.

Then they knock again. Harder.

I stand up, turn to face the window.

Now I jump.

My hand goes to my heart like I'm a comedian faking shock. But I'm not faking. Everything in my body loosens, like I could slump to the floor.

It's Zach Greenfield, his scruffy face pressed to the glass. His eyes wide so I can mostly see the whites.

It's a no-brainer. I slide my phone out of my back pocket. I'm calling 911.

But he starts waving his hands around, asking me to stop. "Please. No," he says. "Listen. Just listen."

His words are muffled by the glass, his breath steaming against the window and then disappearing.

"Go away."

"Please," he says. "Please. Just listen to me. You don't have to let me in, but you have to listen to me."

"I don't have to do anything. It's over. Leave me alone."

"Please," he says. Real emotion is etched on his face, drawing lines of desperation on his cheeks and his forehead. "Just listen. For five minutes."

Against my better judgment, I feel empathy for the man. He's had his life wrecked. He's lost someone he—maybe—cared about a great deal. Do I give him the benefit of the doubt?

I enter 911 into my phone but don't press CALL. It's ready to go if he makes one aggressive step. I walk across the room and pull the door open.

He comes and stands in front of the screen door, which is filled with a storm window for winter. It's filled with glass year-round, even in the summer, because I'm too lazy to change them. But the glass is thin, and he can be heard through it.

"If you have something to say, make it fast," I say. I hold up the phone. "I'm ready to call the cops."

He holds his hands out so I can see the palms. He looks young and meek. And cold. His cheeks are flushed above his stubble.

"I just want to talk about Sophia," he says. "About who really killed her."

CHAPTER EIGHTY-TWO

He stays on the porch, hands still raised like he's surrendering.

"Why the fuck aren't you in jail?" I ask.

"I was because of what I did to you. I'm out on bail, and I'm just going to plead guilty. Breaking and entering. Assault. My lawyer is figuring it all out."

"Good," I say.

"Everybody's saying that Lance did this, that he killed Madeline and Sophia. And that's why he killed himself. But I'm not so sure about that."

"Why? Because he was your friend? Because you used to go to his parties and feel up college girls?"

The flush on his face intensifies, and he looks away for a moment and then back at me. "Lance was my friend. Neither one of us was perfect, but he was my friend, okay? And he looked out for me. My dad was never around, okay? And Lance . . . well, he treated me well. And I'm here trying to help, man. I am."

"Help how? Did you tell Lance the details of Sophia's murder?"

"What are you talking about? The cops never told me *anything* about what happened to Sophia. I was a suspect. They don't tell suspects the details of a crime. I asked them to tell me more about her murder. I wanted to know. To *understand*. I begged them to tell me what happened. Sophia was my wife. We had problems, almost all of them my fault, but she was my wife."

"Did you talk to Lance about Sophia at all?"

"Look, man, that night I came over here and went nuts . . . and I'm sorry about that. I am. But when I did that . . . I did it because the cops came and talked to me. They told me you were a suspect in Sophia's murder. It just . . . It got me really wound up. And I lost it. It's so much pressure. . . ."

"Okay, if you came to apologize for that—"

"Just listen, though," he says. "Will you listen? And then I'll go. Sophia hated Lance. I mean, she couldn't stand him, no matter how much I liked him. She thought he was pompous and lazy and, more than anything else, a sexist. She hated that he used to have those parties and let underage kids drink and get high. It's not that she was a prude. It's just that she thought an authority figure like a professor shouldn't be doing that kind of stuff, especially now. She went to one of his parties one time. Once. That was the night with Madeline, and, okay, I'm not proud of how I acted. Sophia had gone home early because she thought Lance was so gross."

"You should have gone with her. She had good sense."

"I can't relitigate the past," Zach says. "But I'm telling you she hated Lance. And she really turned against him even harder right before she died. She used to just roll her eyes about him, but all of a sudden, she acted like he was the lowest of the low. She told me she didn't want me even agreeing to play golf with him or talking to him. She said I shouldn't have anything to do with him."

"Why the change?" I ask.

"I don't know. She didn't say. But on the news they're saying Lance was sexually harassing Madeline. And maybe Madeline told Sophia. If that's true, that might be why she took such a harsher view of Lance. He went from being a loser to a harasser. And Sophia really hated anyone who abused their authority that way. She really got righteously indignant when she heard about stuff like that."

So far, everything he says tracks. It makes sense.

"Okay," I say, "so Sophia found out about Lance harassing Madeline and confronted him about it. She wanted to protect her friend, her mentee, I guess. She went to Lance, telling him to knock it off, and he killed her to keep her quiet. If it came out that Lance was harassing a student, he probably would have lost his job, even if it happened over two years ago. And it would have been embarrassing for him. He had reason to protect himself."

But Zach is shaking his head. He looks certain.

"Look, I wasn't a perfect husband. I . . . okay, I just wasn't perfect. We got married young. Maybe we rushed it and I wasn't ready. Sophia was so much more mature than I was. Okay? The whole world knows I made my share of mistakes. But I *know* Sophia. We were together for six years, married for three. I knew her, okay? The way you know a person when you share a house and a life with them. And I know this—she wouldn't have gone anywhere near Lance once she learned that about him. She wouldn't have been able to. She would have been so angry, so disgusted. . . . The truth is, she would have been more likely to kill him than to have him kill her. It just wouldn't happen. She'd have avoided him like the plague."

"Okay. So she'd have avoided him. Lance found out she knew and went to her office. He tracked her down and surprised her, killed her in the car. That's how violence occurs sometimes. Unexpectedly. That's how Lance took her down."

But Zach is shaking his head again. "No, man. No. She had a meeting with someone that night. A *meeting*. She wouldn't have arranged a meeting with Lance. No chance. It wouldn't have gone down that way."

Now it's my turn to shake my head. "I think you're blinded, Zach. You have some loyalty to Lance, so you're tying yourself in knots, trying to get him off the hook for killing your wife. And he was loyal to you. The story Madeline wrote says Lance knew the details. It all points to Lance. I think you're casting your line into an empty pool."

"Just think about what I said," he says. "Don't just dismiss me. Think about it."

"It's been a long day, Zach. And I gave you all the time I can. Good night."

I shut the door and flip off the porch light. I take one look out the window and see Zach going down the steps and back out into the night.

CHAPTER EIGHTY-THREE

It's time for me to face the music, so I knock on Preston's door about an hour later.

Grendel barks while I stand outside, the big envelope I was given by Rebecca clutched to my chest, and it lifts my spirits to hear him again.

When Preston opens the door, his eyebrows lift in surprise. He's wearing jeans and a sweater, the sleeves pushed up to his elbows, as if he was expecting company to come by for a cocktail, even though I hadn't called in advance.

"Connor. I've been meaning to call you, but it's been pretty hectic."

"I'm sorry to show up like this, but can I come in?"

"Of course." He steps back.

Grendel comes up and sniffs me. I hold the envelope in my left hand and bend down to pet him with my right. He licks every one of my fingers, his tail wagging. "It's good to see you too, buddy."

"Kelly and the girls are over at a friend's. Do you want a drink or something? I could sure use one."

"Why not?"

I sit on the couch with the manuscript in my lap and Grendel at my feet. Music plays from somewhere in the house. I can tell it's the jazz program that runs on the local public radio station, something Preston listens to almost every night.

He comes back with a bottle and two glasses and pours. He sits down across from me on the other side of the coffee table and drinks. I expect him to make a toast to Lance, but he doesn't. He just throws back his shot and then pours another.

"You're not touching yours," he says.

"Not yet. I'm trying to stay clearheaded. For a change."

"What's in the envelope?" he asks.

I heft it in my hand and then toss it onto the table, where it lands with a splat. The noise makes Grendel jump.

"That's my resignation from the university," I say.

Preston holds his second shot halfway between the table and his mouth. He looks confused. "What are you talking about, Connor?"

"Just what I said," I say, pointing to the bundle of papers. "That's the end of my academic career."

Preston puts the shot back on the table without drinking it. "It's been a long day, Connor. Maybe the longest day ever. So do you mind not fucking around with me? What's in the envelope? How is that giant thing a resignation? And why would you even be resigning?"

I do what I came to his house to do. I come clean. "Preston, I didn't write my book. Madeline O'Brien did. It was her thesis, and when she disappeared, and I needed to get tenure, I passed it off as my own. And published it. That's part of the reason she came back to town. She wanted the money from the book so she could start a new life. I could have admitted it then or at any point along the way, but I didn't. And maybe if I had, we all could have avoided the chaos that's ensued. That's on me. But I'm admitting it now. That's the manuscript in Madeline's own handwriting. And on the top is my resignation letter. I spell this all out in the letter for the dean and the provost to see. The plagiarism and everything. And I resign. I'm going to call my publisher in the morning and tell them. They'll pull the book. And I'll have to figure out a way to pay back the money, most of which I've spent." I rub my forehead. "It's going to be a nightmare. But I deserve it. And I wanted to let you know since you're the head of the department. And you've been a good friend to me."

Some of the color runs out of Preston's face. He stares at me, his eyes intense, glistening. Long moments pass while the music plays in the other room.

"This is pretty shocking, Connor. On top of everything else today, this is pretty damn shocking."

"Lance didn't say anything to you about this?" I ask.

"He made plenty of snarky and degrading comments about your book. But that's just Lance. I didn't listen to a lot of what he said."

"And the police didn't?"

Preston rubs his cheek. "Detective Bowman said something about your book and who wrote it. . . . She seemed more focused on the details in there coming from Lance. And how that made Lance guilty of the two murders. I guess I didn't follow all of it. I was pretty upset by everything that was happening. That's why Kelly took the kids out. She wanted me to gather myself a little. I was listening to some jazz."

"Well, it's all in there. You can take it to the tenure committee and whoever else it needs to go to tomorrow. I can finish the term if you want, but I'm already suspended, so I might as well just stay away. I can start to figure out my next move. If you have any ideas, I'd love to hear them."

Preston leans forward, reaching for the envelope. He places his hands on either side of it, scooping it up. But before he can lift it, I place my hand, palm down, on top of the bundle, preventing him from raising it.

He looks over at me.

"Before you look at it," I say, "I have one question."

He stops trying to lift it. Our hands are close together but don't touch.

"What is it?" he asks.

"It's about Lance," I say. "Do you remember that night, the second anniversary of Emily and Jake dying, and the two of us went out drinking? You said you knew Lance was crossing the line and there was only so much you could do to protect him. Do you remember that?"

"I knew Lance had some problems. Yes. The parties . . . He was reckless. And it clearly ended up biting him in the ass. And led to terrible, tragic consequences for everyone. For two young women."

"Did you know about him and Madeline? That he was sexually harassing her as he helped her with her thesis?"

"Like I said, Lance had a lot of problems. None of it is a complete shock to me. And I bear a certain measure of responsibility for that. If I'd stepped in with a firmer hand, if I'd been tougher, then maybe a lot of this could have been prevented. I was blinded by my friendship for him. Someone in a position of authority can't let that happen. And I need to reevaluate how I do my job going forward. I'm scheduled to meet with the dean and the provost tomorrow."

"That's good," I say.

"It isn't going to be a pretty meeting, but let's hope something positive can come of all of this. If we all grow more aware and more vigilant, maybe we can prevent it."

He reaches for the manuscript again, and again I place my hand on top of it, holding it down. This time Preston looks irritated with me.

"What are you doing, Connor?"

"Did you know Sophia Greenfield?" I ask. "Personally?"

Now Preston leans back, pulling away from the envelope on the table and from me. He blinks a few times.

"Why are you asking me that, Connor?"

"Did you?"

"No, I did not know Sophia Greenfield. How could I?"

I wait a moment, my hand still on the envelope. "You know that Madeline wrote a short story about Lance when she came back to town and left it for me. That's how I knew Lance had been harassing her. That's why I went to campus today. Once I read that story, it all fit."

"I'm with you so far," he says.

"I think Madeline must have told Sophia about Lance's harassment. And that led Sophia to report it to you. Sophia told you about Lance . . .

and then what happened, Preston? Were you trying to keep the story quiet so it wouldn't reflect poorly on the department? So no one would find out you'd been covering for Lance for years?"

Preston swallows. He uses his tongue to moisten his lips. "You're crazy, Connor. This day, the insane events, it's all gotten to you. It's making you irrational. You need to just take a step back and think about all of this. Rationally."

"I spoke to Zach tonight. Before I came over here. You know, Sophia's husband. He told me she wouldn't have gone anywhere near Lance if she thought he'd harassed her friend. But she'd want to report it. She'd want to tell somebody in a position of authority. That's you, Preston. You're the authority. So, tell me. . . . Did she arrange to meet with you? Did you do whatever it took to protect Lance and the department? More important, did you do whatever it took to protect yourself and your career?"

CHAPTER EIGHTY-FOUR

Preston reaches out. I think he's going to grab for the envelope, to see what's inside, but he picks up his glass and raises it to his mouth. He drinks a large portion of it down.

"Your source for all this guesswork is Sophia's husband," he says. "The guy who has been the prime suspect in her murder ever since she died. The guy who came into your house and tried to kill you."

"The cops have investigated him for over two years," I say. "They've turned every aspect of his life upside down. Over and over again. No arrest. And if he killed his wife, why not let Lance take the fall for it? Lance is gone. Everyone thinks he did it. Why would Zach want to stir things up again? Unless he's innocent."

Preston finishes his drink. "Okay, you seem to be getting at something, Connor. Something I'm not really clear on. You're admitting you plagiarized. You're resigning. Your credibility as a writer and teacher and, frankly, as a human being is lacking."

"That may be true," I say. "I have and will lose any credibility I've built over the years. I'm going to lose everything." I raise my index finger. "But it's something I always told my students that brought me over here tonight. I always told them that if a detail they put in their fiction is so unique, so unusual, the reader will think it has to be true. And the police told me something like that when they came to my house a few nights ago."

"What was that?" he asks. And he sounds curious, hooked by my words.

"They told me they thought there was a possibility that two assailants killed Sophia. And I thought that was so strange. . . . Why would *two* people team up to murder a young woman? In a parking lot? With her in the driver's seat. It's all very strange. Maybe all I had to do was think about it and look around me. And then listen to Zach. So maybe a real possibility is that one person was trying to get the other two together, to make peace between them."

"But Lance admitted everything on the roof today—"

"Did he, though? When we were up there, Lance had nothing to hide. He planned to jump, so why not just admit it?"

"Lance was an odd guy. And clearly disturbed. Everything he said was oblique. And you're wondering why he was opaque right before he took his own life."

"Yeah. Maybe." I plunge ahead. "But you knew Lance was crossing the line with students in the past. And you said you were sticking your neck out for him. Just like you stuck your neck out for me when Emily and Jake died. You were willing to do that so I could hang on to my job."

"That's what I'm supposed to do, Connor."

"Right. Preston the Politician. Preston the Peacemaker."

His voice comes out flat. "What are you getting at, Connor? I lead the department. I'm out front. Some people have to do that. Not everyone gets to hide away."

"But is it possible you took that role too far? Madeline and Sophia were friends. And Lance was sexually harassing Madeline. That's in her short story, so we know that. Remember what you always say—we need to listen to women. And Sophia's husband, Zach, told me that Sophia felt very strongly about mentoring and protecting younger women. That's who Sophia was. That defined her. So if she learned that one of her young friends was being sexually harassed by a more powerful man at the university—a university and a department she was already connected to through her internships—isn't it possible she would do something about it? Isn't it possible she would stand up and try to fight back on behalf of that person?"

"She'd confront *that* person, yes. That's Lance."

"Or maybe if she thought that person wasn't worth the effort, or was unlikely to listen, she might go to someone she thought *would* listen. Someone in a position of real power. Someone who might be able to corral Lance and tell him to knock it off. Or actually hold him accountable at the university."

Preston shakes his head. "This is sad, Connor. It's surprising to me that you couldn't write a book since you're spinning all of this fiction right here in my living room. Maybe you need to take another swing at being a novelist. Maybe it will work out this time."

"Maybe it will," I say. "At least I'm admitting I'm a failure as a writer. How's that novel you've been claiming to write for the last five years?"

"It's mine," he says. "Not plagiarized."

"Touché," I say. "Madeline was a better writer than either of us. Sometimes students come along like that, and we have to accept we'll never be as good as we want to be. Maybe we all have to admit that our lives aren't going to be what we hoped for. Fortunately, Madeline left this book and story behind, and she'll get credit for them now. The credit she deserves."

"A lot of good that will do her."

"You're right. I have to live with that. And I will. It's all I can do. I've lived with stuff before, so I'm going to do it again."

Preston just stares at me. So does Grendel.

So I say, "Sophia called the main line to the English Department a couple of times before she was murdered. Not to talk to Carrie about internships, but to talk to you. About Lance. And it all went wrong somehow. I figure you could try to tell your side of things and get out in front of it before the police come for you. You could try to live with it too." I check my watch. "And the police are on the way now. I told my lawyer to get them and meet us here. Now. You called them on me, in this very house. I thought I'd return the favor."

Preston stands up. "Goddamn it, Connor. What are you dragging into my home? Kelly and the kids will be here soon."

"It would be tough for me to believe all of this, Preston, except you left the building this morning. I came roaring in, heading right to Lance's classroom. I expected you to show up behind me, to calm things down. I kept looking for you. But you weren't there. There was trouble brewing, and you weren't around. Why did you leave at the moment that seemed tailor-made for you?"

"I had a meeting," he says.

"Did you? Or were you afraid of what loose-tongued Lance would say in front of me? In front of everybody up on the roof?"

Preston walks out of the room without saying anything. I can hear movement in the back of the house, down the hallway where the bedrooms are. I stand up, and Grendel looks at me and wags his tail. He looks like he wants to go home.

I go in the direction Preston went, down the hallway. I've never been back to his bedroom area, but I hear rustling and follow the noise. I enter the master bedroom, which is large and decorated in a sleek minimalistic fashion. Preston is bent over inside the closet. He doesn't know I'm here, so I say his name. When I do, he spins to face me like I've shouted. And he stares at me without saying anything, his face contorted in a way I've never seen.

"What are you doing, Preston?" I ask.

He turns back to the closet and continues to rummage.

"Preston?"

He backs out of the closet, holding a duffel bag. He turns to me. "I'm going. Away."

"The police are coming. You can't leave now."

"I'm going to anyway."

"What about Kelly and the girls?" I ask. When I say this, he flinches a little. "Are you going to leave without saying anything to them?"

"I will. Eventually."

"Did you pack that bag just now?"

He looks down like he's never seen the bag before. "I've had this packed for over two years, since Sophia was killed. I always thought this day would come." He looks at the bedroom door and back at me. "I started to let my guard down a little and think it might never come back at me."

"The things we push away always come back, Preston. Believe me."

"Connor, we both still have a chance here." Preston speaks in his calmest voice, the one that tries to move everyone toward a consensus. In this case, he's working on me alone. "You know my kids. And Kelly. You know the life we've built here. And the career I have. We can't give all that up. We can't have all this drama."

"It's the *only* thing you can do."

He hefts the bag in his hand and then leaves the room quickly. I follow behind him.

Preston stops at the coffee table, duffel bag in one hand, and picks up the thick envelope containing the manuscript with the other.

"I'll take this outside right now, Connor," he says. "To the grill."

"What exactly are you taking out there, Preston?"

"Evidence. You were dumb enough to bring it here. I'm smart enough to dispose of it."

He makes his way to the back door, but before his hand grips the knob, I say, "Evidence that what I said about the murders is true."

"That's what you said is in here."

"Are you sure it is?" I ask.

He drops the duffel bag and starts tearing open the envelope. He rips into it like a hungry animal. When he's torn the envelope away he sees what's inside.

"What is this, Connor?" he says, his voice snarling. "I thought this was the fucking book."

"It's not," I say. "Madeline's handwritten manuscript is at my house. I lied. But your behavior here shows my guess was right." Something aches inside of me, like my guts are full of ground glass. "I thought you were better than Lance. I so hoped it wouldn't be true. But you just made it clear I was right."

"Fuck you, Connor."

"What happened? Did Lance see her at the reading? I saw Madeline there. Another student did too. Is that what started it?"

"I didn't see her. But she was a fool to go like that."

"But Lance . . . ?"

"Why do you think we came to your house that night?" he asks. "After the reading. To celebrate? No. Lance was terribly jealous that you published that book. You're younger than he is and a constant reminder of what he hasn't done with his life. I admit I was jealous too. A novel . . . Anyway, we wanted to see if you knew anything about Madeline because Lance swore he'd seen her at the reading. He turned white as a sheet when he saw her standing there. It was a dumb move on her part, but she was a kid. And kids do stupid things. And she'd been to your house, right?"

"She had."

Preston shakes his head. "Lance nearly blew his stack. He was so scared. He thought everything would come out. *I* was the one with the most at stake. Not him. I have the better job. A family. A future at the university. His life is—or was—whatever it was."

"So what went wrong?" I ask. "What happened to Madeline? How did she end up dead in the cemetery?"

"I don't know what the fuck she was doing out there," Preston says. "Maybe she was looking for you. Did she know you went there?"

"I think I told her I liked to go there in difficult times. To find peace and quiet."

"Lance was looking for her. I'm sure he followed her. I wanted Lance to get her to leave town, but he . . . he took a more extreme approach. He said we couldn't leave anything unresolved."

"What did she know about Sophia? That you had killed her to protect Lance?"

"Don't be an idiot, Connor. Don't you know who I am? I'm Preston the Peacemaker. That's what I tried to do with Sophia. Make peace."

"How did you do that?"

"Connor, burn it. The book. We're running out of time. If you plagiarized from Madeline, and that manuscript is the only proof, then burn it. Go home and get rid of it. And let it go. And neither one of us has to go down. Let Lance take the fall. He's gone. He's not coming back, and he has nothing to lose anymore."

"Just tell me, Preston. . . . What did you two do to Sophia?"

Preston shakes his head. "I didn't want anything to happen to Sophia. I just wanted her to back off, to let the stuff with Lance go. Then I could keep the department out of the news. I could keep the university administration off my back. Do you know what it would look like for me if that came out? That I knew about Lance's parties and everything else and looked the other way? I want to be dean someday."

"So you tried to convince her to back off? You were going to meet with her at her office?"

"I arranged a meeting. After hours, outside her office, so no one would see us together. No security cameras, nothing. She thought she was just meeting with me. But I told Lance about it and asked him to show up. Eventually. I thought if I got the two of them together, if the three of us talked it out, Sophia might cool down. That was my plan. Madeline was a senior. She was going to graduate with honors and move on. And I was getting through to Sophia, talking to her in her car. . . ."

His face looks distant, contorted again, the way it was in the bedroom. Like he's in pain, remembering.

"Go on, Preston. Something went wrong. Something with—"

"Lance showed up. Early. And he'd been drinking." He looks right into my eyes. "Connor, I wish to fuck I'd handled it on my own. But Lance got in the car, in the backseat, and he smelled like a distillery. And Sophia reacted like a caged animal. She wanted to get out. She immediately started talking about calling the police and reporting Lance."

"And what happened?" I ask. "He killed her."

Preston shakes his head. "Connor, the sad thing is we actually made progress. I'll give Sophia credit—she listened. She calmed down. She listened. Lance said he was wrong to harass Madeline. He said he got carried away with his students sometimes and got too close to them. And he admitted he drank too much. And he wanted to work on that. Sophia wasn't ready to back down or let it all go, but some of the edge left her. She was listening, like I said. That's the damnedest thing, Connor. She was listening. I was bringing them together. I was working it out. . . ."

"So what went wrong?" I ask.

Preston bites down on his lower lip. "Fuck it all, Connor. Sophia just kept asking for more. She wouldn't take what she was given and be happy. You know?"

"Was she supposed to just 'take what she was given'? Is anybody?"

"She wouldn't. She told Lance he should stop having those parties. She said they were risky and encouraged the wrong kind of behavior. Underage drinking. Impaired driving. She said it wasn't the way a mentor was supposed to act, and he should cut it out."

"And Lance said no."

"Adamantly. He maintained it was his right to do what he wanted. And to invite whomever he wanted to his house. And that inflamed Sophia all over again."

Preston grows quiet. He stares straight ahead, and I wonder if he's going to go on without being prompted. But he does.

"They argued. And Sophia grew so frustrated, so angry, that she said she was going to leave. She reached for the door handle . . . and I made a mistake. I . . . I grabbed her hand and pulled it back so she couldn't open the door. I didn't want her to leave that way, not when we were so close to working things out." His voice rises a little. "She stopped listening, Connor. She stopped hearing the good sense I was making."

"She was scared. Two men in the car with her—"

"When I pulled her arm back, she started to fight. Against me. Physically. She started lashing out with her hands."

"She was terrified," I say.

"I had to fight her off. She was attacking me. And Lance reached over from the backseat— Connor, at that point, we were doomed, Lance and I. We were fighting with a woman in her car. How does that get explained? To anyone?"

"You should have stopped it. You needed to be the adult, Preston."

"The scarf was right there on the seat . . . between Sophia and me . . . and I used it."

"Jesus, Preston . . . how could you?"

"Once it was done, it didn't matter what happened. It was better to leave her there and let everyone get back to normal. Let the life of the department go on. I just had to trust that Lance would keep his mouth shut. . . . You know how that worked out."

"It's over, Preston. Everything is over for you."

He stares at me, his eyes burning.

He bends down and reaches into the duffel bag.

"What are you doing, Preston?" I ask.

He straightens up, holding a black object in his hand. I think it's pepper spray or maybe it's a gun.

Preston flicks his wrist, and the device grows in length. It's a telescoping self-defense baton, one of those things I've seen in movies but never in person. Preston grips it tight, the muscles in his forearms bulging.

He takes two quick, long strides, raising the baton over his head as he moves. With a quick, slicing motion, he swings the baton toward my head. I raise my left arm to ward off the blow.

Something cracks as the baton connects with my forearm. The pain sears up my arm and into my brain. I fall back.

Preston stands over me, the baton raised for another blow.

He swings, and I roll to one side. The baton whistles past my ear and smashes against the carpet. I feel certain my arm is broken. But Preston's swing has left him off-balance. I press that small advantage.

I swing my right leg against his left and knock him over. He falls to the floor, the baton still in his hand.

I push myself to my feet with my good arm. Grendel yelps and barks.

I back away toward the door as Preston rights himself. He stands and comes toward me, while I continue to back up. My arm hangs limply at my side.

"It's over, Preston," I say again.

"Not for me," he says.

He charges, baton raised.

I reach the door, try to pull it open.

But the door swings inward before I can.

Someone is here, coming into the house. Several people.

When Preston sees them, he stops his charge. His blazing eyes focus, and he stands in the center of the room, his cheeks red, the baton raised over his head like a torch.

It's Kelly returning with their daughters. They all look at him with horror, coming face-to-face with a part of him they've never seen.

I look past them to the yard. I see flashing lights strobing in the dark.

The police are here. They're coming through the door.

"Daddy . . . ?"

Then the police are inside, and they wrestle Preston to the ground.

Face-first. It takes four of them to get the cuffs on him while his wife and children watch.

I collapse to the floor, my crushed arm cradled against my chest.

Grendel comes to my side and licks my face.

It is well and truly over.

EPILOGUE

ONE YEAR LATER

I wake up early in the morning. Like I always do.

To be honest, my life now isn't much different from what it was in Gatewood. Before I admitted the book wasn't mine. Before I lost my job and tenure and everything.

Now I wake up early in a different state where I teach part-time at a different university. It's colder here. And farther north, closer to where my sister lives. My arm is completely healed. And I don't have tenure or any real job security. But who does, right?

I take Grendel for a walk around the neighborhood. He moves slower than ever now. Maybe because it's cold. Maybe because he's slowing down, as we all are. I tell myself he might have a few good years left. I hope so.

When I return to my small apartment, I brew coffee and feed the dog. And when the coffee's ready, I sit down to write. I try to write a few hundred words before I have to go to campus to teach that day's classes. Some days I don't make it. But most I do.

I'm keeping my expectations low and reasonable.

For someone who hasn't finished anything in a long time, that seems like a good choice.

I open the file I've been working on and start to go.

And what kind of story am I writing now?

A thriller based on everything that happened with Madeline, and Lance, and Preston?

No need to. Madeline's book is now being published under her name. And the money is going to her family. And I'm slowly paying back my advance, a little bit at a time. The police have assured me that as long as I pay back the money, I won't face any further criminal charges related to stealing Madeline's book.

No, I'm writing a story that means a lot more to me. Something I connect to in a real way.

Something *I* want to write. Need to write.

It begins: *My wife and son died six years ago. . . .*

ACKNOWLEDGMENTS

Thanks once again to everyone at Berkley/Penguin for their hard work on my behalf.

Special thanks to Jin Yu and Bridget O'Toole for their marketing wizardry.

Special thanks to Loren Jaggers for his publicity superpowers.

Special thanks to Ann-Marie Nieves, Jen Carl, and Lori Edelman at Get Red PR for all of their hard work.

Special thanks to Kara Thurmond for keeping the website running.

Special thanks to Kelcey Parker Ervick and Jake Mattox for their friendship and advice.

Once again, my amazing editor, Danielle Perez, worked tirelessly to make the book better. Thanks, Danielle!

Once again, my amazing agent, Laney Katz Becker, went above and beyond the call of duty to make everything happen. Thanks, Laney!

Huge thanks to my friends, family, and readers.

And thanks to Molly McCaffrey for everything.